A MEETING OF PRINCES

"Explain yourself more clearly or I'll leave," I said, crossing my arms on my chest.

His face became very serious. "I believe we're all marked for death."

Alright, now he had my attention. "Go on."

"You know of two deaths, but there have been three of these cold choking attacks. Two months ago I witnessed the first one. That attempt failed. But last month it succeeded in killing Hamed. Now Mured has been killed, and in the most horrible manner. Do you see the progression? Whoever is behind this is getting much better at killing us . . . much better."

THE
PRINCES
OF THE
GOLDEN CAGE

THE
PRINCES
~ OF THE ~
GOLDEN CAGE

NATHALIE MALLET

NIGHT SHADE BOOKS
SAN FRANCISCO

The Princes of the Golden Cage © 2007 by Nathalie Mallet

This edition of *The Princes of the Golden Cage* © 2007
by Night Shade Books

Cover art by Paul Youll

Jacket design by Claudia Noble
Interior layout and design by Jeremy Lassen

First Edition

ISBN 978-1-59780-090-7

Night Shade Books
Please visit us on the web at
http://www.nightshadebooks.com

Acknowledgments

I would like to thank my husband Andre, without his support
this book simply wouldn't exist, and my wonderful agent Jenny
Rappaport, for believing in me. Thank you to my friends and
members of my reading group, David, Richard and Rachel,
who were never short of kind words and advice. A special
thanks to Jason Williams and Jeremy Lassen of Night Shade
Books for making my dream come true.

CHAPTER ONE

I sat straight up in my bed. I knew someone was coming because my two insane brothers, Jafer and Mir, were screaming bloody murder. They occupied rooms flanking mine and never failed to alert me of intruders' presences in our corridor. One could not find better guard dogs than my brothers. I'd chosen to live in the palace's old library tower just to be near them. Well, also to be near my beloved books.

I sighed and grabbed the dagger hidden under my pillow. Although I was not ranked high enough in line for the throne to pose a threat to my brothers, I still kept weapons at hand. One could never be too careful—certainly not here. In the Kapisi Palace's Cage, no prince was safe.

The *Kafes* or Cage System—which entailed locking all princes inside one section of the palace until one was crowned as the next ruler—had been put in place by my great-great-grandfather, Sultan Mudel Ban II, after his numerous sons ripped the kingdom of Telfar apart in a bloody fratricidal war. Back then, princes were spread throughout the country, each governing a province as preparation for the throne. The Ban Dynasty never believed the eldest son should automatically become Sultan.

Slinging a blue silk robe over my shoulders and with my dagger firmly in hand, I moved to the door. I slid its small window open and peered through the wooden grid set behind it. A servant stood in the corridor. He was dressed in the yellow and black silk of the Vizier's attendants, with the traditional, striped baggy pants that made them all look like giant bees.

"Prince Amir," he said, bowing to me. When he straightened, the small yellow hat precariously perched atop his head almost fell off.

"What do you want?" I asked, while scratching my short beard. "Speak!"

The servant glanced nervously at my screaming brothers' doors. "Thousand regrets for disturbing your rest, Your Highness, but a terrible thing has happened. One of your brothers has passed away and… and Master Hassan begs for your council."

I couldn't say I was shocked by the news of one of my brothers' demise. Princes died regularly in the Palace's Cage. However, the fact that Hassan, the Grand Vizier's assistant, was requesting my presence certainly surprised me. To ask a prince to leave his room in the middle of the night to see a corpse was highly unusual.

Careful, Amir, this may well be a trap. My eyes went to the mirror set in the corner's end of the corridor. Its angle gave me a view of the stairwell on the right. Its steps were empty. Yet I wasn't reassured. The Cage might have put an end to war, but it had not ended fratricide. Instead, a set of rules had been put in place. Now murder had to be sanctioned by the Grand Vizier. Now it needed a reason. A bruised honor was the one most often used. Princes, like peaches, bruised easily. *Have I offended someone lately?* Dammit, I could not recall.

I returned my attention to the servant. "Why me?" I asked with narrowed eyes. "Why my council? There are other princes in the Cage, why not ask for theirs?"

The servant swallowed hard. "Because… because of the way your brother died." The servant's voice became a murmur, "It's not a normal death—not normal at all. Huh… and because of

Your Highness's knowledge of magic and its dark incantations. Everybody knows Your Highness studies these… things."

I blew air through clenched teeth in frustration. I knew better than to waste my time trying to explain that alchemy, botany and astronomy had nothing to do with magic. These were true sciences, proven things—not superstitions. I glanced at the thousands of precious, antique books filling the walls of my chambers. The palace's old library did hold a great many volumes concerning the dark art. Now that I was thinking of it, only the Grand Vizier owned more magic books than I did. Not that I had ever felt the urge to open one. *Magic*—I shook my head; to me it was nothing but irrational old superstitions. I didn't need to see my brother's corpse to know that magic wasn't involved in his death, some evil certainly, magic—no. Yet my curiosity was stirred, and although this went against my strongest belief—that one should lay low and not attract attention to one self—I agreed to follow the servant. I had to prove my point: I had to prove that magic didn't cause my brothers' death—more so, I had to prove that magic didn't exist.

Clad in a dark blue kaftan, the long overcoat worn by nobles, and armed with the sword I kept by my door—just in case of an attack—I joined the servant in the corridor. I didn't leave right away, though. First I needed to calm down my two brothers. Moving to the door on my left, I looked through its opened grid. Mir, I noted, had hidden deep inside the darkness of his room and was back to his usual mumbling, so I left him alone and crossed the corridor to the facing room.

As I approached Jafer's door, his hand shot out of the broken grid of his door. "Beware of the dark clouds," he said. "Its evil is coming."

I gripped his hand. "Don't worry; I'll be careful of the clouds. Now go back to bed, Jafer."

He squeezed my hand hard. I didn't move. I knew not to

4 — NATHALIE MALLET

fight Jafer; it would only make him hold on longer. So I just waited for him to let go, telling him that everything would be fine, that the demons, ghosts and clouds were all gone. Like always, I had chased them all away. Sometimes I would sing to him—music helped fight his dementia—I wouldn't do so now. I didn't have the time and the presence of the servant bothered me. My singing might have been good enough to sooth Jafer's nerves, but little else.

"They're coming to kill us, aren't they?" I heard Mir ask through his door's grid. Contrary to Jafer, Mir knew that the only demons roaming the palace were our brothers. They were his worst fear. A fear I shared to a lesser extent.

"No, Mir," I said. "Not tonight. Tonight you're safe—you too, Jafer."

Reassured, Jafer loosened his grip. "Promise you won't stay away long."

"I'll be back in no time," I promised, then left with the servant.

The palace was eerily silent at this hour of the night, especially when considering that it housed 5000 people. Built on the fringe of the Oborandi desert 300 years ago, the Kapisi Palace was now three-quarters surrounded by the sprawling city of Tulag. Only its back wall still faced the desert. Made up of dozens of buildings enclosed within high, fortified walls, many had called the palace a town within a city. The Cage alone counted over 500 souls and had its own kitchen, baths, courtyards and stable. It was spacious. It had to be. My father, Sultan Mustafa Ban had produced over 250 sons, of those 117 managed to survive the harem's intrigues and reach adulthood, which in Telfar was fourteen. Father produced just as many daughters. My sisters, however, were less valued than we were. Kept in the harem, they served as bargaining chips to reinforce or create alliances with the rulers of other kingdoms and the nobles of ours. Although Telfar was a kingdom ruled exclusively by men, history told of many decisions influenced by clever harem favorites. And many Sultans owed their crown to their talented mothers.

We took the direction of the Cage's kitchen, traveling in near total silence. I had never seen these somber corridors so devoid of life before, as if the servants, who usually could be seen everywhere, were fleeing before us. I found it quite unsettling. When we turned into a long alley pierced by windows, a chilling breeze hit me. I stopped and looked out the nearest one. "Why did they have to build the Cage on the only side of the palace facing the desert? All we can see through these windows is either sand or one of the palace's courtyards. Is a view of the city too much to ask?"

The servant sunk upon himself, like an overly submissive dog fearing a kick from his master. "Thousand pardons, Your Highness."

I rolled my eyes. Turning back to the window, I gazed at the desert. The full moon's dim light gave the sand dunes the appearance of finely milled gold. "Tulag is said to be one of the most beautiful cities of the world. Is it true?"

"Oh, yes, Your Highness."

For a second I was jealous of this servant's freedom. How could I, a prince, live to the age of nineteen and never see anything besides the ornate walls of the Cage or the harem? This was a sin. Worse still was the knowledge that I might die without having seen the city, like so many of my brothers already had. Could I escape my brothers' traps long enough to see the crowning of the next Sultan? Would I be free after? In the Telfarian tradition the throne went to the prince who proved himself the most capable. Often he was also the most devious and ruthless, and his crowning was almost always followed by bloodshed as he rushed to eliminate his brothers before they could unite against him. So even if I lived to see the next Sultan's crowning, I would probably die soon after. My hands curled into hard fists. *No, not me. I will live, and I will see the city*. I had made that decision long ago, foregoing the throne as the goal of my life. I never cared for it anyway. It was freedom I craved. I wanted nothing else. Freedom was *my* goal.

"Prince, they're waiting," the servant said.

I shot one last glance at the full moon shining above the dunes then followed the servant. Minutes later, we reached the end of this long alley where Hassan and a small group of guards awaited us. The light of their torches made the corner glow bright amber, as though the walls themselves were on fire.

My first thought was that Hassan looked frightened. A young man in his early twenties, he hadn't grown a beard yet. Tonight, his bare cheeks lacked their usual rosy glow. Right now he seemed ill at ease in the striped pants and black tunic his position as the Grand Vizier's assistant required. Hassan was new to the job, less than a year. He got the position after the previous Vizier's assistant lost his head for failing to discover who stole a precious vase given to my father by the King of Karpel. It was certain that Hassan kept his predecessor's fate at the top of his mind, which surely added to his present fear. However, it was his wide-opened eyes that caught my attention. They darted around the corridor as though he was expecting to see something rush out of its shadowy corners.

Finally, his eyes met mine, and he immediately bowed. "Prince Amir, I beg your pardon for disturbing your sleep. But I'm in great need of your assistance."

I frowned. There was too much relief in Hassan's voice. No one could be that happy to see a prince, we were not a pleasant bunch. I looked at the group of guards standing behind Hassan. The two on his left trembled so strongly they were barely able to stand.

"What's going on?" I asked. "Enforcing the Cage's rules is the Grand Vizier's duty. If this is an unsanctioned death, why isn't he here?"

"The Vizier has been called to the Summer Palace by the Sultan and won't be back for a few days."

"Still, why seek me and not the physicians?" I said, more than a little annoyed.

Hassan wet his lips. "Your Highness is… hmm, well-versed in abstract and complicated things." Hassan gestured for the guards to move aside. They obeyed all too gladly in my opinion, revealing the limp body of a young man sprawled on the floor. Despite the fact that he had the fair skin and red hair of the Nordic people, his purple and gold kaftan indicated that he was one of my brothers: only a prince could afford such a sumptuous garment. *So now we're 116!*

I sighed. His look was his downfall. Hard not to attract attention when one was so… brilliant. Being noticed meant having your potential evaluated. Never a good thing when one lived caged with so many power-thirsty brothers. To say that you didn't want to become the next Sultan, that surviving was enough for you, was useless, even if true. For many of my brothers, only dead princes posed no threat. I counted myself lucky for being of average size, for having the dark hair and brown eyes shared by most of my siblings. Because of this I could blend easily in their midst. With its high cheekbones, square chin and short well-groomed beard, my face was one of many alike—unremarkable. I cultivated every bit of this blandness. I slumped whenever I was with shorter brothers, tried to sound dull when with dimwitted ones, and mimicked the affectations of my high-ranking brothers when near them. Even in my choice of clothes, I was careful. Blue and green were the predominant color of the palace's walls, and therefore of my kaftans. Even my name, Amir, was common. There was at least four or five other Princes Amir still alive—a real blessing.

I gazed at my dead brother with some sadness. He was born with little chance of evading attention. I believe his name was Hamed. If my memory was right, his rank was lower than mine, seventy-eight, or something alike. *How badly did they want this boy dead that they couldn't wait a few days for the Grand Vizier's return? Who did you offend, brother? You obviously made a deadly enemy.*

My eyes left my dead brother to find Hassan. "I don't see any marks on him, no blood either. Not on the ground or on his clothes—"

The guards gasped and stepped back. I stopped talking. A ray of moonlight from the nearest window had just fallen upon Hamed's face. My brother's skin was as gray as cold ash.

"Strangled?" I said.

Hassan shook his head. Turning to the two trembling guards I had noticed earlier, he said, "These two saw everything." Lowering his voice to a whisper, Hassan continued. "Prince Hamed was looking well and traveling toward the two guards when suddenly he stopped in front of one of these windows, clutched his throat and began making choking sounds."

"*Poisoned?*" I hushed. "I cannot believe it! Poison is the weapon of women and cowards. Has one of my brothers stooped that low, Hassan?"

Hassan didn't answer, which I thought was very prudent of him; instead he continued, "The guards rushed to Prince Hamed's help only to be pushed back by—" leaning closer to me he whispered the last words—"pushed by some invisible cold hands."

I blinked. I wanted to laugh but the seriousness of Hassan's face prevented it.

"Prince Amir, these men are terrified. They say that an evil power was at play here. That's why I called for you. I'm sure you can find a logical explanation for this bizarre event. It would reassure these guards and therefore the rest of the household."

I was pleasantly surprised. Hassan wanted me to kill a potentially disruptive rumor, to snuff it before it turned the heads of maids, cooks and all other servants and affected their work. My opinion of this young assistant increased favorably tenfold. Nodding, I took one of the guards' torches and moved to the nearest window. With my eyes fixed on the flame, I stepped closer to the window, then left, then back. It should be about here. *Ah, there it is.* A cold draft struck me. Goose bumps instantly covered my skin and the flame of my torch blew sideways. Gesturing toward a second window on the opposite side of the alley, I said. "I think I've found your cold hands. It's the draft running between these windows."

Unconvinced, the guards looked around uneasily, yet didn't dare contradict a prince's words. At that instant a violent breath of wind pushed me forward, blowing out the flame of my torch and molding my kaftan to my body as snugly as a second skin.

"Ohhh!" the guards made.

"See. It was wind. As for what killed my brother, it's poison. I just don't know which kind—yet."

Sighs of relief were exuded all around and the tension in the alley eased. Seeing that things were back to normal, Hassan sent the guards to fetch a stretcher to carry the dead prince away.

I gave the torch back to one of the departing guards then kneeled beside my brother. The grayness of his skin puzzled me. His lips were blue, I noted. "This poison has strange side-effects. I've never seen anything like this before."

Hassan crouched beside me. "Prince Amir, now that we're alone, I think Your Highness should... touch him."

"What?"

"I couldn't tell this to Your Highness in the guards' presence. But there's something about your brother's death that wind and poison can't explain. If you touch him you'll understand."

I studied Hassan's features carefully. Green eyes, pale golden skin with a rosy hue, his look was typical of the inhabitants of the island of Salo. These islanders were renowned for their sense of logic. "I thought people from Salo didn't believe in magic," I said.

"We don't. I didn't…" He cringed. "I don't know anymore."

As we both looked at Hamed, my dead brother's skin paled under our eyes. He was now the color of old bones, and his lips, near purple. Whatever had killed Hamed obviously wasn't done with him. Something else was being robbed from my brother besides his life.

I went to touch his neck and struck a cold wall. Icy knives pierced my hand, traveling along my arm up to my elbow. I reared back, my fingers all crooked with pain. Wrapping my hand in my kaftan's sleeve, I tried touching my brother again. Once more the cold wall blocked me, but this time it was less solid. I could feel it giving away like half-frozen water. Grinding my teeth against the frigid vice circling my hand, I pushed with all my might. As my knuckles made contact with my brother's skin the cold wall vanished, leaving me breathless.

"You broke the spell," Hassan said. "Colors are returning to your brother's cheeks."

Although I was watching my brother's complexion return to normal, my mind refused to believe what my eyes were so clearly seeing. *This can't be. There must be some sensible explanation for this phenomenon, some logic that didn't involve magic. It has to. Yes, I'm sure it does. I'll prove it.*

"Is something wrong, Your Highness?" Hassan asked, making me realize that I was panting loudly.

I shook my head. "Not a word of this to anyone, understand? Not until we know more."

Hassan nodded vigorously.

Without another word, I rose. It was then that I caught a glimpse of a tall silhouette hiding in the shadow further down the alley. After careful scrutiny, I saw that the spy was either blond or wore a gold-colored turban. I moved slightly to the left. Ah, yes, he was blond. I remembered having seen this blond brother only twice before. I couldn't recall his name though. One sure thing, he was better at hiding than poor Hamed.

"Show yourself, brother!" I called. Just then the guards returned with the stretcher, crowding the alley and blocking my sight of the spy. They immediately began the unpleasant business of moving my brother's body. By the time they cleared the way the blond spy was gone. I approached the dark spot where the blond had hidden. There was an alcove cut in the wall, the type used to display statues or vases.

"Show yourself," I said again. No sound. Gripping my sword, I stepped inside the alcove. It was small, dark and empty. I exhaled, relieved. Confrontation never appealed to me. Not that I lacked courage, far from it. But as courage was considered a ruling quality by my murderous brothers, I tried to display as little of it as possible. When I turned around, a familiar smell touched my nose: the dry, dusty smell of old books. I sniffed the air—moldy old books. *That's odd! I thought I was the only prince who loves books.* Yet it wasn't odd enough to concern me further—after all, the palace was filled with antique decorations, and the smell could be of something else.

I was about to leave the alcove when my eyes fell upon a shiny object dangling from a wood splinter poking out of the wall. It was a gold locket hanging on a chain. I cupped it in one hand, turning it around with a flick of the finger. It was exquisitely made. Definitely not a servant's piece of jewelry. I ran my thumb on the star-shaped flowers and swirls of ribbon chased on top of the locket's cover, then flicked it open. Inside was the portrait of a very young woman, a girl on the threshold of womanhood, painted on porcelain. Her beauty took my breath away. She was splendid, a true vision of femininity, with cascading gold curls, eyes wide and warm, and a skin as velvety as a ripe peach. As I gazed upon her lovely face, my throat tightened and my hand began shaking. The force of my reaction shocked me. She wasn't the first exotic beauty I'd seen. The palace was filled with them: dancers from the eastern country of Tomel, singers from the island of Irabus, bath attendants from Erasor. My father was a great collector of exotic beauties. His harem counted over 200 women from thirty different kingdoms. It was also why I had brothers in every skin shade imaginable. So normally I wasn't easily impressed by pretty faces. Still, the locket's beauty did impress me. She had the look of a princess, I thought. The miniature was certainly the work of a master.

I closed my fist around the locket. *Who was she?* I wondered. For all I knew she could be here, in Kapisi Palace. I watched Hamed's body being carried away by the guards. For some reason, I had the feeling that this woman was linked to my brother's death.

CHAPTER TWO

My brain was dull this morning. I had spent half the night searching for the type of poison that could produce the effect I had witnessed in Hamed, without success, and the other half gazing at the picture in the locket. Now, I needed a full carafe of strong tea just so I would think straight.

It was with my head still reeling with the night's event that I took the direction of the kitchen. In general, princes did nothing by themselves—not even wash. They certainly didn't get their own food. Servants did everything for us. They worked nonstop. Over half of the palace's population was made up of servants of one kind or another: bath attendants, cooks, maids, gardeners. They were everywhere. Well, everywhere but my rooms. Perhaps it was me, growing suspicious with age, or maybe it was the many intrigues involving servants I had witnessed with time. Whichever the case, years ago I broke with tradition and decided not to have any personal servants, as they were susceptible to betrayal. Not necessarily by character flaw mind you, but they could easily be convinced by force. So I'd rather get my own meal and ask for services from the palace servants whenever I needed it rather than have a potential spy permanently stationed in my household.

Exiting the long, white corridor of the old palace's section,

I entered its more ornate new addition. Here, instead of plain windows, the walls were pierced with intricate gilded lattice-work. Bright depictions of peacock feathers shimmering in blue, green and gold decorated the walls.

Knowing that I was going to take this route, I'd chosen to wear simple pants, chemise and kaftan in the same hue as these walls—blue-green. This morning I wanted to be invisible. I didn't feel up to playing average, which wasn't a simple thing to do: if one looked too strong one could be seen as a threat, but looking too weak meant one was an easy target. It was a hard balancing act, like walking on the edge of a sword.

I entered the registry hall. As usual my eyes fell on the gold frame and beautiful cream vellum of the registry. The name and birth rank of each prince was artfully penned on the registry. I noted that a black dot covered poor Hamed's number indicating his passing. The registry was updated daily. Tomorrow Hamed's name would be gone and the names below his would be shuffled around a lot before settling in a permanent position. Ranks tended to fluctuate depending on the weight of gold passing from the princes' mothers' hands to the tabulator's. Of course, the Sultan could stop this at any moment. But very few Sultans had done this. And neither did our father. So by now no rank was accurate anymore. Take me for instance; I should be ranked forty-four instead of fifty-five, but having no one to bribe the tabulator, my rank could only go down. Not that it mattered much. The tabulator was rumored to keep an unmodified registry stashed away, and it was this registry that my father would consult in the end. But most princes believed that Father would compare those two registries and choose the prince who had climbed in ranking the most. The other prevailing rumor was that the registry was useless, that only our actions counted and that they were all noted by the Grand Vizier. This rumor I believed.

I shrugged and hurried ahead. In my rushing, I turned the corner leading to the Great Hall a bit too fast and collided with my brother Darius.

"Ah, watch where you're going!" Darius grunted.

Not losing a second, I leaped back and bowed—more by prudence than respect. Darius was the most powerful of all my brothers and in my opinion the most dangerous. No other brother had more deaths linked to his name than he. I cursed myself for making such an avoidable mistake. Darius was certainly not hard to spot. Contrary to me, Darius wanted to be noticed, and dressed in consequence: bright red silk clothing, huge turban and overstuffed kaftan, anything to make him look bigger than he really was. And the thickness around his waist wasn't fat either, an over abundance of silk, no doubt. Darius was too smart to allow his body to become fat and slow.

"My most sincere apology, brother," I said.

Darius didn't reply. He just stared at me with narrowed eyes. A bad sign, I thought. Then again, Darius always looked at me that way, as if my presence alone in his vicinity offended him. I often wondered what incident had caused this profound dislike, a feeling I'd come to reciprocate with time. I believed it had its roots in our youth. Slowly Darius raised his hawk-beak nose high in the air. He hadn't inherited the classic profile of the Ban: a flawless profile I was proud to bare and why most portraits of our ancestors showed them from the sides. Still, Darius was handsome despite his hawk profile, or perhaps because of it—I couldn't tell. One thing was sure though, Darius knew he was handsome; and he wasn't going to hide his good looks under a beard, not even the shadow of one. Clean-shaven men were a minority in the palace. Wearing a beard was a more traditional look for a Telfarian prince. Was Darius's choice to go beardless just another way to get noticed?

I was still pondering this, when Darius closed the space separating us and his towering shadow fell over me. "You struck me," he said.

"It was an accident. I'm truly sorry for it." I meant every word.

"*Really!*" he said. "For some reason, I don't believe you."

I felt my guts twist. I knew what was coming—a duel for his bruised honor. Damn!

Outright murder was forbidden in the Cage. If caught in the act one could lose all rank. But if offended, a prince could kill his brother in an honorable combat—as long as it was overseen and authorized by the Grand Vizier. Sadly, princes got offended at nothing. And although months had passed since the last duel, I remembered a week which held as many as three duels per day. Many of my brothers saw their last days that week. Was today going to be my last day?

Just then I noted a group approaching behind Darius. Composed of eighteen of my brothers and their personal servants, this group formed Darius's court and followed him everywhere he went. Pledging allegiance to a powerful brother was a way of escaping a duel with him and securing one's survival after his crowning. I watched the group circle us. Dressed in Darius's vibrant fashion, my brothers resembled a flock of exotic birds. I peeked at my dull clothes and thought, *Crow*. With a sigh of resignation, I looked back at Darius.

He gave me a predatory smile.

I was readying myself for the words: "You have offended me," to come out of his mouth, when someone behind me said: "Hey, you're blocking our path to the kitchen."

I glanced over my shoulder and saw Ibrahim and his court approaching. Second most powerful brother, Ibrahim had fifteen supporters in his court. It was rumored that he was our father's favorite and most likely to become the next Sultan. Tall and fair-skinned, he favored clothes of dark shimmering hues of gray. His kaftan was trimmed in black fox and a bejeweled saber always hung at his hip.

Ibrahim's eyes skipped over me to settle on Darius. He smiled while twirling the tip of his waxed mustache, an action he often did. Ibrahim was very proud of his thick mustache. "You're in my path, Darius," he said.

"I'm always in your path, this isn't new," Darius replied. "You'll have to wait, Ibrahim. I have unfinished business here."

Ibrahim frowned. "Business, with whom?" He shot me a look of contempt. Ibrahim had decided long ago that I wasn't a threat. To him I barely qualified as an annoyance. Still having his cold calculating gaze on me was by no means pleasant. "You don't mean with our scholarly brother, Amir!" Ibrahim exclaimed; then he burst into laughter.

His supporters looked unsure of what to do, but as Ibrahim's rule over them was one of terror and violence, they followed his example and laughed too.

Seeing this as a chance, I turned to Darius. "Perhaps we could pursue this conversation another day."

Face pinched, Darius made the slightest of nods. Good enough for me. I scurried away, leaving the two factions to face each other. Only when I had put three turns of corridor between me and my brothers did I allow myself a break.

Resting against the wall, I exhaled heavily. This had been too close a call.

Although he was as vicious as a rabid dog, I wasn't afraid of Ibrahim—not much anyway; Darius however worried me. He was smart and saw everyone as a potential rival, even me. I believed this attitude came from not having the protection and push of a high-ranking or influential mother. Like me, and many other princes for that matter, Darius was the product of the "fancy-of-one-night" as it was called. Neither of us knew who nor where our mothers were. Raised by eunuchs and palace attendants, and taught by tutors, princes like us had to be clever to escape the harem's intrigues. Showing too much smarts and potential at a young age was dangerous. In general, smart motherless princes tended to die young. In comparison Ibrahim's childhood had been easy and sheltered.

The son of a Sultana, one of the four official Sultan's wives, he and his four full-blooded brothers were raised in the safety of her apartment. They formed a real powerhouse, those five—a cruel and deadly one.

I sighed. A few years back, I might have joined Darius's court, if he had asked me. Now it was too late—much too late. Things had happened between us that just couldn't be mended. All I could do was to wait for the day when Ibrahim and Darius would confront each other. Sadly that day was still far away. For the moment, they were content to growl at each other while dispatching weaker brothers or bulling them into allegiance. *No more mistakes, Amir. He's aware of you.* With this in mind, I moved toward the kitchen.

* * *

Carrying food for two days and for three persons, I took the direction of my tower. I wasn't bound to bring my mentally ill brothers food; if I didn't the palace's servants would take care of it. However, Mir and Jafer might refuse food from strangers—Mir in particular, his distrust of servants was stronger than mine—and I owed them for guarding my door. So I gladly did it.

Careful of every step, I reached the top of the stair without dropping anything. The huge silver platter I held with both hands bent under the weight of all this food. Aroma of saffron and herb stew teased my nose as I walked. My stomach began growling. I ignored it and looked ahead. As I passed the tall mirror I had placed at the corner of the corridor leading to my quarters (to see people approach from my door's grid), I caught a glimpse of myself. I looked more like a kitchen servant than a prince. I smiled. Pretty good, I thought, and walked to Jafer's door.

He began screaming and howling immediately.

"It's me, Jafer," I said. "I bring you food."

Calmed down, Jafer approached the broken grid of his door's window. His brown eyes were wide and glossy. The dark circles surrounding them seemed more somber than usual. It made me question when he had last slept. It also saddened me to see him this way. If healthy, Jafer would've been serious competition for Darius. Only a few years ago, Jafer was handsome, bright and strong. I sighed; only a few years ago he was sane.

"Evil is afoot. Its stench is everywhere." Jafer's voice was raspy from too much yelling. "Demons! Demons hidden in dark clouds. I hear them. Hear them speak all the time. Their voices are terrible, so terrible."

"I know, I know," I said. "I'll do my best to chase them away."

The deterioration of Jafer's mind had begun in his late teens. By now he was utterly mad. Agreeing with him and offering help was the only thing that soothed him… only to a point though. Jafer had to be kept under lock, because he could become violent without notice. But most times he just hurt himself and couldn't be trusted with anything sharper than a wooden spoon. Once he found a dagger and tried to stab himself in the ears to stop the voice in his head. Jafer was also prone to visions, or as some called it, "prophesying." In my opinion this had more to do with lack of sleep and bad digestion than anything else. These bouts of delirium were usually announced by a powerful sugary smell emanating from his entire body. There was no such smell in the air right now, so I unlocked the slot cut in his door and passed several plates of food to him, pilaf rice and roasted chicken, bowls of olives, dates and apricots and two loaves of bread. I didn't bring any water. Every room in the palace had its own fountain. Once I was done, I bid Jafer good day and moved to Mir's door.

Mir was quieter than Jafer, his door locked from the inside instead of the outside. He barricaded himself three years ago, believing that everyone in the palace was out to kill him. In this he was not that far off. For some, life in the Cage was intolerable. Mir belonged to those who were unable to cope with the constant threats and intrigues of the Cage. Although the stress had not led him to commit suicide, as it had many. But he did live his life in a state of permanent terror.

I knocked and waited. I knew Mir was on the other side, glued to the door, listening. "Mir… if you don't answer soon, I will leave."

Mir's window grid opened. Hard black eyes stared at me. "Are you alone?"

"Yes."

"Have they followed you?"

"No. I was careful." I tried not to smile. Mir always asked the same questions.

His meal slot opened with a metallic clank. I began pushing plates in.

"This isn't right," Mir said after the second plate of fruit and cheese—Mir loved goat cheese. (I suspected it was at the origin of the foul smell coming out of his room—leftover cheese and bad housekeeping.) "There's too much food. What's happening?"

I sighed. "Nothing. I won't leave my room tomorrow, that's all."

A flash of suspicion crossed Mir's eyes. "Why?"

While I raked my brain for some reassuring explanation to give my brother, I noted a bright object on the ground, a shiny brass bell. "What's this bell doing in the corridor?" I said, picking it up.

"EVIL… the stench of evil is everywhere!" Jafer shouted at my back.

"There's no evil, Jafer, please, stop worrying," I said in a voice I wanted light. Pocketing the bell, I added, "You too, Mir. I'm staying in to work, to study."

"Liar!" Mir said. He always caught my lying; I didn't know why I still tried. Stubbornness, I suppose. "There's a plot, isn't it." Mir continued. "That why this man came to see you—to plot! To plot against us!"

I frowned. "What man? What are you talking about?"

Mir blinked repetitively. "A man came after you left. He went into your room. I heard noises, and then he left."

I glanced at my door then back at Mir's eyes. "Who was it? What did he look like?"

"I don't know his name. He was tall and pale. Not a servant—a brother."

"Was he blond?"

"Perhaps, no one can tell what's under a turban." Mir then slammed his grid shut.

I rushed to my door and found it unlocked. With the silver platter precariously balanced in one hand and my sword in the other, I nudged the door open.

I winced. My rooms had been ransacked. Hundreds of books piled up in tumbling mounds dotted the rugs; my writing desk was toppled over with its inkwell spilled over embroidered cushions staining their exquisite designs. I followed the trail of debris to the entrance of my bedroom. This room too was a mess. Disgusted, I turned around. Immediately, my eyes went to the spiral staircase at the back of my reading room. I grimaced, certain that the upper level of my library was in the same disastrous condition as this one. A dark spot bobbing about in my fountain caught my eye; something was floating inside its blue and gold ceramic basin.

Cursing under my breath, I dropped the platter on the windowsill and dashed to the fountain. "Ahh... the bastard!" I let out, fishing a rare and precious booklet out of the water. The booklet was ruined: its meticulously painted illuminations smudged, the gold embossed leather bounding its exquisite verses of poetry drenched... totally ruined. Squeezing the dripping poetry booklet, I stared at my room. Rage abruptly engulfed me. I was so angry, I could've screamed, but instead I walked to my desk and straightened it. *It's going to take me a full day to right this room… better start now.*

I went to fetch the platter and stopped to admire the view outside the window, which was of a tower identical to mine. While staring at its beige brick wall, I took a series of deep, long breaths. The view was boring, yet this blandness was also calming. My worst moments of torment were often spent by this window. In the Cage, one found solace where one could.

Once my temper was somewhat appeased, I bent to pick up the platter. From that position I could see past the corner of the facing tower and into the mausoleum's yard. Through this narrow space between the towers, I saw a blurry figure roaming the court. The faint sound of music touched my ears. I listened attentively. There was no doubt in my mind: this was the low complaint of a cimara, a stringed instrument only played at funeral processions. The cimara's strident, lamenting notes were said to emulate the sound of the human soul. *Hamed's funeral procession.* The music was fading, which meant that the cortège had left the mausoleum some time ago. By the sound of it, they were nearing the third courtyard. So who was this person lingering in the mausoleum yard? I stretched but failed to get a better view. I put the platter on my desk and hurried up the spiral staircase.

"Damn!" I let out once I saw the messy room. "Two days of work, no less."

After a frantic search through the piles of books and scrolls spread about the floor, I found my brass telescope. I twirled the instrument in my hand in a state of utter panic. The telescope was intact, and its precious lens still in one piece. Breathing a sigh of relief, I kissed the shiny brass tube twice. Shoving it under my arm, I went to the closet. Inside were shelves filled with ancient clay tablets and two big apothecary chests stacked one on top of the other. I gripped the top one—a bulky ebony block of small square drawers adorned with ivory knobs—and shoved it aside. Behind this chest was an old unsealed window.

I had discovered it while making an inventory of the chest's contents. The window opened directly onto the mausoleum and its yard. The yard was simple: green grass with a brick path leading to the mausoleum—a white marble building with an arched doorway and a gold domed roof. The figure stood near the mausoleum's entrance with his back turned to me. He was tall and wore a white turban. As for the rest of his clothes they were of a foreign fashion, short coat and skintight pants tied just under the knee with a ribbon. To make matters worse, this garment was of the most ghastly shade of powder blue and embellished with silver arabesques. In my opinion, this was a hue ill suited for a man. I then noted something in the man's hand. I put the telescope to my eyes. At first everything was out of focus. After some quick adjustments, the image became crisper. I moved the telescope slowly, going down the man's shoulder to his hand. I gasped. He was clutching a white tulip. Was he mad? The white tulip was the symbol of our dynasty; therefore all white tulips belonged to my father and were only allowed to grow in one place—the Imperial White Tulip Garden. *How did he manage to get there unnoticed?* I was baffled—totally baffled. Not only was the White Tulip Garden outside the Cage, but it was also one of the most heavily guarded areas of the palace. For good reason, tulips were worth twenty times their weight in gold. Numerous conflicts had been waged over the ownership of a single tulip bulb.

As if sensing that he was watched, the man suddenly whipped around. I quickly focused my attention on his face. His eyes were identical to mine, almond-shaped and light brown, and so was his nose, straight and fine. His jaw was squarer than mine and his skin very fair and without any beard or mustache. I judged him younger than I, and although I couldn't see his hair, the paleness of his eyebrows told me that he was blond.

I lowered the telescope and stared at him. He seemed uneasy and kept looking over his shoulder. After a moment he stopped fidgeting and entered the mausoleum.

I stayed at the window, my head filled with questions. Who was he? I had to admit it: I was a bit vexed that this brother had managed to become more anonymous than I. How did he leave the Cage? Not only was it impossible, it was forbidden. Who did he bribe to get there? Amidst all these questions two things were very clear to me: First, he was a brother. Second... I pulled the locket from my pocket; he'd ransacked my room looking for this.

CHAPTER THREE

I n the days following the ransacking of my rooms, I searched for my tall blond brother throughout the Cage. I looked everywhere and asked everyone—short of questioning my other brothers, that is—without success. My blond brother was good at hiding.

On the third day, I abandoned my search and returned to my routine, which consisted of studying the stars, reading poetry tomes and experimenting with alchemy. I even tried my hand at potion making. But instead of the fortifying elixir I wanted to make, I produced the foulest smelling liquids there were—each stinking more than the next. A lot of my time was also invested in the study of diverse poisons and their effects. My library held an impressive amount of books on the subject. Again I failed to find anything that matched the effect seen on Hamed. Perhaps it was a mixture of several poisons? Or a new and exotic one, imported from a strange and faraway land.

Purposely ignoring the many volumes of black magic stacked on the highest shelves of my library, I went on searching through my botany books. *There must be a logical reason for the cold wall surrounding Hamed's body—a scientific one.*

After days spent bent over books, I grew tired of these blind guesses. Promising that I'd return to it later with fresh eyes, I put these volumes aside and returned to my normal schedule.

Between my regular study and failed potion experiments, I kept myself in good physical form by shadow fencing. Every day I spent two hours practicing fencing with all types of swords. Using a broad wooden post as a target, I struck at it from all angles while keeping my body in constant motion. Like every prince of the Ban Dynasty, I had been taught the art of fencing by the best tutors available. Master Sergio Olivese, who came from the faraway kingdom of Iberse, thought me particularly gifted at handling a rapier: The long narrow and flexible sword favored in duels. At fourteen, I was deemed the best fencer of my class, beating brothers several years older than I was, even Darius, who had been the best before I beat him. Thinking of it now, this could be the root of Darius's dislike of me. Perhaps beating him had been a mistake. But at fourteen, one rarely weighed the consequence of one's actions. I was so proud then. I remember walking about with my chest puffed up like a young rooster. This was before I learned that being the best was... well, bad. I sometimes longed for those carefree years. I certainly miss Master Olivese's fatherly attention and wise advice.

Following Telfarian tradition, my fencing lessons ended when I reached sixteen years of age. On its last day Master Olivese said to me: "Prince Amir, now begins your longest and most difficult lesson. Learning every movement of the great art of fencing was the easiest part. For you and your brothers keeping your skill sharp will be the hardest test. Remember this, my prince, all talent that isn't used dulls and eventually fades away. Don't let it happen to yours."

I did follow his advice. Others did too: Mustafa, Darius, Teric and a few more of my brothers practiced on a semiregular basis in one of the Cage's courtyards. However, as I knew about their practicing and could study their moves, they didn't know about mine and certainly didn't know my moves.

Time passed in the Cage as it did everywhere else. Days, then a week passed. I forgot about my tall blond brother. My search for the cause of Hamed's death slowly drifted to other subjects, and soon I forgot about it too. My life was back as it was before, except that I was now fetching my food at night. Not since my meeting with Darius had I dared going to the kitchen during the day—this even though I was sure he had forgotten about our *unfinished business*.

The only new things in my life were my dreams. Every night the mysterious beauty of the locket found me in my room. In these dreams only I spoke. She listened while I sang or recited poems like some enamored idiot. In other dreams, we'd walk side by side in the palace's celebrated White Tulip Garden. These dreams came every night without fault. I believed that if I didn't spend so much time gazing upon her lovely face before going to bed it might not have been so. But the few nights that I did not open the locket—which proved quite hard, taking most of my willpower—I found myself unable to sleep. I was bewitched. Part of this obsession was due to my self-imposed celibacy. Bringing a woman to my tower, although allowed—the Cage had its own harem—was certain to attract attention. I grimaced. This was an excuse. What really stopped me was that my last visit to the harem had ended in humiliation. No matter how long I lived, I would never forget that day—it was branded in my memory. Just thinking of it twisted my stomach in knots and made me want to break something.

That infamous day when I arrived at the Cage's harem, Darius was already there surrounded by the most beautiful of our women. Which didn't surprise me one bit—women loved Darius. I suppose his good looks and growing status had a lot to do with it. After a quick survey of the women still available, I found a few that didn't pass his standards of beauty but did pass mine. Petite women with slender bodies and lean, gracious limbs are to my taste. But every time I'd approach one, Darius—*may his penis rot off*—would snap his fingers and the woman immediately left my side for his, proving that they'd rather sleep on the rug at the foot of his bed than in the comfort of mine. Everyone present laughed. Well, I didn't find it amusing. My ability to play submissive had its limits, and that evening it came near to its breaking point. For a moment, I wanted to bash Darius's handsome face to a pulp, to pierce his belly with my sword; I wanted to kill the bastard. Then I came to my senses and stormed out of the harem. I hadn't returned since. I thought it safer that way. More than one argument began over a woman, and I certainly was not going to risk my life just because I felt lonely.

A long sigh escaped my lips; I hadn't had any female companionship for nearly three months. For a healthy young man, that felt like an eternity. This state of frustration was made worse by my nightly excursions. If I refrained myself from female comfort, my brothers didn't. The sound of their lovemaking could be heard from every corner of the Cage. With every passing day, my frustration grew, my loneliness deepened. I came to look forward to my dreams, and soon found myself going to bed earlier every night.

Tonight my dream began in the usual way, by taking me in to the White Tulip Garden, where again the locket beauty awaited me. Foggy air surrounded us like a thick moist veil. I stretched my hand toward her, as always trying to touch her, and as always she was a step too far.

"Come closer," I whispered. No answer. She produced only a head tilt and a coy smile. "What's your name? Please, tell me?"

For a brief moment I thought she was finally going to speak to me. Instead she did something even more surprising. She extended a pink rose to me. I had no idea from where the flower came, yet was overjoyed by the gift. But the moment I plucked the rose from her delicate fingers, dark stormy clouds rolled overhead. Thunder roared. Lightning struck the ground, blinding me. When my vision returned, I saw that she was gone. I was all alone. Then I saw that the tulips were gone too. I looked around in panic. I wasn't in the garden anymore, I was… right in front of the mausoleum. The air around me was thick, dark and cold. Thunder rumbled; lightning stabbed the sky, bathing everything in a silver-blue light. It was then that I saw dark shadows streaming out of the mausoleum, like the waves of an angry sea. Long blood-curling howls echoed. Shivers ran down my back. *This is wrong,* I thought in my dream state. *It shouldn't be like this. It's wrong, wrong, wrong!* The thunder drummed louder. My heartbeat sped up. The mausoleum steps were now a mass of boiling shadows. The thundering reached a crescendo, BANG, BANG, BANG.

I gasped, suddenly awakening.

BANG, BANG, BANG. Someone was pounding at my door, and the howling of my dream were my brothers' screams.

In my rush to exit my bed, I banged my toe on the side table. Lances of pain shot along my toe, foot and shin. I nonetheless hopped to the door, slid its grid open, and without any care for formality shouted: "What's the matter with you?"

The servant on the other side of the door paled. A pudgy-faced boy of thirteen, he wore the blue satin outfit of the palace's messengers. Determined to deliver his message, he raised his chin high. His pale cheeks turned bright red. The boy swallowed hard. "Prince Amir, I'm sent by Master Hassan. He requests your presence in the flower room as soon as Your Highness sees fit." The messenger boy let out a long breath.

I noted that Mir and Jafer had stopped screaming. Both were listening attentively, I was sure of that. Then I heard Jafer whisper in a quivering raspy voice: "Evil, dark, dark evil."

I looked at the boy; to question him would be as useless as questioning a courier pigeon: messengers' heads were nearly as empty as birds'. In a sense, their ignorance was the reason why they were often used in the most delicate of situations. The fact that Hassan had used one to carry this message was not a good omen.

I dressed in a hurry, choosing forest-green clothes, then followed the messenger boy to the Great Hall. We parted ways under its gilded dome. The boy returned to the messengers' quarter, while I traveled the many-arched alleys leading to the flower room. Upon reaching my destination, I faced a second bad omen. Two guards were posted on either side of the flower room's majestic, carved doors. This room had never been guarded before. Bowing, the guards opened the doors for me without my saying a word.

The exuberance of the flower room was always shocking at first. Covered with depictions of blooms that were either carved, painted or applied, from its ceiling to its floor, the room resembled some unruly bouquet put together by the hands of a gifted child. Once my eyes got used to all this decadent busyness, I was able to focus on the five men waiting at the back of the room. My gaze was immediately drawn to the stretch of white cotton on the floor, as an exhausted traveler was drawn to an oasis. Clearly someone lay under this draping. Yet something was amiss. The form bumping the sheet seemed oddly thin and misshapen. I took a step toward it. My foot struck something. A silver platter, broken glass and food were scattered on the floor. Sidestepping an apple, I moved on.

"Prince Amir," Hassan said, bowing. I noticed that the four guards framing Hassan were growing increasingly nervous with each one of my steps. And when I reached them, they backed away from me with their eyes cast down. "Leave us," Hassan ordered. The guards obeyed wholeheartedly, exiting the room in a matter of seconds.

This cannot be good, I thought as the doors slammed shut. My attention returned to the white sheet. "I assume this is the reason you called me here."

Hassan nodded. "Prepare yourself, Prince Amir. This is gruesome."

He lifted the sheet. I flinched and stepped back. Taking hold of myself, I stopped moving before my impulse to run away grew too strong. No amount of warning could prepare one for this sight; gruesome was too weak a word. The brother lying on the floor resembled a dried-up piece of meat. His skin was shriveled and black, making him impossible to recognize. Only his clothes indicated his rank. Kaftan of rich turquoise silk embroidered with gold leafs and lined with sable fur. His belt was made of silver and on his shrunken neck rested a thick gold necklace—I nearly choked when I saw those. Belt and jewelry were a clear indication of one's status, especially belts. Linen and cotton belts were for the lowest-ranked princes; silk, like mine and Darius's, for midranked ones; bronze for high-ranked princes, favorites' sons usually; and silver for the highest of all, the Sultanas' sons.

"He's Prince Mured, ninth in the line for the throne," Hassan said.

"How can you tell? I can't recognize his face anymore."

"The belt," Hassan said. "Only the ten highest-ranking princes wore solid silver belts. We did a quick survey, and he's the only one missing."

"Who found him?"

Hassan grimaced. "Kitchen servants. He asked that cheese and fruits be brought here."

My gaze flew to the food spread on the floor then back to Hassan. I must have looked confused because Hassan immediately explained how things had happened.

"The servants said that Prince Mured fell ill as soon as they entered the room. They panicked and called the guards for help. The group of four that stood here moments ago said they tried to help but hit an icy wall. They watched helplessly while Prince Mured was being transformed into this... this thing."

I stared at what was left of my brother. Mured belonged to Ibrahim's court, Darius's rival, so this could be Darius's doing. It wasn't the ruffian's style though. "Who then, who did this?" I whispered. "And how? How can someone do such a horrid thing?"

"With the Grand Vizier still at the Summer Palace with the Sultan, I'm at a loss. I was hoping you would know, Prince Amir."

I shook my head. "I don't know any poison able to do this."

I studied the room for clues and found none. The only thing this death had in common with the previous one, besides the icy wall, was the window, placed high on the west wall. *Hamed died near a window too, but does it matter. The palace counts thousands of windows, and this one is blocked by decorative metalwork that no one can squeeze past.* I walked to it and peered through its gilded wrought-iron work. "It's the full moon again, just like when Hamed died. Huh, but this shouldn't be of any importance."

"Perhaps… " Hassan hesitated, obviously embarrassed. "Perhaps Your Highness should seek answers outside the realms of nature and science."

Before I could ask Hassan to explain himself further, someone knocked at the door. A guard stepped in, shot me a look of fear and bowed. "Master Hassan, the imperial physicians are here."

"Let them wait, we're not finished yet."

The guard left but not before having given me one last terror-filled glance.

"Hassan, why are the guards afraid of me?"

"They believe you're a sorcerer, Your Highness. A yatus, tamer of demons and spirits, to be precise."

"What!" I was shocked. "Why? You know my opinion of magic. What have I done to deserve this title?"

Hassan became silent and his attention turned ton his hands, which he kept opening and closing. Then he let out a long sigh and said: "Rumors have been circulating in the Cage those last weeks. Mostly amongst servants—at first." Hassan finally looked up at me. "They say that strange and foul smells come out of your tower. That loud noises, banging noises, can be heard daily in your room." Hassan shook his head. "They say you're taming demons to do your biddings that you now fear daylight and only come out at night when it's dark."

I was aware that my mouth hung open, yet it took me a moment longer to close it. The smells were my failed experiments, the banging my fencing practices. And as for my night excursions, I was hardly the only one to do so—how could they make up such a story! "I can explain everything," I said between clenched teeth. "It has nothing to do with magic."

"I believe you, Prince Amir. Unfortunately, I'm afraid it will get worse. One of the guards who witnessed Prince Mured's death also witnessed Prince Hamed's. With the rumors already floating around, your name was the first to pop into his head and then out of his mouth. By the time I was called upon the murder scene, the story of your brothers' demise, added to your suspicious behaviors, had spread through the guards, the kitchen servants, the maids. By now it probably has reached the harem." A sad expression crossed Hassan's face. "I believe that by the morning the entire palace will be aware of it."

"There's more to this, isn't it? There's something you're not telling me?" I stared into Hassan's eyes. He held my gaze for a short moment. I didn't care one bit for the apologetic look I could see in his eyes.

"Prince Amir, they already think you're guilty of these crimes."

Although I knew he was going to say that, the words twisted my stomach in knots nonetheless. I looked at what used to be my brother. Perhaps Hassan was right. Perhaps I should search outside the realm of science. I grimaced; perhaps I should look into magic.

* * *

This morning I was out to the kitchen at an early hour. After what Hassan had told me last night, I thought it best to stop my nightly excursion, at least for a while. I climbed down the stair two steps at a time and turned left toward the Great Hall, where most princes took their meals. When I entered the spacious room, all conversation stopped and the dozens of brothers assembled there with their personal entourage stared at me with a terrifying intensity. Stuck at the back, some young messenger boys where stretching and twisting to get a glimpse of me. This display of curiosity was truly humiliating and enraging—and I had to admit it was also quite frightening. (When people stop talking whenever you appear, you know you're in trouble.) With this in mind, I crossed the room as quickly as I could.

This must be how lepers feel: shunned and feared at the same time. How could they believe me guilty of such abominable crimes? I wanted to shout my innocence, but my reasonable side ordered me to hold my tongue and move fast. The conversation restarted as soon as I was out of the Great Hall. I encountered the same, if not worse, attitude in the kitchen. Here however fear dominated, and the word *yatus* could be heard whispered all around the room.

Stoically, I watched a doe-eyed kitchen servant stack my platter with trembling hands. The trip back to my tower went without incident. The fact that I didn't offend any of my brothers on the way there was the only positive thing about this morning. Still, I knew I would have to come out again today. I had no choice. I had to seek my brothers' killer. More so, I had to prove my innocence.

Later that day I decided to revisit both murder scenes. I did the flower room first as it was the freshest. I jotted down a few notes, then moved to the old alley where Hamed had died. Slowly, I walked along the narrow white corridor, running my hand along its rough plastered walls, studying every crack of its tiled floor. I found nothing.

With a sigh, I leaned against one of the windows and stared at the desert's gold dunes for a brief instant, then looked straight down. Linking two towers together, this covered alley was suspended three stories high in the air. No one could climb through these windows. *Well, that option is gone.*

A familiar tingling at the base of my neck warned me of a presence at my back.

"What do you want?" I said without turning. I didn't need to. The mildew smell now saturating the air undeniably belonged to my blond brother.

"To talk with you," he replied. His voice was soft, yet its tone was extremely masculine, every word crisp and clear. A voice meant to carry over crowded halls.

I slowly turned. I had guessed right. My tall, blond brother stood a short distance away from me. His head was bare, leaving cascades of blond curls free to dance in the cool breeze blowing through the alley. Again he wore hideous foreign clothes: tight knee-high pantaloons, white frilly shirt and a form-fitting vest. A wide-sleeved, open coat finished the ensemble. Except for the shirt, the entire suit was the most disgusting canary yellow—just looking at it made me nauseous. As if this wasn't enough of an affront to good taste, the suit was made of satin. I also noted that his hideous garments were wrinkled, as though he had slept in them... in the closet. His face was gaunt, I thought, as if food had been sparse, and rest sparser still. It wasn't so when I had seen him last, about a month ago. While I studied him one thing became very clear for me, the girl in the locket was more than likely his mother. The resemblance was evident.

"Can we talk?" he asked again.

I then realized that my hand was in my pocket, my fist closed possessively over the locket. *It's his, not mine. Give it back,* I ordered myself. *Give him the locket, now.* No use, I couldn't bring myself to part with it. I just couldn't. So I decided that as long as he didn't ask for the locket I would keep it, and chose not to mention his ransacking my room for fear of losing this lovely treasure.

"Why should I listen to anything you have to say?" I finally replied.

"Because you're seeking the one responsible for our brothers' deaths."

I frowned. "For all I know you might be involved in these deaths."

He chuckled, as if I had jested. "But I am involved—we all are... in a way."

I didn't like his attitude one bit. "Explain yourself more clearly or I'll leave," I said, crossing my arms on my chest.

His face became very serious. "I believe we're all marked for death."

All right, now he had all my attention. "Go on."

"You know of two deaths, but there have been three of these cold, choking attacks. Two months ago I witnessed the first one. That attempt failed. But last month it succeeded in killing Hamed. Now Mured has been killed, and in the most horrible manner. Do you see the progression? Whoever is behind this is getting better at killing us... much better."

CHAPTER FOUR

"**B**efore going any further, tell me your name," I asked, while gripping the hilt of the short sword hidden in my belt at the small of my back.

My blond brother blinked in surprise, then smiled as though the fact that I couldn't put a name to his face pleased him. "Call me Erik."

"Erik?" I frowned. "Erik is not a Ban name—not a Telfarian name either for that matter."

"Amir," he said in his soft masculine voice. "You have more than one name yourself, don't you? So do I, and Erik is the one I wish you to use for me."

I shrugged, he was right: We all had at least five names, each linked to some meaningless title. One of mine was Omar, Lord of the Seventh Gate of Irabel. As we were over a hundred princes, introducing us this way took hours… and was extremely boring. Fortunately for us, our full names were only used in very special occasions, like when a foreign king visited our kingdom.

I studied Erik's face, his robust body; he clearly was of Nordic descent. In a way it made sense that one of his names was also Nordic. Yet one thing didn't make sense—his behavior, his lack of fear toward me. "Everyone in the palace thinks I killed our brothers. Some even believe I'm a yatus and fear me. Why aren't you afraid?"

Noises down the corridor made him look around nervously. "This spot isn't safe. Come with me and I'll tell you why I don't fear you."

Squeezing the hilt of my sword tighter, I didn't move from the window. I just stared at him unsure of what to do.

"Oh, come on," he said. "This isn't the time to be so suspicious. Look, I'm unarmed."

Lifting his coat up, Erik turned around, showing me that he concealed no weapons at his back. "See! I didn't lie. You can let go of that sword now. Come, follow me."

Gesturing to me, he started walking.

All right, I thought. If he was willing to turn his back on me, knowing that I was armed, perhaps I could allow myself to follow him. After a brief hesitation, I fell into Erik's tracks. I was not surprised when he entered the servants' alley, and although his subsequent descent in the dark, humid wine cellar was somewhat intriguing, it was what followed that truly shocked me.

Turning sideways, Erik squeezed between two giant oak barrels until he reached the brick wall behind them and waited there for me to join him. I thrust myself along, unable to decide what was more suffocating, the overwhelming smell of wine or the incredible tightness of the place. I had trouble breathing. My malaises increased when I realized that in this confined spot I couldn't pull my sword. I cursed my stupidity. Why had I followed him here? I knew better. Meanwhile Erik was probing the brick wall with his fingertips.

"Found it!" he exclaimed. "I don't often use this road. So when I do I never remember which brick to press." With these words, he leaned against the wall. The sound of stone grinding stone filled the air, then, right in front of us, a door suddenly opened into darkness. A strong mildew smell rushed out.

I stared at this somber opening, amazed. Should I go in? I hesitated for an instant—just long enough for my eyes to adjust to the surrounding darkness—then stepped into the narrow room now visible through the doorway. "How did you find out about this passage?"

Erik made a face. "Hiding from our dear brothers, how else." He lit a lamp. Soft gold lights climbed the walls on either side of us, exposing pigeonholes overflowing with scrolls of all sizes. There were some stacked in baskets on the floor and more piled in precarious pyramids on the massive oak desk on our right. Omitting a couple wooden stools, this desk was the only true piece of furniture in this corridor-shaped room.

"What is this place?" I asked.

"The palace's architect's storing room. Most of these scrolls are plans of the palace's many expansions, rooms, towers and even its catacombs."

I unrolled one of the scrolls. It contained drawings of a portico. Detailed to perfection, the drawing even listed the color to be used for its decoration in the margins of the scroll.

Erik leaned over my shoulder and looked at the drawing. "Ahh, the east portico of the Divan Hall. They used a lotus design instead of the green palms drawn here."

I opened my mouth to ask how he knew about this change of detail, then shut it right back. Obviously the modified plan was somewhere in one of these pigeonholes. Erik probably studied them all, I certainly would have. Oh, yes, I would've happily lost myself in their studies for months, if not years, I thought with a smile. I wanted to stay here longer, but Erik was already moving ahead. Reluctantly, very reluctantly, I placed the scroll back in its hole and trailed him into an adjacent room. A broad square place, it had served as a drawing room, as the slanted-top table pushed against the left wall indicated. Now occupying the center of the room was a low round table with a brilliant blue mosaic top. Layers of rugs blanketed the stone floor and cushions were thrown in piles around the table. A daybed filled the right corner with still more cushions spread on top of it. Nearby stood a tall ebony armoire, through its half-opened doors I could see stacks of clothes, of questionable hues, piled up in a disorderly manner. I glanced at Erik's wrinkled canary-yellow suit and tried not to gag.

"What's in there?" I pointed to a second room opening on my right; the smell of mildew and rotten paper coming out of it was particularly strong.

"More storage."

"Ah! So you live here?" It was a rhetorical question, really. What I was seeing now explained Erik's rotten paper smell and wrinkly appearance.

He nodded. "It's safer than my official apartments." Tugging one of his blond curls, he added, "I make a too-visible target."

I snickered. "Your choice of clothes is more the cause than your hair, little brother."

Looking surprised, he ran a hand on his suit. "You think so?"

It took me everything I had not to roll my eyes at him. And for a second, I questioned his judgment, or lack there of. "Forget that! I'm not here to give you advice on how to dress, although you're in great need of some, but to hear what you know about our brothers' murders."

"Let us sit and I will tell you everything I know."

Once we were both settled amidst his many cushions, Erik began: "Two months ago, I was having a conversation with our brother Rashid in the blue fountain room, when suddenly he began gasping for air. I tried to help him and immediately struck a wall of ice. I managed to push through it and Rashid started breathing again. I thought of this as an oddity and forgot all about it until Hamed skipped one of our meetings. Fearing that he might've fallen in one of our brothers' traps, I went in search of him. When I found Hamed, he was already dead, and you and Hassan were at his side. Not knowing what to do, I hid in the alcove and watched."

"You saw me break the spell that was over Hamed's body, like you did with Rashid."

Erik nodded. "I think that without our intervention, Rashid and Hamed would've both ended up like Mured—a lump of dried meat."

I stared into Erik's eyes. "The others think I'm guilty of these crimes, why don't you?"

He shrugged. "You're no murderer! I watched you often; I know what you're about. You keep to yourself, as I do. We have that in common—besides our father. I've wanted to talk to you for the longest time. But I didn't know how to approach you."

I nodded in agreement. Prudence was something else we had in common, I thought. Approaching a brother was indeed a delicate and risky operation. He'd done well to wait. My suspicion toward this brother lessened. I felt myself relax, but only for a few seconds—good things never seem to last.

A shadow scouring across the doorway on my right sent me to my feet. My sword was out and ready without my having to think about it.

"NO!" Erik shouted. Rolling to his side, he gripped something under the rug and swung it forth just as I thrust my sword toward the shadow. Sparks flew, as my blade was blocked by the very tip of Erik's long Nordic sword, called a claymore.

With a whimper of fear, the shadow moved into the light. It was a slim, young servant boy. Had Erik used a Telfarian saber, which was a good deal shorter than the Nordic sword, I would have pierced this frail youth through and through. The boy stayed frozen in the light with both hands clamped under his nose. His green eyes, the only feature of his face visible, were wide with terror. Breaking out of his frozen state, the boy turned heels and ran out of sight, leaving Erik and I facing each other sword in hand.

I held my ground, eyes fixed on his claymore. I was the vulnerable one here; his weapon was superior to mine. If I had my rapier in hand instead of this short sword, I would have thought differently. And although I believed myself quicker, he had proven himself fast too. To my utter astonishment, Erik lowered his sword to the ground then let it fall upon a cushion. That was the stupidest move I had ever seen in my life. One should never unarm oneself, not under any pretext. But to do it when facing an armed brother, *tsk-tsk-tsk,* I shook my head at his mental ineptitude.

"Amir, please, lower your sword," Erik pleaded. "Rami is my loyal servant. I couldn't let you hurt him. The boy poses no danger—a breath can easily topple him over."

"The boy isn't the one I'm worrying about, little brother."

Erik grinned. "Twice you called me little brother, this although I'm a head taller than you."

"I believe you're younger than I am."

"Right! Two years separate us. I really am your little brother and perhaps with time you'll come to trust me as such."

This time I rolled my eyes—rolled them twice. Wasn't he told that you couldn't trust anyone in the palace—especially your brothers? I supposed not. I decided that I had spent enough time with that idiot. Without saying another word, I returned to my tower.

* * *

The following day began pleasantly enough: The weather was fine; I had plenty of food left and didn't need to go to the kitchen. I was looking forward to doing quite a bit of research. I had already pulled some of the magic books I own from my library and brought them to my reading room for that purpose. The afternoon was barely beginning when my luck abandoned me.

Piercing howls and screams from Jafer followed by a trolley of Mir's filthiest insults, announced that someone was at my door. My heart skipped a beat. I had the terrible certainty that another of my brothers was dead. Erik's face popped into my mind. Visions of his dried, shrunken body followed. Someone that naïve—not to say stupid—was bound to perish sooner rather than later. He was dead, I was sure of it. So when I looked through my grid I was stunned to see him standing there, dressed like a desert Bedouin gone mad. Layers upon layers of cotton and billowing muslin wrapped his body from head to toe—and that lime green color. *Where does he find these ugly things?*

For a brief instant I wondered if I hadn't discovered another mentally unstable sibling—for some reason, they seemed to be attracted to me like flies to honey.

"Good afternoon, Amir," Erik said above the screams and insults of my guarding brothers. "Can I come in?" Grimacing, he glanced over his shoulder. "Are they always like this? This is awful."

I was too shaken by his presence at my door to answer right away. One didn't seek out his brothers. That was seeking out trouble. He had some nerve, I thought, or no brain at all. I settled on the second. "Why are you here?" I asked in a sharp tone.

"To help you solve the mystery of our brothers' deaths," Erik declared, his face split by a broad silly grin.

"No!" I snapped. "Absolutely not! Go away now."

"Why not? I can be helpful—certainly more than Mir and Jafer."

I snorted. "They do a good job guarding my door. As for you, I don't see how you can help me. You can't even dress appropriately. Learn that first." My remarks failed to bring any change in Erik. He didn't even move. "Are you deaf?" I said.

He shook his head, his silly grin still pasted on his face. "We can help each other. Exchange ideas. Rami can do your errands. This way you'll have more time for your studies. We can practice fencing. I'll even let you win."

"WHAT!" I shot through clenched teeth. I couldn't believe the audacity of this idiot. I swung the door open and stepped in his face. "Little brother, leave now before I become offended to the point of demanding reparation."

He blinked, and his silly grin vanished. "I had no intention of insulting you. I apologize to you, my brother." With a solemn look on his face, Erik bowed to me, a mark of high respect. Which was unusual, princes generally only nodded at each other. When he straightened I saw that he was smiling again. "I'll leave as you wish. But I'll be back tomorrow, and the day after and the day after that. I'll continue knocking on your door until you accept my help."

Turning to leave, Erik took a couple of steps back, stopped in front of Jafer's door and tilted his head. "He's making odd sounds, is it normal?"

I was there in seconds. I stuck my ear to Jafer's door. Gargling sounds were coming from inside his room. "He's swallowing his tongue again."

In a rush of panic, I removed the metal bar locking the door and opened it wide. "Oh, no!" I let out upon seeing my brother.

Jafer was slumped against the doorframe, his body looked as limp as wet clothes, and his face had already turned blue. Without losing time, I shoved my fingers into his mouth and cleared his airway. Jafer gasped loudly and, to my utter relief, began gulping air. His face quickly retuned to a near normal shade, yet his eyes remained rolled back in his head.

I noted that Erik was still here. He stood in the doorframe, staring at me with wide eyes. "He's going to be fine now," I said, cradling Jafer's upper body against mine. "You should go, Erik. Your presence is not helping."

Erik nodded and left without arguing.

I carried Jafer inside the room, which wasn't easy, Jafer being of Darius's stature. A part of me, the practical one, regretted having sent Erik away so soon. He could have helped me handle Jafer's limp, awkward body—oh well. When, after much struggling, I finally laid him on his couch, the air surrounding him became thick with the smell of sweets.

Jafer suddenly sat straight up. Gazing into empty air, he began speaking. "The line will be broken. Clouds… forming around the new line." He gasped, and drool dripped from the corner of his mouth.

Using the corner of my sleeve, I dried his chin. There wasn't much else I could do. I knew better than to try stopping him when he was in this state. Nothing could halt these… episodes. By no means would I call the obscure, senseless things coming out of his mouth *prophesies*. There was a logical explanation for his present condition. I believed the many visitors that had knocked at my door recently had strained Jafer's already fragile nerves causing this bout of delirium.

Jafer shivered violently. "The rose and the tulip will unite… unite… the rose...se—" Just as suddenly as he had risen, Jafer slumped back on the couch totally exhausted. It was as though these senseless ramblings were robbing him of all his strength, so much so that it usually took him a few days to recover after each episode.

As usual, I stayed with Jafer until he succumbed to a peaceful sleep and wasn't in danger of choking anymore. Once back in my rooms, I fell into a slumber of my own.

True to his promise, the next day Erik was at my door early in the morning. I rushed to open the door before his knocking awoke Jafer.

"What now?" I grumbled, while rubbing my eyes. I felt in no mood to deal with his stupidity.

With a serious face, Erik extended a small box to me. "I was rude to you, my brother. I can only hope this small gift will help me redeem myself in your eyes."

"Huh…" I made, staring at the box. I was taken off-balance by this gift. That was new to me. As prince the palace supplied everything for me. I just needed to ask and it was produced, as long as it was within my rank. (One couldn't order oneself a silver belt; otherwise we'd all wear one—things of this sort.) But gifts, gifts were different. I had never received one—not ever. Only the princes whose mothers had remained in the palace received gifts.

I took the box with hesitant hands. Superb work of cloisonné enamel in green, yellow and white covered its entirety in an intricate floral motif. The box's weight surprised me; it was as heavy as a brick. Obviously it contained something. I lifted the lid. Inside were a matching inkwell, a sand shaker, and a quill knife, all done in the same cloisonné enamel pattern as the box. *This is too much; the box alone is a royal gift.*

"Do you like it?" Erik asked, beaming.

"It's gorgeous. But… you can't buy my trust with gifts." Reluctantly, I extended the box to him.

Erik shook his head. "*Tsk-tsk-tsk,* such a suspicious mind." He pushed my hand back. "It's a gift, not a bribe. I know I have to earn your trust—and your friendship."

"Friendship! I don't need friends."

"You can't fool me with rudeness, brother. There's good in you. The way you care for Mir and Jafer proves it. And don't say it's because they guard your door. I'm not that stupid. You do a lot more for them than you say. You keep too much to yourself, Amir, that's your problem. Not all your brothers have murder in mind. Many of us just want to survive the succession and leave the Cage… is that so hard to believe?"

No, it wasn't, but old habits died hard. Years of fear and distrust can't evaporate in an instant.

Sensing my uncertainty, Erik stepped back and made a graceful spin. "See, I even dressed boringly for you. Rami chose these clothes for me. I'm making an effort… I think you should reciprocate."

For once Erik wore something normal, so much so, I had failed to notice. I looked at the ensemble. Copper silk baggy pants and vest, cream-colored linen shirt, and a black sash circling his waist that matched his boots, it was… tasteful.

I nodded approvingly. Then, perhaps because I was lonely or just plain curious, or both, I said: "All right, I suppose you can come in. Oh, and from now on let the boy dress you."

CHAPTER FIVE

My time in Erik's company went by fast. So much so that at the end of the day, when Rami showed up to fetch his master, I was stunned to see that it was already dark outside. Although Erik had evaded some of my questions—mainly the ones concerning his parentage, his ability to stay hidden for so long and his appearance at the mausoleum—by diverting the conversation to our common area of interest: books, arts and fencing—I knew there would be other occasions to question him again and didn't push further. Still, I was somewhat sad to see him leave. I suppose I was lonelier than I had thought and spent the rest of the evening reviewing the day's events in my mind. I'd never invited anyone in my tower before. It filled me with a wild mixture of giddiness, uncertainty and excitement. For effect that that night I found myself unable to sleep and decided that a trip to the kitchen for hot honeyed-milk was in order.

As I approached the kitchen's entrance the low buzz of a conversation touched my ears. The mention of my name stopped me dead in my tracks. Flattening myself against the entrance wall, I listened to the cooks and their crews' conversations.

"He's up to no good, I tell you," said a gravelly male voice.

"Yes," a female one replied. "My friend Ali, who valets on the second floor, said he saw Prince Amir commanding a green jinni."

Gasps of fear and yelps of stupor echoed.

"Yes, I swear," the woman continued, "a real jinni, all surrounded with green vapor and with a face too beautiful to be human. Ali said that Prince Jafer nearly died of fright."

I winced. My fists became two white-knuckle stones. *Spies.* All these servants were spies of the worst kind: stupid, uneducated, superstitious ones. That green jinni was no other than Erik in his crazy Bedouin's costume. And he was not *that* beautiful, either.

"Shh," someone hushed. "I hear steps. Not another word; Master Hassan hates gossips."

"Ah, relax, it's only Rami," exclaimed the gravelly male voices.

Rami! Erik's servant is in there. I wonder if he's going to set things straight. My curiosity now pinched to the extreme, I inched closer to the door.

"What news do you bring us, Rami—juicy ones I hope?" Laughter spread throughout the kitchen. "Come on, don't be shy. We know your master sends you out to gather news. Share what you learn with us. Is it true that the Sultan fell ill? Is that why the Grand Vizier was called to his side so urgently?"

There was a long moment of silence. Then a small, fluted, almost girlish, voice said, "Yes, it's true."

"What about Prince Amir? Is he a yatus?"

"A yatus?" Rami said, "Huh, hard to say—he sure has enough magic books in his library for that, though."

Spies! All of them! Rami too. That boy's nothing but a snaky spy. For a second I wanted to step in and rectify their opinion of me. But I knew it was useless. These people would still choose to believe this juicy story over the plain boring truth. And why should I make the effort. I was a prince. I didn't have to explain my actions to anyone, let alone servants. I'd heard enough of this and left the kitchen. My hunger was gone anyway. I took the road to my tower, crossing as many rooms and halls as I could. I needed to exercise, needed to vent the worst of my anger. Because I was so blindingly enraged, I only realized that I had entered the sitting room leading to the Cage's biggest courtyard once I was completely inside it. This was the heart of the Cage, thus a dangerous place to be.

Slowing down my pace, I glided a hand under the loose folds of my kaftan and found the spot at the small of my back, where I usually carried my sword. Damn! It was empty. I ground my teeth, while hissing a series of swearwords. *That's what company and distraction brought me: trouble—heaps and heaps of trouble!*

The short hair on the back of my neck suddenly stood up. Right away I knew I wasn't alone anymore. From the corner of my eye, I spotted two dark forms scattering to the right. I noted two more moving on my left. Sensing a presence at my back, I turned around. A tall man stood a few paces from me. Dressed in the flowing black robe of the nomadic desert tribe, his head and face were covered by the traditional flowing headdress, meant to protect one from the blowing desert sand, leaving only his eyes exposed. My attention paused on the weapon clutched in his hand. I felt my eyebrows rising at the sight of the spike ball topping the metal shaft in his grip. *A mace! Who fights with a mace these days?*

I glanced around quickly and saw that the four other men had surrounded me and were also dressed in a similar fashion. The black flowing garments made it impossible to put names on either forms or faces. *Clever bastards!* This ambush had been well prepared, but by whom? Which members of my family wanted me dead badly enough to plan an unsanctioned attack and risk being stripped of their ranks?

Stop thinking and act, unless you want to die now, a voice screamed in my mind. I urgently searched the room for anything that could serve as weapon. My eyes fell on a tall iron candleholder on my left. The tall man then lunged toward me, wielding his mace with a disconcerting easiness. I swiftly rolled to the candleholder's foot. Missing my head by a hair, the mace struck the marble floor, shattering its beautiful blue tiles. As I moved farther away from the man with the mace, another dark figure ran toward me with a saber raised high above his head. Grabbing the candleholder by its long pole, I blocked his blow with it. Sparks flew as metal struck metal. I pushed on the pole, keeping my attacker's blade at bay. Meanwhile, I could hear the four others closing in on me from behind.

I needed a weapon, and I needed it now. In desperation, I kicked my attacker in the belly. I couldn't afford gallantry right now.

"Ouff!" escaped my attacker's mouth as he doubled over.

Not losing time, I wrenched his wrist until he dropped his saber. Scooping it up, I faced the four men with a saber in one hand and the candleholder in the other.

Twirling his mace, the tallest man of the group began circling me. His accomplices followed his example, their circle shrinking with every turn. I raised my weapons, hoping that my years of solitary practice had kept my skills sharp. Sadly, a part of me was aware that I was grossly outnumbered and that no amount of skill would suffice to save me. Yet I was determined to do as much damage as I possibly could. I would not die alone, I decided, glaring at my approaching enemies.

They were about to pounce on me, when a voice boomed: "Stop, I order you! Halt this unsanctioned combat this instant!"

The men in black robes froze.

My gaze flew to the nearest courtyard doors. The Grand Vizier stood in its frame. A dark figure against the dark sky behind him, only the slim yellow line edging his black kaftan, robe and turban made him discernable from the background. He made a slight hand gesture and half a dozen imperial guards rushed into the room. The black-robed men withdrew from the sitting room at high speed with the guards on their heels.

I let out a long sigh of relief. Lowering my weapons, I

watched the Vizier approach. Nazir Bey wasn't an imposing man. He was only slightly taller than I, yet every time I'd faced him he never failed to make me feel minuscule. He had a dominating presence, well-suited for his post of Grand Vizier, and a stare so cold it could bring the rowdiest of crowds to silence with the briefest of glances. And although Nazir was second in power after my father, it was no secret that *he* was the one who truly ran the kingdom. I looked at his dark angular face, trying hard not to concentrate too much on his long narrow nose.

"Prince Amir," he said, once in front of me. "Why am I not surprised to see that you're the cause of this… disturbance."

My jaw dropped in the most inappropriate of manner. "Grand Vizier, I was the one attacked."

One of Nazir's well-arched eyebrows peaked up. "I heard otherwise. Some say that you've been attacking your brothers—successfully killing two by using dark magic."

"Gossip! Lies! You know better than anyone that these stories of magic, curses and demons are untrue. These things don't exist. It's superstition."

Nazir raised a hand, stopping me. "You're right, Prince Amir. I know these things better than anyone else. And I know it can be done."

I felt the blood leaving my face. I was suddenly very cold. "Surely you don't believe me capable of these acts of villainy, otherwise why come to my help now."

The Grand Vizier smiled—not a pleasant sight. "I can't risk having the true heir denied access to the throne because he has engaged himself in an unsanctioned combat. The next Sultan should come to power without any doubt as to the legitimacy of his right to rule." The Grand Vizier stared straight into my eyes—his were so dark it was like staring into bottomless pits. "As for Prince Hamed and Mured's assassin, I believe he should hang as the murderer that he is instead of dying in a royal ambush."

The coldness that had seized me moments ago vanished and warm blood rushed to my head. My face was suddenly on fire, my ears burning. I was so shocked that I couldn't think. I couldn't speak. I could barely breathe. In the face of my silence, the Grand Vizier bowed and exited the room.

I'm doomed, I thought once alone. *Unless I find who's behind these deaths, I'm doomed.*

* * *

How dare he say those things to me, I thought while storming through the Cage's corridor. I could ask for reparation. After all, I was a prince and the Grand Vizier had insulted me. Deep down, I was far from sure that my father would choose me over him. I feared taking that chance. What was I to Father but one of many expendable sons. I didn't matter. Nazir, on the other hand, had loyally served him for longer that I had existed. Father trusted him; they had a bond.

Still shaken by my encounter with the Grand Vizier, I found myself going in the direction of the wine cellar instead of my tower. This realization only increased my speed. Filled with rage and unclear intentions, I burst into Erik's secret room. The place was empty. I moved about my brother's clutter of oddities, seeking for some clue—to what, I didn't know. I then cast my eye to the adjacent room; the one Rami had come out of on my first visit here. With no candle burning inside, the open room was like the black mouth of some monstrous creature waiting for me to walk into its trap. *Don't,* said my instinct. Dismissing its warning, I grabbed the nearest lamp and walked to its threshold. A retched smell hit me: a mixture of mildew, wet paper, rotting leather, so heavy, I nearly backed off. With a deep breath, I pushed in.

"Oh my!" I couldn't believe my eyes. Books, all kinds of books, by the thousands, were piled from floor to ceiling. They covered every wall of this round towerlike room. I raised my lamp high, trying unsuccessfully to illuminate the ceiling. The books seemed to go on forever. How high could this room be, I wondered, three-stories high, four at the least? Shining my light on the nearest wall, I began scanning through its titles. Volumes of philosophy by great masters, manuals on all kinds of art, tomes on arithmetic and algebra, and every single one of these books was rare and precious.

My eyes jumped a row, settling on an old leather binding circled with brass locks. Although the writing on its spine was faded, I recognized the book as a dark magic manuscript. The black-hand symbol branded on its spine didn't lie. Stacked on top of it was a botany manual, explaining the many uses of plants, herbs and minerals. This manual was used for making cures as well as for making poisons. It was often referred to, in books of my own collection, as the best of its type. I was stretching a hand to grab the botany manual when I heard someone walking in the other room.

"Hurry!" I heard. It was Erik's voice—on the edge of laughter. "Come, this is our last night. We mustn't waste it."

Last night for what? I didn't know what Erik meant, yet the good humor filtering through his voice angered me. I stormed out of the book room ready to confront him.

Gaping in astonishment, Erik stared at me as if I were a ghost while Rami yelped and ran in a dark corner. "Amir, what are you doing here?" He asked once he'd managed to close his mouth.

I glared at Rami's silhouette hidden in the shadows. "Your servant is betraying you, spreading rumors and false stories."

Erik's face furrowed with confusion. "What are you talking about?"

"Tonight, I heard him spread information concerning our father and me in the kitchen."

"Ah…" Erik said. With a wink to the servant boy, he said, "Rami only spreads the news I allow him to spread. Usually its news already circulating in the palace that servants would learn by morning anyway. And the information he brings back to me in exchange is well worth the one he gives them. Rami would never give away personal information. I trust him to keep my secrets. He's my eyes and ears outside this room."

In my opinion, Erik was too trusting, too naïve also. With the right amount of gold his servant would betray him just as quickly as anyone else in the palace.

"Well, I don't trust him or you," I said. I then told him of my earlier attack, of my meeting with the Grand Vizier and his suspicions toward me. Worse to me was that a servant had taken Erik for a jinni—and deemed me a yatus, a sorcerer, *me*, who despised magic—and all this because of his horrible costume. Even though Erik looked genuinely surprised and concerned by my misadventure, I wasn't sure I trusted him anymore. And by the way Erik looked at me now, I assumed that my distrust was written on my face.

"I'm not the cause of your problem," he risked, "your isolation—"

"You're *a* cause!" I snapped. "Not to mention that you've hid all these books from me. I'm not a fool; I know you're hiding something else."

Erik gave me a sheepish look. "You're right. I keep some secrets from you. Think I should tell him, Rami?"

The servant shook his head violently. Why wasn't I surprised?

"I disagree," Erik said, "I believe it's time."

"Time for what?" I was suddenly nervous.

"To share my most precious secret with you." Turning to his servant, Erik said, "Rami, find some dark clothes for Amir. Tonight he's coming with me."

"Where? I'm not falling in another ambush, one was more than enough. Unless you tell me where we're going, I'm not moving." I crossed my arms on my chest to show my resolve, which only brought a grin on Erik's face.

"There's no ambush where we're going, my suspicious brother. But it's very dangerous, because we're going to commit a great offense—a forbidden thing. We're going to leave the Cage."

CHAPTER SIX

I was so excited I could hardly contain myself. Of all the things Erik could have offered me, he had chosen the one I couldn't resist—a taste of freedom. Shifting my weight from foot to foot, I waited behind Erik for him to move ahead. We were both dressed in a mismatch of dark form-fitting foreign clothes. Soft-sole boots covered our feet rendering our footsteps mute.

On Erik's sign, we crossed a dark corridor and entered a supply closet. A secret door at its end led us to a labyrinth of rough stone passages.

Dug when the palace was fitted with running-water for its many baths and fountains, these tunnels crisscrossed its entire length. Most tunnels were mapped; Erik had shown the ones he had studied before we left. There were so many, the architect's scrolls room was overflowing with such maps. Still, some passages remained secret, Erik had said. Those were only known by the Sultan and the Grand Vizier, who used these tunnels to spy on people and make surprise appearances.

"We're almost there," Erik whispered, after a long series of turns.

"Where?"

"You'll see."

We turned left at the next junction and began climbing

a dark, narrow stairwell. Voices touched my ears, women's voices, talking, laughing, singing—so many voices. I climbed faster. The stairwell suddenly shrunk and my head struck the ceiling.

"We have to crawl the rest of the way," Erik breathed. Then he squeezed through what looked like an air pipe to me.

I followed without protest. After a moment of bumping into each other in this confined passage, I spotted a patch of light shining above Erik's somber mass. Seconds later, we were stretched side-by-side peering through the pierced screen of an air vent.

My breath stayed caught in my throat. The sight was enchanting. Never had I seen such beauties. There were at least fifty women occupying this broad room at the moment. Some lounged in small groups upon a mass of cushions thrown about the pink-tiled floor; while others lingered around the giant white fountain that dominated the center of the room. Throughout the room, I could see black eunuchs, the loyal guardians of the Sultan's harem, circulating amidst the beauties.

"This is one of the harem's music rooms," Erik whispered. "These are lesser concubines, new recruits, still in training. The favorites and wives are housed elsewhere."

I nodded. My mouth was too dry to speak. I was transfixed by the vision of such exquisite women. Compared to these beauties, the women in our harem hardly qualified as pretty.

"There are more in other rooms. Father usually keeps around two hundred and fifty women in his harem at all times. That's a bit much, don't you think? I wouldn't have more than fifty."

I gave Erik a side-glance. Modesty sure wasn't choking him. *Fifty women! I'll be happy to get one.* I returned my gaze to the harem's beauties.

Some women stayed in the harem all their lives, while others left as soon as the law permitted, which was one month after having given birth to an heir. But on average a concubine remained in the harem for nine years. Then upon her departure, she was offered one set of diamond earrings, three gold rings, a necklace—of sapphire if she bore the Sultan a son, ruby for a daughter or plain gold if no child had been produced—three pounds of saffron, ten pounds of raw silk, seven silver bracelets and a silver tea set. Concubines weren't thrown into the street like paupers. They left the palace rich and with more options than when they came in. For those born into slavery, this was a way to gain freedom and status, as many noblemen waited to take these refined creatures as wives, for they were well educated in the art of love and carried strong links to the palace.

New women were constantly acquired to replace the departing ones. They came from everywhere. Harem women were either bought, offered as gifts by noblemen or foreign kings, or were war trophies. I couldn't help wondering in which category my mother belonged. What happened to her? Did she die in childbirth? Had she demanded her freedom after my birth and left of her own will? Or was she bullied into abandoning me by other concubines? Intrigues in the harem were as common and as ruthless as in the Cage. Every harem woman's goal was to put her son on the throne: In Telfar the Sultan's mother was the most powerful woman of the kingdom, not his wives. Only she was allowed to ride at the Sultan's side through the palace gate, everyone else had to enter on foot—even the Grand Vizier. For this privilege concubines were ready to do terrible things. No pregnant woman or small child was safe in the harem. I knew this from personal experience, having been raised there. Yet when looking upon such beauties, it was hard to conceive that they could be so cruel.

"Which one do you favor, Amir?" Erik asked.

I studied the women moving about in their wonderful shimmering gauze ensemble. One caught my attention. She had a dark complexion and long limbs, like a spring foal. Although she was extremely beautiful, it was not what had attracted me. What did was her air of vulnerability; she looked lost and scared. There was no greed in her eyes, no hardness, like in the others' eyes. I felt the need to protect her. "That one on the blue sitting bed."

"Good choice." Erik said. "She sings lovingly, but not very often. She hates the harem, like Hamed's mother had."

I frowned. "You seem to have known our poor deceased brother well."

Sadness clouded Erik's face. "Hamed and I were more than brothers, we were friends. He was braver than me. Hamed wouldn't hide, no matter the danger. They won't bully me, he used to say. I miss him very much." Erik produced a pitiful imitation of a smile. "I think Hamed inherited his courage from his mother. She came from a snow-bound country far north. A true woman warrior, used to leading, used to freedom. She never adapted to the harem's life and kept trying to escape. After Hamed's birth she doubled her attempt and once nearly succeeded in escaping with her baby. That's when the palace official took Hamed away from her. She was deemed a bad influence and forbidden to see her son as long as she lived. She drowned herself in the harem's deepest fountain not long after."

We remained silent for a moment. "And you, little brother, whom do you fancy?" I asked—anything to lighten the mood.

"I too prefer petite women with delicate build. There was one I particularly liked. A very young one. She's not in the harem anymore though. She too wasn't meant for this life." Erik then crawled away from the screen. I quietly fell into his tracks.

Next we visited the treasury. I was appalled that we could

enter these rooms so easily—especially when considering the ruckus made for the theft of that vase last year. Erik just had to open a door and there we were, right inside the treasury's jewel-encrusted walls. At that moment, I felt as though I was the younger brother and Erik the older one, showing me wonders. Everywhere I looked, there were shelves overflowing with treasures and chests of gold and jewels piled waist-high. I saw necklaces of opals, sparkling with all the shades of the rainbow, rings set with rubies the color and size of cherries, and gold. There was so much gold, it was mind-boggling.

Erik picked up an object from an ivory table and mimicked drinking out of it. Only then did I realize that it was a tanker. Its exterior was so overly encrusted with gems that it was nearly unrecognizable. "It's hideously beautiful," Erik said, putting the tanker back on the table.

We went from room to room admiring their many treasures: swords with gold hilts and scabbards studded with diamonds, miniatures made of pearls. One depicted a harem eunuch; his upper body fashioned from an enormous black pearl.

"Hey, Amir, look at these." Erik held up a pair of red velvet shoes. He turned them over exposing solid silver soles. Those were our father's shoes. Called the Silver Step, these shoes were worn daily by all Telfarian Sultans—so people could hear him come and either scoot away, bow or prostrate themselves to the ground, depending on their status. They would stay that way until the sound of the silver sole striking the tile floor told them that the Sultan was gone and that it was safe to rise.

I looked at the shoes and shivered. "Put those back!" I told Erik.

"Sure you don't want to try them on first?"

"No!"

"Fine." Erik set the shoes back where he'd found them. "Come, Amir, there's more to see and we only have tonight."

"Why?"

"The Grand Vizier is back. Tonight he's too busy with the

palace's affairs to be moving about, but tomorrow these passages won't be safe anymore. Come, let's not waste time."

The miniatures room was our next stop. Portraits of our ancestors filled three walls from floor to ceiling. Tiny porcelain painting of Sultanas and favorites occupied the last one.

Erik touched an oblong painting placed in the center of the wall. A stunning black-haired woman with smoldering green eyes stared at us from its gilded frame. "It's Çiçek, Father's favorite. She has a son of Rami's age. Soon he will join us in the Cage."

"A spoiled brat, I'm sure. I can't wait to meet him."

"Why do you say that? He's our kid brother."

I snorted, as if we needed another brother. "Erik, we're in this cage because we're all dangerous animals. He won't be any different."

We left the miniatures room and entered the costume hall, where servants and guards' spare uniforms were kept. On a separate stand I saw Viziers, messengers and physicians' suits, plus quantities of entertainers' outfits. There was also a collection of foreign garments from over forty different countries and a whole row of theatrical costumes.

"That's where you get your ridiculous outfits," I said.

"They're not ridiculous," Erik objected. He pulled a buccaneer's outfit from the display. "Wouldn't you like to travel the seas… chances are it will never happen. I'll never board a ship or cross the desert on a camel's back. All I can do is put on the costume and imagine myself there."

"Childish," I mumbled, slightly jealous that he could do such a thing. I doubted my imagination would be able to lead me anywhere outside the palace. The abstract frightened me. Perhaps that was why I didn't believe in magic—it was abstract. Poison, however, was concrete.

"Show me other things," I said, suddenly hungry for more of this false freedom.

Erik smiled. He looked very pleased by my demand.

We'd crossed several small courtyards without slowing our pace and I was about to ask Erik where we were going when we entered an immense square. A tall pointy tower occupied one end of the square and a long building with many archways the other.

"You must see this," Erik said before taking off. I watched him trot to the center of the square. Once there he waved for me to join him. I did, slowly though. I didn't like the look of that tower. It was all black. Although this tower was visible from one of our terraces, I had rarely paid attention to it. "Why is that tower black?" I asked.

Erik made a face. "What! You don't know? That's the prisoners' tower."

"Is that what you wanted to show me?"

Erik shook his head. "No! Look down. Look at the bricks at your feet."

"So, they're red."

Erik made a face again.

So I looked again, more carefully this time. The red bricks formed the center of this cobblestone yard. There was also a large brown blotch right in the middle of the red brick square. "Er... they're stained... "

Erik nodded. "Blood is red. That's why they chose red bricks for this square. But they forgot that blood dries brown."

"Oh! So the stain is?"

"Blood!"

"Yew!" I tiptoed out of the stain. Before I could say anything else, Erik said: "This is the execution square, better known as Chop-Chop Square. That's where prisoners kept in that tower are separated from their heads."

"Charming!"

Erik shrugged. Pointing to the building across the square, he asked: "Want to look inside that one? It's worth seeing, and there's no blood, I swear."

I smiled, and followed him.

Gliding silently on the dark marble floor, we traveled under a series of beautifully ornate archways until we arrived in a corner filled with red velvet couches, rich rugs and low mahogany coffee tables. An overwhelming aura of power floated in this long room, as if important things were discussed here. "What is this place?" I asked.

"Divan Hall," Erik said. "Councils are held here to settle matters of the state."

I looked around in awe. Then I noted that the room was divided by a pierced, white screen. When I walked behind it I saw a mass of sumptuous gold silk cushions spread over rich red rugs.

"Father sits behind the screen and listens in," Erik said. "He addresses the council only by an interposed person. Father never speaks directly to them."

I grimaced. "Besides Blessing Day, Father never speaks directly to us either." Thinking of Blessing Day angered me. For most Telfarians it was a festive day, where fathers throughout the country gave blessing to the good fortune that had given them heirs by kissing their sons on the forehead. But for us Blessing Day was a day of evaluation, where our father would visit the Cage to see which of us was still alive and whose status needed to be reevaluated, either increased or lowered. His decision was based on prowess or mischief done during the year. This part was done in secret with the council of the Grand Vizier. Frankly, I didn't think our father cared much for us. He never showed any emotion toward us, nor did anything that would make me believe otherwise. All my recollections of Blessing Day were of long, boring ceremonies spent standing in line only to be stared at for a few seconds, and then dismissed. I hated Blessing Day.

I put a hand on Erik's shoulder and squeezed. "This place is for neither of us, brother. Let's leave it."

"You're right. There's little time left and I still haven't shown you the best."

As we stepped outside the Divan Hall, I saw that the night was near its end. The sky was fading from black to blue, yet still enough shadow remained to conceal us. We hurried under a long stone porch. Gravel crisped loudly under our feet as we advanced. When we emerged on the other side I was shocked to find myself walking on tender green grass.

I stopped dead in my tracks and gaped at the wonderful sight in front of me. In this dim light, the White Tulip Garden shone as though the moon itself had lain down in its midst to sleep. Something was out of place though. There was a perfume in the air that didn't belong to tulips—a wild rose scent. I scanned the garden yet failed to find the scent's provenance. A seed, brought on by the wind, must have taken root somewhere along the wall, I thought. Following Erik, I moved up the pathway leading to the pink marble kiosk rising against the palace's outer wall. My hands brushed the tulips' heads as I walked, enjoying the dewy softness of their petals.

We entered the kiosk. The air inside was cool enough to cover my skin with goose bumps. The gurgling of its fountain echoed loudly in its otherwise silence. Quickly climbing the spiral staircase occupying the center of the room, we landed on a small observatory balcony set at the back of the kiosk.

My jaw dropped. The desert was so much bigger than I had ever thought possible. Viewed from here, its wide expanse of sands seemed to go on forever. I breathed in its frigid air with delight, and smiled. "Is there a passage leading to the main gate?" I asked. "A place where one can look upon the city?"

"Yes. Yesterday I could've shown you the city—but not today. The tower where the passage ends is too close to the Vizier's rooms. I dare not chance it."

I then noted the solemn look on Erik's face, a look unfitting his optimistic character. "What is it?" I asked.

"We're never going to be free, are we?"

I sighed. "Depends on who will become Sultan. Still, there's very little chance for freedom, brother... very little chance."

"Yes," Erik said. "Unless one of us becomes Sultan... and that's highly unlikely."

I thought I'd heard regret in his voice. I was about to question him further on this when he suggested that we should return to the Cage. I gave the desert one last embracing look, then reluctantly left.

CHAPTER SEVEN

I returned to my rooms at daybreak and dropped on my bed totally exhausted. Within minutes I was deeply asleep and dreaming that I was running barefoot in the desert sand. I awoke in the afternoon with a smile on my face. My joy faded as soon as reality sunk in. The Grand Vizier was back. And there wouldn't be another night of adventure for some time. I hated Erik for having shown me a bit of freedom and then taking it away. But my hatred lasted only an instant. Erik was a prisoner of this golden cage just as I was. However, Erik seemed to have more ambition than I. Or perhaps I had misread his words. Although I knew far more about my little brother, like where he had hidden all these years and the provenance of his odd clothes, still more questions tormented me: What was his rank? (Erik rarely wore belts and when he did it was only to match his odd outfits.) His full name? Was his mother still in the harem? And why were those books stored in his room? That intrigued me the most.

Determined to get answers to at least a few of my questions, I made my way to his hiding place. As I entered his cluttered sitting room, a fleeting shadow dashed out of the book storage room and ran through the scrolls office. I gave chase only to lose the shadow in the dark stone tunnels.

"Rami, you little snake," I hissed through clenched teeth.

Erik was a fool to trust this boy. I turned around and jumped in surprise. Erik stood right in front of me.

"Whoa—you scared me," he said. "For a moment I thought you were the Vizier."

"I scared you? No, you scared me!" I replied, while catching my breath. Once my heartbeat had returned to a normal speed, I asked: "Tell me about the books in the storage room. Why are they there? Who brought them?"

Erik wrinkled his nose. "Suspicious again! Fine, I'll tell you the story. But first I must warn you. It doesn't end well."

Each grabbing a lamp, we both moved into the book storage.

Raising his lamp at arms length, Erik began, "Long ago... actually, a few years before we were born, an architect named Tarim Aled was commissioned to install a fountain on the second floor of the Imperial Library. Tarim thought that having water traveling above two stories of bookshelves could be dangerous and expressed his concern to the Grand Vizier. In Tarim's opinion placing the fountain on the main floor was safer, this way if a breakage in the water conduits happened the leaking would be diverted underground."

I gazed at the multitude of water-damaged books. "The Vizier didn't listen," I said. "By the way, was this Vizier Nazir?"

"Yes, his first year as Grand Vizier. I know you don't care for the man, Amir, and you would like to think him guilty, but Nazir listened and agreed with the architect."

I frowned, confused. I stared at the books, then at Erik.

He made a face as if he had swallowed a bug. "Our father didn't listen. He insisted on having the fountain on the second floor."

"And a pipe burst."

"Exactly! A pipe burst and all these books were damaged."

I looked at the thousands of precious volumes stacked in this room—*what a catastrophe.* "Our father's stubbornness caused this. You were right, little brother, it doesn't end well."

Erik stared at me as though I had lost my head. "This isn't the end," he snapped. "These books are a small loss, bits of old paper. Do you consider books more precious than human lives? Do you, Amir?" I had never seen Erik angry before. It was quite disconcerting, so I choose to hold my tongue and not answer.

"Well, our father thought so," Erik continued, "and as punishment for damaging the books he had Tarim's sons executed and his wife and daughter sold as slaves. As for Tarim, our father had his tongue and fingers cut off, so he wouldn't be able to reveal the palace's secrets neither by speech nor writing. It's rumored that Tarim found his way back inside the palace's tunnels where he wanders aimlessly, waiting to avenge himself."

We both stayed silent for a moment. Then I risked, "Does it really end that way?"

Erik shrugged. "Why would our father spare his life? That's the only part I doubt."

I thought that it was crueler to let the man live, but said nothing of it to Erik. Instead I stood by quietly and watched him pull a thick volume from the pile. He shoved the book in my hands and I rapidly thumbed through its wavy pages. Most of its wonderfully detailed plant drawings had survived the water and still held their original colors.

Meanwhile Erik continued choosing books. Next he pulled the botany manual I had seen the other day, then an herbal-remedy book followed by a medical dictionary.

"What are you doing?" I finally asked.

"Perhaps if we study these, we might be able to find what killed our brothers."

"You don't think they've been cursed with some dark magic."

"No! Like you, I think there's more curse in a bad piece of mutton than in magic."

We laughed. Once our arms were heavy with books, we took the direction of my tower.

* * *

The following two weeks passed as quickly as lightning. Erik and I spent most of that time reading, talking and exchanging notes. We tried blending different poisons together, tried blending them with other nontoxic agents, still we failed to produce a mixture able to explain our brothers' deaths.

During those days of study and discussion, I discovered Erik's profound love of our culture and tradition and also the full extent of his academic knowledge. He was well versed in economy, expert in foreign and domestic politics, knew our history by heart and could recite our book of laws without hesitation. I was impressed. I could only recite poetry, and badly at that. Having decided at an early age not to seek the throne, I'd paid little attention to my politic and economic lessons. I spent most of these classes daydreaming. Yet some knowledge had still found its way into my brain—enough to realize that my little brother's knowledge exceeded what was taught in my group's lessons. *Private tutors*, I thought. Erik had been groomed to rule; there was no doubt in my mind. However, I decided not to question him on his peculiar upbringing, as it would certainly bring him to question mine—a subject I cared not to share with him at this time.

We also spent a bit of time playing chess and a lot of it fencing. Erik proved a better fencer than I had expected, or perhaps it was my lack of sparing mates that had weakened my reflexes. I couldn't tell, yet I believed that our daily practice would improve on this problem. As I became used to having Erik around, so did Jafer and Mir, who now rarely made noises at Erik's approach.

These days, Mir's litany of insults was reduced to "stinky yellow camel," which appeared to be his favorite calling for

Erik. Although I was relieved by my brothers' quietness, a small part of me couldn't help being worried about it. *What if this is a ruse*, a nagging voice would then whisper in my ears. *A ruse to gain your trust, and then* "quick" *slash your throat. Enough!* I would then say. I had enough solitude. And truthfully—I just couldn't bear being alone anymore.

However, there was a problem with having Erik over—Rami was that problem. The boy followed his master everywhere. I hated having the servant in my rooms. I distrusted his furtive manners: the way he covered his face and avoided making eye contact. Rami was always hiding in shadowy corners, always sneaking about, spying, listening. Every time my eyes would fall upon the boy, my face would tense into an involuntary rictus of dislike that Erik never failed to notice. He would then send Rami away. But the next day the boy would trail Erik inside my room like dirt under his boots. Erik seemed to think that with time I might get used to the servant's presence. He was dead wrong.

Erik snapped his book shut. "We've read all morning, I can't concentrate any longer. Why don't we practice fencing? The exercise will do us good."

Leaning back into my chair, I crossed my hands behind my head. "You're in a rush to be beaten again. For all our mock combats you haven't won once."

"It won't happen without trying."

We climbed to the second story of my tower where our daily practice took place. I opened my weapons closet and looked upon my extended collection of swords. I had dozens of blades of all sorts and origins. Sticking to my practice wooden swords would have been more sensible, but we both grew bored of fighting with those and graduated to real blades. The danger they brought to our practice kept us on edge, and the small nicks we inflicted on each other added excitement to our mock fights.

As usual I chose my favorite rapier, a slim flexible blade with a swept hilt decorated with simple yet exquisite engraving. To my surprise, Erik shunned his beloved claymore in favor of a clumsier weapon still, my pirate scimitar, the longest and heaviest blade I possessed. The scimitar was part of my collection more as an object of curiosity than as a true weapon. It had a beautiful etched blade, a brass hilt and a grip of wound leather.

When Erik pulled it out of its metal slot, the scimitar's broad curved blade sent sparks through the room. He slashed the air with it, sending a cold breeze in my face. "I think I will defeat you today," he said.

"Let's see then."

I took position, feet spread well apart and knees bent, ready to move. Like always Erik attacked first. His lack of patience was his main weakness. I easily blocked his scimitar and glided left. Swiftly twirling, he lunged forward, blade extended, blocking my way. I rolled under his blade, rising up a few paces behind him. Erik turned around quickly and brought his blade up just in time to block mine. Then gripping his scimitar with both hands, he swung down with so much force that he nearly toppled over head first.

"*Tsk-tsk-tsk,*" I made while sidestepping his clumsy attack with ease. "Brute force alone cannot win you this match, little brother."

Lips thinned, Erik gave me a dark stare. We exchanged two more hits, and then Erik made the mistake of exposing his midriff. Automatically I thrusted forward. Only then did I note Erik's grinning face and realized that it was a trick. It was too late to reverse my move. Erik brought his scimitar down on my rapier with all his strength. My blade vibrated under the shock of this terrible blow. The vibrations then leapt to my hand. Flashes of pain ran from my wrist to my elbow then shoulder in pulsing waves. Yet I refused to drop my weapon and admit defeat.

"I suppose there's something to say in favor of brute force after all," Erik gloated.

Anger swallowed me whole. Forgetting all pain, my hand tightened around the grip and I raised my rapier. What followed happened in a flash. I swung, thrusted, parried and swung again with so much speed and rage, I astounded myself. As for Erik, he was blocking my tornado of blows the best he could. But with every move I could see his guard falling lower and lower. Then he failed to block me and the side of my blade slapped him on the shoulder, then upside the head.

"OUCH!" he yelled. "The last one was uncalled for."

"You almost broke my arm."

"No I didn't—you're just angry because I almost won." Erik said, cradling the side of his head. "I can't beat you on speed or agility, Amir. I have to use what I got, longer arms and strength. Why are you so mad at me for doing it?"

Erik's honesty was disarming. All the anger that had so completely engulfed me a minute ago vanished in the blink of an eye. And I found myself laughing. After a moment of hesitation, Erik laughed too.

That evening I went out for a late supper. I entered the Great Hall and stopped dead in my tracks. The room was buzzing with activity. Everywhere I looked servants, like bees in a hive, were hard at work carrying furniture, boxes and chests across the room. This was shocking, especially this late in the day. I stopped two valets, who were busy moving a long white damask couch, and asked them the reason for all this frantic activity.

The valets threw themselves to the ground in respect, a courtesy gesture that did nothing for my darkening humor. Then I realized that these valets were new here, as they showed no fear toward me as the other servants of the Cage did.

"Please rise and answer my question," I said.

"Your Highness, these are preparations for Visitation Days.

We're furnishing Sultana Malika's receiving chamber."

"Visitation Days—already!"

Both valets nodded.

I was stunned. Had I lost track of time or had the date been changed. Visitation Days came twice a year. For three days, mothers and their entourage were allowed to see their sons. Receiving rooms and chambers, normally empty and kept locked, were then opened and prepared for the occasion, tripling the number of servants in the Cage. On the last evening of Visitation Days, a large banquet was held where the Sultan would feast with his sons. All kinds of entertainment were brought in for that special evening, and the festivities usually continued until late into the night.

The prospect of the coming Visitation Days killed my appetite. For someone like me, someone without mother, someone without visitation, this was the worst of times.

I went back to my tower feeling rather depressed.

I went out early the next morning. Although I was still without an appetite, Jafer and Mir were hungry and needed supplies. Traffic within the Cage's corridors had increased tenfold. Stewards and valets were everywhere: moving stuff, unlocking doors, redecorating. But now I could also see the tall white eunuchs who were my father's private guards. All blond and blue-eyed, they wore identical baggy red pants, gold sashes with red vests over their white bare chests, and always they moved about in pairs, like twins.

The white eunuchs were busy preparing the Sultan's thirty chambers. These imperial apartments occupied the palace section between the Cage and the harem. To foil assassination attempts, each night the Sultan would sleep in a different chamber. (Fear ran deep in my family.) He alone knew which chamber was chosen—except perhaps for the woman sharing his bed. Lately, it was Çiçek, whose name meant *flower honey*. The woman had managed to remain my father's favorite for the last six years—a record not even his four legitimate wives could approach.

I returned to my tower with food and in a darker mood than when I left.

Erik waited at my door, his face split with a huge grin. Upon seeing me, he immediately began talking enthusiastically about the upcoming Visitation Days.

I listened silently, while passing plates to Jafer. Erik was as excited as a puppy. I believed that had he possessed a tail, it would have wagged. As for myself, I felt as if a giant boulder had been put on my shoulder, as if a veil of darkness surrounded my head, following me everywhere I went. I felt miserable. I hated Visitation Days more than Blessing Day.

"I can't wait to see Mother, and Salima, and everybody," Erik said all dreamy-eyed.

An unpleasant pang of jealousy twisted my side.

My bitterness must have shone on my face, because Erik suddenly stopped talking. "Have I done something to displease you, Amir?" he asked after an instant of silence.

"It has nothing to do with you," I said, moving to Mir's door.

"Liar," Mir whispered from the darkness of his room. "Liar, liar, liar—"

"Enough," I hissed at Mir, then turned to Erik. "I'd prefer not seeing you for a while. I need some time alone. I have personal things to settle."

Erik blinked once, his face twisted. Then to my surprise, he left without arguing.

Resting my forehead against the cold wood of Mir's door, I expelled a long sigh of relief. When I looked up, my eyes met Mir's dark gaze peering through the pierced grid of his door. "You, not a word," I said. Then I locked myself in my rooms.

* * *

I was left undisturbed for two days, during which I fought the urge to seek companionship in our harem. Funny how feminine comfort when my mood was somber never failed to darken it even more, as though instead of filling the hole in my soul it was ripping it wider. Solitude was best, I knew that. Bit by bit, I began to regain hold of myself. My dark mood, although still present, seemed less heavy, less somber. I often questioned the reason of these devastating spells. Was I becoming like Mir, I often questioned. No, my condition was different. Mine was called melancholy. It had nothing to do with terror and everything to do with sadness and despair.

On the third day Erik appeared at my doorstep. He called for me, scratched at the door, begging me to open.

I remained at my desk, staring into empty space with my throat tightly clenched. The darkness I had so fiercely fought back the last two days now tormented me again, and with such force, I feared for my sanity. Seizing my head between my hands, I squeezed my eyes shut. A long moan escaped my lips.

Erik continued knocking. "Amir, I know you're there. Open!"

"Go away!" I finally managed to shout.

"I've good news. Please open the door so we can talk."

"NO!"

There was a loud sigh, then to my chagrin, Erik, instead of leaving, continued, "I figured out why you're so upset. It's because of Visitation Days, because you don't have anyone visiting you."

I ground my teeth until they hurt.

"Listen," Erik continued, "two days ago, I requested the permission for you to share my Visitation Days. Mother said she would ask our father."

"What!" I bolted out of my chair, dashed across the room and swung the door open.

Erik smiled, eyes sparkling. "They said yes."

My jaw dropped. That made Erik laugh. "This isn't customary," I whispered, as if we were speaking about some illicit activity—then again. "I'm not related to the women of your household. It's… improper."

"You're related to me."

"That doesn't count."

"They still said yes."

"But…"

"But what? Why would they say no? It's not like you're going to seduce my mother."

I stopped breathing for a second. My hand sought the locket at the bottom of my pocket. I squeezed it hard and swallowed the lump in my throat.

"So, brother," Erik said, "are you going to accept my invitation or are you stubbornly going to stay locked in your tower."

Although good sense told me that my tower was a much safer place for me to be, I squeezed the locket harder and said, "I accept."

CHAPTER EIGHT

Never before had I paid so much attention to my choice of clothes, other than for the purpose of blending. Surprisingly I found myself enjoying the act of trying to look good, instead of trying to be invisible—so much so that my face hurt from my constant grinning. Today was a special day for me. Today I was going to meet Erik's mother. Today was my very first Visitation Day. For the first time in years, I wore a kaftan that was neither green nor blue, but of a deep wine color and embroidered with a rich emerald vine design. Black sable trimmed the sleeves and collar. My silk shirt and pants were the same emerald as the embroidery, and a wine color sash bound my waist. Crowning my head was a matching wine turban. My only piece of jewelry adorned its side, a gold brooch with a square emerald at its center and pearls dangling all around. Satisfied with my appearance, I left my room.

As previously agreed, Erik waited for me in the registry hall. For the first time, I thought that he looked like a prince. Wearing a gold chemise and pants under a bronze kaftan decorated with silver tulips and trimmed with pale mink fur, Erik was striking. His turban was of the same bronze fabric as his kaftan with a diamond-pavéd brooch in the shape of a tulip set on its front. Knowing Erik's taste in clothes, or lack there of, I strongly suspected that someone else had dictated his choice. The ensemble was too well thought out. Then the true symbolism of the outfit struck me. *All these white tulips,* I thought. Huh—whoever dressed him saw fit to brand him with the imperial flower, symbol of our dynasty, from head to toe, as though to remind everyone that he belonged to our line—better yet, that he could be a contender for the throne. Dangerous, but oh so clever.

Planting his fists on his hips, Erik struck a pose, and then he pivoted. "See, Amir, I too can dress well."

I nodded. "Yes, and very well at that."

"You look very good yourself. That color suits you."

I bowed to him as thanks for the compliment.

We then took the direction of the main floor chambers hall. This section of the Cage housed the rooms of most low-ranked princes.

Trotting in Erik's wake, I readied myself for meeting his mother at every turn. But instead of stopping in front of one of those rooms, as I'd expected, we exited that hall and climbed to the second story, where mid-ranked princes lived.

So Erik is of my rank, I thought, *this despite his age.* For some reason, I began growing uneasy. Perhaps because I could see the exit stairwell approaching. If we didn't stop soon, we would leave this section of the Cage too, and this could only mean one thing: Erik was high rank. *He's the son of a favorite. Damn! Why didn't I question him more?*

As we went down the stairwell, my heart sped up. I rarely ventured in this section of the Cage. Being high on the line for the throne, the favorites' sons were fiercely competitive and extremely defensive—good reasons to stay away from them and their stronghold. I looked around, studying every detail as we advanced. High arches covered every alley, the walls were pierced with gilded latticework, and the floor was imported green marble. It was superb. I admired the burnished bronze of the chambers' doors as we passed them all without stopping. And soon the rod-iron gate that closed the last chamber hall of the Cage to intruders rose in front of us. I gazed at the peacock feather motif decorating the gate with growing fear. My stomach was a ball of knots, my brow painfully furrowed. Every room beyond that gate had its own balcony, its own private courtyard. This hall belonged to the Sultanas' sons.

Erik stopped at the gate. While he pulled a key from his pocket, my eyes traveled to his waist, seeking his belt. I winced. A solid silver belt, richly studded with swirling waves of diamonds, circled his waist.

Pushing the gate open, Erik entered the last hall. I remained frozen on the other side of the gate, staring hard at him with a dumbfounded look on my face.

"Are you mad at me?" he asked in a small voice.

"You should have told me that your mother wasn't a concubine but a Sultana."

"If I had, you wouldn't have come."

I stayed silent for a long time. "Your mother, she's Sultana Livia, Princess of Sorvinka, isn't she?"

Erik shrugged. "Who else could she be?"

Right, he could only be the son of this foreign princess. No wonder our father had acquiesced to her demand for my visit; he wouldn't dare displease her on such a small matter. Sorvinka was the most powerful and richest kingdom of our era. Their border touched ours on the north, and although we were at peace with them, we knew that this peace was fragile, and if broken, Sorvinka's extensive armies could overrun us in a matter of months. The only reason they hadn't invaded us was that Telfar's fat strip of land, with its broad desert and bordering seas, formed a natural barrier against the many quarreling kingdoms of the south—kingdoms that would not view our demise in a good eye and would raise opposition to our invasion, seeing their own borders in jeopardy. It was not to say that Sorvinka had abandoned all plans of conquering us. I peeked at my blond brother. They had just found a more subtle way of seizing the throne.

Erik motioned to me. "Come, Mother will worry if we're late."

* * *

I was shocked by the beauty of Erik's mother, but more so by the fact that she was not the girl in the locket. A small part of me was also relieved by this.

Sultana Livia's face was square instead of the girl's soft oval. Erik's mother was also fairer of skin and hair. Her moon-flaxen strands were braided and pinned around her head, forming the traditional halo of the Sorvinka's coif. Her face was nearly without wrinkles and strongly Nordic in form, with its high cheekbones, pale icy-blue eyes and thin straight nose. Her long elegant neck was partly covered by a broad diamond choker.

Looking like a ray of moonlight in her tight-bodiced silver dress, she glided toward us as silently as a ghost. Following in her wake were two giant black eunuchs. The skin of their bare torso glimmered like well-oiled ebony. I noted two more eunuchs busy opening chests at the back of the room. Princess Livia's decision to choose the black eunuchs instead of the white surprised and intrigued me. As Sultana she was allowed to surround herself with the imperial white eunuchs—a privilege allowed only to Sultanas—so why select the black ones?

"Mother!" Erik exclaimed, seconds before hugging her.

"Let me look at you." She gripped his face between her hands and studied him carefully. Her voice was throaty and a slight accent hacked her words. "You look thin. Are you eating enough?"

"Mother," he lamented, as if this had been a harsh comment.

She smiled and all the severity and coldness of her face vanished. "I'm happy to see you well, my son." They hugged again.

I stared at my feet not really knowing what to do. When I finally looked up, I found Princess Livia staring straight at me. I couldn't decide if this intense stare held curiosity or hostility. Her examination went on for a while, making me feel as though I were some sort of exotic creature whose capacity for harm had to be evaluated. Then the left corner of her lips curled up. "This handsome young man must be your brother, Amir."

Upon hearing my name, fear struck me. I shouldn't be here.

She glided toward me. I stepped back. My back touched the door behind me. There was no way out. I was trapped. Forcing my body to stay still, I held my breath and watched her approach. She was as tall as I was.

"Sultana," I said, and bowed.

"Please rise."

I obeyed. "Thank you for receiving me, Sultana; it's a great hon—"

She raised a hand stopping me short. "If you're to stay here, you must learn a few things. First, call me Princess Livia. Second, if you betray my son, I will see you dead."

"MOTHER!" Erik interjected.

I smiled, for some reason her threat made feel more at ease, as if things were back to normal. "I will respect your wishes, Princess Livia."

She smiled, and then turned to Erik. "Salima is readying your room as we speak. You should go see her."

Erik beamed. "Come, Amir, let's go see Salima."

We crossed Erik's apartments, which were about three times bigger than mine—and mine were by no means small—and entered a newly opened room. This annex held a second set of smaller apartments only used twice a year for Visitation Days.

The bright sitting room boiled with activity. While eunuchs and valets set furniture into place and unpacked precious objects, stewards filled armoires.

Ignoring the servants, Erik walked straight toward the small woman standing in front of a glass-door bookcase. Absorbed in the study of a thick, leather-bound book, she only raised her head when we were at her side. Her eyes lit up as soon as she saw Erik. She dropped the book and clapped her hands together under her chin.

"Oh, my beautiful prince," she exclaimed, nearly in tears.

"Salima," Erik replied, face split with joy. They rushed into each other's arms. Erik grasped Salima's delicate body around the waist and lifted her up in the air while she giggled with pleasure.

My eyebrows rose. I was a bit taken aback by this show of affection and familiarity. This woman was only a servant—then again, Erik loved servants. Rami proved this. While they went on kissing and hugging, I picked up the book she had dropped. Before I could read its title, Salima exited Erik's arms and took the book from my hands.

"Please, let me do this," she said. "Your Highness shouldn't be bothered by an old servant's clumsiness." Salima quickly shoved the book in the bookcase and locked the door. When she turned back, Erik circled the small woman's shoulders with an arm.

"I should introduce you properly. Amir, this is Salima."

The little woman bowed.

"Salima was assigned to my mother on her first day here and has served her since. She was also my nanny. She raised me well—made a decent man out of me."

Salima glowed with pride, as though the tall, blond prince was her own son.

I felt a stab of envy. Erik didn't needed a second mother; he already had one, and a powerful, fiercely protective one at that. It wasn't fair. Princes of his status had everything.

They were raised in private rooms, taught by private tutors and protected by personal bodyguards. While I was raised by palace attendants within a group of feral princes of my age and had to fend for myself from childhood. Biting the inside of my cheek, I plastered a fake smile on my face.

Salima looked at me warmly. She had light brown eyes and hair as black as mine. Her skin was a reddish tan, indicating an eastern origin, probably Maberian. "Prince Amir, Erik told us many good things about you."

"*Really!*" I looked sideways at Erik.

He shrugged.

Salima lightly touched my arm. "I believe he's right. I can see kindness in your eyes. I'm relived that Erik has found a friend in you. To face the multitude alone is…" she paused to bow at me. "I'm happy for your presence at his side and thank you for it."

I was suddenly riddled by guilt for having envied Erik nearly to the point of hating him. "It's me who should thank him," I said. "And thank you also for receiving me so warmly."

For the next hours we occupied ourselves in the bedroom we were to share. It was quite uncommon for two Princes to share a room, but neither of us thought of complaining. Actually, I was rather happy about it. This way we could talk together while servants unpacked our clothes. I now understood Erik's behavior. Unlike me, who had to keep a watchful eye on servants as some were bound to bring to term the wives or favorites' plots to eliminate us, Erik had grown up protected by servants.

"You seem much attached to Salima," I said once the little woman was out of the room.

"Salima raised me as much as Mother. For us she's more than a servant. She's a member of our family." This remark shocked me. Yet I held my tongue.

"Without her I might not exist," Erik added.

"How so?"

"Being a foreign princess, Mother had few friends in the palace, and even less in the harem. Only Salima, given to her at her arrival, understood how Mother felt. She too had been uprooted. Salima is the well-educated daughter of a nobleman. She was forced into servitude in payment for her father's debt."

I scratched my beard. "Tell me how she saved your life. That intrigues me."

Erik grinned as if he had expected the question. "She cared for Mother when she was pregnant. Mother feared being poisoned, being tripped, being pushed down stairs, so she and Salima locked themselves in her apartments for months. No one else was allowed in. Some tried, but Salima couldn't be bribed." Erik smiled proudly. "She kept the door shut and personally took care of Mother's every need. Because of her loyalty no attempt against Mother—and me—was ever made. Finally one month after my birth—the age a baby is deemed viable in Telfarian tradition—the door was opened. I was then a registered prince and therefore under the chief black eunuch's protection."

BONG, BONG, BONG. The gong declaring Visitation Days officially open echoed throughout the palace. I smiled. For the next three days we would be totally safe, as during Visitation Days no attacks or duels were permitted. I found myself breathing more easily. Never before had I been so carefree. Rami, who for once wasn't glued to Erik's side, was taking care of Jafer. To my surprise, Jafer didn't mind the young servant's presence. As for Mir, he had visitations of his own; this was the only time he'd go out of his rooms. So it was with light steps that I trailed Erik to the sitting room where his mother awaited us.

The sight of the man standing at Princess Livia's shoulder almost stopped my heart.

Clad in the royal-blue baggy pants and vest of the harem,

Oroco, the chief black eunuch, glared at me with increasing hostility. The third most powerful man of the palace, after my father and the Grand Vizier, Oroco had power of life and death over all young princes—especially motherless low-birthed ones. For years I had feared his gaze, yet I had feared his indifference twice as much, as it was known that when Oroco ceased acknowledging one's existence, one died.

In the blink of an eye all my childhood terrors came back to haunt me. And when Erik leaped into Oroco's bear hug, I almost shouted a warning to my brother, so visceral was my fear of this man. Fortunately I caught myself in time, only letting a low moan escape my mouth.

As they now stood side by side, I noted that Oroco was taller than Erik, who already had a head above most men I knew. I wondered if Oroco had been made eunuch at an older age than most. His face displayed a masculinity lacking in most eunuchs: squarer at the jaw with more pronounced cheekbones and brow. His body was also more toned than most eunuchs, yet not truly muscular, although some definition marked the part of his chest peeking through his opened vest. Oroco didn't have the smooth layer of fat usually softening the body of other eunuchs.

He definitively exercises, I concluded, and believed that Oroco's fierce determination to remain as masculine as possible was partly the reason he had become chief eunuch. I assumed the other reason was intelligence.

"Prince Amir," Princess Livia said, "you remember Oroco." Turning to the eunuch, she continued, "Prince Amir is Erik's new playmate."

Playmate! I nearly choked. So a nod was all I managed to give to the eunuch.

Staring at me with one eyebrow up, Oroco responded with a low growl.

Shivers ran down my spine. He used to make this growling sound, deep in his throat, when as young boys we would do something he disapproved. Back then, this sound sent me running every time.

When he was done staring me down, Oroco turned to the princess and whispered in her ear. She smiled at him. And an undeniable complicity flowed between them.

This woman is clever. By choosing Oroco and his eunuchs as her private guards she had flattered his ego and increased his status. In return Oroco would protect Erik from other Sultanas or favorites' plots until he was old enough to leave the harem. This was more than clever, this was brilliant.

Standing in front of Princess Livia—which made me feel quite small—I watched Erik and Oroco grip each other's forearm, wrists touching, as soldiers do when they meet.

"Amir," Erik said, "Oroco beat me up so many times I lost track of how much."

I frowned in horror.

"We wrestle," Oroco clarified in a surprisingly high-pitched voice. "Princess Livia forbade me to let him win, unless he truly did."

Erik nodded. "Took me years and more bruises than one can count to win my first match."

"But you did, Prince. And you did it on your own merits."

Erik beamed with pride. Glancing at the two men's imposing frames, I thought that these wrestling matches might have kept the eunuch from softening and developed Erik's uncommon strength.

Leaving Erik and Oroco to their reminiscence, I looked around. The room's decoration was unusual yet splendid. The foreign furniture that filled it was stern compared to ours. A painting, displayed on an easel beside a blue sofa, caught my eye. Gaze fixed on it, I strolled closer. The painting depicted a family at leisure time: a bearded man sitting near an angular, white-haired woman while a lovely blond girl played a harp, with a strapping young man standing at her shoulder.

"My family," Princess Livia said, making me flinch. I had

not heard her approach.

She touched the bearded man. "My father, King Erik the Just of Sorvinka."

"You're the girl playing the harp, I presume."

She made a slight head movement. "Beside me is my brother, Erik the Fair, now King of Sorvinka. All first born of our line bare the name Erik—but you know this already."

"How was it possible?" I let out, blushing by my boldness.

"How?" She frowned. "Ooh! Why was it allowed, you mean. What convinced your father to let one of his sons bare the name of a foreign king?" She snickered. "Keri is Erik's first name. It's a jumble of the same four letters which happen to spell an acceptable Telfarian name. His ruling name would be Keri Erik Ban. Having no intention of letting my son ascend the throne, your father agreed to it."

"Why not? Erik is better prepared to rule than most of our brothers. Certainly your brother the King of Sorvinka can influence my father's choice."

She shook her head, sending a wave of jasmine perfume in the air. "Sorvinkian blood is the reason Erik will not rule. The Sultan believes that my brother is trying to put a relative on the throne, as a way to absorb the kingdom without the bloodshed of a war. Your father might agree to a political union with a Sorvinkian princess but won't go any further. As you know, your father cannot refuse me too many things—I am, after all, the king's sister. But it's different for Erik." She turned a sorrowful eye to her son. When she looked back at me her eyes were as hard as the diamonds surrounding her neck. "In your culture sons belong to fathers, and fathers alone. No link to the maternal side is permitted, which robs Erik of his title of First Duke of Sorvinka. Because my son doesn't have a Sorvinkian title, or link to our family, my brother cannot influence his future or insure his safety—as he does mine."

"You still taught Erik how to rule a country, regardless," I said.

"One can hope." She looked at Erik and smiled. When she turned back her eyes were cold. "Knowing your father, he'd rather put the most inept of his sons on the throne than Erik. A goat might have a better chance of becoming Sultan than he." She sighed. "This is sad for Telfar. Erik possesses a quality few of your brothers have. Compassion. No ruler can be deemed great without compassion." She then aimed her icy gaze into mine. "Are you a compassionate man, Prince Amir?"

"Yes he is, Mother," Erik said suddenly appearing at my side. "He thinks it's a weakness and won't admit to it, but he is."

"Ah, then you are a worthy contender for the throne," Princess Livia said.

Erik burst in laughter. "Amir has no ambition, Mother."

"Everyone has ambition, they just differ." She stared at me with narrowed eyes. "I hope your ambitions don't interfere with mine."

Short for words, I sought help in Erik only to find him back at Oroco's side. *Thank you for the support, little brother.*

"Let me assure you, I'm in no one's way," I said. My eyes traveled back to Oroco and Erik absorbed in an animated conversation a few steps behind us, then returned to Princess Livia. "You saw to your son's safety very well. One thing intrigues me, though. You had the means to eliminate his competition at a young age, why haven't you? Others would've seized that chance."

Her face suddenly hardened. I had vexed her, I was certain of this.

"To have an adult man killed is acceptable—to kill children is not. Such acts are vile." Her mouth twisted in disgust.

My face was burning with shame. I wish I could take my words back. "I apologize for my rude and thoughtless questioning, Princess." I began to bow. She stopped me halfway by touching my shoulder.

"Don't apologize. I'd rather have honest, open skepticism than the usual syrupy false friendliness that is common here.

After all, I agreed to receive you for a reason—to see if you pose a threat to my son." She leaned closer to me, bringing her cheek in line with mine, and whispered in her throaty voice: "You are right to worry, young prince. I haven't yet decided if you're a threat or not."

I swallowed hard. Before I could formulate an intelligent and nonthreatening reply, Erik appeared at my side. "What's that?" He pointed to the red brocade draping a tall triangular shape carried in by two valets.

"Ah, finally—bring it here," Princess Livia said. Once the valets had gone, she pulled on the brocade, revealing a second painting also propped on an easel.

My throat tightened. This was the girl of the locket—no doubt in my mind. She appeared older in this big painting—she was a young woman now. She held a small dog in her lap, her hand playing with the velvet bow on the animal's neck. In my opinion, she had grown even more beautiful than before.

"Who's this lovely young woman?" I asked in a choked voice, which brought me a side-glance from Princess Livia.

"My cousin Eva, King Erik's eldest daughter," Erik said.

"Your cousin," I stupidly repeated.

A powerful scent of jasmine engulfed me. Again Princess Livia whispered in my ear:

"My brother is a stubborn man. If Erik can't rule, perhaps Eva's son will." She paused, and stepped back. "Princess Eva is to become the next Sultan's first wife."

My knees weakened. Then I noted how carefully Princess Livia was watching me.

She produced a rueful smile. "My niece arrives tomorrow."

CHAPTER NINE

I couldn't sleep. Eva's lovely face tormented me, and the thought that she would marry one of my detestable brothers tormented me even more. I shifted in my down-filled bed for the hundredth time. Giving up on finding rest, I rose on my elbow. "Psst... Psst, Erik," I whispered. "Erik, are you sleeping?"

Grumbling, he turned in a rustling of silk. "No, you're making too much noise."

"Sorry. It's just... I was wondering, your cousin is to become the next Sultan's first wife right? But what if you become Sultan? Whom will she marry then?" I knew that in Sorvinka union between cousins was quite common. However, this was a practice frowned upon in Telfar, as it had often produced addled children. A sensible decision, in my opinion; I had enough unintelligent brothers as it was. No need adding inbreeding to the mix. "So, tell me, which one of us will wed her if you're Sultan?"

Erik chuckled. "Well, you, my dear brother. If I become Sultan, she'll marry you." Erik's chuckling became laughter. Then he abruptly stopped laughing and sat up in his bed. "No, I take that back. What I just said was wrong. If I'm Sultan I'll let Eva choose. She'll marry whichever of my brothers she prefers." He sighed. "We both know it won't happen. I think

Ibrahim will be the next Sultan. I heard that Father favors him. Do you know why, Amir?"

"I can venture a guess: because he's the most ruthless of all."

"No. It's because his mother has a title. Father is the son of an ambitious chambermaid who managed to become Grandfather's favorite. Mother said that his mother's humble origin always bothered him. That's why he puts Ibrahim ahead of Darius, who is a much smarter man."

A sharp pain stabbed my chest. Ibrahim was cruel and brutal toward women. *Darius*, I grimaced. He might well be smarter than Ibrahim, but I still wouldn't cheer for him. I'd rather cut out my own tongue first. I looked at Erik's dark silhouette, watched it melt back in the bed. What were his real chances of becoming Sultan? I wondered. Slim, but perhaps they could be improved. This thought was still churning in my head when I fell asleep. Not being in my own bed, I kept waking up throughout the night. At one point I could swear that Erik's bed was empty. Then after much tossing and turning, I finally found some rest.

* * *

The following day was filled with preparation and excitement. Everywhere I looked there were servants hard at work. If the coming of a foreign princess and her delegation was a big event, the coming of a Sorvinkian princess destined to become the next Sultan's first wife was a colossal one. An excited Erik rushed in to the sitting room, where I stood gazing at Eva's portrait.

"Where did you go?" I asked.

"In the courtyard."

"No, I meant last night."

He became very quiet. "I… just… you kept turning. I couldn't sleep." His sheepish look made me suspect that he was hiding something—yet again. Before I could question him further, Erik said, "Come see Eva's tower." He took hold of my elbow and pulled me along. In no time we were out on the terrace.

Circled by a tall brick wall, the manicured grass of the terrace was artistically dotted with benches and fountains. A pathway, bordered by lavender hedges, led to each one.

Squinting against the morning sun, I scanned the vast courtyard Erik shared with the brothers of his rank. We weren't the only princes out this early. I counted a dozen pair of eyes fixed on the tower rising in the east corner of the courtyard. Made of smooth white stone, the three-story tower was topped with a sparkling brass onion dome. The only door visible to us was cut high on the third floor and circled with a small balcony. The tower's ground access was on the other side of the wall, which opened into the harem. This golden cage would be Eva's apartments until an heir was crowned.

My heart sank. The fact that this tower had been chosen had clear implications. It meant that the heir to the throne had access to this courtyard, so that way the princess could watch him from above. I sighed, this time the rumor was true. The next Sultan would be the son of a legitimate wife—a Sultana.

My eyes flicked to Ibrahim and his four brothers. A shameless boisterous group if there was one. They were rejoicing, slapping Ibrahim on the back and bowing low to him, as if he'd already been crowned.

"Let's go back inside," I said.

Erik followed me without a word. In silence, we strolled to the end of the Cage, stopping at the iron gate that separated us from the rest of the palace.

Gripping the bars, I stared at the long corridor housing the Sultan's many rooms.

Eight of Father's best-looking white eunuchs, clad in their red and gold outfits, exited the nearest room and headed in the direction of Eva's tower. I assumed that these eight were to become her private bodyguards. From the moment she'd step into the palace and until she became Sultana, they would guard the door at the foot of her tower and escort her everywhere she'd go. I watched the tall, blond eunuchs leave. I wouldn't say they looked feminine; they were too solidly built for that. However, many of these smooth beardless faces had features dangerously approaching prettiness. Which reminded me—not too pleasantly—that for some Sultans eunuchs also served as male concubines.

I felt Erik shudder at the sight of these men who looked so much like himself. With a side-glance his way, I saw that his face was contorted in a grimace.

His mother had done well to choose the black eunuchs as private guards, I thought. I wondered if she had the same reaction as he toward the white ones, or was it foresight on her part that had dictated her choice? Could be, I wouldn't put it past this woman. She was smarter than most men I knew.

Seizing the iron bars, Erik shook the gate violently. "I need air," he hissed between clenched teeth. "Come, Amir. Let's go ride."

We returned to the center of the Cage. As we crossed the registry hall I stopped in front of the board. Abdul and Mustafa, sons of the first Sultana and rude individuals if there were any, started the list; they were followed by Ibrahim and his four brothers. Scanning further down the names, I halted at number eight. There it was—the one I'd been looking for. Keri Ban... Erik. For a moment I contemplated the idea of running to my tower.

You'll be safer there, a nagging voice hushed in my mind, *much safer than with him. He's only smart enough to get himself in trouble.* However strong my impulse to flee was, one thing was stronger, stronger than all my fears combined: my wish to see Eva, Erik's cousin.

Pulling my eyes from the registry board, I joined Erik at

the terrace door and together we entered the Cage's central courtyard. Much bigger than the Sultana's sons' private one, this courtyard was communal and shared by all princes. A small oasis occupied its left corner while the rest of the yard was taken by a fencing practice circle, a wrestling sand block and a stable with its riding ring. This courtyard was also the Cage's entrance. It was through its giant double doors that everything entered or exited our limited world.

Today the courtyard was cluttered with gifts to be presented to the Sultan during this evening's banquet. A small army of scribes were carefully cataloging each and every gift into thick ledgers. We moved along all these treasures: gilded chairs, mounds of fur, carved elephant tusks, chests overflowing with gems, gold boxes containing spices and glass bottles filled with exotic perfumes.

I wanted to stop and inspect every treasure, but Erik marched on without even a glance at the exquisite objects surrounding him. Looking back on this loot with regret, I stayed in his steps.

As I passed two cases of richly bound books, I thought that perhaps I could pause for a minute to admire some of these treasures. My eyes fell on four ornate saddles set beside the bookcases. Long silk tassels dangled from their sides matching the bridles hung on their pommels. A little farther was an ebony carriage with silver wheels. Two silver dragons were inlayed in the side of its doors. I ran a hand on the dragons. They were so perfectly done that their metallic bodies seemed melted into the wood.

Shouting from the stable tore me from my contemplation. I dashed through its opened doors and found Erik beating one of our brothers with a riding crop. I watched him lift the crop high in the air, while on the ground our brother squirmed in his fineries. Leaping ahead, I gripped Erik's arm before the crop could come down again.

"Are you mad," I said.

"Let go of my arm," Erik growled with a rage I'd never seen him display before.

"Erik, stop! This is wrong; you can't beat a prince like this."

"Like what? Like a vulgar servant? I'm warning you, Amir, beware of your words."

I held my tongue. Erik wasn't one to make empty threats. So instead I searched the ground for our brother and found him near the door, scurrying away on all fours. As he passed the stable door, something at his waist sparkled in the sunlight. *Oh!* I hoped this wasn't what I thought it was. At that instant I wished I had paid more attention to this brother's face. Too late now, he was gone. I released my grip on Erik's arm. "Tell me what happened."

"What's the use! I know how you think." He turned away, walked to the nearest stall and kneeled. "Don't be afraid," he whispered.

Curious, I joined him at the stall. Curled up against the board was a young stable boy, about Rami's age. An ugly red welt marked his left cheek. Then I saw the dozen welts striping his arms.

Erik shot me a stare so laden with anger that I felt the urge to check my chest for a dagger. "Not a word, Amir—not one!" he said before turning to the boy. "Calm down, little one. Shh... You're not in danger anymore. He's gone."

Trembling with fear, the boy listened to Erik's soft words. Slowly his trembling subsided and he began responding to Erik's reassuring tone.

"Can you stand up?" Erik asked.

The boy nodded.

After a close examination of the boy's injuries, Erik declared them minor, yet told the boy that a lady named Salima would visit him and bring ointment for his welts. Mouth open, the stable boy stared at this strange prince with a mixture of adoration and disbelief. After much bowing and thanks, the stable boy ran out the door.

An uncomfortable silence settled between Erik and me. He was the first to break it; I wasn't surprised. He was bolder than I. "Say what's on your mind, Amir."

"*Really!* It's not what you asked me a moment ago."

Erik sighed, then kicked straw around. "I was angry. My blood was boiling. Servants aren't to be treated this way. They should be respected for what they do for us. They cook our food, sew our clothes, care for our horses. Our lives wouldn't be so easy without them. The actions of some of our brothers shame me." Erik bit his lower lip. "Not you, though. I know you would never do something like this. Beat a boy on a whim. You're better than this. Please, Amir, forgive me for my rudeness."

Erik looked at me with pleading eyes.

I felt ill at ease, unworthy of his friendship. Although I didn't like servants, he was right in saying that I had never mistreated one. But I doubt that I would've made an enemy of one of my brothers to save a servant, as Erik had. My instinct of preservation was stronger than his. Or perhaps I was just more selfish than he. Forcing a smile on my face, I told Erik that he was forgiven, that we were still friends. The relief I saw on his face made me feel like camel dung.

* * *

For the next hour, we strolled through the stable, admiring its new occupants. Elephants with tusks covered in jewels and tipped with gold balls, horses of all kinds, cheetahs wearing fat leather collars on their necks like hounds and trained to hunt gazelles, and a small herd of addax, big antelopes with long, twisted horns rising high in the air.

Erik stopped in front of a pen filled with white camels. "Do you ride?"

"I learned like everybody."

"It's not what I asked. Do you still ride, and if so, which mount do you favor, camel or horse?"

"For what!" I replied dryly. "I don't see the interest of saddling a mount just to turn round and round in a small pen."

"One can ride for pleasure. I do." Leaning against the fence, Erik watched the slowly approaching camels. "White camels are very rare, very expensive. Aren't they beautiful?"

I grimaced. "Hell no! They stink, they bite, they spit— they're awful creatures."

Erik's sudden burst of laughter sent the camels running to the opposite end of their pen. "So you're a horse man then."

I nodded—reluctantly. Erik had something in mind. I was sure of it. Then again, he always had some plan brewing, it seemed.

"Ahhh," Erik let out. "You must see my horse, Thunder. He's in the stables. Come."

The stable's left wing was attached to the riding ring and reserved for the horses that were ridden regularly. As we advanced through the lines of stalls, noise rose from the last one. Kicking and stumping, the likes of which I had never heard before.

"He knows I'm coming," Erik said with a wink.

"He doesn't seem happy about it." The corners of my mouth dipped down in apprehension.

We stopped in front of the stall and faced the black nightmare inside. Twice the size of our desert purebred, the Nordic warhorse was scary to behold: It had thick legs with big hoofs that struck the floor like thunder, and a back so broad I wondered how one could ride such a creature without suffering horrible pain. Just looking at it made my groin ache.

The warhorse shook its thick mane, then stretched its muscular neck toward us and tried to bite Erik.

"Don't go near that monster," I said, grabbing my brother's arm.

"It's fine," Erik said. "He's just a little angry because I haven't ridden him in a few weeks. Thunder, stop this nonsense!"

To my amazement, the warhorse calmed down.

"Thunder descends from the horses my uncle the King of Sorvinka brought along when he accompanied Mother here."

"I didn't know your uncle visited the palace."

"Yes, long ago. He was the heir prince then and only a few years older than us. He stayed for a month, the length of the wedding festivity."

"Will he come for you cousin's wedding?"

"No. It's far too dangerous, and Eva won't marry right away." Erik planted his fists on his waist. "Enough talk of my cousin. Pick a mount and let's ride, brother."

We rode a good part of the afternoon, I on a gray mare and Erik on his warhorse. My mare was a delight to ride. She was so intelligent and swift that I was able to run circles around Erik's slower mount as it ambled through the ring. In a show of discontent, the warhorse bumped into my mare with so much force that she almost fell. If my horse was a tool of war meant for fast maneuvers, Erik's was a weapon bred for attack and trained to help his master in any possible way. Therefore warhorses kicked and struck opponents with their front hoofs, bit and rammed other horses. And if one had the bad luck of being thrown down by the ramming of one of those brutes, the warhorse would immediately trample the unfortunate man to a pulp.

I patted my mare's neck. I'd rather stick with her and the fast exit she provided.

As we were readying ourselves to ride back to the stable, I noted that the boy Erik had rescued earlier was waving at us from the fence. "Your Highness," the boy began once we reached him, "Lady Salima is waiting for you at the stable's entrance. She bids you to hurry."

We gave our horses to the boy and rushed to Salima.

"Ah, there you are, my princes." She smiled, with her delicate hands crossed over her chest—as customary for a woman outside her household to do. "Princess Eva and the Sorvinkian ambassador will be here in an hour. You must ready yourselves for their welcoming and for the banquet the Sultan is giving in their honor. You'll both be seated at the ambassador's side. It's a great honor, and you mustn't smell of horses."

My stomach made a flip. *Eva, I will see her in the flesh,* I thought. I had to restrain myself from running all the way back to Erik's apartments.

CHAPTER TEN

When I saw our clothing my jaw dropped. Princess Livia had had matching tunics and kaftans made for Erik and me. They were reverse images: Mine was silver with blue lotus flowers embroidered throughout and trimmed with silver fox. Erik's was blue with silver lotus and also trimmed with silver fox.

A valet set the box containing my ensemble on my bed, stepped back and waited for my order to begin dressing me.

I gazed upon the ensemble for a moment then let my fingers glide over the kaftan's rich brocade. I had never received such a sumptuous gift and had not let anyone dress me since... since I became a man. It made me uncomfortable. I felt like a toy being played with and in more than one way. But fearing I would insult the princess if I refused her gift, I let the valet dress me. Once he was done, I stared at my glistening reflection in Erik's mirror; this ensemble was flashier than anything I had ever worn in my life. Yet it wasn't what struck me. *Yesterday, Princess Livia called me Erik's new playmate. So if that's all I am, why make such a show of dressing us like brothers then?* I thought, as a valet placed a sapphire-incrusted lotus brooch on my silver turban. *Stupid! Because we're brothers.* Somehow I was not convinced that this was the only reason.

The valet went to tighten my belt and I flinched.

"I can finish myself. Thank you." He bowed and left.

I watched Erik make last minute adjustments to his blue turban; on its front a diamond lotus flower sparkled brilliantly with every head turn. I watched Erik hook his saber to his silver belt; my own was tightly wound blue silk. Our clothes might be the same but our rank wasn't.

"Mother had this commissioned from the imperial armory for you." Erik indicated the long mahogany box on the nearby table.

I flipped the box cover open with the same apprehension as if it had been a basket of vipers. Lying on red velvet inside the box was a magnificent rapier. Not one of those overly ornate weapons that were useless in combat, but a true one. The scabbard was made of shagreen, a type of sharkskin, with gilded roses climbing its sides. I gripped the weapon. The hilt twisted and turned elegantly around my fist providing protection for my hand. The pommel had the right weight, giving the rapier a perfect balance. *A true master's weapon.*

"I told Mother you favor rapiers over sabers," Erik said.

"I can't accept this—it's too much."

"No it's not. And Mother expects you to wear it. I wouldn't disappoint her if I were you."

I agreed, and set the rapier to my waist. Now both ready, we made our way to Erik's receiving room.

Large bouquets of white tulips had been set everywhere in our absence, and essence of rose and jasmine perfumes added to the fountain's water. Wearing an elegant midnight blue gown, Princess Livia stood at the entrance door with Salima and Oroco on either side of her. She smiled at us as we approached, apparently satisfied by our appearances.

We had just taken our place at Princess Livia's side when the Grand Vizier, followed by his assistant Hassan, entered the room. After bowing to the princess, the Vizier turned dark eyes toward Erik and me. His gaze traveled from our clothes to our faces to our belts over and over and over again.

Never before had I been scrutinized this closely by this man; it covered my spine in goose bumps. The Grand Vizier then made a slight grimace that was to pass for a smile. However, the deep furrows on his brow told me that my presence here displeased him.

"Shall we, Princess," he said with a flourished gesture toward the entrance.

Princess Livia nodded dryly and took a few steps outside the room. The Grand Vizier took his place at her side while everybody else settled behind them.

Erik nudged me in the ribs. "I hate these ceremonies."

I nodded. Rising on my toes, I peered down the long corridor ahead. Someone was coming. Yes, there they were. I could see the white eunuchs. My heartbeat sped up; my pulse started drumming on my temples. I was breathing too fast and felt lightheaded. Closing my eyes, I counted to twenty. When I reopened my eyes, Erik's cousin was in front of us.

She was stunning and looked so small and delicate boxed between the eight imposing eunuchs. I swallowed and almost choked. She looked at me. Her eyes I noted were a warm brown, her hair, piled in an intricate mound of ringlets garnished with baroque pearls, was the same dark gold color as honey. Some hot exotic blood from her mother's side had warmed the ice-cold one of her father's Nordic line. In fact Eva looked more like Erik than like Princess Livia.

I gazed down the length of her body and smiled. A translucent ivory shawl draped the upper half of her soft coral gown, and heavy gold necklaces were piled around her neck. My eyes flew to the fat teardrop pearl dangling at the center of her forehead. Her attempt to adapt her Sorvinkian clothes to the Telfarian fashion was clumsily charming—truly adorable.

A tall, bearded man then stepped forward. His face was as stern as his plain brown clothing. By the amount of gray intertwined within his hair and beard, I estimated his age at around sixty. First nodding to the princess then to the Vizier, the man introduced himself. "I am Olaf Molsky, baron of the province of Ivra and ambassador of Sorvinka. King Erik sends his best regards to the Sultan and to you, Princess Livia."

The ambassador's attention then jumped to Erik. His bushy gray eyebrows rose up and for a brief instant Olaf Molsky looked stunned. Then a bright smile lit his face. His gaze moved to me. He had the wisest eyes I had ever seen, and the glint of mischief I could see sparkling in them really puzzled me. I had the feeling that this man was playing a game, but which one, and for which prize, I had no clue—yet.

"Without further delay," Ambassador Molsky said, "I present you, Princess Eva of Sorvinka, future Sultana of Telfar."

Eva stepped up and curtsied in front of the Grand Vizier. "I am honored by your presence at my welcoming ceremony, Grand Vizier. I shall not disappoint nor dishonor the Sultan, this kingdom, this house and you who now represent all. I will conduct myself with the grace due to my rank."

The Grand Vizier seemed impressed by Eva's knowledge of Telfarian formulaic courtesies. "You are most welcomed, Princess Eva."

After another curtsy, Eva turned to Princess Livia. "My dear aunt, I have long wished to meet you."

"It has been granted, dear niece. Let me introduce you to my household. First, your cousin, Prince… Keri."

Erik stepped up and bowed. "You can call me Erik. My friends and family do so."

Eva smiled. "Agreed, Cousin Erik."

Gesturing toward me, Princess Livia said, "This is Prince Amir, your cousin's brother."

I took an unsure step forward. From up close Eva was breathtaking. Her skin appeared as soft and dewy as a peach. I opened my mouth and, horror, nothing came out. I couldn't speak. I just stood there, jaw slack like an idiot. Now everyone was looking at me—she was looking at me. Cold sweat ran down my back. I had to do something. In a rush of panic,

I did the unthinkable: I grabbed her hand, bent down and kissed it.

I heard gasps. Oroco let out a growl. From the corner of my eye, I saw the white eunuchs grip their scimitars. *What have I done!* Unwed women shouldn't be touched. This was an unbreakable rule. My eyes flew to the Vizier. I thought he looked pleased by my faux pas, while Hassan looked mortified.

"Prince Amir!" boomed the Vizier. "How dare you insult our guest in such a way?"

"I... I... " I gave up trying to be articulate, it was quiet useless. With Eva staring at me I couldn't even manage coherence.

Ambassador Molsky abruptly burst into laughter. "Pardon my mirth, Vizier. But I believe Prince Amir only returned Princess Eva's courtesy. She introduced herself in accordance with your customs, and he politely greeted her back following ours. A very thoughtful gesture, I might add."

Face pinched with displeasure, the Grand Vizier lifted his long nose in the air. "Perhaps ... perhaps I can let it pass—this time."

Oh my, I couldn't believe it—I got away with it. I looked at the ambassador. For a second, I wanted to grip his beard with both hands and kiss the old man on the lips. As if sensing my thought, Ambassador Molsky turned my way and... winked.

For a few precious hours, Eva stayed with us in Erik's receiving room. At one point in the evening our group split up leaving Eva and me alone with the eunuchs. During that time, we discussed freely on all kinds of subjects. Having regained usage of my tongue, I did my best to prove myself intelligent and educated. Eva laughed at several of my wordplays. I smiled giddily, oblivious to the stern looks her eunuchs gave me.

"You're quite witty, Prince Amir," she declared. Eva had the loveliest of accents and in this unrehearsed conversation it rang with every one of her words.

I smiled. "Thank you, Princess. It is my duty and pleasure to entertain you."

She pouted. "I hope there is more pleasure than duty in it for you."

God, I had offended her. "It's not... I didn't mean... " My cheeks were suddenly burning. I looked at her. To my surprise, Eva didn't seem offended at all. Actually, she appeared to have a great deal of trouble keeping a straight face.

"Prince Amir, you are blushing. How charming."

Now I was mortified. I quickly covered my cheeks with my hands.

"Please forgive me, Prince Amir," she said while twirling one of her golden curls. "I was only jesting. I'm a jester. It's one of my many flaws. According to my father, it's my worst and most inappropriate for a princess." She extended a hand in an attempt to lower mine from my cheeks. Disapproving grumbles from the eunuchs made her retract her hand swiftly. She sighed and looked down. For a brief second I believed I saw frustration on her face, but when she raised her head again, Eva was all smiles.

I smiled back, and lowered my hands from my cheeks.

Her smile broadened. "Had I known you would have reacted this strongly to my jesting, I would have been more careful." A spark of mischief brightened her eyes. "Your blushing surprised me. Slovakian princes lack this ability." She paused. When she spoke again her voice had dropped to a whisper. "Many also lack smarts. It makes them extremely boring."

I nodded. "I'll keep it in mind not to bore you, Princess."

"Interesting," the Grand Vizier said, surprising both Eva and me by his sudden presence at our side. "Has Prince Amir's conversation bored you, Princess? He can be rather tiresome. Individuals of inferior-birth often are." The Vizier's mocking tone was nearly as insulting as his words.

A frown marked Eva's lovely brow for a brief instant. Then

she looked at the Vizier and smiled. "Prince Amir—tiresome? Quite the contrary, my dear Vizier, Prince Amir is far too clever to be tiresome or boring. I cannot fathom that a man in your position and of your knowledge has not noted such qualities before." Another spark of mischief flashed across Eva's eyes. Displaying a look of perfect innocence, she asked the Vizier, "Unless you think otherwise. Oh, perhaps I shouldn't ask this. Are servants allowed to insult princes in Telfar, Viziers are some kind of servants, aren't they?"

The Grand Vizier turned an ugly shade of gray. I bit my tongue not to laugh. This young princess had the Vizier by the throat. I couldn't believe it.

Eva batted her eyes at the Vizier. "Hmm, that's what I thought. I fear to have placed you, my dear Vizier, in some unpleasant predicament, so I will rephrase my question. Don't you think that Prince Amir is clever and bright?"

For a long moment, the Vizier stayed as still and as silent as a wall. Then emitting a snorting sound, he said, "Perhaps. Unfortunately in young men, cleverness often leads to imprudence." As the rest of our group returned forming a small circle around us, the Grand Vizier turned to me. "The next Sultan will be a lucky man for having a wife such as Princess Eva, don't you think, Prince Amir?"

All joy left me. I wished the man would drop dead. "Yes, very lucky indeed," I replied, and left our small circle under Ambassador Molsky's watchful eyes. I walked to the paintings displayed beside the sofa. For months, I had dreamed of the girl in the locket with the certainty that she didn't really exist outside of my mind—to suddenly be in the same room as she, was oddly painful. Why couldn't Eva be vain, shallow and vapid, I thought, while gazing at her portrait. *Misery, she's as kind and intelligent as she's beautiful.* I was lost—painfully so.

"What's wrong, brother?" Erik hushed in my ear. "You're making a face like someone has just kicked you in the groin."

Not far from the truth, I thought, and wondered if Erik knew that I had also been punched in the heart.

* * *

Later that day, while Eva was led to her tower to prepare for the evening festivity and the ambassador was received by the Sultan, the Great Hall, the biggest sitting room of the Cage, was transformed into a banquet hall.

That evening, Erik and I were among the last to enter the hall. His mother had insisted that we waited and thus made a grand entrance, which in my opinion was arrogant, if not crazy. As if we needed this added attention, our seats were near the Sultan's and flanking the ambassador's, who was the guest of honor. That was more than sufficient to stir envy. And sure enough, it was under our brothers' burning glares that Erik and I sat down on the broad square cushions near the head of the table.

Definitively crazy, I thought with a quick peek at my siblings. To their eyes Erik was a threat—one to eliminate. I was glad when Ambassador Molsky joined us and took his place between us. To be near Erik was like standing beside the target circle at archery practice—one was bound to be hit by a stray arrow. I sighed and looked up; my gaze met the Grand Vizier's. "I'm not done with you," the Vizier's eyes seemed to say.

"This man doesn't like you, Prince Amir," the ambassador said. "I'd be careful if I were you."

"Thank you for the advice… and thank you for intervening earlier. It was very foolish of me to kiss her hand."

Ambassador Molsky smiled; it was a true smile that lit his entire face. Not the polite baring of teeth one often saw on most people in the palace. "I've done many foolish things in my youth too—all young men do. Especially when a beautiful girl is involved. In my opinion, the offense was hardly worth a reprimand."

I smiled. I liked this man's easy-going manner and common sense.

"Amir never does these kinds of things," Erik commented, and then lowering his voice he added, "I think he's smitten."

I could've punched Erik in the gut for saying that. But instead I ground my teeth, squeezed my fist and swore to do it as soon as we would be alone together. "I'm not smitten," I said through clenched teeth. "I just forgot my manners."

"Understandable," the ambassador said. "I'm amazed by the complexity of your traditions. For example: Your codes of conduct regarding the proper behavior toward women are stricter than ours—and far more complicated too. But with so many wives and concubines in the same house, I understand that some rules are needed just to keep the peace."

"Your culture only allows you one wife, doesn't it?" I asked.

He smiled again. "Yes. But mistresses are aplenty. They, however, tend to rule our life and not the other way around. Mistresses are free to come and go—freer than wives, who can't leave their husbands." He leaned closer to me; a glint of mischievousness lit his eyes again. "I know for a fact that a mistress's best lure is her ability to leave us."

Music filled the air, an old, languorous melody.

Murmurs circulated throughout the room. "The princess is coming," it whispered.

"There she is," arose from the brother seated near the door.

Seconds later four white eunuchs passed the great archway carrying a richly ornate palanquin—the enclosed litter used by traveling women—on their shoulders. Through the diaphanous cloud of muslin draped around the palanquin, Eva's silhouette undulated hazily like a mirage. And just like a mirage, it was hypnotic and enticing. There wasn't one pair of eyes in this room that wasn't fixed on her.

I resented the fact that she was offered to everyone's sight like some prized stallion, like bait, like a reward for the most ruthless among us. I scanned my brothers' hungry faces. To my surprise, I saw that Darius also was watching my brothers' reactions instead of Eva's silhouette. Our eyes met across the room. We each acknowledged each other with a slight nod and then looked away.

The clang of hard silver soles hitting the ceramic tiles announced the Sultan's arrival. Everyone in the room rose up and bowed at the waist. We remained in that position until the Sultan had taken his place at the head of our table. When the Vizier clapped his hands, we all straightened.

Immediately, I cast my eyes on my father. I winced in horror, while others gasped openly.

A few months ago, my father had been in good heath, although slightly overweight. The man that now sat in his place was all but his pale shadow. His face was gaunt under his brown brittle beard. His red kaftan hung loosely on him, as if he had shrunk or shriveled like a dried-up raisin—even his turban seemed too big. What had happened to my father these last months? What terrible disease ailed him? I was totally baffled by his appearance.

Once the worst of our shock passed, we quietly sat down. Now however there was an uneasiness choking the room which had not been there before—not to this degree anyway. A glance at the other tables told me my brothers were just as distraught as I was by our father's condition. They kept looking at one another with questioning eyes.

On a sign from the Vizier, huge plates of pilaf rice were brought to our table. Then an entire ox roasted from hoof to horn was carried in by six servants. A series of exotic dishes followed. The air of the hall was soon filled with the enticing aroma of spices and venison.

I found myself without appetite. Ignoring the succulent dishes in front of me, I directed my attention to my father. From my seat, I could hear the wheezing of his breath; see the dullness of his bloodshot eyes. He seemed on the verge of collapsing.

A cool breeze blew through the open terrace door behind me. Shivers ran along my spine, as though some ghostly fingers were touching my back. I looked over my shoulder. Hundreds of torches illuminated the terrace, and although their amber glow dancing in the penumbra made for a lovely spectacle, it wasn't what caught my eye: The moon did.

I pinched Erik's side. "Look outside, little brother."

"Outside! What am I supposed to see?"

"The moon."

Erik sucked air in sharply. "It's the full moon—already!"

"Yes," I whispered. "Tonight one of us will die. And I still don't know who, how, or why."

CHAPTER ELEVEN

rik and I didn't swallow one bite during the banquet. We pushed food about our plates, made noise with our utensils, but brought nothing to our mouths. Father didn't touch his food either and returned to his rooms early, leaving us to entertain Ambassador Molsky. I never had such an honor before and didn't really know what to do.

Once the servants had finished cleaning the table, Ibrahim—who had been trying to attract the ambassador's attention throughout the banquet—stepped up. With a smirk on his face and a twirl of his waxed mustache, he pompously announced, "I've arranged for entertainment. I hope it will be to your liking, Ambassador."

He clapped his hands. The musicians began playing a new melody and twenty dancers rushed into the room. Clad in matching red see-through pants and tops, these black-haired beauties looked like sisters. Once lined in two rows, they started dancing. The hundreds of brass bells wrapped around their ankles and calves rang with every coordinated step they made, giving a new rhythm to the music.

"Oh, wonderful!" Ambassador Molsky said. "Shall we move closer?"

"Certainly." Reluctantly, I moved away from the table and Eva's palanquin. It was then that I noticed that more women were entering the room. Soon the entire Cage's harem was with us. This was wrong, I thought, lips thinned.

Meanwhile at my side, Ambassador Molsky enjoyed the spectacle, tapping his foot in rhythm with the music. Then his eyes left the dancers in favor of the harem's women and my brothers. He seemed surprised by their presence among us.

"I'll answer any of your questions," I said.

He laughed. "Was I so obvious?"

I tilted my head. "We are allowed female companionship—nothing permanent, however. The women of our harem are rotated every few months, so no bond can be forged."

The ambassador pouted. "Bonds can form quickly." His gaze traveled to the tight group of women surrounding Darius and Ibrahim.

"Favoritism is what forms here," I said with a smirk. "See the purple ribbons the girls near Darius wear on their wrists—it means they're his and not to be touched by others."

The ambassador beamed. "Fascinating! What would happen if one touches another's favorite?"

"Trouble—lots of it! Why?"

"I see that Prince Keri is well surrounded too—but isn't it ribbons of different colors I note on the wrists of some of the women hanging on his arms?"

He was right. Erik was like a magnet for the girls—I wasn't surprised; he was handsome, tall and wore a silver belt. Some harem women would risk a beating to gain the favor of a more powerful prince—or a more handsome one. Still, any sign of interest by a favorite was bad news, regardless of its reasons. I thought Erik should get rid of those women as quickly as possible instead of charming more of them like he was doing right now. Yet I knew that was too much to ask, Erik wasn't that smart.

I too was attracting some women's attentions. A long-haired beauty strolled close by. She stopped in front of us and studied me openly. The calculation in her eyes made her ugly—I could tell that she was evaluating me, checking my clothes and my belt instead of my face. Then in a shimmer of pink taffetas, she spun around and joined Darius's troop. I had failed her test. But I passed others', and twice I refused women's advances.

"Are your tastes for something—else?" asked the ambassador, eyes fixed on the dancers' undulant movements.

"No!"

"Why reject their offers then, if you don't mind me asking?"

"I don't mind..." I paused to chew the inside of my cheeks for an instant. "It's just... it's improper with Princess Eva here. I wouldn't dare offend her in such a manner."

My reply seemed to please the ambassador. He nodded approvingly to me. With a sweeping glance around the room, he said, "I see a few of your brothers who are also careful not to commit this faux pas." He motioned toward two overly bejeweled brothers accompanied by a small army of pageboys.

I let out a chuckle. Quickly, I stamped a hand over my mouth.

The ambassador looked at me with raised eyebrows then a spark of comprehension flashed across his face. "Ah, I see! And the one who looks bored at the back?"

I followed the ambassador's gaze to a brother dressed in a dark blue kaftan and wearing very little jewelry. His name was Sherif. Right this moment, he appeared absorbed by the inspection of his fingernails.

"Sherif doesn't care for pageboys. He prefers tall, muscular guardsmen."

"Aah!" was all Ambassador Molsky said.

The dancers had finished and were now mingling in our group. A particularly stunning one caught my eyes, not for her beauty but because she was hanging on Mir's every word. I smiled broadly, happy to see him outside of his room and enjoying himself. The dancers had attracted him here. Mir, like many of my brothers, had a weakness for dancing girls. Only they could bring Mir to enter a room filled with his brothers. I wished Jafer could be trusted to behave, but it was no use trying to fool myself. He couldn't.

My eyes went to the terrace and then to the moon. It was getting late. I had the unpleasant feeling that something terrible was about to happen. This feeling hadn't ceased growing since I'd first set eyes on the moon. By now it was so strong I could almost taste it. Suddenly I wanted this evening over. I sought to get Erik's attention and failed. He only had eyes for the women at his side. When I turned back, I saw that Darius had sent his favorites away. He now stood alone in front of Eva's palanquin with a seductive smile illuminating his handsome face.

My stomach churned painfully, while my blood rushed to my face. I rolled my hands into fists. More than ever I wanted this evening to end—but for a very different reason.

* * *

The evening's festivity finally came to an end, and once the ambassador was escorted back to his rooms, we returned to the terrace and waited until the Great Hall was empty to go back in. As for what we were to do now, I had no clue.

"Are you sure about this?" Erik asked again.

"Yes," I said. "The Great Hall is the best place to be. It's right at the center of the Cage and has access to all its sections. It's also near the harem's gate and our father's apartments."

Erik grimaced. "That's not what I meant. Shouldn't we be in a safer place, instead of in the open like this?"

I shrugged. "I don't know where safety lies anymore."

Erik began pacing around nervously. "I hate the idea that we're waiting for someone to be attacked."

"There's nothing else we can do."

"We can look for the attacker instead of the victim," a voice spoke at my back.

I quickly turned.

Darius and his supporters were entering the hall, carrying torches in one hand and their sabers in the other.

Erik looked at me. "Uh-oh!"

My hand found my rapier's grip and squeezed it, but I didn't pull the weapon—not yet. I watched Darius approach. He stopped in front of us.

"How do you know there will be an attack tonight?" I asked before he could speak.

"He spied on us, spied on our conversation, that's clear!" Erik interjected.

I winced, eyes fixed on Darius's mob, now surrounding us. Couldn't Erik shut his mouth? I supposed not. To my astonishment, Darius chuckled. Not the reaction I'd expected.

"You're not the only ones who can add things up," he said with a one-sided smile. "I too think that the full moon is a catalyst. I've read somewhere that it coincides with the rise of power—dark ones in particular."

I frowned. "I didn't realize you were interested in magic."

Darius narrowed his eyes. "I am as much as you are, brother."

"No! I'm not!"

"Doesn't matter, I'm still not letting you out of my sight. If the rumor is true and you're guilty of those crimes, we'll know tonight."

I nodded in agreement. I was somewhat relieved—after all I was innocent. Only the idea of being so grossly outnumbered by my armed brothers bothered me.

Sure enough, Erik had to make things worse by whispering in my ear: "You realize that if no one dies tonight, they'll all think it was because they were watching you."

Hell, I had not thought of that. Still, I wasn't going to wish for the death of a brother to prove myself innocent.

Traveling in a long procession, we began searching the Cage's rooms one by one, going from corridor to corridor. I walked in front, stuck between Erik and Darius. Being the tallest and handsomest of my brothers, these two made me feel like the runt of the family, which I was not. As we moved along, shining our torches at every dark spot, I noted that Darius's eyes never wandered from my face.

"Do you think I'm going to mumble some incantation, if you look away?" I asked.

"Perhaps."

His bluntness stunned me.

"Amir doesn't believe in magic," Erik said. "If you knew him better, you'd understand that."

"Oh, I know him." Darius snorted. "Amir believes he's smarter than all of us—too good to seek our company."

"What!" I was shocked. "I don't—"

"Yes you do," Darius snapped. "That's why you lock yourself in your tower with your precious books. Why do you shun us, brothers of your rank, and only befriend a Sultana's son?" Darius stopped walking and faced me. "Like it or not, Amir, you and I are exactly the same. No better, no worse."

I was too stunned to speak. Was my ignoring him at the root of our discord? That couldn't be. I scanned Darius's court, realizing for the first time that his supporters were all motherless princes, all raised by the palace attendants. They were all like me. I looked at Darius, who I saw was staring hatefully at Erik.

"He's not like us," Darius hissed through clenched teeth.

Erik stepped into Darius's face. He was about to say something nasty, I could see it in his face. I had to do something quick before he put both of us in peril. Just as I squeezed between those two, a blood-chilling shriek of agony echoed through the corridor.

We ran ahead where the shriek originated. A thick fog blocked the corridor further down. When we moved closer the fog vanished under the nearest door, leaving behind the dried-up, disarticulated body of one of our brothers. Before we could as much as formulate a thought, someone hollered.

"It came from that room," Erik said, "where the fog went."

We dashed through the room only to find the dry, lifeless body of a second brother.

"It's working much faster than before," I said.

"I think it's gaining strength with every life it takes," Darius added. "We must stop this thing before it gets too strong."

"What is it?" Erik asked.

"A spirit, a ghost or some low demon even. I don't know exactly." Darius looked at me as if I should know which kind of creature was guilty of these crimes.

"Don't look at me for an answer. I've never believed in any of those things. I thought our brothers had been poisoned."

"Obviously they were not," Darius said.

"There's nothing else in this room," Erik said. "Perhaps it hs had enough."

Just then a series of shouts were heard coming from the kitchen. We made it there at a breakneck speed and found the kitchen crew in a state of terror.

Screaming insults, cooks waved knifes and cleavers at the thick wall of fog in the middle of the room, while behind them apprentices and dishwashers fled through the back door.

Peering at the fog, I saw the unmistakable form of yet another brother wheeling in this mist. Gripping his throat, he looked at us with bulging eyes. Giant fog hands then lift him up and twisted him like a rag. My brother screamed and kicked, his body horribly contorted.

Without thinking any further, I rushed to help. The fog pushed back, refusing to let me in its midst. Pulling my rapier, I whipped the icy haze around me until it gave. I entered the fog. It was like stepping inside a storm, a cold howling wind stirred the fog, making everything in front of me white and blurry. Still, I knew my brother was just ahead. I could distinguish part of his silhouette twirling in the air. I took a step toward it. The wind picked up speed, spinning faster and faster around me. I tried taking another step and failed. I was stuck in a vortex. I couldn't move at all. From the corner of my eye I saw Erik coming to my aid. As soon as he entered the vortex, the stormy fog wall shrunk into a thin tornado and shot out the chimney, leaving its prey behind. My brother fell on the floor with a thump. The kitchen was silent again.

Erik was the first to break the silence. "He's dead," he said, kneeling beside our brother. "I don't understand this. There were other potential preys in this room, all weaker than our brother. That thing, that fog didn't touch them."

"Because it wants us, and only us," Darius said in a hollow voice.

Why, I thought, rubbing my arms for warmth. I was freezing. *Why would this ghostly mist feed on royal blood only?* It didn't make sense to me—none of this did. Even if I had witnessed the entire incident, I still had trouble wrapping my mind around its surreal nature. It went beyond everything I had always believed in, or not believed in depending on how one puts it. Right now, my only hope was that whatever this was, it had had enough royal blood for one day.

We were coming out of the kitchen when a long scream pierced the silence. *I guess I was wrong. This thing is still hungry.*

We ran west. More screaming arose, closer this time. We were getting near. Then we reached the gate separating the Cage from the Sultan's apartments.

"It came from one of father's rooms," Erik said.

We all stared at one another not knowing what to do next. To go beyond this point was forbidden. Alerted by the screaming more brothers had exited their rooms and joined us at the gate, while on the other side a group of panic-stricken eunuchs filled the corridor.

As another scream echoed, someone said: "It's killing our father. Let's bring the gate down."

The gate fell in a matter of seconds. The eunuchs rushed toward us in an attempt to block our path. They were pushed back by the force of our number, which had grown close to thirty. Seeking the origin of the screams, we began advancing along this long door-filled corridor, when suddenly a door swung open in front of us. A woman emerged from the room. Although she was disheveled and her face was reddened and streaked with tears, I recognized Çiçek, father's favorite, from the miniature Erik had shown me the night we had left the Cage.

"Help!" Çiçek pleaded, hands extended toward us. Her knees gave and she dropped to the ground in a cloud of translucent cream muslins. "Your father! Help your father!" Turning toward the room she had left, Çiçek screamed at the top of her lungs.

I rose on tiptoes to see what had frightened her so. The Grand Vizier stood in the doorframe, his face contorted in an expression stuck between fear and anger. At that moment a ghostly mist blew out of the room and darted toward us. I yelled as it passed through me. Hundred of ice needles stabbed my entire body, freezing me to the bone. The pain of it was excruciating. Then it was gone, leaving me breathless and shivering.

Moaning from our father's room made us all move again.

"Stop!" ordered the Grand Vizier. "Don't take another step."

We pushed in anyway.

Because the room was spacious, it remained lost in semi-darkness despite our torches. And although none of us dared approach Father's gigantic bed, there was still enough light for us to see his shadowy form stirring amidst its opulent bedding.

"Who's there?" the form asked. "Çiçek, is that you?"

"I'm here," Çiçek answered. Running back in the room, she stopped at my side as if afraid to go further.

"Father's alive!" exclaimed one of my brothers.

"Our father is well," another said.

Breaths of relief were exhaled by most. I however didn't feel relief. Actually I was tenser than ever.

The shadowy form sat up in the bed. "What's going on here? Why are you in my bedchamber?"

I stepped outside of our tight group. "We heard screams, Father. We thought you were in danger and rushed to your help."

"Screams?" He climbed out of bed and stretched.

I frowned. There was something odd about his silhouette. I squinted to see better, but failed to find anything abnormal about the construction of my father's body.

"All this rich food must've given me nightmares," Father said, moving into our light.

Loud gasps of horror rose from our group. I blinked, totally paralyzed, while beside me Çiçek fainted to the ground.

Our father looked almost as young as we. As he walked forward a wave of residual magic moved with him. Soon this leftover spread throughout the room, prickling my skin, raising the hairs all over my body and filling my nose with it sulfuric smell.

Father stared hard at our stunned faces. "What's wrong? Why are you looking at me this way?" Motioning toward me with his chin, he said, "You, standing outside the group. You're their leader, answer me."

ME, LEADER! Frozen in place, I watched my father approach. *Get back in the group, hurry.* Useless, my legs refused to budge. I had lost all hope when Erik gripped my shoulder, forcing me back inside my brothers' rank.

The Grand Vizier stepped in front of us blocking our sight to our father. And after a brief whispered exchange with my father, he ordered. "Princes, return to your rooms."

"Grand Vizier," I said, "three of our brothers have been slain tonight and our father—"

"Enough, Prince Amir!" the Vizier snapped. Leaning forward, he whispered in a voice low enough so only I could hear: "If you value your life, don't say another word." Then straightening, he declared aloud, "Princes, if you leave peacefully now, we may forget this breaking of rules. Please, don't force me to have you escorted by the guards."

"NO!" I said. Raising my chin, I held the Vizier's gaze, refusing to move. The man had dared threaten me again—openly. This time I would not let it pass, no matter the consequence.

"Amir, please stop," Erik begged softly in my ear. "Come, Amir, we're leaving. Please, do it for me." He pulled me. I resisted for a moment, then reluctantly went along.

Once in the doorframe, I shot one last glance at my father. I found him in front of the room's mirror, staring at his reflection with the intensity of one who had never seen himself before. From my standpoint I couldn't tell if he was pleased by his appearance or devastated.

CHAPTER TWELVE

"**W**here are we going?" Erik asked.

"My tower," I replied dryly.

We both had spent the rest of the night in the Great Hall with Darius and the members of his court. No one dared mention what we had seen in our father's room and what it implied. Heads hung low and in total silence; we waited for daybreak and the safety we hoped it would bring.

"Why go there?" Erik continued. "It's still Visitation Days."

I sighed, wishing I were alone. "Go back then. I haven't invited you to come."

Erik shut up but stuck with me nonetheless. His persistence brought Darius's words at the forefront of my mind. "He's not like us," he had said of Erik. It bothered me—maybe because he was right.

As I entered the corridor leading to my tower, I immediately noticed that my door was cracked open.

"Psst…" Mir whispered from his grid. "The spy is still in there."

I rushed ahead, kicked the door open and charged into my reading room.

"SNAKE!" I yelled, seeing Rami at my desk with piles of books and notes spread all around him. With a yelp, the boy leaped out of my chair and hid in the darkest corner of the room.

"Erik!" I called. "Get your spy out of my rooms."

"Rami isn't a spy."

"Yes he is. You're just too dumb to see it… unless he's spying for you." I watched Erik's face pale. "Tell me, little brother; why else would the boy be sneaking around in dark corners like that? Every time I turn he's there, in the dark, listening. Get him out—right now!"

"Fine!" Erik snapped. Taking Rami by the hand, Erik led him to the door. He stopped in its frame and spoke softly to the boy, telling him that I didn't really mean what I had said, that I was tired and stressed.

I shook my head. I wanted to shout that I meant every word. Couldn't Erik see the boy's sneaky ways? Yet I remained silent; I had given up trying to convince him. Erik was right on one thing: I was tired, far too tired for this. With sluggish hands, I began sorting the books Rami had spread on my desk. Almost all regarded the incantations and control of mythical creatures and demons. I frowned. This fact was disturbing enough in itself, but a new detail had just climbed to the top of my mind, eclipsing the first.

I looked at Erik still standing at the door. "Servants of Rami's class rarely know how to read. Where did the boy learn it?"

My brother's sudden uneasiness made me nervous. Erik stuck out his lower lip and shrugged. "I don't know."

"Little brother, you're a terrible liar." Crossing my arms, I stared at him.

Erik lowered his eyes to his feet. I was pretty sure that he was searching for his next lie—but why was he looking so afraid. I was about to question him about it when a long howl of agony made us both jump. "Jafer!" I exclaimed; we both rushed to his room.

After an agonizing minute of fumbling with the lock, I swung the door open. Jafer spilled into my arms nearly forcing me to the ground with him. The pungent sugary scent of his skin engulfed me so completely, it was nauseating. "Help me," I asked. "He's having another episode."

With Erik's help, we managed to prop Jafer's body against the doorframe.

"The line is broken," Jafer mumbled. "Two kings' fault, two kings' lines twisted together, like vines growing out of the same pot—" Jafer gasped. "Seek the medium. Seek… seek its beginning where all ends. The signs are there… the tool is there… amidst dark clouds. The tool… must be wielded by one and not the other."

I held on to Jafer wishing he would stop this nonsense.

"The stolen gift," Jafer then said in an unusually calm voice.

"What stolen gift?" I asked, humoring him.

"Father's stolen gift… the gift is the key to find the tool."

Erik became dead white. "And the tool is where all ends, isn't it?"

Jafer turned toward the corridor where Erik stood. Although Jafer's eyes were rolled back and therefore blind, they widened as if they had seen something terrible. "The vile one… the impostor… he will kill us all." Jafer began trembling violently.

I looked at Erik, then at Mir whose face I could see peeking through his grid.

"What is he saying?" Mir asked in a panicked voice.

"The lines…" Jafer gasped. "The lines must remain together… together… they must…" Exhausted, his head fell upon his chest. Spasms shook Jafer's body a few times; then he went limp in my arms. We carried him inside and laid him on his bed. Once certain that Jafer would sleep for the rest of the day, I left the room.

While I was locking the door, Mir called to me: "Brother! Hey, brother! Did he say who would kill us?"

I winced; Jafer's ramblings were not things to improve Mir's already fragile state of mind. "No," I said. "You shouldn't worry about Jafer's… stories. He's a sick man."

Mir expelled a long sigh of relief and melted in the darkness of his room. Seconds later, I heard him mumbling to himself as usual.

Good, I thought, and returned to my rooms with Erik.

"Seek the beginning where all ends," Erik said as soon as I closed the door. "This means something, Amir."

"No it doesn't. Jafer is mad. Nothing he says makes sense. If you think it does, you're just as crazy as he is."

Erik slammed his fist on my desk. "Yes, perhaps I'm crazy, because I can swear that last night a foggy ghost killed my brothers—not poison—not a trick of the eyes, either—*A GHOST*." Erik had shouted the last word in anger. As usual, anger never stayed long with him, and within seconds he was calm again. "What we saw in our father's room can't be explained by science. Nothing we read in all your science books can explain what we saw last night. Amir, it's time to look elsewhere."

Sucking on my teeth, I pointed the books on my desk. "Why ask me now? You already began without me. Isn't that what Rami was doing here."

Erik made a face. "It's your fault. You're too stubborn."

I studied him carefully. He was uneasy again. I didn't like it one bit, yet I decided to put my suspicion aside for now. "All right, we'll look into *Magic*." The word rolled off my tongue like a sour piece of fruit. "But don't ask me to take Jafer's rambling seriously."

"Why not!" Erik stubbornly continued, "It may hold some truth. Stranger things have happened."

Well, apparently stubbornness was a flaw we both possessed. But to be honest, I had to admit that he was right about one thing. Strange things did happen last night: unexplainable things, scary things. At this point, I didn't know what to think anymore. I watched Erik pace in a circle while scratching his head.

"Seek the beginning where all ends." He grimaced. "Where all ends? Where all ends?" The look of frustration on his face might have been comical in another circumstance—right now it was just painful to behold. I decided to put an end to his misery.

"He meant the mausoleum. Death is where all ends, isn't it?"

Erik clapped his hands together. "Yes! It makes sense. Ready yourself, Amir, we're going there."

"How? Through the tunnel! You told me it was too dangerous with the Vizier back at the palace. And may I remind you that it's daylight. There are two courtyards to cross before reaching the mausoleum. People will recognize us."

Erik grinned, which really annoyed me. "Amir, let me worry about this."

* * *

Why have I agreed to this? I questioned while putting on the gardener's outfits Erik had chosen for us. Fortunately, the tunnel leading to the costume hall was short and the hall was often deserted in midday. Still, I thought that Erik's idea of crossing the yards disguised as gardeners was a dangerous one. I strapped on my leather apron. "Are you sure about this?"

"I've done it many times. The trick is to stay in character no matter what happens."

We adjusted each other's dark turban, leaving a long piece of cloth hanging down so we could use it to hide our faces, and then left the hall. Once back in the dark underground tunnels, we traveled west for a few minutes then passed a curve connected to a new tunnel.

"Where does this one lead?" I asked.

Looking unsure, Erik rubbed his temples. Then his face lit up. "To Eva's tower."

"Ohhh!" My eyes widened. I stared down the black mouth of this tunnel. Would I be able to find this tunnel alone? I wondered. *Yes, easily*, I decided, and followed Erik along the other road. Soon we reached a bend leading to the outside yard. The buzz of voices touched my ears.

"Wait," Erik whispered. Taking handfuls of wet mud from the floor, he smeared it on my face and clothes, then repeated the action on his own face and clothes. "Don't forget, Amir, you're a servant. Behave like one."

I nodded, and we quietly slipped outside.

I froze. There were guards everywhere. For a second, I thought us discovered, then realized why they were here. This was the guards' court. Their barracks lining the far wall proved it. Erik never said we would cross the guards' court. He purposely hid it from me. Had I known this, I never would have agreed to come.

Erik poked me with his elbow. "Move. You're attracting attention."

Three guards were staring at us with suspicion. Erik took the direction of the barracks; I followed, and to my chagrin so did the three guards. We were almost at the Tulip Garden's gate when the guards caught up with us.

"Halt," shouted the tallest.

I froze. Erik however immediately turned and faced the guards. Bowing he lamented, "Please, don't delay us. We're already late for our duty. This is the shortest road to the garden. We thought we could gain time by using it. Please, good lords, let us pass."

"What duty?" one of the guards asked. His breath reeked of garlic. Striking me in the back with the hilt of his halberd, he ordered, "Bow!"

Grinding my teeth, I bent down. I felt Erik's side touch mine, his hand wrapping my closed fist.

"We're only gardeners," Erik explained "Our duty is to pick the best flowers and bring them to the mausoleum for the three deceased princes."

"The ceremony's already over," the guard said. "You've missed it."

"Let them pass. We got other things to do," said another.

After much grumbling the other guard agreed.

Just as I thought we were free to leave and my hope returned, the rhythmic sound of metal hitting the stone pavers echoed.

"The Sultan!" Garlic Breath said. "The Sultan's coming."

I raised my head and took a peek around. Every guard of this court was now prostrated to the ground. I looked further back and saw my father coming out of the palace's archway. He proceeded in our direction followed by his usual entourage. Throwing myself to the ground, I stuck my forehead to the pavers and waited in complete immobility.

The imperial cortège approached. The hem of my father's kaftan brushed my turban as he passed near me. Suddenly the cortège halted. From the corner of my eye, I saw the black fabric of a long robe. Then I noted the robe's thin yellow trim. My stomach twisted and I stopped breathing. The Grand Vizier was standing in front of us.

"Guard," the Vizier said, "what are these gardeners doing here?"

The tall guard speedily explained everything to the Vizier.

"Tardiness is a punishable offense," the Vizier said. "Ten whiplashes to each for being late. Do it on this spot, then send them to their work. Our departed princes mustn't be deprived of flowers."

No, I thought, suddenly enraged. I wanted to rise and strike the Vizier. But Erik who had kept hold of my fist gave it a powerful squeeze, reminding me that servants never fought back—fighting meant death for them. So I did my best to remain as still as possible. The Vizier swung around. The bottom of his robe slapped me in the face, and I flinched. Then he was gone.

The first whiplash took me by surprise and I let out a whimper of pain. It took all my strength and determination not to jump to my feet and make this guard eat his own whip. I forced myself not to move. Princes were not allowed out of the Cage. If caught, I would certainly be locked into my tower, if not in the dungeon, for the rest of my days. The Grand Vizier would enjoy this very much, I was sure. The second lash made me bite my tongue.

Trembling with rage, I stared at Erik. He was hardly blinking under the whip, while I gasped with each new blow. Following his example, I bared my teeth and waited for it to be over as silently as I could. When the bite of the whip stopped, a low burning began. I could place where every lash had landed on my back just by its pain.

"Now back to work," the guard said before kicking me.

That was too much. I sprang to my feet. Erik yanked my ankles back, making me fall flat on my face.

"What's with that one?" asked the guard.

"He's simple, my lord," Erik quickly said. "Thank you for the lesson, we'll never be late again." Seizing my arm, Erik dragged me past the gate.

Once we were far enough into the Tulip Garden, I broke free of his grip. "How dare you call me simple? You shouldn't have stopped me—"

"Lower your voice." Erik nervously looked around.

"I don't want to lower my voice. My back is covered in welts."

"So is the back of every servant in the palace. If they can bear it, so can we. Are we lesser men than they to cry over a few whiplashes?"

I closed my eyes and took a deep breath. I felt somewhat calmer, yet I still had the urge to seek revenge over the guards. I was also angry at Erik for having put me in this situation. This was something I would not forget easily. I stared at my brother and grimaced. "Did you have to thank him for beating us? That was a bit much."

"I had to compensate for your attempt to rush him. Ten lashes—that's nothing. I got far worse."

"You got worse! How so?"

Erik looked at me, head tilted. "This isn't the first time I did something like this—leave it at that." Without another word, he began plucking tulips randomly, and so did I.

Once our arms were packed with flowers we took the direction of the mausoleum. This time we made it there without incident, which I was thankful for because I strongly doubted that I could support another beating. As I approached the white columns of the mausoleum's entrance, I became nervous. Memories of a dream I had months ago tormented me. In this dream there were dark shadows brewing inside the mausoleum. I remembered their presence being heavy with malice. It was an awful feeling, an ominous one. And the moment I set foot on the steps leading to the door, that unpleasant feeling returned. It was like an invisible hand pressing the back of my neck.

Don't be stupid, it was just a dream, I told myself. *And mausoleums are always creepy places anyway.* With this in mind, I placed my flowers in one of the two giant urns flanking the door while Erik filled the other. Then we entered the mausoleum.

The air inside was cool and echoed with our every footstep. My eyes went to the dark rectangle of the staircase at the back of the room. Descending deep underground, it led to the resting place of generations of Bans. Each taking one of the lit torches lining both sides of the staircase, we looked down into darkness.

"Any clue as to what we should look for?" Erik asked.

"Not one." I said.

The stair led to a white marble chamber with walls filled by niches sealed by heavy bronze doors. Every one of those niches held the remains of a Sultan or one of his sons. I raised my torch to the nearest one, shining my light on the brass plaque affixed under the door. *Abar Ban* was gracefully engraved on the plaque.

"This is the first-generation room. What we're looking for must be in here."

Erik shook his head. "This mausoleum is new and so is

this room. They built it after the original one collapsed in an earthquake sixty some years ago." He pointed to the left corner. "See that opening."

I nodded, staring at a second stairwell; this one was smaller and darker than the first.

"It leads to the old mausoleum's rooms. Most of the niches here are empty, only the names of the Sultans are here. Their bodies are still in the old mausoleum, deeper down. No one goes there anyway, it's too dangerous."

Well, sure! I thought. *Aren't we the lucky ones?*

We crept down the stairs in silence. Fearing the stairwell might collapse under our weight, I kept listening for any sound that might come from it. There were none. Actually there was no sound at all: no cracking, no dripping, no draft blowing. That total lack of ambient sound was eerie. So when we faced an old iron gate, I was somewhat relieved.

"The lock's gone, the gate's open." Erik made a sour face. "I guess I was wrong. Someone did come down here after all."

Traveling through narrow turns and dangerously steep steps for what to me seemed like an eternity, we finally reached the first funerary chamber. The air at this depth was frigid. So much so I could see my own breath. The light of our torches barely breached the darkness of this place. It was like being inside a pot of stirring ink. I followed the line of the wall, seeking more torches to light. I found two and quickly set them ablaze.

"That's only an entrance, the main room is there." Erik said.

I gazed at the old stone archway in front of us, at the darkness beyond it. I had the unpleasant impression that someone or something awaited us there. *Stop this childishness,* I told myself. Raising my torch, I entered the room.

Shadows ran away from my light as though they were alive. I heard a shuffling of feet nearby. I swung around. It was only Erik coming in. His torches added some welcome light to the room. I could now see that the chamber was cluttered with all kinds of objects.

"Jafer said we would find a tool in here," Erik whispered.

I rolled my eyes. "We should start by finding lamps."

"There's a brazier right there."

After a quick survey, we found several more braziers and lit them all. Their warm, flickering amber glow brightened the room enough so we could distinguish specific shapes amidst the pile of discarded objects: dishes, chairs, clothing and cushions. These shouldn't be here. It was as if someone had used this chamber as his own private room.

"This place is a mess," Erik said. Then kneeling down, he picked something up. "Look, Amir, the gate's padlock."

Even though the padlock was rusted to the point of being little more than a flaky red lump, enough of it remained to tell that it had been broken.

"Someone lived here," I said. "But that was long ago. All these things are covered in dust. Obviously, they haven't been touched for years." I foraged through the bric-a-brac for a minute. I found an old tortoise-shell box. Inside were broken bottles, a few intact clay jars containing dry herbs. I cast my attention on the blend of herbs and aromatic salts filling the bottom of the box, and my eyes caught a glimmer of gold amidst the mess: a ring, actually it was a signet.

GLING, GLING, GLING. The sound of bells, like the ones worn by dancing girls, resonated in the air. Pocketing the ring, I rose up in a hurry. Erik, I saw, was looking at the back of the room with a slack-jawed expression. I followed his gaze to the same somber spot. My eyes widened. Clad in the diaphanous red silk of their profession, three dancers emerged from the shadow. Those women were of such beauty that their sight filled me with liquid fire. The air was suddenly as thick as syrup. Breathing became hard. The light dimmed. And suddenly these women were all I cared about. I wanted to touch them, to hold them, to kiss them.

The woman walking in front extended her hand to me. I

went to her eagerly. Seizing my wrist, she pulled me closer. She was uncommonly strong, her hand strangely cold. Noises on my left made me look there. I saw that Erik was being slowly lowered to his knees by the other two women. The one on his left was avidly kissing his shoulder. A rictus of pain distorted Erik's face—it confused me.

I blinked and shook my head. Gripping my face in her cold hands, the woman turned me away. The instant my gaze met her black eyes, I forgot about my brother, I forgot his pain, I forgot everything, even my own name. I watched the woman's mouth open as she leaned into me. *Such a lovely mouth, such beauty.*

The woman suddenly screamed in pain.

At that very instant something snapped in me. I stared at the woman in front of me with a new awareness. Her eyes were two red beads; her mouth, a horrible fang-filled gap; her skin, gray and stretched over sharp protruding bones. My eyes lowered down her body. "OH LORD!" I shouted in horror. From the waist down, she had the body of a giant serpent. There was no doubt in my mind. This was a pairikas, a female demon who seduced men, driving them to their death, or worse, to commit degrading deeds. The charm she had thrown over me was broken, but how?

I didn't question this for long. Rami leapt in front of me brandishing a torch. Swinging the torch around, he pushed the demon back. The servant boy then attacked the demon still latched on Erik's shoulder. The creature had sunk its fangs deep into my brother's flesh and refused to let its victim go. With one swipe of its clawed hand, the pairikas tore the torch from Rami's grip. The boy began a frantic search for a new weapon.

Meanwhile, I tried to help Erik but found myself unable to move. The pairikas' charm still had some effect on me. Rami, on the other hand, was too young to fall under their spell. Had he been a year or two older, I believe things would have been far different.

In a daze, I watched Rami pick up a long sticklike object lying in the dirt and strike the pairikas over the head with it. The she-demon let out a piercing shriek and, with much hissing and spitting, finally abandoned Erik. Armed with the stick, Rami chased the pairikas out of the chamber.

With the last demon gone, I found myself able to move again. I rushed to Erik's side and helped him to his feet. His shoulder was a bloody mess. This, however, wasn't what worried me. Gashes could heal, cuts could close. I just hoped the pairikas' bites weren't venomous. After all, they were half-serpent.

"Aren't you glad that my servant spies on us?" Erik said.

"No, but I'm glad that your servant's voice has not changed yet."

Erik chuckled. "Yes, that's a chance."

Rami was coming back, dragging his stick behind him as though he didn't have the strength to lift it anymore. He stopped in a patch of shadow and looked my way. Although I couldn't see his face, I could swear by looking at his posture, chest puffed out, that the boy was glowing with pride—gloating even. I grimaced. I didn't like owing my life to anyone—and certainly not to Rami, whom I profoundly distrusted.

"Let's leave," I said. "Coming here was a stupid idea to begin with."

Erik probed his wounded shoulder and said, "At least we found the beginning. I think whoever hid here might be linked to what's happening now."

I said nothing. But as we exited the chamber, I thought that Erik might be right.

CHAPTER THIRTEEN

O ur return to the Cage went without incident. On Erik's insistence we returned to his rooms instead of my tower. After we discarded the gardener's outfits, I cleaned Erik's wound. The pairikas' bite was shallower than I'd thought; it didn't appear to be venomous either. Relieved, I breathed more easily. We then applied some much-needed balm on our welts—I wasn't surprised to see that some lashes had broken the skin. Once we were both dressed in our princely garments, Erik left to see his mother who was in the other room. Now that I was alone, I began studying the ring I had found in the mausoleum's chamber. The symbol carved in intaglio was Maberian and vaguely familiar. Old legends said that the she-demons, pairikas, were also of Maberian origin. I shifted in my chair and winced.

"Prince Amir, you look in pain," Salima said. She stood a few steps behind me, arms filled with clean clothes. Unloading her armful on the bed, she asked, "Can I be of any help?"

I smiled. "No, it's nothing. Er...actually, maybe you can help me in another manner. You're Maberian, are you not?"

She smiled broadly and nodded, apparently pleased by my noticing.

Extending the ring to her, I asked: "Have you seen this symbol before, and if so, what does it mean?"

Upon seeing the ring, Salima paled. "No... never seen it before. If you would excuse me, I have pressing work to finish." She bowed, then exited the room rapidly.

She knows this ring or its symbol, I thought. Her reaction had been too strong to mean anything else. So I was right, the ring was Maberian in origin. Now I needed to decipher the symbol. I wondered if Erik had a Maberian lexicon in his book cabinet. Well, there was nothing like checking. Rolling the ring between my fingers, I rose from my chair and tripped over the long stick Rami had used to chase the pairikas away.

"ERIK!" I shouted. "Can your servant pick up after himself?" I kicked the dirt-encrusted stick under Erik's bed. Storing the ring in my pocket, I was about to curse the boy's lack of order when my hand made contact with the locket. Thoughts of Princess Eva filled my mind. Suddenly I needed to see her, needed to talk with her. No doubt, this pressing need was made worse by my knowledge of the secret passage leading to her tower. The ring could wait, I decided.

Erik popped his head into the room. "Did you call for me? I heard my name."

"Yes... " I hesitated. This was pure folly, yet. "I need a favor."

Erik's face lit up. I knew he had been waiting for this moment since we'd first met, waiting for me to lower my guard and show some trust. Asking favors was not something princes did lightly. For a second, I wanted to take it back but instead said, "I wish to see your cousin again. Could you show me the way to her tower?"

"Hmm," Erik made. "Of course, but Eva must agree to see you first. She must know the risk she incurs by seeing you and accept to take it."

"How?"

"Rami," Erik called.

Startled, I jumped as the boy glided out from behind the tapestry hanging on the wall beside me. The snake had been spying on us again and had heard our entire conversation.

"Go to Princess Eva. Say that Prince Amir humbly asks if she'll agree to meet with him in secret. Be sure she understands the risk in this. Now go, Rami. Use the tunnel."

I watched the boy gallop out of the room, with my mouth open.

"What's wrong?" Erik asked.

"Couldn't you ask me before involving Rami in my affairs?"

Erik rolled his eyes. "Stop worrying about Rami. He's the least of your problems. If Eva agrees to see you, *then* you'll have something to fret about."

He was right. And that really annoyed me. Also bothering me was the idea that Eva could refuse to see me. To occupy my mind until Rami's return, I decided to take a stroll on Erik's private terrace—might as well take advantage of this luxury while I could. I was nearing the terrace's doors when I heard voices coming from the adjacent room.

"So Ambassador Molsky, what do you think of our prince?" I froze; this was Erik's mother's voice—there was no mistaking that accent.

"Without a doubt, he's a fine young man," said Ambassador Molsky. "However, I fear that his chances of ascending the throne may be slim, especially with the Sultan's health being so poor. More time is needed for your plan to succeed."

What plan? I knew I should've stopped listening and gotten out. I was behaving just like Rami by staying here, but instead of leaving I moved closer to the room's door.

"More time has just been given to us." I recognized Oroco's light airy voice. "The Sultan appears to have made a miraculous recovery last night."

Princess Livia burst into laughter. "My dear Oroco, miraculous isn't the term that is used regarding the Sultan's recovery—sorcery is. But as long as it fits our interest, the nature of his recovery matters little to me. (Long sigh!) How ironic that I now want him alive, when for so many years I had so desperately wanted him dead."

"Princess, please," Oroco hushed. "The palace's walls can't be trusted. What if someone hears you? To wish the Sultan's death is a crime."

"Oroco is right, Princess," Ambassador Molsky said. "You should be more careful. To return to our problem, we may have gained time, however, there still is the question of convincing the Sultan that our prince is better suited for the throne than the one he favors. Perhaps you should make an effort, Princess. Be more agreeable toward the Sultan."

Princess Livia gasped loudly, reacting as though she had been asked to perform some horrible deed. "How dare you suggest this! I refused to learn the harem's ways years ago. I will certainly not lower myself now and learn disgusting tricks to please this old goat."

Old goat! I slapped a hand over my mouth.

"Never!" Princess Livia continued. "He'll do well to learn how to please me… and there are other means of persuasion."

Rustling of silk told me that they were rising. I quickly exited the room before they could see me. Once on the terrace, I found a bench in a shady corner and sat. I was so baffled I didn't know what to think. Could Princess Livia be behind these recent events? From what I gathered in our brief meeting, she was ruthless enough. She struck me as the type of woman who, not happy to have you skinned, would demand that a generous layer of salt be applied to your wounds—for good measure. But if she were involved, I didn't know how. I sighed; at least I knew why: she wanted Erik to be the next Sultan. Nothing new or surprising there. My mind went back to Salima, to her reaction to the ring. She was educated and from Maberia, Erik had told me. Had Salima called the pairikas? Could she have set the fog against my brothers? Did she have enough knowledge of magic? Why, why, why? I scratched my beard. It just didn't fit. Something was missing—motive was missing. Salima had no reasons to do any of those things. Who else then? Who had motive and the knowledge needed to commit these crimes? I was still thinking about it when Erik joined me on my bench.

"Eva agrees to see you," he whispered.

My heart skipped a beat. "She does?"

Erik nodded.

* * *

Staring in the mirror, I ran a hand on my cheeks. Clipped short against my skin, my beard was nothing more than a dark shadow on my jaw. Erik wanted to shave it off completely, saying that Princess Eva was better accustomed to clean-shaven men, but I refused. I stared at my reflection one more time and made minute adjustments to my midnight blue ensemble—chosen more for safety than anything else.

"Leave the mirror alone," Erik said. "You're perfect."

"Is the map ready?"

Erik looked at the piece of rolled-up parchment in his hands. He hesitated before giving it to me. "You're sure you don't want Rami to guide you?"

"No! And I won't change my mind either, so quit asking."

Erik sighed. I noted that Rami was back with us. The boy was eerily silent in his movement. I believed a mouse made more noises than he did. His sudden appearance always shocked me. I scowled at the boy as he began tugging on Erik's kaftan.

"Oh, yes, I almost forgot," Erik said, pulling a small ivory box from his kaftan's pocket.

"What's that?" I asked.

"A gift. You can't go there empty-handed."

He opened the box. Inside was a brilliant pair of gold ear-rings: beautiful filigreed circles with three coral beads dangling in their centers.

Rising on tiptoes, Rami whispered a few words in Erik's ear. Erik then said, "The coral matches the dress Eva wore on her arrival. It's almost the same shade of red."

I looked at Rami, who swiftly disappeared behind Erik. The boy sure had good taste. The earrings were perfect. Yet one detail gnawed at me.

"Where do they come from?" I asked, suddenly worried. Erik's sheepish look confirmed my worst suspicion. "You sent a servant to raid the treasury," I hissed, barely controlling my voice. I was scandalized.

"Who will notice these are missing? It's our treasure too, isn't it?"

"Yes… but a servant, Erik, having free access to the treasury… day and night. No wonder royal gifts go missing. For all I know your servant stole that vase. The Vizier's last assistant died because of its disappearance."

Erik's face turned crimson. "What would we do with a stupid pot like that? And… and that's not the real reason the man died. The theft was an excuse. Nazir wanted Hassan in that position—everybody knows that."

"Still, it's not right, Erik." I shook my head and clucked my tongue in disapproval.

Snapping the box shut, Erik said, "Fine then, I'll bring this back. Go see Eva empty-handed."

"Damn you!" Without another word, I snatched the box from Erik's hand and walked out.

The hour of my departure finally arrived. The evening had begun and the palace was just busy enough to provide background noises to cover my steps as I moved from one corridor to the next. In no time, I reached the opening leading to the underground tunnel. Lantern in hand, I moved along the dark, humid stone passage, following Erik's instruction. At first I thought this was going to be easy, but after several twists and turns of the road I was lost. Fortunately the markers, scratches on the tunnel's stone walls, were fairly easy to spot with a lantern. I stopped at the junction of two corridors and studied the marks, then my map. I was about to move on when I heard voices coming my way. In panic, I snuffed out my lantern's flame. Darkness swallowed me. As silently as possible, I entered the tunnel junction on my right. Stopping at its edge, I waited, immobile. The voices were closer now, just behind the bend, only a few paces from me.

"Please, give it back," a woman begged. "I know you stole it from me."

The glow of a torch appeared up ahead, illuminating a junction, then a woman stepped beyond its bend. I blinked. *Salima?* What was she doing here? Then it hit me—Erik showed her the way, what else. *That stupid boy!* Movements at the edge of the tunnel brought my entire attention ahead. A tall, dark form had exited the corner and now faced Salima. There was something ominous about this somber, lanky body, something that made the short hair on my arms and neck stand up, something I should know.

"Oh, stop it!" the form said in a voice distorted by the echo. "The whole thing is your fault anyway. I still found it, you know. It wasn't hidden too well."

Salima backed away while shaking her head. "Please, I beg of you, stop."

"It's too late," the form said.

Step into the light. Come on move, so I can see who you are. Sadly the form remained in the shadow.

"Stop crying. Soon it will all be over," the form said in a cold emotionless voice.

Salima's frail body was now trembling. "I don't believe you. You're lying again."

The form let out a sigh of exasperation. "Enough! It needed to be done. I'm warning you, don't interfere anymore."

In tears, Salima swung around and ran away. The form

vanished immediately after.

The form was clearly a man. But who was he? Somehow I had the impression that I knew him, yet I couldn't place him. I waited in total darkness for a long moment. When finally I was certain that I was alone again, I took a hesitant step out of my hiding place. Only then did I realize that without light I couldn't go any further. Maybe I should go back. No, I decided. I remembered where the last mark was on the wall and would continue ahead. Palming the cold stone, I soon found the scratches, a square, which meant turn left. I did. I followed this tunnel to a broad opening. There I searched the walls for another mark and found none. *Oops!* Perhaps further, I thought. Moving through tunnel after tunnel like a blind man, I sought my way out of this cursed place with a growing despair. I had long passed the point where I could go back. Hell, I had passed the point where I could remember my last turn. Just as I came to the realization that I was lost and could be stuck here for days, a light appeared at the end of this tunnel. For a brief instant I was so happy I nearly called out to the ones holding the light. Then I came back to my senses. I wasn't allowed here. Worse, I had a stolen treasury's piece in my pocket. I quickly hid in the nearest tunnel opening then shot a peek at the approaching men. My stomach flipped. It was the Grand Vizier and Hassan.

"We must find it, our future depends on it," said the Vizier.

"It's a risky business, Master. Shouldn't we wait before taking this final step?"

"We've passed the point where we can afford hesitation, Hassan. We must now act. Our biggest mistake is to have waited. The theft of the Slayer is a catastrophe." The Vizier sighed heavily. "I thought I had hidden it well. What a terrible error. We must get it back, by any means necessary."

I frowned. What were they talking about? I was totally confused. As their footsteps grew closer, I sunk deeper into the dark tunnel, hoping they wouldn't enter it. When they passed my tunnel without stopping, I let out a long breath of relief. Suddenly a warm body brushed against mine. I leaped sideways, arms beating the air.

"Shh... it's me," hushed the darkness.

"Rami?"

There was a rustling of clothes, and then a small silhouette in a hood appeared. Rami had hidden his lantern under the heavy fabric of his hood so its light wouldn't be seen. I wished I had done the same thing with mine instead of snuffing out its flame.

"Follow me," the boy said.

For once I didn't ask any questions and trailed the boy as closely as I could, and only when Rami stopped in the middle of a narrow corridor did I venture to ask: "Are we lost again?"

"No, we're here."

"Here where?"

"Princess Eva's rooms. This passage leads inside her tower." Rami raised his lantern. The light fell on the round hole of an air conduit high on the wall.

I was suddenly nervous. My hands were all sweaty, my stomach twisted in knots. Filling my lungs in one long gulp, I climbed up the hole with Rami on my heels. In no time we were at the metal screen closing the conduit. On the other side was what, to me, looked like a storage room. Linen, dishes, lamps and other necessities filled this room's abundant shelves.

"Where are the eunuchs?" I whispered.

"Downstairs," Rami said. "They're not allowed into her private chamber. Keep your voice low and you should be fine. I'll wait here for you. Don't stay too long."

I nodded, opened the grid and lowered myself down. Once at the door, I paused to gather my courage then stepped out of the storage room and into a luxurious suite.

A round daybed covered with a bright red satin throw occupied the left side of the room. Shear organza drapes, suspended from the ceiling, cascaded around the bed, and in its center rose a mountain of cushions of all shapes and colors. The front of the bed was taken by a low table made of dark wood inlayed with brass. I turned to the right. My eyes fell on a long backless bench upholstered in blue velvet; then they traveled to the antique harp resting on its seat.

I approached the bench and studied the instrument. The burnished gilding covering its wood was cracked and chipped; otherwise the harp was in good playing order. I pinched a string. The sound was clear and crisp.

"Good evening, Prince Amir," Eva said at my back.

I had lived this instant in my mind a hundred times; I was ready. I turned. The moment I saw her, my mind became blank. There was no word that could describe her beauty. She wore traditional harem clothes. Soft pink shear baggy pants that fell low on her hips and a short-sleeved top that left part of her belly exposed. Her wrists and ankles were heavy with gold bangles of all sizes. They clinked and clanked with her every movement. A transparent veil, pinned on the summit of her well-coiffed head, cascaded down to her elbows. As she walked toward me, this airy cream veil floated behind her like a sail in the wind.

Finally regaining my wit, I bowed. "Princess, I'm honored by your invitation." I straightened and gave her my most charming smile—well, I hoped it was.

"You're late," she said with a serious look on her face.

My smile faded. "I apologize. I lost my way and…"

"Because of your tardiness the tea I prepared for us is almost cold." Eva tapped a foot on the floor with humor a few times, then began giggling behind her hands. "Prince Amir, you look devastated. I was only teasing you."

"Oh!" I was suddenly without words again. My cheeks were burning. Once more I was blushing like a teenager who'd just seen a dancing girl for the first time.

Eva stuck out her lower lip. "Now I feel terrible for having teased you. I warned you about my jesting. You mustn't take everything I say so seriously. Promise me you will stop that."

A small smile curled my lips. "I will try my best, Princess."

"Why not skip all these ceremonies. Call me Eva."

I nodded. "It would please me if you called me Amir."

Eva smiled. "I prepared some tea. Amir, would you join me? I assure you, it's still very warm."

I agreed wholeheartedly. We sat on the daybed and talked while sipping sweet tea in crystal glasses as is customary in Telfar. Eva had numerous questions about the palace, about its rules and more so about the next Sultan.

"I can't believe I have to stay in this tower until an heir is chosen. Aunt Livia said it's a good thing. That it will give me time to learn your laws and traditions and most importantly how to break them without losing my head." She grabbed her neck with both hands and stuck out her tongue in a grimace.

I cringed violently. "Don't… ever do that."

Eva tilted her head. "Do what?"

"That thing… with your tongue."

"Oh, why?"

"It's not proper. If you do it in public, everyone present will take it as a personal insult."

Eva smiled. It was forced and sad. "Apparently I still have a lot to learn. Aunt Livia might be right about my time in the tower being good for me. She also said that if I'm lucky, I might be here for a year—I hope not. I'm not used to confinement. I find it hard to bear." Eva's eyes became very bright, as if filled with tears. She squeezed her hands hard together, took a deep breath and lifted up her chin. "Then again, your father might choose an heir faster than we expect." Her voice was firm and full of optimism, and her eyes back to their normal brilliancy.

Eva was stronger than I had thought. I was impressed.

"You're right," I said. "There is a good chance that it will be soon."

"In your opinion, which of your brothers will be Telfar's next ruler?" Eva asked.

"I can't say—nothing's fixed yet."

"Then yours and my cousin's chances are still good." She stared at me with hopeful eyes.

"It's... I fear that we're not favored." An uncomfortable moment of silence followed. Seeking to relieve the tension, I looked at the harp. "Do you play?"

"Yes, would you like to hear a piece?"

"I'd be delighted."

We moved to the long bench. Eva picked up the harp and began playing a slow melody from her homeland. Humming the first few bars, she then sang in her native tongue. I was surprised; Eva's singing voice was lower and deeper than her speaking one. Usually harsh and cutting to my ears, this foreign language when sung in her low-toned voice was hauntingly beautiful. And even though I didn't understand the meaning of the words she sang, I enjoyed every single one just the same.

"It was beautiful," I said when she finished.

"It's an old ballad, the story of a maiden who falls in love with a water spirit."

"Huh... I'm assuming that it doesn't end well."

Eva shook her head. "The maiden dies of a broken heart, but she's reborn as the reeds that grow along streams and brooks and sings their glory in high winds."

"So it's not such a sad ending after all."

She smiled. "No, not that sad."

From the corner of my eye, I noted that Rami had poked his head out of the storage room and was gesturing at me. Was it time to leave already? With a heavy heart, I rose and thanked Eva for the tea and her delightful company.

Staring into my eyes, she asked. "Will you come see me again?"

I felt my heart melt. "If you wish it, I will come again."

"Not only am I wishing it, I command you to visit me as often as you can."

Then I noted that Rami was still motioning to me. The boy kept pulling on his earlobes. *The earrings, clumsy, you forgot to give her the earrings.* I immediately presented the ivory box to Eva. "Please accept this small token of my friendship."

Her eyes widened when she opened the box. "Oh, Amir, they're lovely. The color is perfect." Eva put the earrings on right away. They dangled gracefully against her neck. "I'll think of you every time I wear them."

We bid each other goodbye, but only after I promised to be back the next evening. Then grinning like an idiot, I followed Rami out.

CHAPTER FOURTEEN

I spent the following day dreaming of the coming evening when I would see Eva again. Unable to concentrate on anything else, I just sat in a corner and waited for time to pass. My only occupation was to decide what gift I would bring her that evening. For the first time in my life, I was in love. It was a much stronger feeling than I thought. Unaccustomed to dealing with such powerful emotions—not of that euphoric nature anyway—it overwhelmed me totally, rendering me quite useless in our search for my brothers' killer. So much so that Erik became impatient with me. And the morning that Visitation Days ended and I moved back into my tower, he made quite a scene.

"Amir, you need to wake up. We have little time to waste. Stop this dreaming and help me seek out a solution."

"Solution to what?" I snapped. "The enigma of our brothers' deaths. We don't know enough to solve it. We don't even know what to look for."

"We know that the Vizier is involved in some way. You heard him speak about a stolen object when you got lost in the tunnel. Plus, he's educated. And he's Maberian."

"The same can be said about Salima." It was time to tell Erik what I knew about his beloved nanny. I should've done it earlier, I thought and quickly told him all I had seen and heard in the tunnel.

Erik paled. "No! You're wrong. Salima would never hurt anyone."

"I don't think she has. Actually, she was trying to stop someone from doing something… I don't know what. It was never mentioned, except that the person she spoke with stole something."

"See! For all we know she might've been confronting another servant about stolen bread." Erik folded his arms on his chest. He had that stubborn look on his face again, the one I knew meant that he would hold his ground. So I decided not to argue with him any longer, even though I knew that Salima wouldn't have cried over stolen bread. When it came to servants, Erik was too trusting. In my opinion, he had shown the secret passage to too many servants: Rami, Salima, who else was on that list? Yet I was certain that if I asked about it, Erik would deny telling anyone else. Could it be true, I thought with a peek at Rami, the leak might come from another source? Still, the fact remained: there was another person who knew the secret underground tunnels. I sighed; perhaps Erik was right. Perhaps I'd been daydreaming for too long. After all, there was a killer about.

"Think we should concentrate on finding that Slayer the Vizier so desperately wants back," Erik said.

"All right, but first promise me you'll ask Salima who she was with."

After some hesitation, Erik consented. We spent the rest of the morning looking through books. We discovered that pairikas could be called to serve a master and with the right magical binding they would do his bidding. However, pairikas' powers were limited; they couldn't transform themselves into vapor, fog or smoke. Only certain types of demons could: jinn, ghosts or spirits and efreets.

"Which kind do you think it is?" Erik asked while stretching in his chair.

"I don't know. One thing is sure though. One needed the darkest of magic to control one of these demons."

We went back to work, this time refining our search to books or stories concerning jinn and efreet. To my surprise, I had very few books on the subject. Had I overestimated my collection? I thought not. Then again I'd never really paid attention to any book concerning the supernatural. Still, I could swear I had more.

"I wish we had access to the Vizier's library," Erik complained. "I'm certain he has documents that would shed some light on this."

I shrugged while keeping my nose in the books.

After hours of deciphering obscure legends, we decided on a break and descended to the kitchen in search of something sweet. I was taken aback by the reception the kitchen crew gave Erik. They all rushed to his service with genuine pleasure. They really seemed happy to see him. I didn't understand it. Servants were never happy to see princes. We were bad news. We meant trouble. We inflicted pain. I was stumped. Even the head baker—an old crone who usually threw me dark, hostile looks whenever I would come into the kitchen—was overjoyed to see my brother.

"Ah, my handsome and good prince," she said, clasping her hands under her whiskered chin. "We don't see you often enough."

Erik bowed in front of the head baker, who turned pink with delight. "Dear Amkel, I'm glad to see that you're well," he said. "Has your son become head navigator?"

"Yes, yes, he has. All thanks to your letter of recommendation." The crone flashed a sparsely toothed grin at Erik. "I've got fresh börek still warm from the oven—I know you love these flaky pastries—and five different kinds of honey I kept aside just for you."

She disappeared at the back of the kitchen. The sound of pots and pans being banged rang for a brief moment, then she came back carrying a platter filled with goods: Rolls, pomegranates, tangerines, a plate of baklava dripping with honey and walnut—my personal favorite—and five small jars of honey that were as ornate as perfume containers.

"Theses jars are reserved for the Sultan and the Grand Vizier. The Vizier's sweet tooth is well known in the kitchen. He's consumed so much sweets, I'm surprised the man still has teeth." The crone placed a bony finger to her wrinkled lips meaning that we should keep this bit of information to ourselves.

Tapping a bony finger on the first jar, the crone said, "Çam bali, a pine-scented honey from young forest growth. It is rich, dark and full-flavored." She tapped the jar next to it. Its content was almost as dark as molasses. "Siyah Çam Bali, black-pine honey, has a stronger, deeper flavor. This one is Portakal, or orange-blossom honey. Don't be fooled by its light color and thin texture, it's the sweetest." Grabbing a jar of amber-colored honey she dangled it in the air. "That's your father's favorite; it's good, full-bodied. It's called Çiçek, the flower honey." She winked at us. "In my opinion, it's too thick and very common."

I chewed the inside of my cheek not to laugh. I didn't know servants could be so bold as to criticize my father's favorite. It was amusing though. I touched the last jar. "And this bright gold one, what's its name?"

"Ahh," she made. "You got better taste than your father. Ogul Bali, or virgin honey, it's the first honey from a new swarm. None is more subtle in taste."

She went on adding food to the platter until it overflowed. There was a bowl of tarama salstasi, red caviar in mayonnaise, half a watermelon, plates of pit-roasted lamb and more wheels of cheese than I could count. I then noticed how she avoided looking at me and kept her eyes fixed on Erik at all times, as if she wanted to tell him something but didn't care to do it in my presence.

"This is too much, Amkel," Erik said. "Amir and I can't eat all this."

She glanced at me and said. "For your poor ill brothers, they too should get some sweets."

"It's very kind of you," I replied with a slight nod.

She gave me a long evaluating look, as if she could judge my character just by looking at me—somehow I thought she could and felt myself shrink a bit.

"Hey, leave something for us!" someone boomed behind us.

I swung around and saw Ibrahim and his four brothers entering the room. The kitchen crew scattered away from these princes as quickly as mice from hawks. With the room now totally cleared of all servants, I noted that Ibrahim's entire court was also entering the kitchen.

Something was wrong. I could sense it deep inside my bones. I watched the five brothers walk straight toward us. As they were closing in, Ibrahim moved left and I caught a glimpse of the brother following in his tracks. My stomach dropped. This was the prince Erik had struck with the riding crop. He still bore the crop mark on his jaw.

Sensing what was coming, I gripped Erik's elbow and attempted to make him back away. But before I could, Abdul, Ibrahim's right-hand man and the most brutish of all my brothers, pushed me aside and collided with Erik, who struck the table that was behind him. Jugs of fruit juice and plates of meat in thick gravy toppled over, splattering Abdul's clothes. Abdul let out an exclamation of horror, which was quite unconvincing in its artifice. I grimaced; what a poor actor he was. This was a planned accident.

"It's stained, it's ruined!" Abdul barked, while picking pieces of meat off his kaftan.

In my opinion it wasn't a big loss. Eyeing Abdul's garnished purple and yellow ensemble, I had trouble finding the stain amidst its busy pattern. Yet I knew he was going to make a scene, I knew what was coming.

"You didn't look where you were going," Erik said, making things worse, which didn't really surprise me. Erik had a way of making bad situations worse. I looked at Abdul. The son of the first Sultana, Abdul was a big muscular man used to being feared by all. The fact that Erik displayed no fear at all made Abdul's blood boil.

"You were in the way," Abdul said, his face now red with genuine anger.

"No, I wasn't! You hit me on purpose."

"How dare you!" Abdul exclaimed. "Not only did you stain my clothes, you insulted me! I demand reparation!"

"So do I," Erik replied with his chin high in the air.

I winced. This had been Ibrahim's goal from the start; I could see it in his devious little smile. I looked at Erik then at Abdul. I had no idea who of these two would win that fight, and that frightened me. I stepped up. "Wait a minute. I was pushed first. I demand reparation."

Abdul turned a stunned face to me, while behind him his brothers held their sides laughing.

Erik frowned at me. "Amir, what are you doing?"

"Abdul pushed me first. The law is clear, he must fight me first as I was the first to be offended."

Abdul's bushy eyebrows rose, then he grinned. "Fine! I'll kill you first and then I'll kill him—suits me just fine. It's a pity you're so puny, I doubt you'll provide me with much of a warm up." He burst into laughter. The rest of Ibrahim's court joined in.

Puny! Now I was really insulted; I swore I could have killed him right then and there.

"Brothers, please," Ibrahim said, calling everyone to silence. "We must choose a location for these combats. I suggest the third courtyard, as two of the opponents—" he pointed to Erik and Abdul—"have rooms there. More precisely at the foot of the white tower, so Princess Eva can watch the combat from her balcony." Ibrahim smiled at me. "She might find it entertaining, don't you agree?"

I narrowed my eyes and held my tongue.

Erik shrugged. "Doesn't matter to me."

Ibrahim bowed. "In an hour then."

"In an hour," I said.

Once Ibrahim and his followers had departed, Erik jabbed me in the shoulder. "Why did you do that? You don't think I can win—is that it?"

I took a moment to gather my thoughts before answering. "I think my chances of winning are better than yours."

"No! Abdul and I are better matched. We're closer in size and strength."

"Exactly! Abdul knows how to fight strength—speed and agility, I don't know."

Not saying a word, Erik pouted.

I felt a tug on my kaftan's sleeve. It was the crone. This time she looked me in the eyes. Apparently sticking my neck out for Erik had softened her opinion of me.

"Princes," she whispered, "before you leave I must inform you of the rumor floating about the palace. Listen carefully." Her voice dropped to a murmur. "A growing number of princes believe that the floating mist that killed your brothers is at the Sultan's service. They think that he's absorbing his dead sons' essence like some youth potions and that he will slowly kill you all."

I couldn't say I was surprised that my brothers thought our father guilty, but that they had dared say it aloud, that really surprised me.

"These are dangerous words to utter, my princes," the crone said. "Even when one thinks one's alone. In the palace, there is always someone taking note. My advice to you is to stay away from the ones who utter them. Please, don't mingle with those princes."

Erik and I exchanged looks of worry. "It's good advice, Amkel," Erik said. "Amir and I will try to follow it the best we can."

Smiling sadly at us, she bowed. "I wish you luck, good princes. We'll pray for your victory."

We thanked her and left. There was no time to waste; we had duels to attend.

* * *

Within an hour, the news of our forthcoming duels had spread throughout the Cage. So when Erik and I stepped into the third courtyard's sunlight, I wasn't shocked by the crowd assembled at the foot of Eva's tower.

Amidst my brothers' colorful kaftans was a dark spot: the Grand Vizier's black robe. Following our law, he was to witness the duel—first, to ensure that no rules would be broken; second, to confirm the loser's death. As usual Hassan was at the Vizier's side.

Holding a book and a quill, the assistant danced from foot to foot, clearly unnerved by the event. Called by a palace messenger, Hassan then left the Vizier's side with obvious relief and exited the courtyard with the messenger boy. This better be important news to pull Hassan from recording this duel, I thought, before returning my attention to the Vizier's dark figure. His face was as devoid of emotion as always. Yet I knew that Hassan's impromptu departure displeased him; I also knew that he would not chastise Hassan, whom he treated more like a son than an assistant. Nazir was the last of a long line of Viziers. Last because he didn't marry nor produce any children that I knew about. Although I assumed that he, like most men, had needs, I'd rather not think of it. Picturing Nazir in an amorous embrace was like picturing snakes mating—it made my skin crawl. I looked away and moved on.

Without a word, Erik and I made our way to the blue-tiled

terrace that surrounded the base of Eva's tower. Throughout my advance, I had to fight with myself not to look up the tower. I thought it better if I didn't see Eva and kept my eyes straight ahead. I noted a patch of gold on the ground. Using a generous layer of sand, a broad circle had been drawn on the tiles. The combat would be held inside this sand circle.

Once at the circle's edge, I found my gaze being pulled toward the tower. Unable to resist the temptation, I looked up. The tower's balcony was empty, the door behind it closed. Eva had chosen not to watch the gruesome spectacle to come. It was for the best. I was relieved. I scanned the mob of overly dressed spectators assembled beside the sand circle. Most bared rejoiced expressions. *One less brother to worry about, with luck perhaps two.* I was sure that was what they were thinking right now. I noted Hassan making his way back beside the Vizier. He whispered something into the Vizier's ear that produced a look of utter disbelief on the stern man's face. More bad news, I supposed, and looked elsewhere.

My eyes met Darius's; he bore an odd expression, one I couldn't read. Then Darius shook his head at me, making his thought clear: I was a fool for risking my life for Erik. Well, I had to agree. Not because of Erik's status, but because it went against everything I had done in the last four years—gone was my anonymity. Damn, I was really stupid!

I turned my attention to my opponent. Abdul had stripped down to his puffy pants and sandals. Coarse black hair covered his chest and back. The man was as hairy as a monkey. My gaze glided to the weapon in his hand: a mace. Or should I say *the mace*. It was the same metal shaft topped with a spike ball that had nearly killed me a month ago. *Well, well, well, so we meet again.* I shed my kaftan and pulled my weapon. As usual, I had chosen a rapier, the one given to me by Erik's mother.

As I was about to take my first step inside the sand circle, Erik gripped my shoulder. "Don't hold back. You can't hide your skills any longer."

I patted Erik's hand then entered the circle.

Abdul glanced at my rapier and laughed. "What's that? A needle? Do you plan to prick me, brother?" With surprising speed, for a man his size, Abdul swung his mace. The metal shaft of the mace struck my blade, sending a wave of pain down to my elbow.

Grinding my teeth, I held on to the rapier and sidestepped my assailant. The sound of a door closing and the shadow of a shape moving on the balcony distracted me. Without thinking, I looked up the tower. Abdul chose that moment to strike my hilt. Taken by surprise, I nearly dropped my weapon. Before I could move away, he swung again. The mace's spike ball grazed my shoulder, ripping my shirt. The crowd roared. I glided left. Abdul turned awkwardly, leaving his side exposed. I could have easily plunged my blade between his ribs, but I hesitated. The crowd booed. I saw Erik urging me to act and Darius looking confused and angry. I blinked, and then it was too late. The moment had passed. Abdul was now attacking again. For a while I twirled, dodged and danced around the lumbering Abdul with ease. He had no chance of touching me. He knew it; I could see it by the tension distorting his face.

Stop showing off, my pragmatic side ordered. *Kill him—kill him fast.* Yet I continued floating around him, unable to bring this cruel dance to an end. It was now clear to me that no matter how long and hard I practiced fencing I would never be a killer. Damn! I was in more trouble than Abdul.

As if sensing my weakness, Abdul pounced at me with utter disregard for his safety. His mace zipped a hair away from my face. I let myself fall backward. Landing on my back, I immediately rolled aside as the mace shattered the tiles where seconds before my head had been.

Hushes and shouts of regret and frustration rose from the crowd.

I jumped to my feet. Abdul moved forth. My blade slashed his left bicep.

"Ahg," he growled. But instead of backing away, he rushed toward me like a bull stung by a bee, while swinging his mace in a broad circle. My road was cut. My heels were almost touching the sand. I was out of options—this was a live-or-die moment. Swallowing hard, I watched Abdul approach. I stood frozen, my mind blank. Then at the last moment my survival instinct took over, I dropped to my knees and leaned forward, bringing my rapier under his guard. The blade sunk deep inside Abdul's chest. The crowd gasped.

Abdul stared at the hilt sticking out of his chest then at me. His jaw dropped and he fell backward. An oppressive silence fell upon the terrace.

Out of breath and still on my knees—I doubt I could have stood anyway—I looked around. Every eye in the courtyard was on me. Forcing my body not to tremble, not too much at least, I fought back the urge to bend over and vomit. Once the nausea gripping me had passed, I found the strength to rise. Although wobbly, my legs held. I approached Abdul's body. My blade had pierced his heart. He had died almost instantly. I was grateful for this.

Hassan made his way to our sides. He kneeled beside Abdul and after a brief examination declared him dead. Pulling my rapier out of my brother's body, he extended it to me. Hiding my repulsion, I took it. After having bowed to me, Hassan returned to his spot by the Vizier. I looked at the crowd; my brothers appeared quite shocked to say the least. *They all thought I would lose.* I sought Erik and found him gazing at his feet. Darius, on the other hand, stared directly at me, he seemed intrigued. As for the Vizier, he displayed no emotion. Leaning toward Hassan, the Vizier whispered a few words to his assistant. Hassan quickly scribbled notes.

When I turned away, I noted Ibrahim's rueful smile. I was confused. I just killed his right-hand. He couldn't be happy about that—*a trick! This was a trick.* At that instant, Abdul's full-blooded brother, Mustafa, stepped up to the circle's edge.

Tall and slender, his slim appearance enhanced by his dark blue clothes, Mustafa had a thin mustache and broad protruding cheekbones. His dark eyes settled on me.

"Prince Mustafa," the Vizier said, "your brother's demise is unfortunate but well within the rules. However, if you wish to avenge him, you must allow Prince Amir an hour to recuperate."

Mustafa glared at me. There was murder in his eyes. "I don't want to avenge Abdul," he hissed between clenched teeth, "I wish to preserve his honor instead."

A low mumble ran through the crowd as everyone spoke at the same time.

At least I'm not the only one to be stunned by this.

"Silence!" the Vizier ordered.

Everybody obeyed.

"Your decision to forego avenging your brother is duly noted; you are now bound to it and cannot return on your word," the Vizier told Mustafa. In my opinion, Nazir looked quite dejected by Mustafa's decision not to fight me. "Please, state your demand."

Mustafa stepped into the sand circle. "My brother made two duel appointments. I wish to fulfill the second." Facing Erik, he declared, "I wish to fight Prince Keri and complete my brother's appointment."

I felt the blood leaving my face. This was not good, not at all. Mustafa was an expert swordsman. Damn, the man had lightning-fast reflexes. Erik was as good as dead.

CHAPTER FIFTEEN

In a state of panic, I reviewed the rules of engagement in my head. I had to find a loophole fast, otherwise Erik was lost. *Think, think, think, Amir.* It was useless. Nothing came. As my eyes fell on two brothers shoving each other in the midst of a heated argument, a light came on in my mind. *A fight, a good old brawl!*

I walked to Erik and whispered in his ear. "You're allowed to change the terms of the combat, because you're the one offended by Abdul's death. Make it a wrestling match. It's your only chance to win."

To my surprise, Erik didn't argue. He just nodded. I suppose he had some sense after all, or perhaps it was witnessing Abdul's death that had wised him up; either way it was good. Stepping inside the sand circle, Erik announced his wish to wrestle Mustafa.

A mixture of booing and loud cheering rose from my assembled brothers.

Wrestling, although highly entertaining, was not deadly. I scanned my two most powerful brothers, curious to see which cheered and which booed. Ibrahim was glaring at me with a sour face, while Darius chewed the inside of his cheek in order not to laugh. As for the Vizier he looked perplexed, as if this show of smarts on my part was so utterly unexpected that he

160

couldn't truly believe it yet. Hassan was overjoyed and grinned from ear to ear. I believed pulling a blade from a warm body was an experience he'd rather not repeat—at least not right away.

The two wrestlers began preparing for the match. The moment Erik took off his shirt I knew that he was in trouble again.

The crowd gasped at the sight of his back. A series of fresh red welts and old white scars marred Erik's pale skin. On his shoulder was the ugly purple blotch of the pairikas' bite mark.

Eyes narrowed, the Vizier addressed Erik: "Prince Keri, what are those marks on your back? They oddly resemble a whip's bites. I'd like to know what caused them."

"I was thrown against the riding-ring's fence by my horse," Erik said. "The rough edges of the planks made those marks."

The crowd let out a communal "Ahh," as if reassured that no prince had been whipped and that their world remained undisturbed. The Vizier however seemed far from convinced.

"By the state of your back, this happened more than once. And if I'm right about the wound on your shoulder, the beast also bites. Perhaps you should find a different horse."

Erik shook his head. "I like spirited horses."

The Vizier smiled, if one could call his baring of teeth a smile, then turned his gaze to me. "And you, Prince Amir, have you also fallen from your horse lately."

I swallowed hard. He knew. Nazir remembered the gardeners and put two and two together. I searched my mind for a reply. Should I lie? Should I say yes?

Darius solved the problem for me by shouting: "Is this wrestling match going to begin soon, or are we to wait until it's too dark to see."

More brothers joined his protesting. With a face pinched by displeasure, the Vizier clapped his hands together three times announcing the start of the combat.

Erik and Mustafa began circling one another, carefully studying each other's moves. Lacking Abdul's great size, Mustafa was lean to the point of being gangly—especially when compared to Erik, whose chest rippled with hard muscles. However, I knew that Mustafa's fencing training gave him speed, endurance and agility. This could help him, but more so it was Erik's tendency to underestimate his enemies that worried me. Mustafa would not make that mistake.

Sure enough, Erik was first to attack. Mustafa evaded him easily. Then dropping to the ground, he swung a leg in the back of Erik's knees. Erik fell flat on his back. In the blink of an eye, Mustafa was on top of him, trying to pin him down.

Oh no, I thought, biting my knuckles. He couldn't lose this quickly.

Erik however looked unconcerned by Mustafa's presence on his stomach. Flashing a brilliant smile at his opponent, Erik swiftly embraced him in a bear hug. Panic flashed across Mustafa's face. He struggled wildly and managed to slip away, but only for a second. Erik was on him again and now had an iron grip on Mustafa's arm.

In a desperate attempt to free himself Mustafa rammed Erik's chest, pushing him amidst the nearby group of princes. Erik bumped into Ibrahim, who immediately raised his fist to strike Erik in the back. The crowd shouted in protest.

As Ibrahim's fist came down I saw a red flash of light. Then I saw Erik bare his teeth in a grimace of pain. Swinging around, Erik grappled Ibrahim by his kaftan, pulled him closer and punched him in the jaw.

Face livid, Ibrahim opened his mouth—to demand reparation I'm certain. But before he could utter a word, Ibrahim realized that he now stood inside the combat circle and that Erik's blow was not only allowed but also irreproachable. Ibrahim speedily jumped out of the circle and the fight continued.

It was then that I noted the long cut, a fresh bleeding one, marking Erik's back. Without a doubt, this was the work of one of Ibrahim's rings, and the red flash I had seen earlier, the spark of a ruby in the sun.

Erik feigned moving left, Mustafa rushed right and fell into Erik's wide-open arms. Seizing Mustafa around the chest, Erik lifted him off the ground, swung around and fell on top of him. A loud *Ouff* shot out of Mustafa's mouth as he hit the tiles. Stunned and breathless, he lay motionless under Erik's weight while Hassan verified that both his shoulders touched the ground. After a brief count, Hassan gripped Erik's hand and raised it into the air. "Prince Keri is the winner."

Cheers and congratulations echoed from most of our brothers, except for Ibrahim and his supporters, who all remained silent and stone-faced. Ibrahim's cold reaction didn't surprise me, however, my other brothers' show of enthusiasm certainly did. I never thought they would cheer for Erik. Even Darius was clapping. Erik for his part seemed unaware of the divided assembly. Boasting a look of self-satisfaction, he bowed to the crowd then tried to help Mustafa to rise. Humiliated, Mustafa slapped Erik's hand away with obvious resentment. This made the crowd laugh and humiliated Mustafa even more.

"The princess!" someone shouted.

Suddenly all laughter died, replaced by a hush of admiration.

"Yes, I see her," a brother whispered. "I see her."

"She's been watching," another said.

I immediately looked up.

Leaning against her balcony rail, Eva peered down at us. She wore a pale blue satin ensemble. Clear pear-shaped aquamarine gems hung from her ears and neck, glimmering in the afternoon's dimming light like frozen raindrops. A diaphanous veil covered the lower half of her face, yet did nothing to hide her beauty or expression. She was relieved. That was obvious. Her gaze then glided to Abdul's limp form and her expression darkened. Eva looked at my assembled brothers smiling back at her, at Erik waving, at the Vizier and Hassan bowing to her. Eva looked at everyone—except me.

Please, Eva, give me a sign, a look, a smile, I silently begged.

Instead she sighed and reentered her tower without even giving me as much as a glance.

Why this sudden distance toward me? What fault have I committed? Had she seen me fight? Had she witnessed the terrible act I'd been forced to commit? Not only had I killed a man, I had killed one of my own brothers—I had committed fratricide. Eva was repulsed by me. There was no other reason for her behavior. I couldn't blame her; I couldn't blame her at all. The truth was I never felt so disgusted with myself in my life.

* * *

We were coming back from our dueling, when the news that a thief had been caught by the palace guards reached our ears. I hastened to the small group of brothers assembled ahead of us from whom the rumor had echoed.

"Pardon me, brothers; I couldn't help overhearing part of your conversation. The guards caught a thief, you said. When?"

"Just before your duel with Abdul. They caught him in the Grand Vizier's room no less."

Beside me, Erik stiffened and paled at the same time.

"Who would dare attempt such a feat," I said.

"A cretin," a dark-skinned brother replied.

"Where is that thief now?" Erik asked in a quivering voice.

"In one of the dungeon's cells; where else would he be? He is scheduled to be *questioned* later this evening, I heard."

Erik sucked air in sharply. "Questioned!" He backed away from the group, rubbing his pale cheeks with both his hands. "He's going to be questioned," he whispered.

I nodded, not in the least shocked by the fact. *Questioned* was the delicate way of saying tortured. It was a common practice and a proven way of obtaining information, although I often questioned the veracity of the information acquired in this manner.

Darius appeared at the bottom of the stairs. "Have you heard the news?" he asked.

"About the thief, yes," I replied.

Darius aimed his attention at Erik. "It's a servant boy; his name is… Ramo, Rama… no, Rami."

Uh-oh! I did my best to keep a straight face. Taking a step back, I brushed against Erik. He was shaking like a leaf. I gripped his hand in the hope of calming him, and then feigning indifference, I told Darius that I didn't know that servant and didn't care about his fate; after all, the boy was a thief and had what he deserved.

Darius frowned, his eyes jumped to Erik. "Why is he so visibly upset, then?"

Nosy bastard, I thought. I couldn't find any reason for Erik's present state. My mind was blank.

Fortunately for me, Hassan's presence at my side brought this unpleasant conversation to a halt. "Prince Amir, Prince Keri, may I speak with you in private."

Under Darius's suspicious gaze, we moved near a fountain, so the gurgling sound of the water would cover our words.

"Honored Princes of Telfar," Hassan began with his usual rigid formality. "You are awaited in Prince Amir's tower and must present yourself there at once."

"Awaited by whom?" I asked. "I don't like having someone in my rooms without my consent. Who has the nerve to do such a thing?"

"The Sultan, your father," Hassan answered.

Well, that shut me up right away. Erik and I exchanged frightened glances and without further ado rushed upstairs.

The Sultan was staring out the window when we came in. He slowly turned. His kaftan was a deep, rich maroon with gold arabesque motifs running along its edge. The shirt and bouffant pantaloons visible underneath it were a golden tan color and made of brushed silk as was his turban. His belt was a tight circle of chased gold links.

My eyes focused on the bejeweled sword hanging on his hip. Never would I choose such a useless weapon, I thought, while bowing to my father.

"Please rise, my sons," he said.

Obeying, I looked at my father as though I were seeing him for the first time—as in a strange way it was. I'd never seen him look like this. A handsome man in his thirties with classic straight features, his mother's eastern origin was visible in my father's pale skin and the blond strands mixed in the brown of his short beard. Sadly his mother, who was reputed as being brilliant, died only a few months after Father's ascension to the throne. Some said that if Grandmother had lived longer Father would've been a better Sultan. I also recalled what Erik told me, that Father saw his lack of nobility as a shortcoming and that was why he was so adamant in choosing a Sultana's son as the next Sultan. Could it be true? To his eyes was I less valuable than Erik? I looked at the stranger that was my father and wondered about this.

Father walked away from my window, the silver soles of his shoes clanking against the tiles of my floor with every step. He stopped right in front of us. His eyes danced from me to Erik. "So different, yet so alike." He concentrated his attention on me. "I recognize you. You're the one who led your brothers into my chamber to help me."

Staying silent, I rolled my sweaty hands into balls to hide their trembling. I had never been this close to my father before, it was unnerving, like being near a lion—they too sometimes killed their young, didn't they. And although I was dying to ask him the reason of his presence here, in my rooms, I knew better than to speak without having been asked to. Clenching my jaw tight, I waited.

Fortunately my wait wasn't long. With a long sigh, my father said, "As you can see I am presently no more than twelve or fifteen years older than you." He paused to let us digest this bit of information—as if we had not noticed his appearance. "As you know, I'm kept informed of everything happening in the kingdom, city, palace—the Cage makes no difference."

Erik reacted to this news by gluing his side to mine.

"I was told that you've been working together at solving the terrible problems that are affecting us lately. Is this true?"

I cleared my throat. "Yes, but without much success, I'm afraid. We lack clues. And so far our brothers' deaths remain a mystery to us."

The Sultan smiled. "Perhaps I can supply you with a clue." He indicated the window. "Look at the sky. It's darkening fast—in an instant the moon will appear behind the west tower."

I cast my eyes on the tall, white tower, moments later the tip of a partly filled moon pushed past its corner.

"Now look at me very carefully," the Sultan ordered.

We did. At first I saw nothing besides the healthy complexion of a young man. Then one white hair popped into his well-groomed beard. *It was there before*, I told myself. *It's my imagination. It's stress from the fight.* Suddenly more white hairs sprung in his beard, tiny wrinkles spread from the corner of his eyes to his temples and the laugh-lines around his mouth deepened.

Erik made a strangled moaning sound, which he quickly muffled behind a hand. For my part, I couldn't lie to myself anymore: our father was aging right under our eyes.

"Every night, I grow a little older," Father said. "It started a few months ago. Since I've become younger and younger with each full moon rising. But I'm also growing older faster in between each one. Nothing we have tried to stop this curse has worked. You saw me before the rise of the full moon. I was barely alive."

"Yes," I said. "I remember being shocked by your appearance. But… er… why tell us about this curse? Surely more competent men than we can help you—the Grand Vizier for instance."

The Sultan's mouth twisted in a sad smile. "Because my time

is counted. I doubt I'll live to see the next full moon. I'm aging too fast this time, stopping this curse before hand is my only chance. For this I must engage every good brain the palace holds. Yours, I'm told, is particularly apt."

I blinked. Was this a compliment? I looked at my father and saw that he was studying me carefully and at length. Then his eyes pierced mine with a terrible intensity.

"They say that for certain faults there are consequences one can't escape—errors that will haunt a man, even a Sultan, to his death. They say that such mistakes have a way of righting themselves on their own accord. I never believed in those things before."

"Neither did I," I said, wondering what mistake my father had made. Could it be linked to the flooding of the library? So many questions—and so little time. I needed help to solve them. An idea formed in my mind. "Erik and I will do our best to help you. I will also recruit some of my brothers to help us. I—"

"No!" my father boomed. "I forbid you to tell anyone about this."

"But, surely you want the false rumor floating in the palace rectified."

The Sultan raised a hand ending my protestation. "For many of your brothers, it's already too late. I'm aware of the rebellion brewing against me. The truth won't undo their actions or erase their words. I chose to tell you because your names don't appear on the list of princes who are plotting against me." He moved to the door, and with a stern face added just before leaving, "I hope, for your sake, that it stays this way."

CHAPTER SIXTEEN

ather had left an hour ago, leaving Hassan behind to meticulously sort out all the notes Erik and I had accumulated in the last few months. At first I thought that he was going to call some scribe to have it copied. No such luck. Hassan just packed the entirety of our work into a box, thanked us for our contribution and then exited my room with the loot.

"This is a shame," I said, fuming. "I thought he wanted our help."

"What did you expect?" Erik snorted. "That we would sit down with the Vizier and exchange thoughts? For my part, I'm not surprised at all—and frankly I don't care about our father's fate."

"Shh… Watch your tongue, little brother. He has ears everywhere. You heard him; he knows everything happening in the Cage, our brothers' plotting, our search. Be careful."

Erik gripped his head with both hands. "I…" he mumbled, letting himself fall into a chair. "I can't think straight anymore. I'm sick with worry, Amir. If I don't do something to help Rami, I think my head will explode."

I studied my brother's face; he looked frazzled to say the least. His face was too pale and his eyes were too red. Erik was taking Rami's capture hard. I knew he would take it harder still if I spoke my mind, but what else could I do besides speak the truth. I sighed. "Your servant's a thief. He got what he deserved."

Erik rose up so abruptly his chair toppled over. "NO!" he shouted. Lowering his voice, he continued, "You don't understand. It's my fault. *I* sent Rami in the Grand Vizier's rooms to search for books and clues while we were fighting. I'm the guilty one, not Rami."

I was appalled. "How could you be so stupid? Once they see your family brand on the boy, they'll know you've sent him. That's if Rami doesn't betray you first. Damn, Erik, you might as well have done the deed yourself. Because once the boy opens his mouth, you'll be in just as much trouble as he is. I'm surprised they haven't picked you up yet."

Erik shook his head. "You're wrong. First, Rami will never betray me. Second, none of our family's servants bare marks of any sort. Mother's against it, she says that people aren't animals to be branded."

"That's smart! It's probably why the palace officials haven't come for you yet. They don't know that the boy's yours and that you sent him."

"See," Erik said with pleading eyes. "I told you that Rami wouldn't say a word."

I looked at Erik's guilt-ridden face. I didn't know how to break the news to him, yet I knew I had to. "Rami will speak. If not of his freewill, he will under torture."

Erik went dead white, and for a brief moment I thought he was going to faint. No matter how hard I tried I failed to comprehend my brother's distress over a servant's fate. Then again, he had been raised by servants, not me. Still, I thought Erik's attachment to that boy was abnormally strong. For the first time, I questioned the nature of Erik's relation with Rami. Not that it would be shocking to me if Erik favored boys over girls—many of my brothers did. Somehow I found it hard to believe. Usually I could figure out my brothers' preferences quickly and without fault. I was certain that my little brother loved women. Could Erik be partial to both sexes—perhaps? I shrugged, why question this anyway. It was without importance.

Kneeling in front of Erik, I laid a hand on his shoulder. Something occupied my attention. Something I couldn't escape. I had a debt toward Erik to repay. When I had sought a favor from him, he had agreed to it without hesitation and arranged my first meeting with Eva. However, the hardest thing for me to admit was that I also owed a debt to Rami for coming to our help in the mausoleum.

With clenched teeth, and despite my thoughts that I'd lost my mind, I said, "Don't worry, little brother, I'll find a way to rescue your beloved Rami."

* * *

We quickly made our way to Erik's hiding place. Once there Erik pulled maps out of the architect's working post.

"There should be one for the prisoner's tower and its dungeon." Erik said, his arms overflowing with rolled-up parchments. "Don't stand there. Help me."

I began unrolling parchments one after the other. The fifth one was the plan of a bedchamber ceiling. The detail of the medallion carved in center of the ceiling was exquisite; however, it wasn't what held my attention. What did was the seal stamped in black wax at the bottom of the drawing. This emblem was identical to the one carved on the ring I had found in the mausoleum.

I poked the blob of wax. "Erik, I think I found something."

"Me too." Erik laid a detailed plan of the prisoner's tower and its dungeon over my drawing. "See, there's an access tunnel leading to the tower, just as in the rest of the palace."

I studied the plan carefully for a moment. We could make

our way inside the tower without being seen, but once there we would have to cross several corridors and halls in the open before reaching the cells where Rami was *presumably* held. Tracing the line of the main corridor with a finger, I descended along the length of the tower to the dungeon underneath it.

"Is there a way to access the dungeon besides walking all the way down in the open? That's... dangerous." *Insane* was the word I really wanted to say.

Erik shook his head then shrugged. "Yes, I believe so. I must've misplaced it, because it's not here. That's the only plan I can find. Should we spend more time looking for another?"

I thought about it for an instant. When would they start questioning Rami? *It might already be too late,* a nagging voice blew in my mind. Thinning my lips, I looked at Erik. "No. It'll have to do. There's one thing though—the tower's guards—how can we pass them and make it down to the dungeon without raising their alarm?"

Erik's eyes suddenly widened and his mouth became a perfect circle. "Oh, oh, I know. We'll go to the costume hall and get guards' outfits."

I grimaced. That was risky, I didn't like it one bit, but knowing that every minute wasted might lead to Rami's fall and therefore Erik's, I kept quiet. So it was against my good judgment that I left with him for the costume hall.

Erik's uniform was dangerously small. The white shirt had ripped at the shoulder the moment he put it on. Fortunately a red vest covered this fact. However, the matching red bouffant pants left far too much of his shin exposed. Well, I thought, these bare patches of skin on his legs matched the ones on his arms—his shirt's sleeves were also too short. Erik was obviously taller than the average guard.

As for me, I had always considered myself average in height. But as I floated in my own disguise, I supposed that when it came to guard's standards I might have been on the small side. That kind of annoyed me, making me feel somewhat substandard. It also made me nervous. With Erik bursting out of his outfit and I looking like a dressed cat, not to mention the long, cumbersome halberds we had to carry—unused to the length of these weapons, we kept scraping the walls with them—whom were we to fool? I consoled myself with the fact that we had a few minutes of practice walking in uniform before reaching our destination. It could only improve... I hoped.

We made it to the prisoner's tower too soon for my taste. Glued together in the darkness, Erik and I listened for the guards. Footsteps. Loud ones. They were moving away, though. After a moment of hesitation, we pushed out of the secret passage and found ourselves right at the end of a short procession of guards. In panic, we hurried into the line, matching our steps to the guards in front of us, even though we were going in the wrong direction. I looked at Erik. His face was tensed, yet determined. I watched him scan the area ahead. Because of his height, he could see farther than I could—the back of the guards in front of me was all I could see.

Erik made a slight head nod left. Seconds later an alcove appeared in the wall. We hid in it and waited for the column of guards to vanish behind the corridor's bend.

"Come," Erik said. "I think it's safe now."

To my astonishment, we made it to the entrance of the dungeon without incident. Considering how we looked and behaved, this feat made me question the efficiency of our army. Perhaps its training should be revised. Not my problem, I thought, and looked ahead. As we were nearing the dungeon's thick iron gate, two guards stepped in front of us.

"Halt!" the guard on the left barked. "State the reason of your presence here."

Erik snorted. "Nothing official—don't worry."

Both guards immediately abandoned their rigid posture

and slumped against their halberds. "What then?" asked the same guard.

"Our commanding officer dropped his dagger sometime during our shift. He just realized he lost it now. Because we're both new recruits," Erik rudely poked a thumb at me, "he sent us to toss every corner of this dark hole for his *precious heirloom*." Erik then spat on the ground. "Dirty son of a camel!"

The two guards burst in laughter. The guard on the right, a fellow with a big flat nose and a mouth that displayed more gum than teeth when he laughed, said, "I pity you, my tall friend. If you spend the night bent in half searching the ground, you're in for one hell of a backache. Your companion, however, won't have that trouble. His eyes are much closer to the ground."

I gasped. This man had insulted me—he called me short, not in those words, but I knew what he had meant. A white-hot flash of fury seized me; I wanted to shove the blunt end of my halberd into this man's belly. Fighting this violent urge with all my strength, I squeezed the weapon hard. Suddenly, the hair at the base of my neck stood up. I was being watched, I clearly sensed it. I looked up and saw that the other guard was staring at me. His dark eyes seemed to question my being in this uniform.

"The Guard Corps isn't what it used to be," he said. "Now, they take pretty much anyone. *Tsk, tsk, tsk.* All right then, good luck in your search." He then moved aside.

Not wasting any time, we took the direction of the dungeon's second level where the questioning-cells were. Upon entering the level, we both froze in horror.

The place stunk of urine and waste. Covering my nose, I took a few steps in the dark cold air of the room then stopped and scanned the surroundings. The walls were full of moving shadows and cobwebs. Questionable debris littered the straw-covered stone floor and rats could be heard squeaking in every corner. Two giant braziers occupied the center of the room. My eyes went to the huge square block of wood placed between the braziers. I shuddered

This is where they brand servants and slaves crossed my mind. Then my nagging inner-voice whispered: *Fool! That's to cut off thieves' hands.*

Shaking myself, I grabbed a handful of Erik's shirt and made him cross the room with me. We passed a torture room. I stopped and took a morbid peek inside. A long wood table outfitted with iron restraints occupied most of the space. Resting on top of the table was a fat barrel of water and a funnel.

"They fill prisoners' stomachs with water until it bursts," Erik whispered in my ear.

I swallowed hard, glad that the room was empty of suppliants. Right now, I strongly doubted I could witness a torture session and do nothing.

We moved along. This time it was Erik who took the lead. Soon we entered a broad area occupied by the holding-cells. Cries, moans and calls for pity rose from all corners. I tried covering my ears but it was useless. The sounds still reached me. I looked around, squinting against the penumbra. Cagelike cells lined both sides of this long narrow room. Inside these cages, shadows stirred, and when we approached the bars, they rushed in mass at the back of their cells to huddle together. The stench here was so strong I could hardly breathe.

Erik seized the bars of the first cage. "They brought a boy here not long ago. Where is he?"

No answer came. While Erik continued asking, I followed the alley between the cages to its end. There, hidden behind a bend, I found a heavy wooden door with a small peeking-slot cut in the middle. Slouched in a chair in front of the door was a sleeping guard. The man snored loudly. His breath reeked of bad wine. The key ring dangling from his belt caught my eyes.

I smiled and tiptoed to the man. I winced; from up close this man's stench was strong enough to knock down a horse. Well, strong enough to make my eyes water. Holding my breath, I tried taking the key ring without waking the guard. I pulled gingerly. It refused to budge. I pulled harder. Still nothing. I peeked at the man's face. Drool dripped from the corner of his opened mouth. *Ah, that horrid stench!* For a second I wanted to close his stinking trap. Instead I lowered my eyes to the key ring and give it a good yank. There was a ripping sound, and the piece of cloth tying the key ring to the guard's belt finally broke. My prize in hand, I stepped back, grinning.

The guard stirred. My grin vanished. The guard opened his eyes and sprung to his feet.

"Don't move," I said.

The guard blinked, looked at the key ring in my hand then at his belt then at me. I could see some intention forming in his eyes. At first I thought he was preparing an attack but when his eyes glided to the opening on my left I realized that he was about to flee. I moved right, giving him more space to run, just to see if he would take it. Sure enough, he rushed ahead with the uncoordinated movement of someone still under the effect of alcohol. As he squeezed to my left, I brought the shaft of my halberd down on his head. Knocked out, he spilled on the ground in a cloud of dust. Ah, the courage of a drunken guard was a thing of beauty.

Without more delay, I moved to the door and opened the peeking-slot. Before I could peer into the slot, the sound of footsteps coming from behind made me look over my shoulder. I sighed with relief. It was only Erik, joining me. He was making quite a racket, I thought, while staring at him. He walked sluggishly and almost tripped over the guard's sprawling body. This ordeal was testing my brother's strength. He seemed as physically spent as I knew he was emotionally.

Better hurry before he collapses. I turned and looked through the slot. It was pitch-black inside the cell. *Empty. Damn, Rami is elsewhere.* I was about to close the slot when I heard the shuffling of straw inside the cell.

"Psst," I hushed. "Psst, Rami, is that you."

There was a gasp followed by whimpering then a hiccupping yes.

"Erik, the boy's here," I whispered.

Erik roughly brushed me aside and began fighting with the door. "It's locked and too thick to be brought down. What do we do?"

Shaking my head, I stretched over Erik's shoulder and dangled the keys in front of his nose. "Move aside," I ordered.

The third key was the right one. The door opened with a whining complaint of rusted hinges. I stepped in and almost fell down the threshold's step. It was so dark inside, I couldn't see anything. Even with the door wide open and the torches burning outside, it took my eyes a moment to adapt to the surrounding darkness. Slowly, darker shapes appeared against the cell's gray walls: two benches, a bucket and... *Oh*, a severed head. I turned away from the head and spotted Rami's small silhouette at the back of the cell.

Curled on the dirty stone floor, the boy was propped against the wall, his slim wrists captured in a wide iron cuff attached to a thick chain.

Erik rushed past me like the wind and scooped Rami in his arms. The boy let out a moan of pain and fought the hug.

"Erik, leave him. He's hurt," I said, kneeling beside Rami. The boy's tunic was torn, the left sleeve missing. On his exposed arm was a fresh brand, a swollen red hand, the mark of a thief.

Erik stared at the brand with shiny eyes, his face distorted with a rictus of anger. "How dare they! They'll pay for this. They'll pay, I swear."

For my part, I thought that it was pure luck that Rami wasn't in worse shape... well, he still had his hands. Thieves were usually punished by cutting one if not both of their hands off. Then again, they weren't finished with Rami, they were just beginning. While freeing the boy from his chains—fortunately the right key was on the ring—I asked. "Have they questioned you? Don't lie!"

Rami raised his chin, and for the first time since we'd met he looked straight at me without hiding his face—in this penumbra I still couldn't make out his features. "I held my tongue," Rami said. For some inexplicable reason, I believed him.

"I told you he wouldn't betray us," Erik said in a soft voice.

Rami nodded then lowered his head into the crease of Erik's shoulder. "I didn't speak, even when they branded me. They said they would come back later with the chief torturer and that he would make me speak." The boy gripped one of Erik's hands into his. "I was so afraid. Not so much of the chief torturer, but of failing you."

While Erik whispered reassuring words to Rami, I scratched my head. A new problem had appeared to me. "Uh... how are we going to get out now?"

"What do you mean?" Erik said. "The same way we... Ohhh, damn!"

I slapped my forehead with the heel of my hand. How thoughtless of us not to have planned this part—really stupid. "There's no way we can pass the guards with him in tow. So how do we get out?"

Rami's head swung from Erik to me. At first he looked confused, then scared, then finally appalled. "You didn't use the dungeon's passage?" he whispered.

We didn't answer.

Rami's jaw dropped. Quickly he covered his mouth with a hand. "You risked your life for me," he mumbled before throwing himself into Erik's arms again.

I rolled my eyes. Now was not the time for long displays of gratitude. "Rami, where's that passage? Can you show us the way?"

The boy nodded, and within seconds, he was on his feet and

out of the cell. After locking the knocked-out guard in the cell, I followed Rami and Erik into one of the torture chambers. Brightly lit by torches, this chamber had clearly been used tonight. Another clue of its recent use was the unpleasant smell of brunt flesh lingering in the air. The image of Rami's fresh brand rose to the top of my mind, and I had to fight the urge to look at his arm. Instead I stared about the chamber. A stretching table occupied its center and all kinds of torture implements hung from its walls: whips, tongs and branding irons. I noted that an iron—the one probably used to brand Rami—was still in the glowing brazier. Cringing, I turned away. My eyes fell on the three iron maidens lined against the back wall. These metal sarcophagi had interiors filled with puncturing spikes.

Rami, I saw, had stopped in front of the third one. The boy gazed at the image of a woman with her arms crossed over her chest that decorated the exterior of the iron maiden for a brief instant. Then he opened it, exposing the deadly spikes that riddled its inside.

"This can't be the way out," I complained, staring at this death trap.

"Wait!" Rami said. He slipped his hand over the maiden's face and poked his fingers into her eyes. There was a horrible sound of rusted metal grinding together, the spikes retracted inside the wall of the maiden and a trap door opened in her back. The cool wet breeze of the sewers hit our face with force. Took me all I had not to gag.

Filling our lungs to capacity, we entered the iron maiden. Once on the other side, Rami pulled on a lever and the maiden closed back, preserving her secret. With Rami guiding us, we took the route back. I was surprised to see Erik dragging behind. And when he bumped into a corner for the fourth time, I questioned the acuity of his night vision. The muffled sound of voices in the distance made me forget Erik's clumsiness. The voices became clearer as we moved along. When we reached the tunnel leading to Erik's secret room, we discovered the origin of the voices. There was a rush of activity ahead of us. I spotted over a dozen guards moving about. The glow of their torches and lamps cast amber and gold lights on the gray tunnel walls, giving them a richness they otherwise did not possess. Our road was totally blocked.

"The Vizier," I hissed. The man was having the tunnels searched. Could it be for Rami? I wondered. Had they already discovered his escape? It seemed a bit soon to me. Still, why chance it. "We need to find a good hiding place for Rami—fast," I said.

"My hiding—" Erik started.

"No, I've seen the Vizier in these tunnels one too many times. We need a better place…" I tapped my lips with a finger. "Ah, I know the perfect place."

"Where?" Erik asked.

"Come, you'll see." I took the lead, going in the direction of my tower. Soon we were out of the tunnel and at the entrance of the corridor leading to my rooms. After verifying that the corridor was clear, we tiptoed to Jafer's room. I unlocked his door while keeping an eye to Mir's grid. Mir didn't like Rami; he didn't like any servant for that matter. But knowing that the boy had been caught stealing—somehow Mir always learned this type of news faster than I did—he wouldn't hesitate to call the guards, who might come running. On the other hand, if Jafer called the guards, they would ignore him. Nothing Jafer did or said was taken seriously anymore. I only hoped he wouldn't harm the boy.

We rapidly entered Jafer's room. It was so dark inside that it took me a minute to realize that Jafer was calmly seated on a couch right in front of us with a strange little smile on his face, as though he had known all along that we were coming.

"Jafer," I began, "I need your help."

Jafer tilted his head and his eyes glided to Rami, who was hooked on Erik's arm.

"Will you allow the boy to stay with you?" I asked.

To my dismay, Jafer's smile broadened. "I welcome his company," he said in a voice so sane and so reasonable that for a moment I feared that the man in front of me wasn't my brother but a talented impostor.

"Are you sure it's safe for Rami to be alone with him?" Erik whispered in my ear.

"Yes," I lied. No one would ever search this room for Rami, of that I was sure—but of nothing else.

CHAPTER SEVENTEEN

Erik spent the following hour preparing Jafer's spare bedroom for Rami. In the meantime, I fetched some balm to soothe the boy's wound.

Rami ground his teeth bravely while I applied a copious layer of ointment on his burnt skin. When I was done, I noted that Jafer was patting the boy's hand in a supportive manner while Erik looked on disapprovingly. My little brother's face was pale and sweaty. He looked exhausted. This day had been hard for him. And I too was feeling tired. I supposed we'd do well to retire to our respective chambers for a good night's sleep. But first, we needed to change into our Princes' clothes, which meant going back to the costume hall where we'd left our garments—we couldn't afford to have them found.

The trip back to the costume hall proved more difficult than I had imagined. News of Rami's escape had spread to every corner of the palace like grains of sand after a sandstorm. Every room was bursting with activity, every hall, every corridor cluttered by traffic. Fortunately our guard costumes served us well. If only Erik would stop tripping over his own feet, we would have made better time.

Finally we reached the costume hall, waited for the people in it to leave, pulled our clothing from their hiding places and changed. Our return to the Cage went without problems. As soon as we stepped into its corridors we bid each other good night and took the direction of our respective quarters.

* * *

Solid knocks on my door pulled me from my sleep. My first thought was that they had discovered Rami and now were coming for me. Seizing my rapier, left hanging on a chair, I rushed to the door and opened its window. Instead of the army of guards I had expected to see standing in front of my door, I saw a lone servant, a boy in a valet uniform twice his size. Immediately I recognized the stable boy Erik had saved from a whipping. The boy's face was twisted with anguish.

"Prince Amir," he said in a quivering voice. "Prince Keri demands to see you."

"What? Can't he wait until morning?"

The small valet became very agitated. "Please, Your Highness, you must come at once, Prince Keri has fallen ill. Please, he needs you at his side."

Erik, ill! I just left him. How could this be? I dressed in a hurry then followed the valet across the Cage. Upon entering Erik's rooms, I saw four imperial physicians clad in the long gray robes of their functions assembled in front of my brother's bedchamber. They were in the midst of a heated argument, seemingly unable to agree on the best way to treat Erik's ailment.

"He must be bled," declared the one with the long white beard.

"No, his humor must be soothed first with a camphor potion," a short fat one argued.

I winced. In my opinion both suggestions were harmful.

Seeing me approach, the physicians bowed.

"How's my brother?" I asked, ignoring all etiquette.

After a moment of uncomfortable silence and hesitation, the chief physician spoke up. He was a tall bony man with stringy white hair and long spidery hands that always seemed in constant motion. Looking at me kindly, he said, "I'm afraid that Prince Keri is on Death's door."

The news struck me like a punch in the gut. "No! This can't be!"

"I'm afraid it is so. Come, Prince. Come see for yourself."

I trailed the physician into Erik's chamber. When I saw my brother's pallid face, my breath caught in my throat. His lips were blue, his skin gray and his eyes partly rolled back in his head. Erik was sweating so profusely that it had drenched the bed linen, forming a dark halo all around his body. I touched his forehead, his skin was boiling.

"We're unable to determine the cause of this sudden illness," the physician said. "Its symptoms are very unusual. Perhaps it's something... he ate."

I stared at the man. I understood what he meant by that—poison. He thought Erik had been poisoned. I returned my gaze to Erik. "We ate the same things," I said.

Upon hearing my voice, Erik stirred. "Amir," he breathed, extending a hand at me.

I gripped his burning paw. "I'm here, little brother. Don't worry. Everything will be fine now." Deep down, I feared for Erik's life. He looked terrible, as if something was eating him from the inside. Reviewing the day's events in my mind, I sought for the cause of my brother's present state—was he offered something to drink or eat without my noticing? I tried to recall our every action—after the combat perhaps. Suddenly a flash illuminated my mind, a red flash, just like the one produced by Ibrahim's ring when it had cut Erik's back.

"I think it happened this afternoon, during the combat. I need to see his back to be sure."

With the young valet's help, we rolled Erik onto his belly. I lifted up his nightshirt over his head, exposing his scar-riddled back.

"Ohh," I let out, gazing upon the pus-swollen cut slicing his left shoulder blade. The cut was oozing and the skin around its edges was blotchy and purplish. I was right. Ibrahim had sunk his ring into Erik's back for the purpose of poisoning him. This was an act of utter cowardice, an act so devious it left me trembling with rage.

"This is where the poison entered his body," I said.

The physician leaned closer. "You're right." Then to my surprise, he stuck his nose to the cut and—smelled it. "Lemony," he said. "Smells like lemon, which means the white desert spider's venom is the poison used on him. That's unfortunate."

"Are you sure... can you tell just like this?" I was hoping he was wrong. This spider was infamous, its venom a death sentence.

"I'm afraid there is no mistaking that smell."

My knees weakened and I had to grip the bedpost not to fall.

The physician placed his long-fingered hand on my shoulder, patting it gently. "Look at me, young prince."

I obeyed. His face was thin; his eyes, a pale washed-out blue. They should have been cold—being the color of ice—yet they were warm and kind. These pale eyes were also filled with wisdom, to me that was comforting. Surely a man with such knowledge and experience would find a cure. He had to save my brother, he just had to.

The physician smiled at me. "All is not lost, my prince. There's an antidote. The only problem is that I'm missing one ingredient, the essential one. Sadly it's also very rare. Perhaps you know of it. It's black willow bark. Some call it weeper's dust."

"Weeper's dust!" I shouted in relief! "I have it in my apothecary chest in my rooms. Start your brew, physician. I'll go fetch the dust."

When I retuned with a bottle of weeper's dust, I found Erik soaking inside the basin of his bedroom's fountain. I saw that his wound had been lanced and cleaned and that a generous layer of honey was now smeared over the cut. Honey was an old remedy. There was nothing better to keep infection away. I gave the weeper's dust to the physician, who immediately added three good pinches of it to a fowl-smelling yellow brew. Then he spoon-fed this mixture to Erik. "Now let's hope we are not too late," the physician said.

As we were laying Erik back in his bed, the double doors of his bedchamber suddenly burst open. The Grand Vizier marched in with a small army of guards in tow. He stopped in front of me, fists firmly planted on his waist. "Where's the boy, Prince Amir? I know you and Prince Keri are somehow involved in this thief's escape."

"What are you accusing us of, Vizier," I spat between clenched teeth. I hated that man more than ever. I hated his presence in this room in this dire moment, hated his arrogant stand, hated his assurance of our guilt, hated his accusing tone, this despite the fact that he was right to suspect us.

"You know all too well what I mean, Prince Amir. However, I'm willing to refresh your memory." The Vizier stepped closer to me. His eyes, I noted, had become two thin slits. "Two men dressed as guards entered the holding cell where a thieving servant was held—in all accounts this thief is Prince Keri's servant boy."

"Was this servant marked as his?" I demanded.

The Vizier's stare darkened. "No, but—"

"Then he's not my brother's servant!" Waving a hand at Erik's limp body sprawled in his broad bed, I added, "My brother is too ill to have committed the act you're accusing him of anyway."

The Vizier's dark eyebrows rose in surprise at Erik's sight. His gaze swung to the chief imperial physician, who bowed and said, "Prince Keri has been poisoned during this afternoon's combat. His condition, as you see, is too grave and too advanced for him to have run around the palace in secret, let alone do the things you've mentioned. Only someone possessing an abnormally strong constitution could've done it in this state."

The Vizier made a face like he'd just sucked on a particularly sour lemon. He was still unconvinced, I could see it in the way he kept twisting his mouth. So I did something I rarely do: I gambled. I called Erik's new valet. The boy rushed to my side.

Throwing an arm around the boy's narrow shoulder, I smiled at the Vizier. "As you see, Erik's servant boy has never left his room. The one you caught belonged to someone else."

The Vizier studied the boy carefully. A guard then whispered a few words in his ear. A cold calculating smile stretched the Vizier's thin lips. "I'm informed that the captured servant was branded with the thief symbol. This is easy to verify."

"Show him your arms and back," I told the young valet.

Under the Vizier's intense hawkish glare the boy removed his tunic, exposing a back marked by whip but not branded in any way.

The Vizier's eyes roamed over the boy's small frame for a long moment then flicked to Erik, who was mumbling deliriously in his bed, then to me. His dark complexion turned sallow. He looked totally lost, which made me realize that the Vizier had no other suspects and didn't know where to look next. It was with a sense of triumph that I watched him squirm and bow before me.

"My most sincere apologies, Prince Amir, I was sorely mistaken."

When I judged that the Vizier had done enough groveling, I allowed him to leave. Once we were alone again, I turned to the physician. "Do you think my brother has a chance of surviving this?"

"It's difficult to tell at this stage." The physician then smiled at me. "However, I do believe that he has an abnormally strong constitution. And that might serve him."

* * *

The hours that followed were the longest of my life. This long wait made me realize how attached to Erik I had become.

And when by midmorning his fever subsided and his coloring returned to something closer to normal, I was so relieved I nearly cried. But Erik was far from out of trouble yet. Around noon, the physician forced Erik to swallow a new potion, one fouler than the first, with the result that my poor brother spent the rest of the day vomiting and evacuating all kinds of disgusting humors in any possible manner one's body could. Soon his bedchamber was reeking of bile... and other horrid bodily ejections.

The imperial chief physician seemed pleased by this terrible reaction. "This will eliminate all poison from his body. Now I believe he will get better."

"If he survives the remedy," I mumbled, yet I was grateful, immensely grateful for Erik's recovery and thanked the physician profusely before he left. Then I settled on the chair beside Erik's bed, determined to spend the day by his side. As time passed, Erik's condition improved: his breathing, which had been shallow and hacked, deepened. His fever dropped and a slight pinkish hue colored his cheeks. With each new improvement, I felt some weight lifting from my shoulders, and I too began breathing more easily. Just as I told myself that I could rest and close my eyes without fearing Erik's death anymore, a bawling Salima dashed in the room.

Rumor of Erik's imminent death had reached every corner of the palace, including the harem and Princess Livia's quarters. I felt guilty for not having sent word of his state to his mother; then again, I wasn't certain myself that he would make it. Truthfully, I had been worrying too much myself to think of it. I made up for my thoughtless behavior by explaining the situation in length to Salima. Once reassured, Salima went to work cleaning Erik's room, saying that its stuffy air was bad for him. I had a hard time convincing her that she should instead return to the harem and ease Princess Livia's heart. Even then, Salima was reluctant to leave Erik's side.

She raised him, I told myself. *Salima is as much Erik's mother as Princess Livia.*

Later that day, I made my way to Jafer's room to see how he and Rami were doing and gave them news of Erik's state. I found them playing chess in the sitting room. That took me aback. First, where did a servant learn to play chess—and play well, as I could see that the boy was winning? Second, Jafer's illness affected his concentration, and because of this he hadn't been able to play chess in years.

As Rami stood, eyes wide with worry for his master, I forgot about the chess game and reassured the boy on Erik's condition. This done, I returned to Erik's side and made arrangements to have him moved into my tower.

I didn't like having him living so close to Ibrahim and his brothers. And sure enough, when we left for my tower, Erik lying flat on a litter carried by four servants, with me walking beside it, Ibrahim and his brothers lined the corridor to see us depart.

The bastard twirled his mustache with an air of self-satisfaction while his brothers made rude comments and laughed.

As we walked in front of this boorish group, I squeezed Erik's hand hard. My brothers' predatory gazes sent shivers down my spine; I felt as if we were wounded gazelles passing a den of hungry hyenas. Well, from now on this gazelle was going to fight back. I glared at Ibrahim, letting all the loathing and disgust I had toward him pass through my eyes. I kept my gaze fixed upon his until my head was twisted backward to the point of being painful. Only then did I face front. It was enough, I thought; the message between us had been clear: next time we would meet one of us would die.

Back in my tower, I arranged to have the young valet boy and Rami dressed identically. This way the boys could change places whenever need be. This seemed like a good solution to a problem I knew was to come—namely Rami. By now, I knew the boy enough to figure that he wouldn't stay in Jafer's room for long. He would move in and out, or worse, stay glued to Erik until he was well again—and this no matter what I'd tell him. Rami often disobeyed Erik, so I didn't expect him to obey me at all.

We had just settled down when shy knocks brought me to my door's window. I saw a red-eyed Salima frozen in the corridor in front of Mir's door. My brother was glaring at her through his door grid with a fierce intensity. Mir was obviously unhappy to see this stranger there. Poor frightened Salima stared at him as if she had been caught in fault. I hurried out before Mir began spewing his usual litany of insults.

Salima gripped my arm like a drowning woman seizing a floating log. "I need to know more about Erik's health... and so does Princess Livia. She's awaiting my return as we speak."

"He's much better. Come see for yourself."

Under Mir's intense glare, I escorted Salima inside. She rushed at Erik's side, fussed over him for a good hour and left only when she was certain that he was out of danger.

That night I looked at the moon with a feeling of helplessness. How much time before the full moon? Not enough. Maybe it was because I was exhausted or my nerves were frayed, but lately time seemed to fly by faster than it ever had. Or maybe I was just busier. With these fuzzy thoughts in mind, I fell asleep on the bench by the windowsill. I shivered, while dreaming of Eva dancing in a thick wet fog. Her silhouette became fainter and fainter as she was slowly being absorbed by the fog. I ran after her, calling her name. Soon I too was lost in the mist. The moment I stopped running I felt something rubbing against my shin. I looked down and screamed. Tendrils of fog had transformed into hands. They were scratching at my legs. More hands shot out of the misty ground. There were hands everywhere. One grabbed my ankle. I stumbled and fell into a bottomless black hole.

I awakened on the floor, shivering from cold. *Eva! I must see her, give her news of Erik. With all the false rumors circulating through the palace, she may think him dead.*

I knew this was an excuse to see her, yet I hurried to wash and change. Once dressed and cleaned, I filled a copper platter with the traditional Telfarian breakfast: honey, butter and a loaf of bread. It was with a light heart that I left for the secret tunnel with the breakfast platter. I found my way without any problem and without meeting anyone. As my hand grabbed the doorknob of the storage room and I was about to enter Eva's room, I abruptly came to my senses.

Eva didn't expect me. I didn't ask her for permission to visit. Recollections of her reaction toward me after my combat with Abdul again haunted me: her refusal to look at me. The hint of repulsion I had seen on her lovely face.

"Stupid!" I whispered. "Stupid, stupid, stupid!" My hand slipped off the knob. I had taken one step away from the door when it swung open. I flinched so violently I almost dropped my platter. Eva stood in the doorframe with a look of fear on her face.

"It's me," I said, and winced. *Damn, Amir, she's not blind.* I could have kicked myself for uttering such a platitude.

Eva placed a hand on my forearm. "I'm so glad to see you. I've been waiting for news since yesterday. How's my cousin?"

"He's well. Totally out of danger."

Eva let out a long sigh of relief. A painful stretch of awkward silence then followed.

Gathering my courage, I said, "I thought we might share breakfast."

She looked at the platter and made the slightest of nod. It was only then that I noticed that she was dressed in the fashion of her motherland. Her tight bodice-flaring gown of green brocade swept the floor. Gone were her loose curls; now her hair was tightly pulled, braided and rolled at the back of her head. A white cornet, with a long lacy veil, was pinned through the braid. I supposed that her love affair with our culture had died while she watched us trying to kill each other. I felt ashamed but more so angry, this for a reason I couldn't really pinpoint.

Hiding my feelings, as they were far too confusing anyway, I entered the room. We sat on her long bench close together. I mixed the butter with some honey. For this I had chosen the best and rarest, Ogul Bali, the virgin honey with no aftertaste. I then spread the thick creamy mixture on a piece of fresh bread and offered it to Eva.

"It's delicious," she said after having nibbled the corner of her bread. Eva didn't care to eat, that was clear, she was just being polite. I couldn't blame her; I too was suddenly without appetite.

Forcing a few bites down, I proceeded to explain what had happened to Erik in detail, elaborating profusely on his improving condition. Eva listened in perfect silence. I noted how she kept her eyes fixed on her hands, which she wrung continuously. Something was bothering her, and with every passing minute it seemed to weigh more and more heavily on her mind. Finally she raised her eyes to me.

"I can hear my eunuch guards' conversations from my other room. They said that the Sultan is ill again… and might not live very long. I also heard that Prince Ibrahim will probably be the next Sultan. Is he the man who poisoned my cousin?"

I looked down at my own hands, one was clenched in a white-knuckled fist while the other was about to crush my breakfast into a sticky mush. I forced myself to relax. I sighed. "I'm afraid so."

She nodded, showing no surprise. "So, in other words, my future husband is a despicable man."

I squeezed my eyes hard for a second. "He's worse than that… far worse."

To my utter surprise, Eva patted my back as if to reassure me. She let out a chuckle. The sound was full of spite. "I thought this might happen. I prepared myself for the idea of marrying a man I dislike. However, I have to admit that this Ibrahim sounds worst than anyone I ever imagined." She raised her chin in a display of courage and fortitude. "I will not worry now. As long as he is not officially Sultan I can still hope that things might change. The eunuchs said that the only other serious contender for the throne is Prince Darius. Is he a better man? Shall I wish for him to take the throne instead?"

I swallowed hard. I wanted to shout, *NO! Wish for me!* But I said, "Yes. He's better."

She nodded silently.

I gazed upon her beautiful profile. *Hope,* she had said. She needed hope. I knew what I needed to say for this, but letting the words out was torture. "I think... I think I might be able to tip the scale in Darius's favor."

Eva's fingers grazed the back of my hand; her touch was as light as butterflies' wings. "Thank you," she whispered.

It was my turn to be silent. I dropped my piece of bread on the platter. I couldn't swallow another bite. When I raised my eyes, Eva was looking at me.

"How strange," she began with a sad little smile, "less than a week ago I couldn't wait to leave this tower. Now I dread the day I will leave it."

"I wish I could..."

"Please, Amir, we both know wishing is useless." Her delicate hand touched mine. "However, if it's true that we have little time left to us, perhaps we should spend more of it together, don't you think?"

My heart jumped with joy. And even though I knew this was utter insanity, that Eva would never be mine, that this was extremely dangerous, that I would get deeply hurt, I said yes immediately.

CHAPTER EIGHTEEN

My next days were spent in a mixture of misery and delight. I was delighted when in Eva's company; as we grew closer and closer, every touch of her eyes or hands filling me with euphoria, but I was miserable the moment I left her side—and horribly tortured every time I saw Darius. Although I had promised Eva that I would help him become Sultan, not only did I fail to make contact with him, I fled Darius like the black plague. A week passed in a flash. On the night of my seventh meeting with Eva, I got an idea. Why not get some disguises and visit the palace together, Eva and I, just like Erik had done with Rami and me.

That evening, I showed up at her room with an armful of clothes. Not gardeners' costumes, which were linked to unpleasant memories, but bakers' ones: long white tunics, linen aprons and white turbans with long scarves to hide most of our faces.

Eva was overjoyed by the idea of seeing something new. She grabbed the clothing with an enthusiasm I hadn't seen her display before. Once dressed, we left her tower giggling like children. We moved through dark tunnels at a brisk speed and soon reached the first dangerous crossing. We needed to exit the linen closet and enter the dark alcove located further down the corridor without being seen. That was the tricky part. We were at the heart of the Cage. After careful scrutiny of the surroundings, I grabbed Eva's hand and led the way.

We were almost at the alcove when a dark figure burst out of it and collided with us. Eva let out an exclamation of surprise in her foreign tongue.

As if shocked by this strange sound, the dark figure whipped its head toward Eva, while I, having taken the hit full front, struggled to stay on my feet. Once my balance was regained, I studied the dark form. It was a woman, tightly wrapped from head to toe in a black haïk—the traditional oblong cloth worn as an outer garment by Telfarian women. She peered at Eva a moment longer, then, half-bent, scrambled away before I could see her face. A dancer, or just a servant girl returning to her station after having entertained one of my brothers, I assumed. Not wasting time, we hurried into the safety of the alcove.

"Where are we going?" Eva asked as we walked under the many archways leading to the treasury.

"It's a surprise," I said. Having stepped outside the Cage only once myself, I knew very little of the palace and could only show Eva the places shown to me by Erik. I dared not venture into strange places for fear of getting lost. Eva's safety was too important to risk. *Idiot! You're risking her safety right now*, a voice nagged in my head. I blocked it and moved along.

Once inside the treasury I was a bit disconcerted by Eva's reaction to its contents. She moved about the shelves of bejeweled articles with a slight expression of boredom.

She picked up a small gold statuette of a ram. "Your father collects beautiful things."

"He collects all kinds of things. Would you like to see his other collections?"

She smiled. "Certainly."

Hand in hand, we made our way to the miniatures room. Eva gasped upon entering the room. I too was impressed.

Although I had been in this hall before, I didn't really pay much attention to it then. Perhaps it was being with Eva that made me see things differently now. I looked around with wide-opened eyes. Every parcel of the walls was taken by hundreds and hundreds of small portraits done either on metal, porcelain or ivory. All these faces looking down on us were intimidating, to say the least.

"Are they all your ancestors?" Eva breathed.

"No, only the men on the east wall are. The rest are portraits of wives, Viziers, favorites and persons who had some meaning for the present or past Sultans." Stepping to the east wall, I pointed up. "See the first row. Those are the Sultans of the Harik Dynasty. Then come the ones from the Tolem Dynasty and the Mefenkal and finally the Ban. So far we're the longest ruling dynasty."

"Why's the Tolem Dynasty so short? I see only three Sultans. Were they bad rulers?"

"The Plague wiped out all their heirs. It also killed seventy percent of the people living in the city. The Mefenkal ruled until my ancestor, Mured Ban the First, toppled the dynasty in a military coup." I poked a finger at the portrait of Mured, the only Ban facing forward. All the other Ban Sultans were painted in profile.

"Aunt Livia told me about your renowned perfect profiles." I felt Eva's eyes on me. She was suddenly scrutinizing every detail of my face. Once content, she whispered, "I'd like to tell you that you have a very beautiful nose; however, I fear it might make you blush again... oops, too late."

A mischievous smile curled Eva's lips. Making me blush had become one of her favorite things. Mine too, because it always involved some flattery. With her attentive nature and sharp mind, Eva had quickly discovered that I was unused to compliments, and that I didn't know how to react when given one. It was the surest way of making me blush. After much head scratching, I finally found some reply. "Your nose is prettier than mine."

She tapped a finger on her nose while wrinkling it. "Not really. It's too short. It lacks character. I wish my nose had a bump." She pushed her lips together and tried to look at her nose—which only made her cross-eyed. "Just a little one," she said, "to show strength." Then turning her focus back to the miniatures, she asked: "Why isn't the first Ban showing his perfect profile like all the others?"

I leaned against Eva until our cheeks touched. "He had a broken nose. It happened in a brawl."

Skipping over a series of stern-looking Viziers, we moved to the other walls and concentrated on portraits of beautiful women.

"Here's Aunt Livia!" Eva exclaimed.

The portrait had been painted the year of her arrival. Princess Livia looked like a girl, I thought. The hard edge that was now permanently etched on her features had not yet marked her. She appeared soft and kind... and almost hopeful in this painting.

"Who's that one, right in the center?" Eva touched an oblong gilded frame. I looked up at the dark-haired beauty in the frame. She seemed to stare straight through me with her sultry gaze.

"Çiçek, the present favorite. Her name means flower honey."

"She's gorgeous," Eva said.

I thought that *she* was the gorgeous one. Without the help of rouge, jewels, or fancy garments, Eva, in my eyes, outshined every woman in this room. I watched her move along the wall in her simple, white baker's outfit, with my eyes fixed on the slow movements of her hips. I smiled in awe.

"Amir, this one looks like Salima. Come see."

I kneeled in front of the small ivory miniature, set at the foot of the wall—indicating that although this woman was important enough to be in the hall, she was of lesser importance than the others. "You're right. She looks like a young Salima."

I picked up the miniature and turned it around. The woman's name had been scratched off.

"Is it Salima?" Eva asked, leaning over my shoulder.

"No, it's impossible. No concubine of the Sultan can be made a servant."

"Why? Aren't most harem women former slaves? Servants still have freedom; it's a higher status—and a better fate in my opinion."

I shook my head. "Some harem women may have started their lives as slaves, but once in the palace they're concubines of the ruler and therefore cannot be reduced to the servitude of others. They're to leave the palace rich and free. To make an imperial concubine a servant is a grave insult."

Eva squeezed my shoulder. "Aunt Livia would argue that between concubine and servant, the servant's position is the lesser insulting of the two."

I chuckled. "I am sure she would." I turned the portrait face up. "This woman might look like Salima, but it cannot be her. She is from Maberia though, just like Salima. That's probably why they look so alike."

"Amir…" Eva said, straightening up, "is your mother on these walls?"

I winced. After a moment of hesitation, I decided to tell her what little I knew about my mother. Eva listened attentively and without interrupting. Still, I could tell that she was confused by part of the story and hadn't yet grasped the rules of the harem. When I was done, she smiled emphatically at me. If she found my humble state off-putting, she was too considerate to show it. Instead she offered me some suggestions.

"Perhaps you should look into the registry. Aunt Livia told me that everything is noted there. You might be able to at least learn her name."

I shrugged. What for? It wouldn't change anything in my life. Regardless of what I thought, Eva's suggestion stayed in my mind and I found myself thinking that maybe I should look it up anyway.

* * *

Our next stop was the Divan Hall. Eva let herself fall on my father's cushion rugs with the most delightful disregard for the power it represented. It was a real pleasure to see—probably because it was so improper. To have a woman in the Divan Hall, sitting in the Sultan's designated place, was sacrilegious to say the least. For the average Telfarian man nothing could be worse. With this in mind, I gave Eva my warmest smile.

"So, this is where all is decided," she said, looking around.

I shrugged. "Small matters, I'm sure. Telfar is relatively quiet."

"You know, I'm amazed that a kingdom where every habitant is a potential slave isn't in more turmoil."

I thought that if I'd shown her Chop-Chop Square she might not be so amazed. Then again, Sorvinka was known for its thousand gibbets. Eva looked up at me from her seat in my father's cushions. She seemed oddly at ease there. Much more than I would be—if I dared sit there.

"Have you assisted at one of these meetings, Amir?"

I shook my head. "It's forbidden."

"Why? That's insane! My father's hall was always open to me and my sisters. We spent hours sitting at his feet listening to him render judgments and settle conflicts."

"Really!" I was shocked. "You were allowed there?"

She tilted her head. "Yes. In his war room, too, in his banquet hall, and in his council's chamber. I would see plays, hear minstrels, or converse with the brightest minds of our kingdom. Father welcomes new ideas and inventions. Oh, Amir, you would love being there." All joy abruptly vanished from her face. Hugging her knees, she added, "Father allowed me to see and learn everything his heir would have. He often said I would've made a great ruler. If *only* I had been a boy." She sighed.

I stared at her in disbelief, not at her father's words, but at another fact. "Your father, the great King of Sorvinka, has no sons… not one. I thought this was a false rumor, surely…"

Eva shook her head. "I know it's hard for you to understand, but Father has only one wife—my mother. He loves her very much you know. He might even be faithful to her. As far as I know he hasn't produced any illegitimate sons either—and even if he had, in Sorvinka bastards rarely ascend the throne." She shot me a hard glance. "Your father doesn't have this problem. He has so many sons they're killing one another."

I felt as though she had just slapped me in the face. My first impulse was to defend myself, insist that I was forced to fight, that the only choice I had was to kill or be killed, but I did nothing of the sort. Like her, I thought that what we were doing was wrong. So I changed the subject. "Could Erik be named as your father's heir instead?"

She laughed. "To be an heir one must carry the Orson name which comes through male lineage only, or have a Sorvinkian high title. Erik has neither; worse, he's a Ban. For my countrymen, he's the son of a foreign Sultan. They'll never accept him as their king."

"Who is the heir then?"

Eva grimaced. "My cousin Lars, a dull-witted imbecile, who keeps picking his nose whenever he thinks no one's watching. He's going to be a weak king." Her lips thinned. She was angry. Baring her teeth, she said, "This is unjust. I can rule as well as any man. I know everything one has to know—even the most elaborate military tactics. As for Lars he barely knows which side of his tunic is front." Eva punched one of the cushions surrounding her. Then her mouth turned downward in a bitter grimace I had never seen her display before. "But as a royal daughter my duty is to marry well and forge a bridge with our enemies. And until the law of my country is changed to allow women to rule, it's sadly all I can do." Her voice was muffled by frustration.

I wanted to say that this would never happen—that no woman could be king. But the look on her face kept me mute. At that very instant I knew that if I dared utter these words I would lose her forever. I knew she would hate me.

Hooking her fingers into the lattice screen separating the room, Eva rested her forehead against it and in a small voice begged, "Please, Amir, show me other things... beautiful, joyous things."

Next we visited the stables; Eva wanted to see beauty, and there were few creatures more beautiful than our horses. After, I showed her our elephants, with their broad foreheads painted with red motifs and their tusks encrusted with gold and gems. And before leaving the stables, we stopped to pet cheetahs and the imperial salukis, an ancient race of greyhound bred to hunt antelopes. Eva laughed as the dogs licked her face and hands while she ruffled their silky coats. I was overjoyed by her pleasure and let her pet the dogs as long as it was safe to do so. Then I led her to the White Tulip Garden. Under the moonlight, the tulips glowed like mother-of-pearl carvings, each one shimmering brighter than the next.

"Oh, Amir, it's magnificent," she sighed, sliding her arm under mine.

We strolled slowly among the tulips and halted in front of the pink marble kiosk at the back of the garden.

"It was built in honor of a woman named Alisha."

"Was she a favorite?"

"Yes, but the kiosk was built by her son, who would never have become Sultan without her help."

We climbed to the second story and stood on the small balcony where nearly a month earlier Erik and I had spent some time. With our faces turned to the cool desert wind, we stayed silent, enjoying the peacefulness of the night.

"Being here is harder than I've thought," Eva said in a hushed voice. "I miss so many things. Walking alone in a field, riding my horse at breakneck speed through small villages, dancing with my sisters through the halls of my father's castle—all things I will never do again. No wonder Aunty Livia is so bitter. I wish… I wish I could go home." She sighed. The shadow of a smile grazed her lips. "I know, I said that wishing was useless." She poked me with her elbow. "What is your greatest wish, Amir?"

"To be free," I answered without hesitation.

She chuckled, sadly. "We are both of royal blood, yet we have less freedom than peasants. A peasant girl can kiss whomever she wants without it being a crime."

My eyebrows rose. I looked at her. Part of her long scarf waved lazily in the breeze hindering my sight of her face. I gently pulled the scarf aside, exposing her lips and chin, and let my fingers glide over her cheek. She closed her eyes. I moved closer, circling her small waist. As I bent down, she rose on tiptoes, meeting me halfway. Our lips touched, hers soft and fresh, mine burning. Eva molded herself against me with total abandon. That took me aback. But at the same time it set fire to my entire body. I wished we could have kissed all night. Sadly, it came to a halt too quickly. When the shouts of the change of guards echoed, we pulled apart in common accord, knowing it was time to return to our respective prisons. We hurried out of the garden and soon we were back inside the palace, then the Cage.

"Take my hand," I said when we exited the first tunnel to cross a brightly lit corridor.

Eva stayed glued to my shoulder, her face well-hidden under several layers of scarf.

Just as we neared the cellar's entrance, Ibrahim and his troop of arrogant followers shot out of the kitchen, blocking our path. With reflexes honed by years of combat practice, I dodged a collision with him and struck the wall instead. Eva, on the other hand, bumped straight into Ibrahim, bounced back and landed on her butt.

I immediately threw myself on the ground beside her. Forehead on the icy tiles, I begged pardon for our clumsiness.

Still stunned, Eva was slower to react.

"You, get down!" Ibrahim barked, then went to kick her.

I moved in front of Eva, taking the blow in the ribs. This enraged Ibrahim.

"How dare you interfere with my punishing!" he boomed. Then I heard the distinctive *swoosh* sound of a sword being unsheathed.

Covering my face with my scarf, I looked up. Seven brothers were with Ibrahim, too many for me to beat—not to mention that I was unarmed. If I had been alone I would have attacked them anyway. But I couldn't risk Eva being discovered. If we were caught together, the consequences would be terrible for her. She would lose her reputation—perhaps more that that—perhaps her life. Only one option was left to me, I readied myself for the repulsive act I had to perform—begging for our lives, begging Ibrahim.

"What's this commotion about?" someone said at our back.

I glanced furtively over my shoulder. Darius, accompanied by five of his supporters, was coming our way. He looked down at Eva and me. Our eyes met. Darius's eyebrows rose in a quizzical manner. I quickly turned away.

"Are you to duel with bakers now?" Darius asked Ibrahim. Laughter followed.

"Mind your own business!" Ibrahim snapped.

"Everything happening in the Cage is my business, brother—especially the unsavory things that bring dishonor to our name."

Ibrahim stepped up; his foot almost crushed my hand.

"What are you insinuating?"

"I'm talking about poison, brother. It's a vile weapon and viler still are the ones who use it. And you, Ibrahim, are one of those vile individuals."

I blinked. Was Darius defending Erik? I thought he hated him.

"The next Sultan cannot be a user of poison," Darius said in a terribly reasonable voice. "I'm certain most will agree with me on this. So, Ibrahim… do you agree or disagree?"

I glanced at Ibrahim. He was bright red. He was also trapped. Darius had only given him two choices: a duel to clear his name or admit his fault and step out of the succession race. I couldn't believe Darius's boldness. I knew those two would eventually confront each other—it was inevitable—but I never imagined that it would be like this. I watched Ibrahim squeeze the grip of his saber; then I sought Darius and found him standing just beside Eva. He was much closer to us than I thought. I wished Eva and I could leave this dangerous spot. Knowing this was impossible, I looked back at Darius. The expression on his face was one of strained patience.

Folding his arms, Darius said, "So, what's your answer, I'm waiting."

To my utter amazement, Ibrahim turned around and left without saying a word.

Gasps rose from all my brothers. Then Darius's supporters cheered, while Ibrahim's just stood there in total shock. Suddenly realizing they were now without a leader, Ibrahim's supporters bowed to Darius. My brothers' loyalty was an inspiring thing to behold.

For my part, I still couldn't believe what had just happened. Ibrahim had been ousted. Darius had done it without any bloodshed, without a fight. He had used his wit and cunning—and it proved far more efficient than any open combat could ever be. Now, Ibrahim had absolutely no chance of ascending the throne—simply because cowards didn't make good Sultans. I had no doubt that in the space of an hour every detail of what had just happened would make its way through the palace, touching the Grand Vizier's ears, then my father's. Favorite or not, Ibrahim's name would then be scratched from his list.

Meanwhile Darius gracefully accepted congratulations from everyone present. "Can you please leave me for a moment," he demanded. "I want to speak with these bakers."

I screwed my face and waited for everyone to exit the area.

Darius nudged my side with the tip of his foot. "Stand up, we're alone."

I rose up and so did Eva. I was grateful that her costume left only her eyes visible because Darius's attention had shifted to her. While scrutinizing Eva very carefully, he moved closer to us. Staying put, Eva stared right back at him, which made Darius smile.

"Lovely eyes. I'm sure the rest of her also is." Turning to me, he said, "I'm assuming she's one of our brothers' favorites, otherwise you wouldn't be in disguises."

A wave of relief washed over me. I nodded.

"Indeed, dangerous game, my brother," Darius said, looking at Eva once more.

I cleared my throat. "You shouldn't talk after what you just did. By the way, how did you know Ibrahim wouldn't fight you?"

Darius smiled broadly; obviously he was happy that I had asked. Leaning close to me, he whispered. "Have you ever seen him fight?"

I shook my head.

Darius touched the tip of his nose. "Neither did I."

My jaw dropped.

"Exactly—Ibrahim makes others fight. He never does himself. I always suspected he was a coward. When he used poison on Keri, I was certain of it. You, on the other hand, are better with a sword than I thought. I was impressed. You could have killed Abdul much faster, though. You hesitated, and that almost cost you your life. I wouldn't do that again if I were you."

The hell if I needed him telling me what to do. He had some nerve. I began backing up, showing him that we needed to go.

"Wait!" He paused to moisten his lips. "I need a favor from you."

Argh! I closed my eyes and breathed deeply. Sure, no good deed comes without strings attached. "What do you want?" My tone was too sharp, I was a bit mad.

"To know more about Princess Eva."

At the mention of her name Eva's head tilted upward.

Darius suddenly looked embarrassed. "Now that I'm first in line, I'd like to know how she is. You spent time with her... actually talked with her. Surely you must know her character."

"She's very beautiful," I dryly stated.

Darius sighed in exasperation. "I'm sure she is. I want to know the quality of her mind. Is she quick or witty? Does she read? That's what interests me—pretty faces are common enough and can become boring after a while. However, a good mind, like a good blade, never dulls."

"Why are you so inclined to know this? Are you planning to fill your harem with brilliant-minded women?"

Darius's face became very serious. He shook his head. "I don't intend to have a harem at all."

My eyes widened, while Eva's darted on Darius. I hated the way she was drinking him in. Didn't she just kiss me? I stared at Darius. I wanted to stab him right in his pretty face, I was so insanely jealous. I cursed his good looks, tall stature and heroic nature. I wanted him dead and rotting. I forced myself to breathe, then to speak. "Darius, you're not serious, are you?"

"I won't have my sons caged; they won't live fearing from

one another as we do. I'll end this cruel practice. I'll break down the Cage, I swear. I'll change everything."

Seeing that spending more time with Darius would only make him look better, I arranged a meeting with him for the next day and left. Our return to Eva's tower went without incident. As I was about to leave for my own tower, she made me promise to come back the next night. Somehow, I thought her enthusiasm had more to do with Darius than with me. I said yes, regardless of what I thought.

I left, dreading my meeting with Darius the next day. I had always feared him, knowing he was intelligent and strong. But now I feared him for different reasons—reasons dear to my heart. No harem. No Cage. Change. Only one wife. Well, he didn't say that one, not exactly, but... Dammit! I should've spoken those words in front of Eva, not him. Damn, I hated myself more than I hated Darius.

CHAPTER NINETEEN

I returned to my tower and found Erik waiting for me in my sitting room. With the help of a tonic sent by the physician and Rami's constant care, he had recuperated very quickly.

"You're up," I said, closing the door.

Erik shook his head at me in a disapproving manner. "What are you doing, Amir? We've promised Father we'd help. Time is running out. You can't spend what little is left of it with my cousin. That's stupid."

"Lower your voice, little brother." I glared at Erik with undisguised anger. In my opinion, he wasn't one to make reprimands. "Shall I remind you that you've done more than your share of stupidities? Don't ever sermon me again."

A wounded expression flashed on Erik's face. Obviously, I had just touched a particularly sensitive area. But instead of being satisfied for having won my point, I felt guilt. Lowering my head, I sighed. "You don't know how it feels to love a woman who belongs to another."

"Maybe I do," Erik said in a small voice.

I snorted. "Stop this charade. You can't hide your preferences from me any longer—I don't care anyway."

Erik's eyebrows rose high on his forehead. He and Rami exchanged wide-eyed stares and shrugged. "What about our promise to Father?" Erik asked.

"I didn't promise him anything. And how are we to help him now, he took our work, our notes. It's all gone. "

Erik shrugged again. "Our notes were useless anyway. Maybe it's for the best that they're gone. Maybe we need to start over, look in different places, but we have to do it now. Things are speeding up. Amir, please stop your nonsense and help us."

I looked at Erik's red-rimmed eyes—although looking better, he was still weak from the poison. Sadly it had not diminished his stubbornness. "Go back to bed," I said, "We'll discuss it tomorrow."

"But—"

"No but," I snapped before disappearing in my bedroom.

* * *

The next morning I sneaked out of my tower while Erik was still asleep. I was determined to see Darius early and rid myself of the debt I owed him. The idea of sharing my knowledge of Eva's character, tastes and talents made me sick to my stomach. Yet I knew I couldn't escape this duty. When I neared Darius's door, I noted that it was cracked open. Instinctively my hand traveled to my rapier. Without a sound, I pulled the blade out and slowly pushed the door wider.

The muffled sound of a struggle touched my ears. I rushed in. Darius's sitting room was empty and undisturbed; the chessboard set on his low brass table, unmoved. The sound had stopped. I looked around unsure of what to do. There were two doors on either side of this room. Should I check inside, I wondered, or leave altogether? Just then the crash of glass breaking echoed from behind the left door. I dashed to the door and kicked it open. What I saw inside the room shocked me down to my core.

Two brothers were holding Darius down on his bed, while Ibrahim sat across his chest trying to make him drink some dark brew squirted out of a goat's bladder. No need questioning what this liquid was. Poison mixed with wine, I was certain of it. I knew that Ibrahim was vile, but this was a truly disgusting behavior. I focused my attention on Darius's face. He looked alert, and by the state of his bed linen, which were soaked and stained, Ibrahim didn't have much success in making him drink the mixture—so far.

Stunned by my sudden presence at the door, my devious brothers froze for a short instant.

Ibrahim was the first to snap out of it. He turned to his helpers, one of which I recognized as his youngest brother Khaled. "Don't stay there like idiots; Saïd, get him. Khaled, you stay with me."

I raised my rapier. Saïd abandoned his grip on Darius and grabbed his saber. Before he could pull the blade out, I lunged forward and slashed his hand. Shouting in pain, he backed away. Meanwhile Darius, having fewer opponents pinning him down, was breaking free of Ibrahim and Khaled's hold.

"Saïd, kill him, kill him now," Ibrahim ordered. Fear peaked through Ibrahim's voice. That pleased me. And I would have smiled, if I hadn't suddenly been struck by horror. Ibrahim had dropped the poison. He was now aiming a knife at Darius's chest.

A *katar!* The triangular knife was an assassin's weapon. Its unusual grip, in which one had to insert one's forearm through ladderlike rungs to wield it, prevented the loss of the weapon in combat; releasing one's hold on its grip only made the blade dangle from one's forearm.

I leapt onto the bed, swinging my rapier in an upward motion just as Ibrahim was stabbing downward. Our blades struck together. The sound echoed in the room, and threw a bright metallic spark in the air. Because he was hooked to his katar, the blow propelled Ibrahim backward. He rolled off the bed, temporarily vanishing from sight.

I looked at the two brothers still on the bed. Now freed of

Ibrahim's weight, Darius had swung around and seized Khaled around the neck. Both were now struggling madly amidst the bed sheet. Believing Darius able to fend for himself, I walked to the edge of the bed, seeking Ibrahim.

Ibrahim suddenly dashed from behind the bed and ran for the door. I went after him. He grabbed a bronze vase on the nearby table and chucked it at me. I ducked. But Saïd, who had been sneaking up on me, didn't. The vase struck his head. Knocked out, Saïd spilled to the floor.

"Arghh!" Ibrahim growled in frustration before sprinting out of the bedroom.

I gave chase until he disappeared down the corridor. Then I returned to Darius's bedroom to see him still choking a now blue-faced Khaled. Taping the tip of my blade under Darius's chin, I said, "Let him go."

"Why? He was ready to kill me. Given the chance he would've killed you too."

"Because we're better than they, are we not? To kill him now will only lower us to their level."

Darius blew air through tightly clenched teeth. His hands loosened around Khaled's neck and Khaled immediately began gulping air in deep loud gasps. Slowly the color of his face returned to normal.

Leaving Khaled, Darius rolled off the bed and onto his feet. "You realize that they'll only get three days of confinement in their bedrooms for this."

"They'll lose more than three days of freedom. They'll lose their names, ranks and status; that's enough for me." After a moment of reflection, Darius nodded. Apparently it was also enough for him.

Once Saïd had regained consciousness, we escorted him and Khaled to the Grand Vizier's chamber. In the Vizier's absence, it was Hassan who registered my brothers' offense and delivered their sanctions. Just as I had thought, both brothers were stripped of their silver belts. A search for Ibrahim's whereabouts was also ordered. As ringleader his punishment was to be harsher. He could expect months of confinement, if not years.

"Where are you going?" Darius asked, as we left the Vizier's rooms.

"None of your business, brother. As it stands, I no longer owe you anything. I saved your life, so we're on equal footing again."

Darius studied my features, as if he could read my thoughts by looking closely at my face. "She's mine—like it or not."

My blood boiled instantly. Perhaps the bastard could read me after all. I glared at him.

"No, she's not!" That was all I said before leaving him.

On my way to the cellar, I passed the kitchen. Thinking I'd recognized someone inside, I back-stepped to the entrance. It was Mir. He was busy filling a plate with all kinds of pastry. I knew Mir didn't like sweets, but this early in the day nothing else was available in the kitchen. By the way he slapped cakes and hazelnut rolls onto his plate, Mir seemed rather unhappy with his lot. I felt a surge of guilt. To leave Erik and his boys in charge of Mir's food was wrong. I was the only person he trusted not to poison him. My neglect had forced him out of his hiding. This wasn't good for his nerves in normal circumstances—there was nothing normal about the Cage's atmosphere lately. Fortunately, Jafer didn't mind Rami's presence. It still didn't ease my guilt though.

Promising to pay more care to my ill brothers in the future, I continued on my way to the cellar. I entered the dark secret tunnel without a lamp; I didn't need one anymore. I had grown accustomed to the darkness. Also I had traveled the tunnel leading to Eva's tower so often by now that I could've found my way there with closed eyes if I had to. Tiptoeing to the storage room's door, I scratched on it three times. Then with a stomach filled with butterflies and a silly smile on my face, I waited for

Eva to open the door.

When it finally opened, my heart almost leapt out of my chest. My silly smile turned into a grimace. It wasn't Eva in the doorframe, but Oroco's imposing black body.

"He's here, as expected," Oroco said, glaring at me.

"Bring him in," a female voice demanded.

Moving to the side, Oroco waved me in.

Seeing no other option and still in shock, I stepped inside the room.

Dressed in a simple blue satin gown, Princess Livia stood beside the velvet bench. She was as straight as the prisoners' black tower and looked just as menacing. My eyes traveled to the bench where Eva was slumped. Raising a sorrowful face from the cradle of her hand, Eva looked at me with teary eyes.

I gave her a reassuring smile—well I hoped it was. Maybe I just managed a sneer, I couldn't tell. My face was numb—I was numb all over. My brain however was churning at high speed. *Erik, bastard! You betrayed me.* He was the guilty one. I was certain of it. I swore to take revenge. Oh yes, Erik would pay for this.

Princess Livia wagged a finger at me. "Prince Amir, I welcomed you into my family, introduced you to friends and relatives, and this is how you repay my kindness—by putting my niece's reputation and life in jeopardy? I'm sorely disappointed. However, I must admit that my niece's behavior isn't without reproach."

"Princess Livia," I said, bowing as low as I could. "I'm totally at fault. Princess Eva has nothing to do with it. Let me assure you, her virtue is intact."

Princess Livia's right eyebrow rose. She shot a glance at Oroco, then with a snort said, "Don't lie to me, young man. I know my own blood. Eva's as guilty as you are. It's fortunate that we were informed of your escapades before you engaged in improper conduct." Princess Livia's voice had risen steadily with each word spoken. Oroco approached her, and with a peculiar gentleness placed a hand on her shoulder. She instantly relaxed. When she spoke again, her voice was back to normal.

"Fortunately for you, I cannot disclose this incident and have you punished as you deserve, without endangering my niece. So I'll have to take another course of action."

Oh, that made me very nervous.

Princess Livia crossed her arms. "To ensure that neither of you will see each other again, Oroco and I will stay here with my niece until she weds."

Eva rose up. "No, you can't. Please, Aunt Livia."

"Sit down, child!"

Eva stomped her foot. "NO! And I'm not a child. I am the future Sultan's first wife. My title is higher than yours. You cannot order me around."

"AH!" Livia let out a throaty laugh. "Your title! You don't have it yet. Right now you are nothing but an imprudent princess who is on the verge of losing her pretty head. What you have done this last week can cost you your life."

Eva paled. Then her chin rose, as it always did when she was gathering her courage. "I have done nothing wrong, and neither has Amir. You have no right—"

"SILENCE!"

I stepped up. "Don't speak to her in that tone."

Princess Livia turned calculating eyes to me. Somehow I thought that I had reacted exactly as she wished. "Young man," she said with a hard smile. "You have absolutely no right to her—not even to protect her. She belongs to the next Sultan, this you cannot change." Crossing the distance separating us, she leaned to my ear and whispered, "However, the line of succession can be changed. It already has changed once, yesterday. I was informed that the Sultan's chosen heir has fallen into disgrace and that the new heir is some motherless rogue named Darius." She paused, as if to give me time to prepare myself for what was coming, as if I hadn't guessed yet. "You can change it again. Look at Eva."

I obeyed. Eva looked at me then at her aunt. For the first time since I had met her, Eva looked scared. But when she spoke it was anger that filled her voice. "Aunt, I hate you."

Princess Livia rolled her eyes then turned her attention to me. "Eva's fate is in your hands, Prince Amir. You know what to do." She straightened. "One last word of advice, hurry up. Your father is gravely ill. Rumors say he has only a few days left."

I ran all the way to my tower, and when I grabbed its door-knob I was still shaking with outrage. Princess Livia wanted me to kill Darius so Erik would become Sultan. Now everything made sense: they both had used me right from the very beginning. I was so furious, I could've killed someone. And for once it wasn't Darius I wanted dead. It was Erik. But I knew better than to rush in my room and confront Erik in this state.

Resting my forehead on the cold wood of the door, I began filling my lungs in deep, long breaths. Soon the racing of my heart, which had been drumming in my ears, dissipated. I was now aware of another sound—mumbling: Mir talking to him-self—no doubt. *He's right not to trust anyone. He was right about Erik too. Damn, why didn't I listen to him?* Well, now I knew the truth. Things were going to change. I went in.

Erik and Rami were deep in the study of my books. This too, I thought, was suspicious.

"Get out!" I ordered. "Both of you—OUT!"

Erik looked at me, mouth open, while Rami, as usual, avoided direct eye contact. I hated that sneaky creature's refusal to look me in the eyes more than ever.

Erik stood up. "What's happening with you? Your face is all red."

"Shut up and leave!"

Erik flinched. He looked genuinely surprised. He was quite the actor, I thought. It wasn't really surprising. Erik liked dress-ing up and role-playing, he told me himself.

"Don't play innocent. You've betrayed me. Our meeting,

the gift, the invitation to meet your mother, that was all part of your plan, wasn't it?"

"I don't understand what you're talking about."

"Yes, you do! I can understand that you have ambition, but to use Eva as a pawn, that's…" I shut my eyes and grimaced. Although it pained me to part with it, I pulled the locket from my pocket and flung it in Erik's face.

He frowned. "My locket! I thought I'd lost it in the dark tunnels."

"Liar! You knew I had it. You turned my room upside down to get it back."

"I never did such a thing."

"Mir saw you, so stop denying it. You're a liar, Erik, and if you don't leave my room now, I'll tell the Vizier about your thieving friend." I poked my chin toward Rami.

Erik turned dead white. Dragging Rami along, he exited the room, slamming the door hard behind him.

I suddenly felt weak, as though part of my strength had left with Erik. I let myself fall on the bench by the window. For long minutes I raked my brain for some means of revenge. Nothing came. Lying and duping one's brother was not a crime in the Cage, it was a way of life, a way of survival. There was nothing I could do about it besides demand reparation through combat. I doubt Eva would view my killing her dear cousin in a good light. As for Erik and his mother's possible implication in my father's illness and my brothers' deaths, I still needed to think things over before making a formal accusation.

Tomorrow—tomorrow your head will be clear then you'll know what to do.

* * *

Later that evening, a violent episode of delirium and vision struck Jafer. I found myself having to cradle him in my arms for hours while he called out for our father's stolen gift. Never before had one of his episodes lasted this long.

"The dark cloud," Jafer suddenly said. "They're his—his to obey. The alliance... the unholy alliance... with... with the black one. They're bound to each other."

I frowned. "What kind of alliance?"

"One that defies nature... one that cannot be undone. But he has a weakness—he thinks he's someone else."

"What?" This was confusing. "Who is he? What's his name?"

Jafer looked at me, really looked at me.

"What's going on, what did he say?" Mir asked from Jafer's opened door.

I should have closed it, I thought, my mistake "Shh," I made.

"Ah, I knew it. You're both plotting against me."

I rolled my eyes. "Please, Mir, Jafer is trying to say something, something important. Go on, Jafer, tell me his name." One glance at Jafer and I knew that he wouldn't say another word. His stare was vacant, Jafer's mind was gone. I was holding on to his empty shell. I reckoned that this was the worst day of my life.

Later, I dragged Jafer's limp body to his bed, where I rocked him for hours with Mir's obsessive mumbling playing in the background. Finally, Jafer fell asleep from exhaustion. Not long after, so did I.

I dreamed that dark shadows were seeping out of the mausoleum. They moved through the palace's many yards, killing everything in their passage. When they floated over the White Tulip Garden, the flowers turned black and rotted. I began shivering in my sleep. My teeth chattered painfully. Then the sound of bells, like the ones worn by dancers, rang softly in my ears.

"DEMON, AWAY DEMON," someone screamed at the top of his lungs.

I sat right up in my bed, believing a pairikas in the room. I looked around and was lost for a moment. This wasn't my room, nor was I in my bed. I was still in Jafer's room, on his couch with a thin blanket crumpled around my body. I heard a shuffling behind me.

Turning, I saw that Jafer was out of bed and looking around with a slight dazed expression.

"They're everywhere now," he breathed.

"Who?"

"The dark clouds. They'll kill us all, you know."

Ignoring Jafer's ramblings, I listened for other sounds and found none. All was calm, this was only a nightmare—apparently one Jafer and I had shared. Then a breeze blew through the room, raising goose bumps on my skin. I didn't remember having left the window open.

Tossing the blanket aside, I went to close it. I grabbed the window latch and froze. There was that bell sound again. It came from outside the tower. I leaned over the windowsill and peered down.

A pairikas stared right back at me with glowing red eyes. My knees weakened. The she-demon was only a few paces under the window, hooked to the stone wall of the tower with its talonlike nails and the rough scales of her serpent's lower-body. Lifted by the breeze, the airy magenta fabric of its dancer's costume waved in the air, rendering this vision the more surreal. The creature emitted a low throaty growl then slithered down the tower in a flurry of flapping fabric and bell ringing.

In a hurry, I locked the window from the inside.

"I knew it was coming," Jafer said. "I heard the bells and knew it was there. I chased it away."

"You did well," I said. Obviously, crazy men couldn't be seduced by pairikas. A chance, otherwise we both would be dead. A weight settled on my shoulders. The she-demon had come for me, I was sure of it, yet I refused to speculate on who had sent it.

You know who did, a nagging voice whispered in my ears. *Stop deluding yourself, he's guilty. Erik's the one behind this.*

CHAPTER TWENTY

E ven though I'd barricaded Jafer's window, I didn't feel
safe. Perhaps it was Jafer's attitude that made me feel
so insecure. He watched me work with a defeated look
on his face, as if this was all for nothing, as if our fates were
already sealed. Sure made me wonder if he knew something
I didn't. I hated thinking this way, it was not rational. Yet
nothing was anymore.

"Where's our brother?" Jafer abruptly asked.

"Which one?"

"The one who cares about us."

I squeezed the hammer's handle. "We're not speaking anymore. He lied to me."

"Yes, small lies," Jafer said in a light tone. "Nothing meant
to harm."

"Is there something you're not telling me, Jafer? Something
I should know."

He shook his head. "Nothing I can clearly remember."

I watched Jafer make a series of faces as he tried to find
words or put orders into his mind, either way it looked extremely painful. Despite his best effort, Jafer failed to recall
anything useful and remained silent from then on.

Once I had finished blocking Jafer's windows, I thought
I should try convincing Mir to let me do his. I crossed the

corridor and knocked at his door.

A clank of toppled copper vessels echoed from inside Mir's room followed by footsteps running toward the door. Seconds later, I heard the clink of the door being locked from the inside. I frowned; my brother was the last person who would forget to lock his door.

"Mir?" Silence.

Then I heard the ringing of brass bells. The hair at the back my neck stood up. My heartbeat sped up. I gripped my sword. "Mir, it's me, Amir."

Behind the door, someone exhaled loudly. Then Mir's face popped at the door's grid.

Relief washed over me. "Can I come in?"

Mir shot one glance at my hand, which still gripped my sword, and hissed. "You're just like the others. You'd kill me if you could. I'm warning you. Try entering my rooms and you'll be the first to die. Don't think I won't hear you, I will. I set bells on strings all around my rooms. No one can enter without tripping them." To prove his point, Mir shook a string of bells in front of the grid. "See! See!"

"Mir, you know I mean you no harm. I j—"

"Enough! You plot—you plot like all the others. I heard them speak in the Great Hall, they're planning an attack."

Before I could question him, Mir slammed his grid shut. Usually, I paid no mind to Mir's obsessive fear of plots, but this time I thought that he might be telling the truth and that his fear might be well founded.

I went to my rooms and boarded my own windows, then sat down at my desk. The books Erik and Rami had been studying were still there, opened at the last pages they'd studied. I cast my eyes on the volume Rami had been sifting through. Something on the corner of the left page caught my attention: a stain… no, a blotch of something.

"That boy and his dirty fingers." I leaned closer.

The blotch was light beige and had a crusty texture; a bit

of green stuff was stuck in it, too. By the look of it, I deduced that something had been smeared on this page with a thumb. I brought my nose to the blotch. A sour smell wafted from it—a familiar smell. Where had I smelled it before? At a loss, I stared at the book's title. This was my library inventory book. I looked at the information written on that stained page. I was more lost then ever. That page listed all my esoteric material. Why would Rami study this list? What was the boy looking for?

I scanned the many volumes piled on the desk. Those were the books listed on this page. I did a quick count. One book was missing. I moved my inventory book aside; under it I found Rami's notes. I brought the small square piece of vellum to my eyes. The boy's writing was graceful and flourished. For a moment its elegance occupied my entire attention. This wasn't the handwriting of a servant; besides scribes, only nobles and princes wrote this well. Then I focused on the words Rami had written: *Chronicles of the Blue Mage*—it was the missing book's title.

* * *

Later that day, I went down to the Great Hall. Upon entering the hall I was struck by its unpleasant atmosphere. A suffocating tension filled the air. Too many brothers were assembled in this room. Fear was visible on most of their faces, and for once it wasn't the fear of one another. I didn't like this at all.

"The full moon is only a few days away," someone declared. "We all know what this means."

A roar of acknowledgement rose from the princely mob.

"We have to do something," someone shouted above the growing noise.

"Let's escape!" another declared.

"No!" came from the back. "We can't escape a curse. We need to find its source."

A heavy silence followed. Then a brother said: "We all know

what we need to do. We've talked about it already. If we plan it well, we can succeed."

"Yes, let's do it!" was repeated throughout the hall.

Get out of here, my instinct ordered. As I turned, I noted Darius staring at me from across the room. His face was all furrowed; I'd never seen him this anxious before. Mir was right, my brothers were planning something, but what—surely not an attack like he had said. They couldn't be this stupid. I stared at the overexcited mob while backing away.

From the corner of my eye, I saw Erik coming toward me with a face paler than usual. My lips thinned; he was the last person I wanted to see.

"We need to talk," he said.

I grimaced. My throat was too tight to let out words.

"Please, it's important."

"We have nothing to say to each other," I managed to blurt out, and walked away, leaving a desolate-looking Erik behind. Once back in my room, I locked myself in.

Dark, desperate thoughts harassed me all day—so I spent most of it brooding in a corner. The night that followed was not any better: Sleepless and full of fear for my brothers and myself, I paced my room until the first ray of sunshine slipped through the cracks on my boarded window. Determined not to sacrifice another day to dark thoughts (or by hiding like a petrified mouse), I exited my rooms and went downstairs to gather news.

This morning, I found that the tension in the Cage had increased to the point of being palpable. Terror had replaced fear on my brothers' faces. Some were even shaking. When Darius entered the sitting room, I decided to talk to him. Perhaps he knew what had brought this on.

"Terrible isn't it," he said.

I frowned.

"What! You don't know?"

I shook my head. My mouth was suddenly dry.

"Two brothers died last night."

"A duel?" I asked. It wasn't the full moon yet.

Darius made a sour face. "If only it were true. They were mauled to death by some demonic creature." He grimaced. "I saw their remains, Amir. It was horrible. Their necks and chests were all torn up. What bothers me the most is that their rooms were in perfect order, their beds hardly crumpled. Those two didn't fight back. They just lay there as if welcoming death." Darius gripped his temples, as though his head was suddenly too heavy. "It makes no sense. What evil trickery is behind this?"

I knew the trick involved. Pairikas' charm was the trick; they had done this. I looked at the brothers assembled in the room. "That's why they're so scared."

"Yes, they're scared to the point of speaking foolishly and behaving even worse."

My curiosity was aroused. "What do you mean?"

For a moment Darius looked unsure if he should continue. After hesitating, he scanned our surroundings then said. "I've been advised to stay in my room this evening."

"Advised by whom?"

"The Grand Vizier. I suggest that you do the same, Amir. No matter what you hear tonight, stay locked in your rooms. Don't go out—not even for a peek. That's my advice to you." Without another word, Darius left.

I took Darius's advice to heart and returned to my tower. On the way there I noted that the quantity of guards patrolling the Cage had tripled. The glare of suspicion they shot me as I walked past them sent chills down my spine. I was relieved when my door came into sight. But before locking myself in, I stopped at Mir's door. I might as well warn him too.

I knocked gently. "Mir, you were right. Something's brewing."

"Yes," he said, surprising me. I didn't believe him to be so close to the door. "It's bad downstairs, very, very bad. I don't like it at all."

"Stay in your room and everything will be fine. I won't move either."

"Yes, yes, yes. Stay hidden, that's good, that's safe." Mir's voice lowered to his habitual mumbling.

Next I went to check on Jafer, even though I knew he couldn't leave his room. I discovered him seated on his couch, gazing in empty air, prisoner of a catatonic state. Touching his shoulder lightly, I tried to bring some reaction out of him.

Jafer's head slowly rose toward me. His mouth opened. A thick strand of drool escaped from its corner. "The Slayer—find the Slayer," he breathed before returning to his previous position.

I wrapped a blanket around his shoulders and left. There wasn't much else I could do for him anyway. As for Erik, I debated if I should warn him too, but only for a second. His mother probably already did.

"I'm sure she knows what's going to happen, if she hasn't fomented it herself." I still had not digested her suggestion that I should dispose of Darius. It burned in the pit of my stomach like a red piece of coal.

I returned to my room and threw myself in the study of Erik and Rami's notes. Most of their annotations concerned the control of jinn, efreet and pairikas. Rami's were especially well-ordered. The boy's elegant handwriting and beautifully turned sentences made reading easy and pleasant. Jinn, Rami had written, could be linked to objects and were gaseous creatures able to take any form. They were mostly good by nature, but in the wrong hands jinn could be used to do harm. Made of smoke, efreet were far more dangerous and harder to control than jinn. They were also extremely powerful. Efreet could even command lower-demons, or easily summon wandering spirits and old ghosts of an area, forcing them to do its bidding—so to control an efreet was to control a dark army.

Efreet and jinn had one thing in common though, they both craved sugar. I went on reading until my eyes started to close and my chin dropped on my chest.

I was awakened by the gentle ruffling sound of muslin. A bit dazed, I glanced about the room, seeking the origin of the sound. I was shocked to see Eva standing a few steps from my chair. She wore the coral dress she had on the day we first met. It was its many layers of shifting fabric that had pulled me from my sleep.

"How did you find your way here?" I asked, standing up. I was painfully aware of my state of disarray—disheveled and wrinkled didn't begin to describe my appearance.

Putting a finger to her lips, Eva made, "Shh." Smiling, she then opened her arms.

"I've missed you too," I whispered.

As I took a first step toward her hug, a shadow brandishing one of my swords popped up behind Eva.

"NO!" I shouted.

Eva turned around just as the shadow swung the blade. Three things happened at the same time: the room became icy cold, the light dimmed and a deep blood-curling growl resonated.

Without thinking, I dove in front of Eva and grappled the shadow's arm before it could finish its move. I was shocked by how easily I blocked the blow. This creature wasn't very strong. I pulled it near my desk, so the lights of my candles could bathe it. I gasped. This was Rami, twisting in my grip.

"Amir, don't hurt him." I recognized Erik's voice.

Peeking left, I watched him come out of a dark corner of my library as if he had walked straight out of the bookshelves. How had they gotten in? The burning sensation in the pit of my stomach intensified to the point of becoming molten lava. Rage swallowed me. "Why should I spare him, Erik. Not only is this boy a thief but he's also a murderer. Without my intervention, he would've killed Eva."

"Let me go," Rami ordered in his girlish voice. "Let me kill her." By contorting his slim body, the boy almost slipped out of my grip. Rami might not have been strong but he sure made up for this shortcoming with agility. Holding on to him was like holding on to an eel. I was determined not to let him escape and managed to keep a good grip on him.

From the corner of my eye, I saw Erik moving toward me. I needed a weapon. I tried disarming Rami.

The boy spun around with the speed of a feral fox and bit my wrist.

"Ahg," I hissed, and circled Rami's chest with both arms. Right away, I realized something was wrong with this boy. But then Erik was on me and I had no time left to think. Seizing Rami's weapon-holding hand, I aimed the boy's blade at Erik. Its tip pierced his kaftan, ripping its front.

"STOP!" Rami shouted. "Amir, stop! Look at her. It's not Eva."

"Shut up, snake. This is…" the rest of my words died in my throat.

Eva was gone—standing in her place was a tall, dark creature with broad batlike wings sticking out of its back. Totally naked and exquisitely beautiful in a confusing kind of way, this creature was neither male nor female but rather a mix of both. Its skin was black, not the black of Oroco's, which in fact was dark brown although called black. No, this skin was a matte-black so deep that it seemed to drink the ambient light.

Turning bright yellow eyes toward me, the creature smiled amicably, as if this was a game it had been playing with me and that I shouldn't be mad at it. And for a second, I wasn't. Damn, I'd almost smiled back at the thing.

Rami broke free from my grip. And while Erik and I stood frozen in place like statues, the boy pounced on the creature, his sword swiping left and right. The blade sliced through the dark demon repetitively, sending puffs of smoke and a sulfuric smell in the air instead of blood. Rami went on slashing nonetheless. The boy swung so hard he almost fell down, only catching himself at the very last moment on the backrest of a chair.

His turban and scarf, however, pursued their trips to the floor revealing silky black hair grazing Rami's shoulders in a pageboy cut. Once his balance returned, the boy went on fighting the demon for another minute. Then, out of breath, Rami retreated to Erik's side.

The creature threw its head back and burst into laughter.

I plugged my ears; this was the most disturbing sound I'd ever heard: It was metallic, as though big chains were being rattled at the bottom of this creature's throat.

Then in the blink of an eye the creature turned into a puff of smoke, which slipped under my door. Only then did I realize that I could move again, that I had been paralyzed and almost completely under this demon's control. By the look on Erik's face so had he.

I rushed out the door, even though I knew it was useless—one couldn't capture smoke. Sure enough, the corridor was empty. So after having verified that Jafer and Mir were safe, I returned to my rooms.

Erik and Rami were still there waiting for me.

"What was that thing?" Erik asked.

"I'll guess an efreet."

"Why didn't it kill us when it had the chance?"

A good question. The creature had not struck once, not even to defend itself, although Rami's effort to kill it proved quite useless.

"The more I think about it the less I believe it was here to kill me," I said.

"Why then?"

"I don't know. Perhaps it was looking for something?"

"In my opinion, the demon was looking to trick you into giving him information—then kill you," a small yet firm voice declared.

I cast my eyes on Rami, who was carefully keeping his back to me. I noticed that his turban was back on his head. *No, not "his" or "him,"* I corrected myself. This wasn't a boy. Boys didn't have breasts. And I had definitely felt breasts wrapped under some kind of binding when I had gripped him... er, her, gripped her. "Who's she, Erik, another one of your lies? What are you both doing in my room by the way?"

To my utter surprise, Rami walked strait to me and slapped me across the face. "That's for calling me a thief and a snake."

Quickly scooping her up, Erik pulled Rami away from me. I was certain that if he had not, she would have struck me again.

"Please don't be mad," Erik pleaded.

"Don't apologize to him," Rami ordered. "We just saved his life. He should be apologizing to us."

Cradling my stinging cheek, I watched the girl struggling in Erik's arms. She sure had spirit. Now that I looked at her, I couldn't believe she'd fooled me into thinking she was a boy. Her facial features were far too delicate to be masculine—no wonder she kept her head low or half-hidden under a scarf—her wrists and ankles too gracile. She'd done it though; she fooled me and the entire palace to this day. "Who's she?" I asked again.

"Her name is Mira." Erik grinned. "Mira—Rami, I rearranged the letters into a different name, like Mother did with mine." He paused and looked down at his feet. "You know we're not supposed to form permanent bonds; I had to keep her identity secret. With shorter hair and loose clothing, I thought she could be mistaken for a boy. She's tiny." Erik ran a hand through her pageboy haircut. "I sorely miss her long locks, though. Her hair used to fall down to the small of her back. I made quite a mess when I cut it."

"It's just hair, it grows back," she said.

"Mira's right, that's not important," I said. "How long have you been together?"

Erik shot me a stern look. "That's not important either. And please, keep calling her Rami. It's safer; we can't afford a name mix-up in public."

I nodded, looking at the pair. My conversation with Ambassador Molsky floated back to the top of my mind. I remembered telling him that the women of our harem were changed every few months to prevent bonds forming. *Bonds form quickly*, Ambassador Molsky had then replied. He was right. Myself, I had fallen in love with Eva in the blink of an eye. "You stole her before the rotation took place."

Erik chewed the inside of his cheek. "Yes, I stole her."

A light dawned in my head. "That's why the pairikas couldn't seduce her in the mausoleum. Because she's a girl."

"Yes! I was so scared you'd figure it out then. Or that night when I left the room we shared to go see her. When you asked me where I went, I panicked and lied... I hope you're not too mad at me for this. You can't blame me for preferring spending the night with her than with you." Erik's grin had returned. He looked relieved, as if a heavy burden had been unloaded from his shoulders. He was rejoicing a bit too soon for my taste; I wasn't done questioning him.

Folding my arms on my chest, I asked, "You still haven't told me how you entered my room."

Erik gave me a sheepish look. Then he walked to the bookshelves. "There's an opening leading to the underground tunnel between these two shelves. That's the reason I wanted to talk to you today. If I wanted to ransack your room, I would've used this passage, not walk down your corridor. Mir must have seen someone else. And that person wasn't looking for a locket either."

"I know. I'm missing a book."

"Oh, then we can start looking..."

I raised a hand stopping him in mid-speech. "Erik, first I need to know something. Did you tell your mother about my meeting with Eva?"

"NO! I know how you feel about Eva, and more so about not being allowed to love her." Erik wrapped an arm around Rami's shoulders. "I told you that I understood your position. Someone else must've told her—a servant, a cook or a valet. Someone definitively recognized you or Eva when you went out of the Cage."

The image of the wrapped-up woman, a dancer probably, we'd bumped into popped up in my mind. I recalled her reaction at hearing Eva's language. The more I thought of it the more I believed that this woman had recognized Eva. I couldn't link the dancer to Erik's mother though. However, I could link other things to his mother—dreadful things.

"Why the long face?" Erik asked.

"What if we discover that your mother is underneath our brothers' deaths… Are you ready to deal with this?"

"What are you insinuating?" Rami said, with her fists firmly planted on her hips. "Princess Livia knows nothing of magic."

"She knows a lot about scheming," I replied. "She's using Eva to manipulate me, to force my hand." I closed my eyes hard and breathed deeply. "Your mother wants me to eliminate Darius so you can become Sultan."

"You're wrong," Erik said. "Mother would never…"

"Come on, Erik. She raised you to govern; you were educated for that explicit purpose."

"So were you."

I shook my head. "My upbringing is far different than yours." I sighed. "Fine! Your mother didn't openly say the words *kill him*, but she made her wish very clear to me. She asked that I change the line of succession."

Erik sat down on the floor. He looked extremely rattled, distraught even. In view of his reaction, I decided to skip the fact that I had also heard his mother wish for our father's speedy death. The way things were going, Erik would figure it out by himself quickly enough. After a long period of silence Erik announced that whatever truth we would discover, he would accept it and behave accordingly. This settled we agreed to work together again. He informed me that Father was dying and I told him of Darius's advice.

"It's our brothers," Erik whispered. "Rami heard them talking about revolting a few days ago."

"So has Mir," I said. "But something has changed this morning. There is something far worse than revolt in the air."

"Yes, I can sense it too."

* * *

The next hours were spent inventorying my entire library. In all, I was missing four books. The two on magic didn't surprise me, but the two volumes of ancient tales and myths sure did. What would one need old tales for? Rami argued that there might be some truth in them—some lost bit of knowledge. I found it hard to swallow at first, then the picture of the dark creature imposed itself in my mind, as if to tell me that I needed to keep an open mind, to refuse seeing the obvious might cause our loss.

"I wish we had copies of these books," Rami said.

An idea emerged in my head. "Maybe we do. Erik, do you have a list of the damaged books in your hideout."

He grinned from ear to ear. "Yes!"

We were about to leave when a long wail pierced the air. I immediately recognized this lament as Jafer's and rushed to his door with Erik and Rami on my tail. I burst into my brother's somber room and nearly stepped on him.

Convulsing violently, Jafer lay on the rug near the door.

Knowing nothing could stop these spasms, I did what I could to help. I turned Jafer on his side and checked that his tongue was not in his throat. Today his convulsions were over quickly enough and Jafer opened his eyes. I thought that for once he looked lucid. His eyes roamed our faces for a moment, and then he smiled. There was such relief in his expression, as if some wrong had been righted. With Erik's help, I carried Jafer to his couch. While Rami placed cushions under his head, Jafer took her hand and pulled her into a hug. He whispered briefly in her ear, and then let her go.

"Yes, I'll do that," Rami told him.

Joy illuminated Jafer's face, it was as if he had accomplished the mission he'd been set upon. Letting himself fall on the cushions, he said, "Now stay together. Always stay together." Exhausted, he fell asleep moments later.

As we left Jafer's room, I noted Mir's worried face glued to his grid.

"How is he?" he asked.

"Better, much better. I think that by tomorrow he's going to be well again."

A wave of sadness washed over Mir's eyes. "You really think so?"

"I'm sure of it."

Mir sighed heavily and closed his grid.

I doubted that Mir believed me, but at least he had not spat on Erik. We returned to my room. Once there Erik showed me how one of my bookshelves could be pivoted to the left, exposing the passage behind it. Knowing that little time remained before nightfall, we quickly entered the dark tunnel and ran in the direction of Erik's hideout.

CHAPTER TWENTY-ONE

Tonight, there was a foul smell floating in the tunnels. It lingered in the air like a bad omen. Not daring to light a lamp, we stumbled along rough stone paths in almost complete darkness. Fortunately Erik, who led our column, had good night-vision and an excellent memory of the direction we were to take.

Last in our line, I trotted with my hands gripping Rami/Mira's tunic. I still had a hard time getting used to Rami being a girl. I was also a bit envious of Erik's relationship with her, mainly of the fact that they could go everywhere together, like Eva and I had done that night. I wondered how long those two had been together. A year perhaps. Yes, for some reason, a year sounded about right.

Erik abruptly halted and I slammed into Rami's back.

"OUFF," she let out as she was crushed between us.

"Someone's ahead," Erik whispered.

We flattened ourselves against the tunnel's wall. Within seconds, the cold wetness of its stones pierced my skin. I began shivering. The glow of a lamp appeared down the tunnel. It moved toward us, illuminating the path ahead. There was a junction there. I could now see the dark mouth of the connecting tunnel. Seconds later, the lamp-carrying silhouette disappeared through it.

"Where does that tunnel lead?" I asked.

"Don't know," Erik replied.

We continued on our way and soon reached the architect's office marking the entrance of Erik's hideout. The damaged book inventory list was scribbled in a thick volume. I was shocked to see that it took nearly half its pages. There were far more books in this room than I had previously thought. With Rami's help—the girl proved an efficient scribe—copies of three of my four missing books were quickly located in the inventory: the tales and mythologies books and the guide of magical usage of plants. As for my incantation manual, it seemed to have been a unique and precious volume. However, finding the three books amidst the multitude stacked in the back room took quite a bit of time. And to access the last one, piled all the way up the wall, Erik and I had to make a ladder of our bodies for Rami to climb on.

Standing on my shoulders, she stretched as much as she could while I held on to her calves. "Almost have it. I can touch its spine with my fingertips."

"Amir, rise on tiptoe," said Erik, who was on all fours under me.

"Hold on to something, Rami" I warned before rising to the tip of my feet. Holding my breath, I tried to maintain balance. After a long minute, the muscles of my calves started burning. Then my knees began knocking. I looked up at Rami. She was almost there. I pushed up a bit more and watched her hand close on the spine of an old brown volume.

"Got it," she said.

I fell back on my heels, then gently lowered myself down so Rami could hop off my shoulders and I from Erik's back.

He rose with a grimace and some bone cracking sound. "That's going to hurt tomorrow."

"Then you'll complain tomorrow," Rami told him, which made me chuckle.

Grabbing the precious books, we returned to the tunnel. As soon as we reached the first Cage's crossing we knew we were in trouble. The corridor was buzzing with activity. Guards were everywhere. And sounds of fighting echoed from downstairs.

Stuck in a linen closet, we watched the guards through the holes of the latticed door. We dared not go back into the tunnel for fear of making too much noise.

A guard stepped in front of the latticed door and bowed. He wore the red and gold uniform of the palace. His turban, I noticed, was adorned with a white feather, the indication of a commander's rank. The commander straightened. "Grand Vizier, this section of the Cage has been expunged and all its rebellious princes captured."

Nazir's black-robed figure moved into view. "What of the other sectors?"

"There's still fighting on the lower level. It'll be under our control within the hour."

"And the gate to the Sultan's apartments?"

"It's intact, Grand Vizier. We stopped the attack before the princes could reach it and bring about their plan of murdering the Sultan. This group is already filling our holding cells."

The Vizier crossed his long-fingered hands under his nose. "The others will join them soon." Satisfaction laded his voice. My dislike for this man grew tenfold.

The commander suddenly seemed ill at ease. Shifting his weight from one foot to the other, he asked: "What about the ones who didn't plot against the Sultan but are joining the fight now? These are just defending their brothers."

"Helping rebellious murderers is just as reproachable as being one. Arrest every prince who comes out of his room tonight. In the morning we'll see which prince had the good sense of staying in. Now I must leave you. I have other cats to whip." In a twirl of black fabric, the Grand Vizier turned around and left.

Soon after the commander moved away from the door we returned into the tunnel.

Erik rested his back against the cold stone wall. "I thought the goal of their rebellion was to flee the Cage, not kill Father."

"It's our father's fault," I said. "His silence led our brothers to believe he's the killer. Worse, some believe he's using us to rejuvenate himself." I wanted to help my brothers, yet a part of me refused to take that risk. Too dangerous, it said. I was torn and could see the same conflicting feelings on Erik's face.

Rami stepped up. "No, this is their doing. Your brothers knew the consequences of their act. There's nothing you can do for them now. It's better for us to return to the hideout and wait for the morning."

I raised the book I was carrying, ran a hand on its beaten leather binding and looked at Erik. "We can use that time to learn what we can. Perhaps we'll find another way of helping our family."

* * *

With so many of my brothers in prison, I found it hard to concentrate on my reading. Thoughts of them kept churning in my mind, muddling everything. Sighing in frustration, I shot a peek over my opened book.

Absorbed in the study of a thick book of tales, Erik and Rami were nestled in each other's arms at the back of the daybed, like two lovebirds. While reading, Erik played with a strand of Rami's hair. By the satisfied smile on her face, she seemed to enjoy it.

As if sensing my gaze on her, Rami looked up. Our eyes met. She held my stare without flinching, and then her left eyebrow rose as if to say, "So."

I looked away, thinking that for a commoner she had quite the attitude. Minutes later, I slammed my book closed. A puff of dust and musty-smelling mildew wafted out of it. This volume had taught me nothing new or useful. I grabbed the last book. Bound in green leather, this volume held ancient myths going back a thousand years. I skipped quickly from one story to the next until I found one about a hermit living in a cave who one day in the midst of a deep meditation contacted an efreet.

The story narrated how the efreet, suffering from the same painful loneliness as the hermit, seduced the man. The efreet soon became the hermit's wife, transforming his life of poverty into one of immeasurable riches. The hermit grew famous and earned the title of Sultan; in fact he was the very first Sultan. And when this first Sultan went to war with his neighbors to expand his kingdom, the efreet called an army of demons to do battle for him. But with time, the Sultan grew tired of the efreet and seeking new companionship began building a harem. Scorned, the efreet sought revenge by killing the Sultan's favorites and plaguing his land with a drought so terrible that half of his kingdom remained a desert to this day. The story continued with the Sultan defeating the efreet by renouncing his life of power and luxury and returning to his cave—but not before producing a son. This boy started a long line of Sultans. There were several stories like this. The one where a man who had all his wishes granted by an efreet and then had to repay the demon by sacrificing his first born stuck in my mind. A third story involved a jinni who was enslaved by a fishmonger. The jinni brought this man all kinds of riches, even a marriage with a Sultan's daughter. This story, however, ended with the fishmonger's death. I didn't know what to make of these tales. If they held clues, I failed to see them.

I turned my attention to my companions. "Have you found anything helpful in your book?"

"Well," Erik said. "I found that pairikas originated from Maberia. These creatures' link to their native land is so strong that only a person with Maberian blood in his veins can call upon them. They're mostly depicted as protective spirits set to guard shrines and precious objects."

"Maberian blood." I rubbed my beard. "That's the Vizier's blood."

"It's also the architect's. Anyway, the thing with pairikas is that they can only leave their assigned area if the charm binding them to their duty is broken. Left to their own device, pairikas revert to old habits of seducing and killing men. But once free they'll also seek to return to their homeland."

That's interesting, I thought. The pairikas were now free. I had seen it with my own eyes. I wondered if it was because of something Erik and I had done in the mausoleum? Could entering the place be enough to break the charm? Perhaps it was taking something out? The ring—maybe it was taking the ring? Another question remained though: Who had set the pairikas as guardians of the mausoleum?

"And you—find anything?" Erik asked, pulling me from my thoughts.

"Huh, my book mentioned jinn being enslaved and efreets and men marrying."

"Yewww!" Erik grimaced. "That horrible creature!"

"Efreets can take any form they wish," Mira said. "When we saw it first, it looked exactly like Princess Eva, but we knew it couldn't be her. Erik's mother is watching over her like a hawk."

I nodded, thinking that I should have figured it out myself. My joy of seeing Eva had blurred my mind then. "Regardless of their appearance, these unnatural, *unholy* unions between men and demons seemed to have always existed, and they cost men dearly: a son, a wife, a limb."

Rami/Mira's head tilted to the side. An expression of deep concentration veiled her delicate features. It made her look slightly older than the fifteen years I had given her. Maybe she was older, closer to Erik's age. She certainly behaved that way. Rami tapped her pink lips with her index finger for a brief moment then poked that digit at the air. "It cost those men their future. Not all of it, but its main path—the one they should have normally traveled. By claiming those paths as sacrifices, the demons drove these men's lives in different directions... and to different futures."

"Hmm!" I rubbed my chin. I was a bit confused and far too proud to demand more explanation. Instead I mulled over what Mira had just told us. To change one's future seemed complicated at first. But if one thought about it carefully, the easiness of it was quite frightening. Every little change made to one's life could bring bigger ones. However, some changes were more drastic than others. For example: the loss of a wife meant different children or none at all, the loss of a limb meant a change of work and status, the loss of a first born meant a new heir.

"You're right. I hadn't seen it that way. Still, these are only tales. The amount of truth they hold is highly questionable."

"What else do we have to go by? Tell me," Rami/Mira said.

"Right!" I plunged back in the study of my book.

This night seemed without end. And when it finally did end, every muscle of my body was stiff from having sat too long in the same position... or maybe it was just that hard chair I was in. Without a word, we picked up our notes and took the tunnel leading to the cellar. As it was facing the kitchen, we hoped to eavesdrop on the crew of cooks and their help's conversations. I was pretty sure that they would be talking about last night's event. With luck, we might learn more of our brothers' fate.

We had not taken ten steps in the tunnel when we heard someone crying in the distance.

Erik pointed west. "It's coming from over there."

Without further discussion we moved toward the sound.

As we got closer it became clear that it was a woman crying. Seconds later her silhouette appeared at the junction of two tunnels. Wrapped from head to toe in a black haïk, and with her face buried in her hands, she was now bawling uncontrollably.

Gripping Erik's arm, I said, "Don't rush. This could be a trap. She could be another demon."

Cautiously, we inched toward the crying woman. Erik's posture abruptly changed, his back lost its stiffness and his entire body relaxed. "Salima!" he exclaimed.

The woman's head popped up. Although her face was twisted with grief nearly beyond recognition, it was Salima, all right. Upon seeing us, her eyes widened with a mixture of shock, fear and disbelief. She rushed into Erik's arms. "Oh, you're safe. I was sick with worry." Salima stamped little kisses all over Erik's face. "I looked everywhere for you. I thought you'd been captured with the others."

"We're fine," Erik whispered in her ear. "We spent the night in my hideout, you should've known that."

Salima suddenly looked embarrassed. "I didn't think of it. When I saw the Vizier coming out of Prince Amir's rooms, I was too scared to think straight."

"The Vizier was in my room?"

Salima's head bobbed up and down very quickly. "Yes, yes, he was! He looked very angry. I thought he was mad at you." She pulled herself out of Erik's arms. "I must leave now—I must find your mother, reassure her that you're well."

After one last hug with Erik, Salima vanished down the tunnel.

"She looked really happy to see us alive," I said.

"Yes," Erik replied in an oddly monotone voice. Something was bothering him. He kept staring in the direction taken by Salima with a furrowed face. But when I asked about his state, he refused to say anything, only shrugged.

We returned to the cellar. Once we'd squeezed past the giant wine barrel, Mira put her turban and scarf back on. Stumping her shoulders and head, she then took a masculine stand and became Rami once more. "I'll go gather news. Wait for me here."

As soon as she was gone, I turned to Erik. "How long have you two been together?"

He shrugged. "Some time."

"Where's she from? She looks Abesian, but these islanders are darker? So where?"

"I haven't really asked."

"Oh, come now, you can tell me."

He shrugged again—never a good sign with him. I waited for something more to come. But Erik apparently didn't want to say a thing.

"She's well educated," I continued, eyes fixed on Erik's face. "More than the women who usually make up our harem."

I thought he paled at my remark, but in this cellar's dark corner I wasn't completely certain. Erik looked as if he was about to speak when Rami returned. "It's safe to come out. The guards are gone. No one's getting captured this morning."

"Did you learn how many brothers are left in the Cage?" I asked.

"The kitchen crew doesn't know yet. They said that Hassan has posted the names of the captured princes in the Great Hall, and that the registry listing the succession line has already been modified on account of all of the rebellious princes that have been disowned by the Sultan."

Erik and I gaped at each other. Without another word being said, we rushed in the direction of the Great Hall.

I was shocked by the emptiness of the Cage. Only our footsteps broke its oppressive silence. Upon entering the Great Hall, I saw that the Cage wasn't totally void of life. Darius and seven of his supporters stood in front of the registry. Their clothes, like ours, were wrinkled by too many hours of wear. They too had the tired eyes and the dull looks of ones who had spent the night awake. However, I sensed that their state went beyond simple physical exhaustion, their nerves were also frazzled.

Darius's eyes flicked from me to Erik then to me again. He shook his head and clucked his tongue. Then he motioned for us to approach.

Erik gripped my elbow. "Is this wise?"

"Yes, Darius won't do anything rash."

As I got closer, I regretted my statement. Darius's eyes had remained fixed on Erik throughout our progress. I feared that he might be seeking some stupid reason to demand a duel. With this in mind, I hurried to divert Darius's attention. "Where are the rest of your supporters?" I asked with a peek at the remaining seven standing behind Darius, like obedient dogs behind their master.

"In a holding cell." Darius pointed the scroll nailed to the wall, listing the names of all the dishonored princes in red ink. "I warned them to stay in. They wouldn't listen to me."

"How many are left—surely there are more than just us."

A sad chuckle escaped Darius's lips. "No one who counts, Amir."

I frowned.

"Come see." Darius walked in front of the registry. I moved to his side and looked up.

"OHH!" I breathed at the sight of the list. I was struck not only by how few names it held and their placement, but also by the color of the ink used, a rich, bright purple. This wasn't a list made by the tabulator, but one coming straight from the Sultan's lips. This was the succession line as Father wished it. The fact that Erik's name was just below Darius's made me nervous. The other surprise was that Mir, whose full name was Amir like me, followed Erik. Then came Darius's seven supporters, Rashid, which no one had seen for over a month, Jafer, me and last was Ibrahim. I shook my head. At least my father saw fit to put me ahead of a poisoner. Yet I was less regarded than Darius's thoughtless supporters and my mentally deranged brother, Jafer—that was disturbing all in itself.

"Shocking, isn't it?" Darius said.

I nodded, speechless.

"What's going to happen to our captured brothers?" Erik asked.

Darius's handsome face twisted into a rictus of anger. "They've already been stripped of their titles. I don't know what else they'll do to them."

I thought he knew. I had an inkling myself of which terrible fate awaited my brothers—treason was punishable by death. The stained, red bricks of Chop-Chop Square appeared in my mind. I had no doubt that the square would be my brothers' last destination. I swallowed the lump lodged in my throat, and just like Darius, chose not to speak of it. In common accord, we both moved away from the registry.

Darius then cast his attention on Rami hooked on Erik's arm. His eyes narrowed. At that instant I thought he looked like a cat which had just spotted a fat mouse. Crossing the distance that separated him from them in two long strides, Darius cupped Rami's chin in his hand and raised the girl's face up to the light.

"Hey!" Erik shouted, brushing Darius's hand away.

Darius smiled. "She might fool others but not me. You should hide her better."

Just as I dreaded, Erik stepped in Darius's face. A staring contest began. The tension in the hall abruptly climbed. Unable to suffer more drama, I moved between the two men.

"There's been enough life wasted today, don't you think?"

To my surprise it was Darius who backed away. Then again he was without a doubt smarter than Erik, or perhaps just more cunning, more used to dangerous games.

Pouting, Darius said, "You're right. For today, I can concede to a truce—for today only though." With one last glance to Erik, he left with his group.

With Darius gone, my attention returned to the registry once more. "So few names."

"I wouldn't be surprised if there are more princes left in the Cage than what's listed there," Rami said. "Your scribes are careless. They often make mistakes. The next Sultan should see that their work is verified."

I stared at the girl with curiosity. "How can you know that?"

She bit her lip and looked at her feet. "I just do," she mumbled.

I watched her return to Erik's side with increased curiosity. I had hit a nerve—I could see it in the way she kept fidgeting. But more so by the expression on her face. She'd just made a blunder and wasn't too happy about it. Was she a scribe herself? I wasn't sure—in Telfar women were not permitted that position. On the other hand, Mira was a foreigner. No, I decided, she was too assertive to be a scribe, who were little more than educated servants. So who was she and where did she come from? With these questions churning in my mind, I climbed the stair leading to my tower.

I knew something was horribly wrong the moment I stepped into my corridor: Jafer and Mir's doors were both wide open. I dashed to Jafer's room first. I took one step inside and froze in horror.

Face blue and distorted by pain, Jafer lay dead on his couch. At first sight I knew that this wasn't a natural or accidental death. Jafer had been murdered. The way his hands where rolled into fists told the story. Jafer had fought back. I stayed in the doorway, stuck in an odd numbing daze, while Erik gripped my shoulders and Rami whimpered.

Forcing myself into motion, I slowly approached Jafer's lifeless body. I closed his eyes, then touched his forehead, then his cheek. His body still held some warmth. This shocked me to my core. All of the demon's kills had been icy cold to the touch. This was not the work of a demon, but of another type of monster—a man. And sure enough Jafer's neck still held the imprint of the hands that had strangled him. Normal man's hands. *Oh God, Mir.* I ran out.

It was much darker inside Mir's quarters than in Jafer's. I took one step in and bumped into a small table placed near the door, rattling the plates of leftovers and empty glasses stacked upon it. A sour smell rose from a plate of old cheeses, stinking up the whole place. I took another step and stopped. There was something under my foot, something round and hard. When I picked it up it rang. The object was a small brass bell.

Erik came in with a lamp, shedding some well-needed light into the room.

"Whoa, what's all this?" he said.

I looked up. Mir's room was entirely crisscrossed by strings; each one had a series of bells tied to it.

"Mir's alarm system," I said. "He told me about it, said it would warn him if someone tried to enter."

Erik shone the light on the ground. "Someone did. The strings tied to the door are all broken."

Looking down, I spotted five bells rolling about on the floor.

For the next half hour we searched Mir's cluttered rooms and found no trace of him, alive or dead.

"He wasn't locked in," Erik said as we exited the room. "With his system of strings and bells, he heard the intruder coming in. There's a chance Mir might've escaped."

I put little hope in Erik's reassuring words and stayed mute. My focus moved to my own door. As expected, it too was open. Whoever had done this had obviously planned to get rid of me too.

"Do you think it's the Vizier?" Erik asked.

I mulled it over for a moment. "It doesn't make sense, Erik. The Vizier could've had Jafer and Mir arrested as traitors like the rest of our brothers, if he wanted to get rid of them. Why cover it up? Why have their names put on the registry? Why kill them? They pose no risk to the succession, anyway."

"Perhaps they saw something they shouldn't have."

I slapped my forehead. "You're right. Mir did see someone, back then I assumed it was you. So I didn't question him further—damn!" I was so angry at myself, I wanted to kick myself. Worse than my anger was the guilt that ate at me from the inside. This was my fault—all of it.

I went back into Jafer's room and kneeled beside Rami, who had stayed beside my dead brother. The girl was crying softly, her head lying in the fold of her arm. Placing a hand on her back, I leaned closer to her. "Jafer whispered something in your ear last night. What was it?"

She sniffed and swallowed hard. "He said... get the Slayer, you will need it." Fat tears rolled down her cheeks. She squeezed her eyes shut, as if this action could stop such a heavy downpour. "I didn't know what he meant, but thought that if I agreed, he would calm down. I should have demanded an explanation."

Laying her head back down, she whimpered in small hiccups. I patted her back. "Don't feel guilty. It's not your fault. Jafer mentioned the Slayer to me too, and I didn't question him either. It was a mistake, considering that the only other person to mention the Slayer is the Grand Vizier. Nazir was desperately looking for it, and contrary to us he knows what the Slayer is."

"Maybe we've been looking in the wrong places," Erik said.

"Or at the wrong things," Rami added. She looked sadly at Jafer. "But first, we ought to cover him."

I fetched a blanket from his bedchamber. When I came back, Rami was gently crossing Jafer's arms over his chest. Something sticking out of his fist caught my eye: a small crumpled piece of parchment. Careful not to rip it apart, I gently pulled the little bit out of my brother's death grip.

Yellowed and with fraying edges, the strip of parchment held only a few words in Yalec, an ancient language few could still read. Having spent years alone in my library, I had taught myself several languages and Yalec was one of them.

"Ek leima elta oreh," I read aloud.

"What does it mean?" Erik asked.

"My Yalec is rusty, but I think it means, I offer my blood in a near future."

"No, that's a bad translation," Rami said. "The correct one is, I sacrifice the essence of one future."

"Where did you learn Yalec?"

"Doesn't matter. What does is that this sentence is part of an incantation—probably from your missing book. Whoever has this book killed Jafer."

The Vizier knows Yalec, I thought. *He has a collection of dark magic volumes, keeps a supply of sweets, which demons crave, knows his way through the tunnels and was desperately seeking the Slayer. How many more clues do I need? The man has to be guilty.* Still, deep down, I felt that something was missing. But no matter how hard I tried I couldn't find the missing piece of this puzzle.

I sighed, covered Jafer's body and said. "Let's fulfill his wish. Let's find that Slayer."

CHAPTER TWENTY-TWO

While we made our way to the imperial tabulator's office, I kept thinking about Jafer. I wished I could turn back time. I wished I'd paid more attention to his words. He had given me the key to this enigma, I was sure of it. But this precious key was wrapped in obscurity. For example, Jafer had spoken of a tool, a tool linked with the Sultan's stolen gift. I still failed to see the use of a vase in all this.

Unless the vase contained something? Jinn live in vessels, don't they? What about an efreet? Could one live in a vase? I doubted it. Perhaps only a small part of Jafer's vision was useful, the rest could be delirium. If so which part was valid?

A soft noise at my back roused me from my thought. I stopped and glanced over my shoulder. The corridor was empty, yet the hair at the back of my neck stood on end. We were being followed; there was no mistaking that sickly feeling at the pit of my stomach. Scanning the area, my gaze fell on the dark shadowy arch of an alcove—a good hiding place if any.

I was about to inspect the alcove, when Erik called: "Amir, there's no time to waste. Come, hurry."

I scrutinized the dark alcove for a minute longer. Slowly the unpleasant feeling in my stomach subsided. Convinced that it had been my nerves affecting my senses, I joined my companions who were waiting at the tabulator's office's door.

I had never entered this office before, so I was rather unprepared for what it held. Just the number of scribes, a good hundred at least, hard at work in this room was enough to astound me. For some reason, I had imagined a handful of old men scribbling by candlelight in a dark, dusty room. No such thing here; this office was clear, orderly and very bright. Huge windows filled the south and west walls while lamps were planted in rows on the east and north ones. Twenty-five desks occupied the long narrow office, each shared by four scribes. A small army of errand boys, their arms overflowing with scrolls and books, added nonstop activity to this crowded room by constantly moving from desk to desk. These errand boys were like experienced dancers. Their every gesture was timely and filled with purpose, not once did they drop a book or stop at the wrong desk. Moving among the drab sea of beige tunics of the scribes, a spot of color caught my attention.

The imperial tabulator was coming toward us. The long emerald robe and matching square hat of his position made his identity unquestionable. The man was slightly bent forward—due to years of slumping over books, I assumed. His eyes although small and beady, were clear and swift.

"Princes, what an honor," he said with an awkward bow, which I assigned to the state of his back. "We rarely receive such dignified visitors. Please excuse the state of the office…" The man paused, hesitating. "There's been tremendous changes—events that needed recording."

While speaking, the tabulator's small eyes scrutinized our faces. I could tell he was trying to put names to our faces. The bulk of his attention was focused on me, I noted. Erik was an easy guess. I was the problem. And by the lost look on his face, I believed that if I had told him I was Prince Amir, he would have replied, Which one? I could hardly blame him; I had spent years trying not to be noticed. Still, I found it a bit insulting and had to bite the inside of my cheeks not to show my displeasure. This wasn't the time to behave rudely. I needed that man's cooperation, so I smiled amicably at the tabulator.

"Perhaps princes should pay more attention to the palace's records. Prince Keri and I would like to do just that."

"We are at your service. Please tell us your needs."

I gave him the list of documents I wished to examine. The list was swiftly transferred to the nearest errand boy, who immediately went to work searching through the cabinet and bookshelves lining the walls. The tabulator then led us to a private reading room adjacent to the office. Well lit, the room had two comfortable-looking blue couches and a big rectangular reading table at its center. We settled around the table.

The chairs were hard and uncomfortable. *Perfect,* I thought, *they're meant for working not sleeping.*

The errand boy was back less than a minute later with the first load of documents. Not knowing what we were looking for, I had asked for a bit of everything: princes' birth registry, ambassadors' visitations account, harem turnover and the treasury inventory. Now that the documents were piled up on the table, I thought that perhaps my search was a tad too broad. The mass of parchment was so high it obstructed my sight of Erik who was sitting right in front of me.

"I'll take the princes' birth registry," Rami said.

Erik grabbed the harem turnover before I could touch it. "I'll check those."

His voice was oddly strangled, I found. Well, that left me with the ambassadors' visitations account and the treasury inventory. *All right, let's find this stolen gift then.*

Turning to the visitations account, I easily found the date and event I was looking for. Almost a year ago, the ambassador of Karpel came to the palace, bearing gifts and a peace treaty from his new monarch, King Avel the Fourth—a war baron rumored to have risen to the throne by the tip of his sword, who now wanted to make an alliance with his neighbor, thus stabilizing his precarious position. On all accounts, the visit had been without incident. However, it was noted that the Karpelian Ambassador, a boorish individual more at ease on a combat field than a palace hall, had consumed too much wine and, in an advanced state of drunkenness, toppled his glass, soiling perfectly good table linens. Later that evening, the barely standing ambassador presented a list of royal gifts to the Sultan. How many faux pas had the man made, I wondered. I turned the page and my eyes fell on the red ink and gold vellum of the ambassador's list. I couldn't believe my luck. The original list was right there, pasted to this page. I looked at it and smiled. Another faux pas, the list was written in their language and not ours, as it should have in accordance with proper etiquette. *Commoners!*

"I found something!" Rami said. "Actually, I found that something's missing." Holding up the birth registry, she pointed to the thin ragged line of paper at its center. "Someone ripped some pages out. It's missing four years."

I did a quick survey of the missing years then flipped quickly through the remaining pages.

"Who was born in those years?" Erik asked.

"You and I." I snorted. "Darius too! Thinking of it, pretty much all the princes still left in the Cage."

Erik rolled his eyes. "Well, that's not very helpful."

I blinked. Gazing at the missing pages again, I declared, "No, it *is* helpful. Rami go ask the tabulator who has last looked at this book."

"Good thinking, Amir," she said, and was out the room before I could remind her of my title. Erik might tolerate this lack of formality considering that she was sharing his bed, but this wasn't my case.

"This can't be!" Erik exclaimed. He put his book down and rubbed his eyes.

"What is it?"

Grabbing his book again, he said, "I'm not sure. It has to be someone else. It can't be her."

"Erik, who are you talking about?"

He stared at me over his opened book and said: "Salima! She's listed as one of father's concubines. It has as to be a different woman baring the same name."

My eyes widened. The portrait I had seen in the miniatures room sprung into my mind. "Show me the book." Sure enough, Salima's name was there and inscribed beside it were a date and a moon crescent indicating that she had been chosen to spend that night with the Sultan. I flipped a few pages back and found this Salima woman's full registration into the harem. "Aled Salima, daughter of Tarim Aled—seized as payment of debt. *Aled?* I heard this name before. Erik, did you know it was Salima's full name."

Pale as death itself, Erik kept shaking his head. "I never heard her full name before. Mother said I should never bother Salima with her past because it was painful to her. Now I know why." Erik paused to let out a long, ragged breath. "Tarim Aled is the architect punished by our father for flooding the library. Salima is his daughter."

"She's showed you the tunnel. Not the other way around as I've always assumed."

Erik nodded. "This morning when she said she didn't know where I was. That bothered me, because of all the places to look for me she knew my hideout was where I would be." Erik buried his face in his hand. He seemed devastated.

"Could she be… involved in—"

Erik didn't let me finish. Raising tear-filled eyes at me, he snapped, "No! I refuse to believe Salima capable of hurting anyone. She's not strong enough to kill our brothers. You see, Amir, it's somebody else's doing." Erik's eyes suddenly widened. "Do you think that her father is still alive? That he's taking his revenge on us."

The memory of my first meeting with Eva came back to me. I remembered Salima arguing with a dark figure, pleading with him to cease what he was doing. The dark figure, I recalled, spoke easily. The architect was known to have lost his hands and tongue. So unless his tongue and hands had magically grown back, she had a different accomplice—one with hands strong enough to strangle my brother.

"Her father died long ago," I said. "Salima found someone else to help her. Erik, I'm afraid she's behind this… one way or another."

Just then Rami came back in. She was out of breath as if she had run all the way. "You won't believe this. The last person to flip through the birth registry is the Grand Vizier."

"When?" I asked.

"Last night. There's more. The Vizier also demanded to see the unmodified registry, the one reserved for his and the Sultan's eyes only."

So the rumor was true. There were two registries. "Where's the registry now?" I asked.

"The Vizier took it with him." Rami then noticed Erik's reddened eyes and nose and my solemn face. "You look—what happened? What did you find?"

I told her what we had discovered. Rami didn't hide her surprise.

"One thing bothers me in this story," she said. "Why, after two years in the harem, humiliate Salima by giving her as a servant to Erik's mother."

She had a point; I couldn't figure that one out either.

"I think I know," Erik said. "Father didn't want her to leave the harem and marry a nobleman like other concubines. As Mother's servant Salima remained in the harem, which forbids her to marry. This way she wouldn't have any children and the architect's bloodline would truly die with her."

So far my father had proven himself vindictive enough for me to believe him capable of such a spiteful act. However, I sensed that we were, once more, missing some crucial pieces of this puzzle. I cast my eyes on the royal gifts list. This missing vase pricked me like a tick pricked a dog; it just wouldn't leave me alone. Yet I knew we couldn't waste more time in this room. With a peek at the door—to be sure we were still alone—I ripped the royal gifts list out of the book. The sound of fine vellum tearing was awful to my ears.

"What are you doing?" Erik whispered.

"Shh... not a word. Jafer wouldn't shut up about this missing gift. I will find where this vase went even if it's the last thing I do."

Erik glanced at Rami, then to me. "You're wasting your time with that; it doesn't matter in our search."

"Somehow, I think it does." I couldn't help noticing how uneasy Erik and Rami were, they didn't know on which feet to dance. *Huh... well now I'm sure it's very important.*

Opening the treasury's inventory to the pages listing the Karpelian royal gifts, I ripped out those pages too and pocketed the lot. I was determined to study these pages, if not now, later. "The Grand Vizier is probably busy preparing the grounds for a new Sultan. Not mentioning all our brothers in the prisoners' tower. I'll be surprised if there's anyone left in his chambers right now."

I glanced at the window behind me and was shocked to see how low the sun was in the sky. We'd stayed in the tabulator's office longer than I had thought. Gathering our notes, we thanked the tabulator for his help one last time then pushed through the palace's darkening corridors. Once more the feeling of being followed chilled my spine. I continued moving with the others, but kept looking over my shoulder while doing so.

We were nearing the Grand Vizier's apartment when Erik, who was walking in front, stopped dead in his tracks. Turning pleading eyes to Rami, he said, "We should tell him. I can't carry this secret any longer."

At the mention of the word secret, my ears pricked up and my head swung forward. I watched a panicked Rami shake her head, her hands gripping Erik's arm.

"Please don't," she begged. "Nothing good will come of this."

Erik caressed her cheeks softly. Then with a determined look on his face, he said, "He's going to find out anyway. You saw him take those lists."

Burying her face in Erik's chest, Rami let out a moan. With an arm wrapped protectively around the young woman's shoulders, Erik motioned for me to come closer.

Forgetting about the oppressive feeling of being spied on, I obeyed.

It was Rami who spoke. "Take the two lists out, please."

I did, flattening the creased pages the best I could.

"Look on the Karpelian list. Can you see the mention of a vase being given?"

I scrolled along the list twice. For a second, I questioned my capacity of reading Karpelian—only for a second though, my knowledge of this language was more than adequate. "No! There's none… but the vase is clearly mentioned in the translated version of the treasury."

Rami made a tongue clucking sound. "Haven't I told you that your scribes aren't the best? They're lazy and careless."

Frowning, I looked back at the original list. What word had been mistranslated? I began linking both inventories together: ten camels, six horses, nine dancers, it went on without a glitch for quite a stretch. The new King of Karpel had been very generous. Then I spotted the mistake. I felt the blood leaving my face. Coldness seized my entire body. I stared at Erik and Rami with wide eyes. "You're right, they translated it wrong. The mage's vase is in fact the mage's daughter. The scribe confused the word vaspor-daughter for vaspora-vase."

There was a long moment of excruciating silence. Mira was the only one courageous enough to break it. "I saw the scribe make the mistake. I thought it was my chance to escape the harem. If one doesn't exist, one can disappear without raising anyone's attention. So I said nothing about the mistake."

I blinked, still a bit under the shock. "Why would the daughter of the king's mage be…" I stopped in midsentence. "Oh, I see. Your father was adviser to the old king… not the new one."

Rami produced a sad smile. "Father warned the old king against the baron. That filthy man had too much ambition and not enough honor. But the king didn't listen—not until it was too late… too late for everyone." Hugging herself, she let out a long trembling sigh.

Rami/Mira's knowledge of magic, chess, etiquette, and over-all abilities suddenly made sense. No wonder she was so well read. She was a palace-educated woman, probably a lady-in-waiting to the old queen, and of all things a mage's daughter. Then it struck me, she also was one of Father's concubines. I glared at Erik. He looked away.

"Don't be so hard on him," Mira said. "I'm the one who engaged him. I saw his shadow behind the harem's ventilation grid. I knew someone was spying on us. As days passed, I became sure that this wasn't the Sultan and I dared approach him."

Erik kissed the top of Mira's head. "I'll continue from here," he said. "The first time she spoke to me through the screen, I panicked and ran away. When no word of a man spying on the harem was mentioned, I figured that she wouldn't betray me if I went back. Mira told me of the clerical mistake. I checked it out and sure enough she wasn't listed in the harem's registry, or anywhere else. She didn't exist. Knowing that she wouldn't be missed or looked for, I helped her escape."

My jaw dropped. I was totally shocked, although I had expected these exact words to come out of his mouth. Maybe it was hearing it aloud that left me so shaken—I couldn't say for sure.

"Amir, you saw these women. You know that some aren't meant for this life. She's not meant for that life. It's not like Father was going to miss her either. He didn't even know she existed. I didn't steal anything. One can not steal what isn't there."

Erik failed to convince me that his actions were without consequence. His face was much too pale for that. To steal a concubine was punishable by death, not only for him, but also for her. I opened my mouth to chastise him, but before any word could come out, the sound of broken pottery echoed behind me.

Turning around, my eyes settled first on the remains of what used to be a magnificent porcelain urn now smashed on the floor in bits and pieces, and then on Ibrahim exiting from a dark corner.

Glaring at us, Ibrahim produced a malicious grin. He'd heard every word that Erik had said; I had no doubt about it. Now he was going to run to the prisoners' tower in search of the Grand Vizier. Of this too, I had no doubt.

"You don't need to tell," I risked.

He burst into laughter. "Have you lost your mind? This information can redeem me."

In a swift move, Ibrahim pulled his saber and began backing away. I stepped toward him. He ran. I gave chase. Soon we reached the stairwell. Taking two steps at a time, I landed on the ceramic tiles at the bottom of the stairs with a loud bang.

Ibrahim, I saw, was fleeing in the direction of the Great Hall. Then he stopped, petrified, in the entrance. That was odd, I thought. Why wasn't he running anymore? Why was he standing there with his saber hanging loosely in his hand? As Ibrahim began backing up, my eyes floated ahead of him.

Darius and the rest of my brothers were coming out of the Great Hall, thus blocking Ibrahim's exit. I smiled. This time Ibrahim would have to fight his own battle.

Obviously, Ibrahim thought so too. He backed away, his head moving back and forth between Darius and me as if trying to choose an opponent.

I sighed. I knew which one of us he was going to choose.

To my surprise, Ibrahim turned to Darius and his supporters. "My brothers," he said, "listen to me. Keri has fooled us all. That boy at his side is in fact one of Father's concubines—he stole her."

Oh no, my heart sank. I thinned my lips in anger, I should have guessed he would take the low road, I should have run faster, stopped him before he opened his filthy mouth.

Darius stepped up. "Keep your breath, Ibrahim. You're a coward and a poisoner! No one believes your lies—Father's concubine." Darius chuckled. "The boy's a girl all right! But she certainly didn't belong to Father's harem; otherwise her disappearance would've caused a huge scandal."

"She is," Ibrahim insisted, "I'm telling the truth, Keri stole her…"

"ENOUGH!" Darius snapped. A thin smile then spread across his lips. "Tell me, Ibrahim, where have you been hiding these last few days—in which dark corner, under which bed?"

An explosion of laughter erupted from the brothers assembled behind Darius.

"Your luck has run out, brother," Darius said with narrowed eyes. "This time you'll have to fight me."

"No, he will fight me," someone boomed over my shoulder.

I turned.

Erik stood at the bottom of the stairs, his claymore in hand. "Darius, Amir," Erik bowed briefly at us. "I demand reparation! I demand a duel. Ibrahim's offense against me is the gravest—he poisoned me. I deserve to fight him first."

"NO," I shouted. "He attacked me first, two months ago. He was dressed in the black garment of the nomadic desert tribe then, still I know it was him and his brothers."

Ibrahim stared at Erik; his eyes ran along his sturdy body then on his imposing claymore. Turning to me, he began scrutinizing me in the same way he had Erik. Obviously, he was calculating his chances of winning.

Ibrahim smiled. "You're right, Amir. I led the attack on you that night. As you were the first to be offended, you'll be the first to die."

CHAPTER TWENTY-THREE

While Ibrahim and I discarded our kaftans, my brothers formed a circle around us. I was first to step in the circle's center. Ibrahim soon joined me. As we faced each other, I noted that we were dressed alike, rust-colored baggy pants and white linen shirts. I also noted that for the first time since he had grown it, Ibrahim's mustache wasn't waxed. Its tips hung down, giving his face a cynical appearance. Was Ibrahim a good fencer? I tried to recall his combat method, his favorite moves, but my brain was suddenly blank. So I just squeezed the grip of my rapier and waited for his attack.

We slowly circled each other, like dancers studying their partner's every movement before beginning a difficult pas de deux. Suddenly Ibrahim pivoted in the opposite direction he'd been moving and launched forward. I leaned back just in time and his blade grazed my shoulder and chest instead of piercing me. We exchanged a series of blows. Every one of mine blocked or parried.

Ibrahim was faster than I had thought and his blows almost as strong and as hard as Erik's. *Fight him like you fought Erik, then*, I said to myself. *Get close, get under his guard.* I knew there was no other way. So when he made a swiping move with his blade, I crouched and launched forward. I rose up inches from him. Ibrahim let out a startled growl. Taking advantage of his surprise, I seized his sword hand. Ibrahim's eyes widened. Then he tried slapping me with the back of his free hand over and over again.

I thought that it was a very odd move... until Darius shouted, "Careful of his rings—they're poisoned."

Ibrahim was trying to scratch me. *The bastard!* But when I attempted to move away from him, I realized that I was trapped. I couldn't move without putting myself in harm's way. I looked up at Ibrahim's face. The bastard was grinning at me. Something inside me broke. The invisible barrier keeping my savage side at bay suddenly dissolved, and the volcano of scorching rage which had been sleeping at the bottom of my stomach for years finally erupted. Clenching my teeth, I stopped moving and waited for Ibrahim's ringed hand to come toward me. Seconds before it could hit my face, I abandoned my grip on his sword hand and seized the ringed one. His ruby ring sparkled like the evil eye of a demon. I saw that the gold claws holding the stone in place had been sharpened; they gleamed in all their deadly glory. Twisting his wrist around, I pushed the ringed hand against Ibrahim's own neck. The ring dug deep into his flesh, letting blood out.

Ibrahim's mouth dropped, in shock. His eyes bulged out as the reality of what had just happened sunk in. With a hand clasped on his neck, he backed away from me.

"You—You!" he kept repeating.

His sword slipped from his hand. The blade hit the tiles with a resonating metallic clank. This noise made me realize how silent the room was. I looked at my brothers. They appeared unsure of what to do now. They looked at each other, cleared their throats or scratched their heads, before turning to Darius for guidance. Darius nodded then stepped aside, opening the circle that had enclosed us. The combat was over. Following his example more brothers broke line.

"Leave," Darius ordered Ibrahim. "Your fate is sealed. Go die elsewhere."

Picking up his sword, Ibrahim slowly exited the circle. But the moment Darius turned his back on him, Ibrahim raised his sword and charged Darius, well intending to stab him in the back.

"Watch out!" I shouted, lunging forward. For an instant, time seemed to stand still. In that brief moment, I saw Darius's stunned expression as *both* our blades went straight for him. "Down!" I yelled. Darius ducked, and my blade met Ibrahim's. With swift automatic reflexes brought on by years of practice, I rotated my wrist upward then forward, Ibrahim's blade flew out of his hand, while mine plunged deep into his chest.

Ibrahim's eyes grew the size of saucers. He gripped the blade still sticking out of his chest, looked at it then looked at me and blinked. I doubted he was seeing me, these were only reflexes. He was already dead. *Maybe it's you who'd rather not look at him*, a small voice nagged in my head. Seconds later, Ibrahim slipped to the floor.

A hand clasped my left shoulder.

I flinched, realizing only then that my eyes were still glued on Ibrahim's dead body.

"Once more, I owe you my life," Darius said with a mixture of annoyance and amazement.

I ignored him; my gaze had turned to the terrace, mainly to the darkening sky above, which I could see through the Great Hall's opened doors. The moon was rising—the full moon. "Darius," I said, pointing at the moon. "I don't think this debt matters anymore."

Darius made a sour face. "Perhaps we too should have risen against our father. How many of us will die for him tonight."

"Tell him," Erik said. "Tell the others too. They deserve to know the truth."

I agreed and told everything I knew to my brothers: the pairikas, the efreet and our father's curse.

"So Father is innocent!" Darius exclaimed when I was done. He seemed extremely relieved, as if the thought of our father killing us for his own profit had been too painful for him. "How long do you think this curse will last?" Darius asked.

I shrugged. "I think the curse is linked to Father's life... actually to his death. So it should stop with his passing. However, I'm not sure we're meant to survive him. The more I think about it, the stronger I believe that we're supposed to all perish together."

Darius sucked air sharply. "At last news, Father wasn't expected to live through the night. That leaves little time. Do you know who's behind this?"

Erik, Rami and I exchanged looks. But it was I who spoke. "So far the Grand Vizier is the only one with the means to do it."

Erik moved to my side as if to give me his support. "We were on the way to his rooms when Ibrahim showed up."

A scream of agony filled the air making us all jump.

Indicating the darkness outside, a brother said, "It came from the prisoners' tower."

As one we all moved to the terrace's doors and stared westward where the tower rose. Its somber spike was out of focus like a mirage. Streams of fog swirled slowly around it like a lazy tornado. Once in a while, when the fog moved out of the way, the light of lamps could be seen shining through its windows. More screams echoed from the tower. Seconds later we watched two forms jump out of the tower's highest window, and although we couldn't see it from here, we all knew they'd splattered on the square below.

"Amir," Darius breathed. "Go. Find the guilty one. We'll stay here and do our best to stop this abomination so you'll have more time."

I wanted to say, you can't stop this thing, Darius, no one

can. But the determined glare in Darius's eyes kept me silent. He slapped a hand on my shoulder. "You're our last chance, Amir. Find the dark mage behind this and kill him. Go!"

* * *

I only stopped running when I saw the door of the Grand Vizier's rooms appear at the end of the corridor. Still sprinting, Erik bumped into my back almost knocking me to the ground. Once our balance was reestablished, we tiptoed to the door. I rested my ear to its wood. No sound. Nothing. Then I heard a slight rustling. Goose bumps pricked my arms. That was a bizarre sound, like something or *someone* being dragged on a rug. Without hesitation, I pushed into the room—only to freeze at the threshold with my hand still squeezing the doorknob.

The room was in shambles: There were bits of paper everywhere, the furniture was toppled over, vases, statues, and plates smashed on the ground. Moaning made me look behind the door. To my utter dismay, I saw the Grand Vizier sprawled on his carpeted floor. Blood streamed out of a horrible gash opened in his belly.

The Vizier looked up at me with an ashen face and stretched a bloodied hand my way.

I kneeled at Nazir's side while Erik remained paralyzed at the door, mouth agape. "Who did this to you?" I asked.

The Vizier gripped one of the many loose sheets of paper spread on the carpet and shoved the crumpled page into my hand. "He's not… " Nazir managed to say between laborious breaths.

While the Vizier fought to regain his breath, I looked at Mira. (I didn't see the need of calling her Rami anymore—Father was dead, the Vizier dying and everyone else knew she was a girl, so why continue this charade.) Mira was picking up the scattered sheets. Once she was done, she joined me at the Vizier's side. "These pages are from an old incantation book—it's in Yalec, like the book you're missing."

The Vizier made a hissing sound. "He came for the book… for my copy. He knew I could use it against him… he…" Nazir coughed. "He tried to take it from me. I fought but…" His hand touched his bloody belly and he grimaced.

"Please, go on," I begged, fearing he might lose consciousness at any moment; the man's time was counted.

Nazir's eyes reopened; for a moment they floated around aimlessly then finally fixed themselves on me. They brightened. "He's wrong about her—he doesn't know!"

Grinning victoriously, the Vizier pulled two squares of yellow parchment from the fold of his garment and shoved it in my hand. There was no mistaking what he had given me; one was a page of the modified birth registry, while the other belonged to the Sultan's registry—the book we were not allowed to look at.

"Your father was right about you… he was right to make… changes," Nazir said. "We argued about it… I thought it was your doing, thought you were guilty."

"Well, I thought the same about you."

The Vizier tried to laugh, but instead coughed up blood. He didn't have long to live, no need being a physician to know that.

I squeezed his hand. "I need a name. Give me his name."

"Amir—Stop him," the Vizier whispered. "Stop him." His breath became raspy and the light of his pupils dulled. "He can't… he can't kill her sons. Remember that… remem—" The Vizier's head limply rolled onto his shoulder.

"Wake him up, Amir," Erik said in a thin voice. "Wake him up so he'll give us a name."

"He's dead, Erik." I grabbed my head with both hands. We were back to the beginning. We had no suspect. Right now I was totally lost. My eyes fell on the registry pages Nazir had given me. I was brushing creases out of it when Mira gasped.

"There it is!" She exclaimed, brandishing a page of the incantation book. "Look at the last words of this page. They're identical to the ones on the bit of paper Jafer tore off."

I gave one look at the registry pages in my hand and pocketed them, choosing to study the incantation Mira was showing me instead.

After reading the incantation three times, I came to a daunting conclusion. "That's senseless gibberish! I don't understand any of it. The chosen path, only the killer can snuff its light." I glanced as Erik kneeled at my side. He looked more lost than I was—if that was possible.

Mira rolled her eyes. "Bad translation, again! You're just as inept as your father's scribes. Let me explain to you this paragraph's meaning." She took a deep breath and began, "To please his partner of dark descent and gain one's dearest wish. I'm not sure about the exact wording of this section, but I'm pretty close. One must sacrifice the main path of his future to give place to a new one. But beware of the Demon Slayer, as whoever wields it can destroy the darkest of fiends and bring back light to our world."

"It still makes little sense to me. Frankly, it's as confusing as Jafer's vision."

Mira took one of my hands into hers. Her fingers were cool and a little callous—those were working fingers. "I know how you feel. My father had visions too—they were less taxing than Jafer's though. Visions are often hard to interpret—they're enigmas even for the ones having them. It's I who convinced Erik that there could be some truth in them."

"I wasn't hard to convince," Erik said. "It was clear that Jafer knew who Rami was from the start—the first time he mentioned Father's stolen gift, I nearly fainted I was so afraid he would tell everyone."

I frowned. I remembered that day too, more so I remembered Erik's pale face, but this was not what tickled my mind.

There was something in what Erik had just said that suddenly seemed very important—something about Jafer's visions. Damn, he had had so many, and most of the time I was alone with him, why couldn't I remember it now. It had to do with Father's stolen gift. *Yes, that was it.* So if the gift wasn't a mage's vase containing a jinn, as I'd first thought, but the mage's daughter, how could Mira lead us to the Slayer—how could she help us. I just needed to remember Jafer's exact words. If only I had paid more attention. I was frustrated—time was running out—why couldn't I put this together.

Beside me Erik was strangely quiet. He just stood there, head hung low, chewing on his lower lip, being useless.

I sighed, now totally discouraged. "I think we should leave…"

"Shh," Erik hushed at me. Tapping his index finger on the tip of his nose, he went on chewing his lip a moment longer. Suddenly his face brightened. "Ah!" he exclaimed. "Remember what Jafer said the day we went into the mausoleum?"

Being whipped was my only recollection of that awful day. I shook my head no.

Erik smiled. "Yes you do. Jafer said we would find a tool there, a tool we needed."

I screwed my face. It was coming back. "That's not what Jafer said. He said Father's stolen gift would help us find the tool. But… Ohhh!"

Jafer's words rushed back to the forefront of my mind with the speed and violence of a flash flood. "He spoke of the faults of two kings; of their lines intertwined like vines growing in the same pot. He also said that this mysterious tool should be wielded by one and not the other."

Erik nodded along, even though his expression was one of utter confusion. "Go back to the tool, Amir."

I scratched my head. Back then I believed that Jafer meant the stolen gift was the tool, but now I knew otherwise. My eyes went strait to Mira. How could I be so blind? "When Jafer said the stolen gift would find the tool, he meant you, Mira. You're the stolen gift."

She blinked. "Yes, that could be why Jafer asked me to get the Slayer. The Slayer has to be the tool." She wrinkled her pretty nose. "Should I have it already? I don't have anything!"

Closing my eyes, I recalled our evening in the mausoleum. Once more I was in the cold arms of the pairikas, then came the dizzying feeling of being drunk. Through this distorted vision, I remembered watching *Rami* attacking the creature with a stick. I searched further, yet found nothing else. "Mira, that long stick you used to chase the pairikas. What did you do with it?"

"That wasn't a stick. That was—OHH! That was an old rusted sword."

"Where is it?" Erik and I both asked.

"I don't know. I brought it back with me. I remember that. The last time I saw it, it was in Erik's bedroom then it just disappeared."

Erik rose up. "What are we waiting for? Let's go look for it."

* * *

The corridors of the Cage were eerily silent. Never before had they been so quiet—and so empty. I couldn't see a soul anywhere, not even a maid or a valet. Had they fled the palace like rats from a sinking ship, or were they just hiding in dark corners? *Either way, this can't be good,* I thought. One good thing though was that because of this emptiness we made it to Erik's rooms without being stopped or slowed. Once there we split up and each began searching a different room.

Stuck with the reading room, I did a fast examination of every corner. The book cabinet was my first stop. I rattled its glass doors. They were locked. I remembered Salima locking a book inside it when we were introduced. I recalled her insistence in taking the book back from me; the nervous glint in her eyes, the speed in which she made the book disappear. The cabinet's shelves then were tightly packed with volumes—now as I peered through the glass I could see an empty space amidst the first row of books. My eyes moved to the lock again. Its brass was shinier than the rest of the cabinet's fixtures. The old lock had recently been replaced by a new one. Someone had broken in this cabinet. Memories flooded my mind. "You stole it," Salima had told the dark figure in the tunnel. I smiled. *Oh yes he did. And you know who he is, don't you, Salima?* "ERIK, ERIK, come here."

He appeared from his bedroom. "What?"

"Where's Salima?"

Erik frowned. "I… don't know, with Mother I suppose?"

Just then Mira exited the sitting room. "I can't find it anywhere. I brought it. I'm certain of this. Someone must have stolen it. A long, cumbersome piece of metal like that cannot disappear all by itself."

"Cumbersome!" I said with excitement. "You're right, it was cumbersome. You left it on the bedroom floor and I tripped over the damn thing and almost fell down. I was so angry I kicked it under Erik's bed."

Erik immediately vanished inside his bedroom. Seconds later he was back at the door, this time carrying a dirt-encrusted long sword blade. Although the leather that had once wrapped its grip had long since rotten away leaving the metal underneath naked, the blade could still be wielded.

Using my sleeve, I rubbed some of the dirt off it. Engraving ran along the center of the blade. I cleaned off the rest of the dirt so I could decipher the words engraved on the Slayer.

"Only a drop of Telfarian royal blood is needed to satisfy the Demon Slayer, but a drop he must have," I read aloud. "Keep it for now." I gave the blade back to Erik.

"It's almost as imposing as my claymore," he said, twirling the blade expertly. "Where do we go now? Should we chase the demon?"

I looked at the blade then at Erik. "I'd rather find the dark mage behind it. But for that we need to know his intentions, his goal."

"Perhaps we do," Erik said. "We have clues that don't seem to fit together, or appear meaningless. But I think they do go together. I mean, it's a riddle—like with this blade."

I had the unpleasant feeling that Erik was right again, unpleasant because it implied that I should now know where the dark mage was, and that my failure to solve this riddle could have terrible implications for my brothers and myself. I gazed about the room, seeking a clue, a hint, anything that would lead me on the right path. I saw nothing and began pacing back and forth like the cheetah caged in our courtyard. I found myself in front of Eva's portrait.

Touching the rough surface of the painting, I let out a sigh. This painted replica was a pale replacement. I missed Eva and wished she were here. *Stop this; she's another man's future wife, Darius's probably.* As this painful thought stabbed its way across my mind another surfaced, a darker one. Eva was the next Sultan's future wife. This was a certainty, regardless of who this Sultan would be. *She* remained fixed to this position; *she* was the main path of the next Sultan's future—the one that was to be sacrificed.

In panic, I turned to Erik and began gesticulating like a madman.

"What's the problem, Amir? Why are you so pale?"

My throat was so tight, I had trouble breathing let alone speaking. After much swallowing, I managed to blurt some explanations.

Erik grabbed his chest. "Eva! You mean Eva is going to be sacrificed."

"I think so."

Erik didn't ask by whom or why, he just said, "To her tower."

CHAPTER TWENTY-FOUR

We had not yet entered the Great Hall when we heard the sound of fighting coming from it. I sped up and reached the arched entrance first. I saw that the terrace doors were closed and that rolled-up carpets and cushions were stuffed in every crack in an attempt to stop the fog from seeping in. It was as successful as trying to stop the rain from falling by yelling at it. The fog was still coming in, swirling in thin plumes until big enough to take shape.

Meanwhile, Darius and my other brothers stood back to back in the center of the room, with their swords drawn. They were circled by an increasing number of ghostly creatures, whose appearances seemed in constant mutation, passing from beautiful nymphs to grotesque ghouls, as if unsure of their intentions: Should they seduce my brothers or terrify them? Darius split one of these vaporous beings in half with his sword, only to see it reconstitute itself moments later. Darius turned my way. Our eyes met. ~

"Get out!" he ordered through clenched teeth, then went on attacking the foggy ghosts.

Not wasting time, I turned to Erik, gripped his tunic and hauled him away.

"Shouldn't we help them," he argued, yet offered little

271

resistance to my pulling. Like I, he knew ghosts couldn't be killed—not with swords anyway.

"There's a better way of helping them," I said, "like finding another way to get to the tower, for instance. This one's blocked. Any idea would be welcomed now."

Mira stepped up. "Remember the tower's balcony, the one facing the courtyard where you fought Abdul? Maybe we can climb the side of the tower and access her room through the balcony."

"We'll need a rope and a grapple," I said, and ran faster.

An amber glow escaped Eva's chamber, spilling onto her balcony. Careful not to make noises, I climbed the rope Erik had successfully grappled around the balcony rail. Fortunately, the rope was sturdy enough to hold all three of us.

As I neared the balcony's edge, voices touched my ears: low male mumbling... and female sobs—*EVA!* I wanted to go faster, to rush ahead, but I knew this was ill advised.

Surprise him, a soft voice whispered in my ears. Listening to its wisdom, I silently hoisted myself onto the balcony, then helped Erik and Mira. Together, we tiptoed into the room.

The air inside was thick and hot, as if some giant braziers had been kept burning all day in this room. And although I couldn't see any torches lit, an eerie amber glow bathed everything. A quick scan of the room told me that it was empty. I also noted that the adjacent chamber's door was cracked open. Bright orange light shone through this opening. They were inside that chamber; I could hear more voices now, different voices than the ones coming from inside the chamber. These new voices were muffled, as if coming from behind a closed door. I listened attentively. Yes, people were screaming and banging... as if to get in. The image of the narrow service door set at the back of Eva's room arose in my mind. *The eunuchs,* I thought, *they're locked outside.* Pulling my rapier, I dashed to the door with Erik and Mira in tow. At the slightest nudge of my shoulder, it swung open.

For a short moment, I was blinded by the bright orange glare of the room's four braziers. Then my eyes adjusted to this unnatural light and I gasped in disbelief.

Bound to a table, transformed into a makeshift alter, lay a terrified Eva. The ivory silk of her nightgown spilled over the table, exposing her alabaster legs. I looked up at the man leaning over her. "Mir!" I nearly dropped my weapon in shock.

With the long, dark mage's robe covering his brown tunic and pants, Mir seemed to have stepped straight out of the book of old tales Erik and I had read recently. I hardly recognized my brother. Mir stood differently—straighter, although I didn't remember him being bent or misshapen. The arrogant set of his jaw and cold calculation of his eyes were new to me. Mir looked dangerous. For some reason, the clear lucidity of his eyes only increased this impression of danger. I felt my throat tightening.

"Don't move," Mir said, pressing a knife on Eva's neck.

I obeyed; it wasn't very hard as I was still frozen by shock. "You!" I breathed.

Mir smiled smugly. "I thought you'd figure it out earlier. Jafer did." He sighed, displaying an unconvincing sadness. "I had to dispose of him. A real annoyance. I couldn't stay in my room after that. By the way, did you like my alarm system? All these bells and strings, convincing wasn't it. Only a crazy man would've come up with such an invention."

My face was burning with anger, my hand tightening around the grip of my rapier.

"See, the bells were to cover the presence of a dear friend of mine."

I frowned, watching Mir's eyes flick across the room. The ringing of hundreds of small bells echoed. I turned toward the sound.

A figure was coming out of the darkness. Its movements were as graceful as a seasoned dancer, but its form was somewhat distorted as if stuck between the mirage of a beautiful woman and its own ambiguous one. "The door is secure," the creature said above the banging and shouting coming from the chamber's second door. "I charmed its wood. They might bring it down but still won't be able to pass its threshold."

Amid the many voices of the people trying to get into this chamber, I recognized Oroco's light tone. At that instant, I did something I thought I would never do, I wished for the eunuch to be at my side.

"I believe you've all met Likos," Mir said with obvious pleasure.

Likos gave us a disturbing grin. "Yes, they have," he replied in a growling voice.

"Efreet, evil demon!" Mira shouted.

Mir burst in laughter. "Please, mind your manners; my friend is very sensitive… and noisy. I'm astounded that you didn't suspect his presence in my room. You never questioned with whom I was constantly speaking. The bells alone were a clue, Likos keeps losing them."

The efreet produced an expression of pure contempt. "Don't blame me; you're the one with a taste for dancers."

A shiver of disgust ran down my spine; I'd rather not think about what went on between those two. I shook my head. How many of those stupid bells had I picked up? Too many. And Mir's mumbling, a crazy man talking to himself, I had assumed. I was the fool. I looked up and found the efreet staring at me. The demon stepped closer to us.

At my side, Erik took a deep breath. Then without warning, he launched forth, brandishing the Slayer. As the blade sliced through its midsection, the efreet bared his teeth in a nightmarish grimace while Mir screamed.

Likos leapt back. Half curled upon itself, the demon held his belly. "How dare you. You'll pay for this," the efreet growled. When Likos straightened itself, I saw that it had dropped all charm. The efreet was once more the black-skinned, winged creature that had stood in my room. And to my horror, I also saw that its belly was intact. The Slayer might have inflicted some pain to the efreet, but it didn't wound it.

In one leap Likos was at Erik's throat, the demon's fingernails dug into my brother's flesh like small daggers. I rushed to Erik's help, attacking the efreet with my rapier, piercing its side without effort... and without effect.

Erik raised the Slayer, but before he could strike Likos again, the efreet knocked the weapon out of Erik's hand with one broad swap of his clawed paw. The Slayer slid across the room. From the corner of my eye, I saw Mira chase after the blade.

As I returned my attention to the efreet, a new form rose up beside Mir. I immediately recognized Salima's delicate frame.

"Please stop him," she begged Mir.

Folding his arms, Mir smiled with satisfaction while watching the efreet choke Erik, who by now was barely conscious.

Meanwhile I continued striking the efreet, even though my best effort to wound Likos remained without success. Yet I couldn't stop. Erik needed my help, I could see his strength waning, his face turning blue. Then Erik's hands fell alongside his body and he stopped struggling. I gasped, horrified, as the efreet raised Erik's limp body above his head and looked at Mir for further instructions.

"Please stop, he's your brother," Salima went on begging. "You promised you wouldn't hurt him."

Mir sneered. "All right—Likos, let him go."

The efreet chucked Erik against the wall. My brother hit the stone wall with a sinister thump and slid to the floor where he lay motionless. Salima rushed to Erik's side. In tears, she lifted his head and rested it on her lap. Erik let out a moan. My heart leapt. He was alive. I nearly crumbled to the floor under the force of my relief.

"You promised not to hurt him," Salima lamented while rocking Erik back and forth.

"Oh, stop it!" Mir snapped. "This is your fault. You should've killed the Sultan years ago, as Grandfather wanted. The poor man had no tongue, he couldn't recite the incantation. He counted on you, the last member of his family still alive, to do it. You failed him and almost betrayed me. You were weak then, and are weaker now, Mother."

Mother! Salima was Mir's mother. I was shocked.

Mir glared at her with obvious rancor. "Even after the Sultan threw you away, like a vulgar object. Even after he made you the servant of his foreign bitch, even then you refused to avenge our line."

Salima looked at me with watery eyes. "I tried to stop him," she said apologetically. "I went to his room, but he was already gone. That's when I saw the Vizier. I searched the tunnels for him. I did my best, but I failed. It was I who stole your book and hid it away, so he wouldn't use the dark magic it contains. He found it anyway."

"So you're the one who ransacked my room," I said.

"No, I did," Mir interjected. "I'd been reading and stealing your books one at a time for quite a while, you just didn't notice."

This revelation hit me like a slap in the face. Suddenly everything became clear. That smudge in my book, that familiar smell, it was herb cheese, Mir's favorite snack.

Grinning, Mir continued, "But that day I couldn't find your Yalec magic book, the one containing the curse I was using; I thought you had stored it in a secret place. So I turned everything upside down to find it—in the same time raising Jafer's suspicion. And to think it was you I was worrying about. I even sent Likos to check on your progress." As he spoke, Mir lifted his knife from Eva's neck and took a step forward.

Eva immediately began struggling on the table.

I was debating if I should attack Mir now when a low purring, like that of a tiger, blew near my ear. Then a burst of heat struck the back of my neck. From the corner of my eye, I saw that it was the efreet's breath; the creature was that close to me. I twirled, facing it.

Keeping its burning gaze on me, Likos addressed Mir, "What are your orders, my sweet?"

My sweet! I grimaced. Then I cursed myself, as I recalled Mir picking up pastries in the kitchen. Efreets love sugar. Damn! He fooled me for so long and so completely.

With a wink at Likos, Mir ordered, "Have your demonic army kill all the Sultan's sons except for Salima's sons."

Sons? How many did she have? I looked at Likos. I could swear that the efreet was confused if not divided. Likos stared at Mir then at Erik then at me. Although I knew it was useless, I raised my rapier. The efreet didn't move. It looked uncertain.

"Are you sure this is what you want?" Likos asked. There was a new expression on the efreet's face, an unpleasant smile on its lips, as if it had just now realized what was demanded of it.

"Yes!" Mir shouted. "Father's dead. There's no use dragging this on any further. Leave only Salima's sons as heirs and you'll get your sacrifice. Go—do it. And stay with your army until they're done. One cannot trust night spirits and ghosts to work unsupervised. At first chance, they'll return to the dark holes we pulled them from. Go, now!"

I flinched as the efreet vanished in a puff of smoke. I had not expected that. I assumed the efreet would kill me before leaving.

"Arghh!" Mir shook a fist at the disappearing efreet. Apparently, he too was stunned by the demon's choice of action. "Why couldn't you start with him?" Aiming his gaze at me, Mir sighed. "It seems I'll have to take care of you myself, brother."

In a surprising show of agility, Mir leapt over the table. Shedding his long robe, he exposed the sword hanging at his side. I suddenly realized that I'd never seen Mir wearing a sword before. Pushing back the sleeves of his tunic over well-muscled forearms, he unsheathed his blade. Lord! It was a cutlass.

I had seen these long serrated swords in the armory before. Mostly used by naval officers—because it could saw through ropes faster than a regular saber could hack through them—I'd always considered cutlasses as somewhat of a curiosity. I never imagined that one could actually fight with such a gruesome weapon. I easily pictured the type of damage this serrated blade could do. It would chew up my flesh just like a good kitchen knife would a mutton leg.

"You're not the only one to practice in secret, Amir." Mir said. "However I, *contrary to you*, know my opponent's strengths and weaknesses."

Taking a combat stand, I watched Mir advance.

He moved with ease. His body was more muscular than I had imagined—I realized that I had never really looked at him, because I had never considered Mir a threat.

Clicking his heels together, Mir saluted me then extended his cutlass toward my rapier. The instant the tips of our blades touched, the fight began.

I attacked first, trying to sneak under his guard. Mir blocked me effortlessly. I tried gliding my blade along his to get closer. But my rapier got caught in the teeth of his cutlass. I couldn't use that move against this weapon.

"Not so easy." Mir smiled. He then swiftly twirled his wrist. As my blade was still hooked to the teeth of his, my arm was pulled downward and my weapon nearly torn out of my hand. The tip of my rapier struck the floor, and before I could raise my guard again, Mir's cutlass ripped through my right shoulder.

Grinding my teeth, I fought the pain and kept my hold on my weapon. To be disarmed now meant death. In a broad sweep, I struck his blade sideways, pushing it away from me and ripping more of my flesh at the same time. Clutching my shoulder, I stepped back. Steaming hot blood gushed through my fingers.

"I'm disappointed, I thought you were better than this," Mir said in a steady voice.

Damn! He wasn't even breathing fast—while I was already winded. Thinking of it, I believed my state had more to do with blood loss and shock than true exhaustion.

The next few minutes were lost in a flurry of blows, each coming at me faster than the last. I was having more and more trouble blocking them, and when I raised my blade to block the last one, I knew my angle was wrong. The cutlass hit the side of my rapier, shattering its blade close to the hilt. Continuing in the same sweeping motion, the cutlass dipped low under my guard. "Ahhh!" I screamed as its teeth sliced through my side. My legs gave and I found myself on my back with only a knob of a blade to protect me.

Through the burning pain eating my side, I watched Mir plant his feet on either side of my shoulder. The tip of his cutlass was now grazing my throat.

Beaming with pride, Mir addressed Salima: "See, Mother, even the best swordsman of our family can't approach my skill."

Looking terrified instead of proud, Salima clutched Erik's shoulder harder, making my wounded brother grimace. Her reaction brought a sour pout to Mir's lips.

His eyes narrowed. "You always loved him more than me. He's your favorite son. The one you wanted. He's your personal revenge against Father."

What was he talking about? I was lost. I stared at Salima's frightened face. Erik wasn't her son… he couldn't be… he… Could he? My eyes returned to Mir. I could almost see the dark thought brewing behind his eyes. Movements farther back in the room caught my eyes.

Mira was silently crawling toward us with the Slayer in hand.

My eyes swung back to the blade near my throat. *I can stab his calf with the bit that is left of my rapier.* Yet I knew this action would only hasten my death. Mira needed more time, she needed a diversion. I cast my eyes on Mir. "Why?" I asked.

"Why!" he spat. "How dare you ask me why? Our father ruined our entire family line on a whim—that's why." The venom in Mir's words was hard to bare. "But, I haven't told you the worst. A few years ago, I used the secret passage to enter Father's room. There I found that he'd left specific orders concerning my treatment after his death. I was to remain caged and childless for the rest of my life, regardless of who became the next sultan. That's when I decided it was time to avenge my family." Mir smiled at me viciously. "That's why I chose this curse, so he would suffer month after month like Grandfather had. I only wish it'd lasted longer." Mir spat on the ground. "Do you know what the Vizier told me before I ripped his belly open?"

I shook my head, very slightly; his cutlass's blade was on my neck.

"He said that Father had done well to put my name behind Jafer's in the succession line, as if I would be surprised by that."

I had to admit that it all sounded like something our father would do. The man was petty enough to have left such orders. However, I could argue that it was my name behind Jafer's and not his—but something else came out of my mouth. "It's your efreet that betrayed Eva and I to Princess Livia, isn't it?"

Mir burst into laughter. "My efreet—Nooo! It was my mother."

I stared at Salima. She looked ashamed for a brief instant then raised her chin and said, "You were endangering the princess. I couldn't... I had to tell. Please forgive me."

"Ahh, you're back!" Mir exclaimed looking at the door. "Just in time to see me finish Amir—" He shot a glance at Erik, and added, "And maybe that one too."

Salima let out a long wail.

Twisting my neck, I saw that the efreet had returned from its mission. With careful steps, Likos began circling us, its glowing red eyes fixed on Mir. A low growl escaped his throat as it neared us.

I looked up at Mir.

He smiled down at me. "Farewell, brother."

Before Mir could push his blade in my throat, I sank the rest of my rapier in his calf. If I was to die, I would fight all the way there. To my surprise, the cutlass never touched my neck. Instead Mir was propelled across the room by some invisible hands. He struck the wall and landed on the floor in a tangle of tapestry.

Stunned, I gazed at Likos now standing at my feet. The attack on Mir was no doubt its doing—but why? Why turn on his master?

"What's wrong with you?" Mir said, standing up. "I told you all the Sultan's sons—but Salima's."

The efreet's shoulders stiffened. An odd expression crossed his face. I thought that for a demon Likos looked quite sad. Then I regained my senses, stopped eyeing the efreet, and instead pulled the two registry pages out of my pocket. I scrolled down its list of names until I found Salima's. She had given birth to a son named Amir; however the second registry's page showed a different birth date—the tabulator's registry had Mir's birth date linked to Salima, while the Sultan's registry had... mine. The Grand Vizier had purposely mixed our birthdates, keeping my true descent hidden from everyone but himself and my father. *That's why the Vizier disliked me so, and why when Father looked at me he said he couldn't escape his mistake.* Then something else hit me. My name wasn't at the end registry anymore; I was third for the throne. Those were the changes Father had made before dying, the changes he and the Vizier had argued about.

I tried sitting up. Pain drilled my shredded side. At my third attempt, I succeeded.

"Likos!" I heard Mir say. His voice was angry. He still didn't understand that the efreet was going to kill him.

"Mir!" I shouted. "Mir, run!"

But instead Mir walked straight to the efreet. "Likos, go back and kill the last son. You hear me."

"NOOO!" I screamed.

The efreet looked my way torn by our mixed orders.

Mir punched Likos in the chest. "Don't look at him. I give the orders… agh!"

In a lightning-fast move, Likos grabbed Mir by the throat, lifting him off the ground, and before I could shout another word, I heard a snap. Mir's head fell loosely upon his chest.

Salima screamed and quickly buried her face in Erik's shoulder. I then noticed that Mira had made it to their side. I watched her pull the Slayer from behind her back. With a peek at the efreet, she slid it to me.

I winced, as the blade clamored against the tiles. The sound stopped when the Slayer hit my thigh. I immediately covered it with my leg. When I looked up, the efreet was approaching. It stopped at a safe distance from me and began a careful scrutiny of the room. "It is done," Likos said in a thundering voice. Tendrils of fog seeped through the floor and began swirling up the efreet's body. Likos's demonic army had returned. Covering its leader in a ghastly mist, it entered the efreet's mouth as soon as the demon started gulping air. I could swear the creature was swelling in size with each new gulp it took. I thought I should say or do something before it got too big. "Likos, why didn't you tell Mir he wasn't Salima's son?"

Likos's head tilted. "He never asked."

"I'm Salima's son, am I not?" I risked. I wasn't going to make Mir's mistake.

The efreet smiled; well, I thought it was a smile. "Yes. You are her son."

"And Erik."

"Him too."

I looked at Erik's fair skin and strapping physique. For true brothers we looked almost nothing alike. "How do you know?"

"I'm an efreet. I have the answers to all questions, as long as they are asked."

"Then tell me how he is my brother."

"You have the same mother but not the same father. You are Sultan Mustafa's son, while he is the offspring of King Erik the Fair of Sorvinka. Years ago, when still a young prince he accompanied his sister, Princess Livia, here. He stayed a few months, long enough to seduce Salima and conceive a son."

My attention turned to Salima; her face was soaked with tears. "Is this true?"

She nodded. "Yes. When Princess Livia learned of my condition, she immediately knew it was her brother's son and that I and my unborn child were in grave danger. I was forbidden to have more children." Salima lovingly brushed Erik's blond curls from his forehead. "Princess Livia couldn't bear the loss of the future King of Sorvinka's first born. She couldn't bear to lose me either. So she conceived the plan of passing Erik for her own child. By wearing loose clothing and spending most of my term locked inwith her, we thought I might hide my pregnancy. It worked. We fooled everyone into thinking Erik was Princess Livia and the Sultan's son." Salima kissed a stun-looking Erik on the forehead. Obviously, he didn't know this either.

I touched my face. I had thought our similar facial features and pale brown eyes came from our father—now I knew they were Salima's. No wonder the fog didn't hurt me or Erik when we walked inside it. That was also why we were both able to break the spells trapping our brothers, me with Hamed, Erik with Rashid. If only we had known earlier. Then I noted the faces Mira was making and I turned back to the efreet. "Couldn't you spare Mir?" I asked, while my hand closed around the Slayer.

"No, he captured me with an old incantation that forced me to obey his every command. As long as Mir paid me for my army's services with his family's blood, I was chained to him." The efreet's lips stretched. This time I had no doubt, it was a smile. "However, now I am not chained to anyone—anymore."

I felt the blood drain from my face. But before I could move an inch, the efreet's ice-cold hands circled my neck. My face was so close to Likos's that our noses almost touched. The creature's breath was as fowl as rotten meat. I kicked, punched and struggled uselessly—the efreet's grip on my neck was unbreakable. My vision began darkening, its periphery shrinking. With my last strength, I raised the Slayer and plunged it into the efreet's belly. It felt like stabbing butter. The demon howled. Next thing I knew I was hitting the floor.

With the Slayer sticking out of his belly, Likos went on a tornado-like rampage across the room, hitting and destroying everything it could grab. I had assumed that the creature would die quickly—like in the tales—not go berserk like this. Its howls were thoroughly ghastly.

My eyes went straight to Eva who was still tied to the table. I made a mad dash for her and toppled the table over before the efreet could seize her. I undid Eva's bonds in a hurry. Then we hugged each other tightly while around us the room broke apart.

As if it had burned all its energies, the efreet suddenly stood very still. The high wind subsided. Debris and objects of all kinds rained down to the floor. Likos emitted a low growl. Then in a puff of smoke, the demon vanished. The clank of the Slayer striking the tiles immediately followed.

With Eva's help, I stood up and joined the others.

Mira had already gathered up the Slayer. She extended it to me. "Wielded by one and not the other, Jafer said. It now made sense. You're the one with the drop of royal Telfarian blood needed for the Slayer to work."

"Yes." I smiled sadly. "Erik and I are the intertwined lines he talked about, the tulip and the rose grown in the same pot. We both are the faults of two kings. Jafer was right. I…" I swallowed hard. The memory of Jafer still pained me. Taking the Slayer, I made the silent promise of honoring his memory the best I could. With the efreet's charm now gone, the chamber's doors burst open.

Led by Oroco, an army of eunuchs and palace guards spilled into the room with Hassan and Princess Livia in tow.

Hassan's eyes focused immediately on the Slayer. "The Demon Slayer, the first Sultan's sword. We searched everywhere for it. The Vizier was extremely distraught that someone managed to steal it from the pairikas he conjured up to guard this precious heirloom."

"We too looked for this tool." I explained, how we had found it, the reason for our presence here, and what had happened in this room. (But I kept the fact that Erik wasn't the Sultan's son, secret. He was my brother. I dared not risk his life with this truth.) Motioning toward Mir's disarticulated body, I continued. "He caused this horrible killing by cursing Father and setting an efreet on us. In the end, the demon killed him too."

Hassan's mouth dipped downward. "Demons are rarely loyal."

I thought that Likos had been loyal enough.

Hassan then walked to Erik and bowed. "Your father, the Sultan, is dead, and with the exception of Prince Amir so are all of your other brothers. Prince Keri, you are now the highest ranking prince, therefore you are the new Sultan."

Erik slowly rose. His legs seemed unsteady yet they held him. Shaking his head, Erik looked at me. "You're the real heir, Amir. You should be Sultan. The choice is yours. Command and we'll obey." Erik bowed to me.

To my surprise so did Princess Livia and Oroco. Soon everyone in the room was bowing to me.

CHAPTER TWENTY-FIVE

I looked at all these bowing people. "No," I breathed in a voice so low that only Erik, who was closest to me, seemed to have caught. Yet the look of confusion on his face indicated that he was unsure of what he had just heard.

"N… n… n," I tried again but did even worst than before. My throat had clamped shut. Nothing was coming out. I couldn't speak anymore. Panic suddenly seized me. Now I couldn't breathe, couldn't think. My head was spinning.

"Amir," I heard someone ask. I turned. It was Eva. She gently placed a hand on my forearm. "Amir, you're trembling! What's wrong? Do you need a seat?"

I shook my head, unable to speak. Then on impulse, I rushed out of the chamber and ran in the direction of my tower only to realize moments later that I was on the wrong side of the Cage. Fortunately, the guards were still too shaken by recent events to think straight and opened the gate for me without question. Once I had reentered the Cage, I stopped in the Great Hall where servants and physicians were tending to the business of removing my dead brothers' bodies from the room. Among this group, I recognized the tall bony silhouette of the chief physician, the man who had saved Erik's life. I watched him bend down beside one of my brothers. My heart dropped. It was Darius. Joining the physician, I kneeled beside my dear departed brother. Darius looked as handsome in death as he had in life. At least his body had not been desecrated. It was a very small consolation.

The kind old man gave me an apologetic look. "There's nothing I can do for him or the others." Then his expert eyes roamed over me for a few seconds. "You however could use my care."

"Later," I said. With a sigh, I lightly glided my fingertips on Darius's forehead as a last farewell gesture, then left for my tower.

I wasn't there for more than half an hour when I heard knocking at my door. I didn't answer. I just stayed seated on the bench by my window, looking out.

"Amir," a voice called behind the door. "It's me, Erik. Open up."

I took a deep breath. "It's not locked."

Erik immediately entered and seated himself in front of me on the bench. His left arm was in a sling and a nasty looking bruise already colored one of his cheekbones.

"Why did you run?" he asked in a soft voice.

"I needed to think… alone."

"Have you?"

"Yes," I said with a firmness that surprised me. "There are things I need to ask you. If you were to become Sultan what would you do with the Cage?"

Erik's face twisted. "I'd tear down all its gates."

I smiled satisfied. "And Eva?"

"I've already told you that. Eva would be free to do as she wishes—considering that she's my half-sister that's the least I could do." Erik suddenly frowned. "Why are you asking me these questions? Amir, when you said no earlier… You're not really thinking of abdicating in my favor."

I nodded.

"Have you lost your mind?" Erik cried out. Then lowering his voice, he murmured, "You can't... not to me. I'm not a Ban... not even a Telfarian."

I seized my brother's right hand. The gesture reopened the wound in my side making me wince. "You are more a Telfarian than I am. You have more love for this country than I ever will. And honestly, the thought of becoming Sultan suffocates me. It is not what I dream about. Being Sultan is the last thing in the world I want."

Erik shook his head as if he was refusing to understand my reasons.

"Listen to me, little brother. I'm not prepared for this position. You, on the other hand, are ready for it. Father thought the same. That's why he put you ahead of me on his list, because you're more apt to rule than I am."

For the following hour, we stayed seated and discussed this matter at length. Many times Erik asked me if I was sure of my decision, that if I wanted it I could still change my mind and that he would understand. But each time my response stayed the same. He, Keri Erik Ban, would be the next Sultan of Telfar, while I would remain a prince—a very rich prince, however. Erik insisted that I take half of the treasury. I declined the offer. It was too much. Instead I settled for a fifth of its contents and the ownership of my father's summer palace. Its view of the Irvel Lake was said to be sublime.

"You need the care of a physician, Amir," Erik said once we had reached an accord.

Carefully, I probed the skin around the gash on my shoulder. "They're only flesh wounds, but you're right. They should be tended to. Also I think it's time for me to leave this tower... for good."

Erik offered me his arm as support. I took it. Both wincing, we painfully stood up.

"We make quite the pair," he said.

"Yes," I agreed.

Slowly we exited my room only to stop in front of Jafer's. As I stared at his door, tears welled up in my eyes. I had another reason for refusing the throne. One I kept to myself. Jafer had prophesied that the Ban line would be broken. I would never go against his last wish. "Farewell, my dear brother," I whispered, "may you find peace in the afterlife."

Then, supporting each other, Erik and I left the Cage.

* * *

"See the four little arms inside this crocus flower?" I said, bringing the purple bloom near Eva's eyes. "They are called stigmas."

"These orange things?"

"Yes. Well, that's where saffron comes from."

She looked shocked. "From these flowers." In a sweeping gesture, she pointed to the crocus field that surrounded us. We were seated right in its center on a bright blue blanket.

"Saffron is dried up stigmas."

With great care, Eva plucked a stigma from the crocus's heart. She crushed it between her fingers and then breathed in its aromas. "Hmm, it's wonderful," she said with her eyes closed.

I nodded, gazing at the vast expanse of purple and white flowers that was offered to our eyes. Although it was still early morning, the Telfarian sun was bright and the field was already filled with workers. Most were women; their delicate fingers were better suited for harvesting saffron. I grinned, suddenly overwhelmed by joy. Only a week had passed since I had left the Cage. Yet I had taken advantage of every minute of my new freedom and visited as many places as I could. I tried bringing Eva along in these escapes, but it proved a challenge because, according to our tradition, noblewomen needed to be accompanied by a male relative every time they ventured outside. This enraged Eva, and the long costume that left only her eyes exposed, which she was forced to wear every time she exited the palace, angered her even more. So we usually went out in disguise… like today. Dressed as wealthy commoners we could pass for a married couple and go most everywhere, as long as no one recognized us. We had been lucky so far.

I raised my face to the sun and breathed in the morning air. The scents of wet dirt and crushed saffron tickled my nostrils. I loved it. Beaming with delight, I turned toward Eva. I frowned. She looked too serious. "What's wrong?" I asked.

"Nothing," she said, staring straight ahead. "We should return to the palace. Erik's crowning is at noon. We should get ready."

"Our crowning is different than yours. No one is putting a crown on anyone's head. Ours is more of a presentation."

"I know," Eva interjected with humor. "It starts with a procession through the city, so the people can see their new ruler, followed by a formal introduction to the nobles and dignitaries of the kingdom."

"You forgot the months-long celebration."

"No," she said, rising up. "You forgot that you must prepare yourself. You too are riding in this procession… while Mira and I will contend ourselves with watching you from a balcony with Salima." The sharpness of her tone worried me. Had I offended her in some mysterious way? But before I could ask her, Eva grabbed my hand and said, "We also need to talk. There is something you need to know… it concerns both of us."

I was immediately on my feet. "What is it?" I asked, my stomach suddenly in knots.

"Not here," she said. "I'll tell you once we've returned to the palace."

The trip back to the palace was a real torture for me. What had started as a slight apprehension had quickly transformed into fear. What if Eva said that she didn't love me anymore?

What if she had fallen for another? This terrible idea kept churning in my head nonstop. So when we finally entered my new apartment and Eva said, "Amir, I love you very much, I thought I should tell you." I was immediately relieved. Then seconds later, Eva verbally stabbed me right in the heart.

"However," she said, stepping inches from me, "regardless of my feelings toward you I have requested permission to leave Telfar."

"No!" I exclaimed. "You can't leave. Oh… I see. You're jesting again."

Eva caressed my cheek. "Amir, would I jest with something like this? You know me. I would never be this cruel."

A sharp pain ran across my chest. I brushed her hand off my cheek and backed away from her. "If you leave me, you are cruel."

"Amir," she said in a reprimanding tone. "Be careful not to say something regretful. I did not make this decision lightly. I thought it through."

"Please, you must reconsider… do it for me."

Eva raised her chin. My heart sank. I knew the meaning of this gesture too well. She was going to hold her ground. "I'm sorry, Amir. I cannot live here. I cannot live with the constraints of your traditions."

"Give it time. You'll grow accustomed to them," I said, hating the begging tone my voice had taken.

Eva shook her head. She crossed the space separating us and brushed her soft lips over mine. Stepping back, she said, "I love you, but I won't stay here. You, however, are free to follow me." She then dashed out of my room.

Feeling totally gutted, I stayed in my apartment mulling over dark thoughts until a steward knocked at my door announcing that I should prepare for the procession. Without any enthusiasm, I put on my ceremonial clothes: silver chemise and pants covered with a bright blue kaftan. Then for the first time in my life I set a silver belt around my waist. Sadly, it brought me no joy. I was too devastated by the thought of losing Eva to find joy in anything. Then grabbing my blue turban, I hurried to the palace's main entrance.

* * *

A small group of people, mostly nobles, already waited near the entrance door when I arrived. In her blood-red dress, Princess Livia stood out from this crowd. As the Sultan's mother—although Salima was Erik's real mother, Princess Livia would go on playing this role for Erik's safety—she would ride at his side. She must be overjoyed by this, I thought. Then she turned her gaze toward me. Murderous hate filled her eyes. I blinked, confused.

"Prince Amir," she said as she made her way toward me. Without ceremony she gripped my arm and pulled me aside. "You," she hissed at me, "you ruined everything. Because of you the next Sorvinkian King will be a weak one."

"Princess Livia, I don't understand."

"Listen carefully, foolish boy, I will not let you ruin my niece's future as you ruined Erik's. Stay away from her or beware my wrath."

"Do not threaten me," I shot in a strong voice.

All conversation in the entrance abruptly ceased. Everybody present was now looking at us. A heavy silence followed, during which Princess Livia and I glared at one another.

Erik's appearance in the entrance brought cheers from the assembled nobles and relieved the tension which had built up in the place. He was dressed in white from head to toe; even the fur that was trimming his kaftan was white. After having acknowledged the bowing nobles, Erik joined us. "Mother, Amir, come. We must climb on our mounts. The population is clamoring to see us."

Princess Livia darted a hate-filled eye my way and whispered, "If you think that you can ruin my plans and get away

with it, you are sorely mistaken. You'll pay for this, I promise."
Then she stepped outside.

I took her threat seriously, and although it worried me to
some extent, I was more intrigued by it than anything else.
What have I done to deserve this? I shrugged. I would know
soon enough, I supposed.

"What are you waiting for?" Erik asked, with a big smile
on his face.

"For you, little brother," I replied.

Erik's smile got bigger still, and then it abruptly vanished.
After a peek over his shoulder, he said, "I hope Mother wasn't
giving you trouble about Eva."

"How do you know?"

"Since she learned that Eva had asked me if she could return
home, Mother became very 'convinced' that the two of you
should not see each other alone anymore."

I punched Erik in the shoulder.

Gasps of horror rose from the nobles waiting at the entrance.

I ignored it. "Why did you have to say yes?" I snapped.

Erik's eyebrows rose. "Amir, we discussed this before. You
knew I would set her free. I've already wrote to her father announcing Eva's wish to return home. I also mentioned in my
letter that you would probably accompany her on this trip."
Erik made a face. "I hope the King will take this news well."

I clutched my belly. "Oh, I feel sick."

"Why, Amir? I thought you wanted to see the world."

"Yes… but…" I wringed my hands. "Once in Sorvinka, the
King might decide to marry Eva to someone else."

Erik threw an arm around my shoulder. "True. He's her
father. He can certainly do that. Face it, Amir, there is a strong
chance that you will have to *win* Eva's hand. So once there
try gaining the King's esteem, it might help. However, it's
going to take months before we get the King's reply, so in the
meantime if I were you, I'd spend as much time as I could

with Eva." Bending to my ear, Erik whispered. "Just be careful that Mother doesn't catch you."

"Why is your mother so angry at me, do you know?"

Erik blew out a long breath. "It's complicated. If you don't mind, I'll explain it to you tomorrow. Today we have a procession to attend."

I nodded in agreement.

As we walked toward the entrance's doorway, I thought about Erik's suggestion. It was a smart one. And I vowed that at the first chance I would get, I would find Eva and savor every minute we had together. With this in mind, I followed Erik under the shaded portico of the entrance. We emerged on the other side in the bright midday sun. The roar of the crowd assembled behind the palace's fortified walls to see their new Sultan was deafening. Yet I paid no mind to it. The bulk of my attention was taken by our mounts. Three giant elephants, their bodies covered with red decorative motifs, gold tassels and ornaments, awaited us.

"You cannot be serious!" I exclaimed, staring at Erik.

He nodded vigorously. "Mother doesn't mind," he said.

I turned back. Seated in a palanquin set atop the second beast, Princess Livia, her face partly hidden under a veil, was glaring at me. My eyes lowered to her mount. I shook my head. "Elephants are not traditional Telfarian mounts."

"Actually, two other Sultans have ridden elephants before, though not in a crowning procession, I'll concede you that. Consider this my last folly, Amir. Once I return to the palace I'll be a Sultan. I won't be able to do anything amusing anymore." Then nudging me in the ribs, he added, "Also, I think that when one is offered the chance of riding an elephant, one must take it."

I stared at the huge animals with some apprehension, then reluctantly said, "All right. After all, it is your day."

CHAPTER TWENTY-SIX

Leaning against the balcony rail of my luxurious apartment, I sipped a glass of steaming tea, savoring this quiet morning—the first since Mir's death two months ago. I was happy to see the end of the crowning celebration. It was tiring in the end. I blew on my tea while gazing at the city. My eyes danced on the white wash of the houses, the red tiles of their roofs, on the golden onion domes of the official buildings. I never tired of this view—it was constantly changing. There was always something new to see. It amazed me. Even its smells, a mixture of spices from the nearby market and camel wool, wafting up to my balcony was pure delight. My only regret was that my brothers had died without having enjoyed this freedom. I found myself thinking of Darius often, lately. How badly I had misjudged him. I wished I could go back in time and befriend him. He might still be alive if I had, and therefore Sultan. Now I knew that he would've made a good one. The fact that he was willing to sacrifice his life for us proved it. I suddenly felt guilty for having survived.

"Ah! There you are," Eva said, pulling me out of my sad reminiscence. I was grateful for her interruption. Dwelling on such events wasn't good for me, as I was by nature prone to melancholy. I turned and welcomed her with a broad grin.

Although it was very early in the morning, Eva was already in her finery. So many jewels hung from her hair and ears, I wondered how she managed to keep her head straight. In a ruffle of silk, she joined me on the balcony. I looked at her and smiled. With the pink morning glow on her cheeks, she was more beautiful than ever.

She wagged a finger at me. "You should've come with me, Amir. The ambassador asked for you before leaving."

"I know. I should've seen him leave. But that meant a close meeting with your Aunt Livia. She's still angry at me for the choice I made. I didn't think she could hold a grudge that long."

Eva chuckled adorably. "She'll survive."

I kissed the top of her head, feeling a bit guilty. I liked Ambassador Molsky and would miss him greatly. I regretted not seeing him off. However, I rationalized my action with the notion that I would soon see him again. Eva's wish had been granted. She was returning home and I was accompanying her. Her father took the news of her return well, I thought, and even sent word welcoming me into his castle. He ended the note by saying that his halls had ghosts needing expunging. I hoped he was only jesting, because I had my fill of ghosts.

The sound of hoofs striking the brick road made me look down at the palace's majestic entrance. A huge black warhorse passed the gate. Erik, clad in a plain brown kaftan, was back from his usual morning run. He was never one for fashion, I thought. Why should it change now that he was Sultan? Erik was practical. And in these garments, he could inspect the kingdom's true functioning without being recognized. I knew he would take the role of Sultan very seriously. He might not bring about all the changes Darius would have—Erik loved our culture and tradition more than Darius and I—but perhaps it was for the best. Once more, I thought I had made the right choice. From the height of his horse, Erik looked up at us and waved. We waved back.

"Why did you refuse the crown?" Eva asked, leaning against me. "People keep asking me that question."

"Erik... Keri, I should get used to his new name, is a born ruler. He has the temperament for it. I never wanted to be Sultan. I said it many times."

My eyes returned to the city's rooftops. I smiled. I had thought Princess Livia wanted Erik to rule Telfar—I was so wrong. Erik had explained everything to me. The conversation between her and Ambassador Molsky wasn't about Erik. The prince they were talking about was me. A poor spy I made. It was me she wanted as Sultan. As for Erik, she had grander plans for him: mainly Sorvinka's throne. Once the identity of Erik's father was revealed, he would've, without a doubt, become Sorvinka's next king. But for this she needed the next Sultan to love Erik enough to spare him regardless of who his father was. As Erik's friend and true brother I was the perfect candidate. "Are you a compassionate man?" she had once asked me. I smiled, what a cunning woman. Yet I had foiled her plan, though not voluntarily. Princess Livia couldn't safely divulge Erik's true birth anymore. He was now Sultan Keri Ban, the king's nephew, not his son. No wonder she was so mad at me. Somehow I doubted that Princess Livia had forgone her goal though. She'd soon foment another plan, I was quite sure of it.

I wished her luck. With Mira now Erik's first wife, she would need it. Theirs promised to be a difficult relationship. Princess Livia and Sultana Mira were both strong, determined women, each pushing to influence Erik on matters dear to their hearts. You may change the Sultan, but in this kingdom some things never change.

As for my mother, Salima, she still cried over Mir's death. I understood it; she had believed he was her son for so long—these feelings couldn't be dismissed so easily. I could only hope that with time we'd grow closer. These days, I often wondered if I would have become mad with revenge like Mir, had Salima nurtured me. Hard to say—I suppose I would never know, and didn't really care either. My life had changed and for the better.

I nuzzled my nose in Eva's neck. She giggled and twisted in my arms. It never failed to produce that reaction. She was ticklish; this was one of the wonderful things I had discovered since we began our courtship—a secret courtship, mind you. But I had high hopes for us. Soon I would meet with her father. With luck the King would deem me worthy of his daughter, and then there would be no more secrets.

"Do you really want to know why I refused the throne," I whispered in her ear.

"Yes," she breathed.

"For me, becoming Sultan only meant that I would've exchanged one cage for another. But as a rich prince I'm truly free. Free to see the city. Free to see the entire world." On this I squeezed Eva tighter against me.

Don't Miss the continuing adventures of Prince Amir in *The King's Daughters,* **coming Summer 2008.**

THE KING'S DAUGHTERS

[An Excerpt]

Chapter 1

Bitter cold stung my cheeks and transformed my breath into vapor. The snow squeaked under my boots as I walked along our caravan in search of survivors. Corpses; so far I'd found nothing but corpses. I spotted a column of steam rising from one of our fallen men. I rushed to his side only to discover with much chagrin that the white cloud of steam wasn't coming from his mouth... but from his opened gut. I touched his neck—no pulse. This one was dead too.

"Arrh! What kind of frozen, bandit-infested hell is this?" I cursed aloud in frustration and anger. This was the seventh attack by brigands we'd suffered since we'd set foot in Sorvinka. The elite soldiers, who had escorted us upon our departure from Telfar, had long since been decimated. We were now reduced to using Eva's Farrellian eunuch guards as our last defense—those eunuchs were a *parting gift* from her aunt, Princess Livia. At first, I did not fancy having them around. Now... well, now was a different story. I cast an uneasy glance at our dead guards. Their numbers were dwindling fast too. At this rate we'd soon be left without defense. I looked at the frozen, barren landscape. I hadn't been long in Sorvinka, and already I hated this country. Although I knew it was Eva's home, I couldn't understand why she wanted so badly to return to this frigid, inhospitable land. How could one miss this miserable place? *She missed her family, not this*, I told myself. I understood her desire to rejoin them, yet I wished we had stayed in Telfar, my homeland, warm, beautiful and safe Telfar. I let out a long sigh, and then continued my search for survivors. Even though I was still sweaty and warm from having fought in a battle, I tightened my kaftan around my body knowing that in a moment I would be shivering from the cold in this gray morning air.

"Aaah… Your Highness." The lament came from my left. I turned toward it. Clutching his bloody side, Ely, one of Eva's eunuch guards, was trying to rise. I rushed to his aide and gripped him just as he was about to fall forward. His eyes widened. "Your Highness, behind you!" I swung around. First, I saw the brigand coming at me; then I saw his blade aimed straight at my chest. With my own sword sheathed and my arm circling Ely's convulsing body, there was no way I could block his blow. The man was nearly upon me. Gritting my teeth, I braced myself for its impact. But just as his blade was about to plunge into my flesh, the brigand was rammed sideways by one of Eva's guards. With two efficient swipes of his sword, the tall eunuch easily dispatched the brigand. I didn't question myself for an instant the identity of my rescuer: it was young Milo. I recognized him immediately, not only by his unique swordplay—which was without flourish and done with an economy of movement—but also by his wispy blond hair. All the other eunuch guards had the bright red hair most common to Farrellians; while Milo's had only the slightest touch of copper. If one looked closely, one could spot freckles of the same hues dusting the bridge of his nose. This was the second time Milo had saved my life; although I was glad to be alive, a small part of me dreaded being indebted to the young eunuch. To my relief, a few more surviving guards joined Milo. Relinquishing Ely to the care of others, I made my way to Milo's side. Looking proud of himself, Milo bowed to me. With his lean athletic body and long limbs, Milo reminded me of a young colt, a bit clumsy yet very powerful, an unusual look for a eunuch… and a deceiving one too. And when one added Milo's square jaw, aquiline nose and overall masculine facial features to the mix, all that was left to betray his physical state as a eunuch were his light airy voice and smooth, beardless cheeks.

"How many guards survive? Do you know?" I asked.

"Seven, counting myself, my lord. Three are gravely wounded though. Those men won't be able to fight if we're attacked again."

I turned my sight to the gibbet still visible on the horizon and grimaced. "Sorvinka is known as the land of the thousand gibbets. If you ask me, they would do well to double that amount. I haven't seen that many ruffians in all my life." I shook my head. "This country will be the death of us."

"Yes, my lord," Milo said, while stomping his feet and beating his side for warmth. "And if the brigands don't get us, the cold will."

I looked at the shivering Farrellian. Milo was on the skinny side for a eunuch. Without this protective layer of fat, he tended to get cold quickly. I patted his shoulder. "You fought well today, Milo."

"So have you, my lord," Milo replied with a bow. When he straightened, I saw that he was beaming with pride. "I am pleased to have served Princess Eva as well as expected and, more so, not to have disappointed you." Milo paused, as if unsure if he should continue. I gave him a nod of encouragement. "I know that many… no, actually, most people don't consider us, eunuchs, as… true men, capable of true men's actions. I… I am overjoyed to have been able to prove myself to you, Prince Amir." On this Milo bowed at the waist. His show of gratitude made me uncomfortable, and I was glad when Eva poked her head out of her carriage.

"Amir! Amir!" she called. "Are you hurt?"

"I'm fine. Please stay inside the carriage. It's safer there. We'll join you in a moment." I turned to Milo. "You'll take Ely's place beside Eva."

"It will be my honor."

Rubbing my short beard, I inspected Milo's clothes. His costume, a red and white mock copy of the Farrellian military uniform, was torn and stained with blood. "Do you have a spare?"

"This *is* my spare."

"Come with me," I said. "I think I have something that might fit you." I made my way to the wagon containing my belongings. When I opened the back door, I caught a glimpse of my reflection in a polished bronze mirror propped against a chest, and flinched. I didn't recognize myself; for a moment, I thought I was looking at a ruffian. All I could see were piercing brown eyes and sharp cheekbones. Then I recognized my flawless profile with its perfect straight nose—the trademark of my family, the Ban—yes, that was me all right. I didn't look my best. I had lost my turban in the battle, and my short, thick black hair was all tussled. Also my beard was clipped too close to the skin for my taste, looking more like a shadow then a true beard. *Eva likes it this way*, I told myself as a consolation. It was a pain to maintain however. After a quick search in my garment trunk, I found a loose beige tunic and a dark green kaftan with sleeves ample enough to cover Milo's long limbs. Although Milo was clearly sad to part with his mock uniform—I had noted how proudly the young eunuch wore the garments—he took the clothing I offered him with good grace. Leaving the eunuch to change, I made my way to Eva's carriage. I wasn't surprised to see that Eva was outside. She never followed orders… especially mine. She was staring at the horizon, her black mink cape hanging loosely over her blue velvet dress, as if its addition had been an afterthought. For some reason, she seemed unaffected by the ambient cold. Petite and finely built, Eva had golden curls, warm brown eyes and a peachy complexion. Despite her ethereal look, my beautiful ice princess was not a delicate creature. In the course of this trip, I had discovered that Eva was as robust as a peasant girl and as headstrong as a mule. I found this new knowledge a little disconcerting, yet I let none of my feelings interfere. "You should've stayed inside the carriage," I said in a tone of reprove. "It's not safe for you out here."

"Hush!" she whispered, and then closing her eyes she took a deep breath. I watched a content smile stretch her lips. "Hmm," she made, as if she could taste the air. "I love the smell of spring in the air."

"Spring!" I stared at the snowy landscape with its naked, dead-looking trees, then at the depressing gray sky. "If this is spring, I dare not imagine what winter is like."

Eva burst into laughter. "You would love it," she said amidst billowy clouds of vapor breath. "You complain, but I know you would love it."

I smiled, but quite frankly, I doubted I would ever get used to this miserable cold, let alone enjoy it. Setting my gaze on the road ahead of us, I said, "I hope we can reach your father's castle before nightfall. I fear we may not survive another attack."

"Oh stop worrying. We're almost there. In a few hours we will be warming ourselves in my father's court." Eva's attention slowly glided to the yellow-covered wagon behind us. "Maybe then I will finally get to see all those mysterious gifts you've brought." Her nose wrinkled a bit, a sign that she was annoyed. "I don't understand why you have to be so secretive about them."

"What! And spoil the surprise?"

Eva rolled her eyes. "Fine." This settled, a brilliant smile lit up her entire face, and she squeezed my hand. "Oh, Amir, I can't wait for you to meet Father." My stomach clenched painfully—as it always did at the mention of my forthcoming meeting with her father.

"Amir, what's wrong? Why is this dreadful look on your face?"

I shook my head. "I fear… (Sigh). What if your father doesn't see me as a good enough prospect for you and denies me your hand? What if your father dislikes me on sight?"

"You worry too much, Amir. It's your biggest flaw, you know. You are very endearing, my prince. Why would my father dislike you?"

"I don't know. Your Aunt Livia despises me… well, let's be honest, she hates me. She never forgave me for refusing the Telfarian crown and making her son, Erik, the Sultan. She wanted him to be the next Sorvinkian King, not the ruler of a small country. I'm surprised your aunt hasn't exacted her revenge on me yet, she certainly threatened me that she would often enough."

Eva gave me a patient look. "Amir, my aunt does not wish you ill."

"Perhaps. But you can't deny that she distrusts me. That's why she surrounded you with eunuch guards, so they'd keep you safe… from me. We've been traveling together for months, and this is the first moment alone we have had since we left Telfar. Those guards were never meant to be a *gift* as she said. They were meant to be a barrier."

Displaying a charming pout, Eva ran a finger along my jaw. "Aren't you happy that she did so? As I see it, if it weren't for my guards, we wouldn't be alive now." Eva's carefree expression morphed into a somber one. She gazed at the grim surroundings. "Something has changed. When I last traveled these roads, Sorvinka wasn't a dangerous place. I don't understand what happened to my country. It worries me, Amir." Throwing her arms around my waist, Eva rested her head against my shoulder. "Let's leave this spot. Leave now. Let's not waste another moment here. I'm dying to see my family."

"Yes. Anything you want, my love," I said, bending down to kiss her.

"Huh-huh." Milo cleared his throat behind me. "My lord." I turned and was shocked by how a change of clothes could transform someone. Milo looked like a totally different man. The dark green kaftan accentuated the color of his eyes, which were soft green; it also made him seem blonder and gave his shoulders a more squared appearance. As it was right now, Milo could have passed for a young nobleman. "We are ready to leave, my lord."

"Then we should," I replied.

Eva applauded with enthusiasm. "I cannot wait to see Father."

"Yes… me too." I smiled at her. Deep down, however, I was petrified by fear… and given the choice I would have rather faced a horde of brigands than her father. *Enough*, I told myself. *The king has no reason to dislike me. Just don't give him one and everything will go well.*

* * *

I stared at the tall, fortified walls surrounding the castle. *Why won't they open the gate? Don't they understand me? It cannot be my accent. My Sorvinkian is near perfect.*

"OPEN!" I shouted one more time. "I am Prince Amir of Telfar. I accompany Princess Eva, the king's daughter. OPEN THE GATE!"

The gate remained closed. I turned my gray mare around and rode back to our caravan. I had reached its first carriage when I heard orders being yelled behind the wall. I looked back and saw armed men lining up behind the fortification and, *oh dear*, bows' strings being drawn. I felt my stomach drop. I couldn't believe it; they were going to shoot at us. Before I could order Eva's Farrellian guards to take cover, a volley of arrows flew in their directions, piercing their chests and necks. As the guards fell dying on the ground, the carriage door flew open and Milo appeared in its frame. "My lord, what's happening?"

"The king's castle has been taken by enemies; I see no other reason for this attack. Stay inside with Eva. Keep her safe. You hear me, Milo?"

"Yes, my lord," he said, and shut the carriage door.

Pulling my sword, I pushed my horse toward the front of our caravan. Before I could get there, the castle's gate opened with the loud clicking of well-oiled chains, and a small army of soldiers rushed out. Within moments, the entire caravan was surrounded.

"Drop your weapon," called one of the soldiers.

"NO!" To my surprise, the soldier seemed unsure of what to do.

"Obey."

I shook my head.

"Make way," a voice ordered from the back of the troop. The row of soldiers circling me parted and four knights riding black warhorses approached. Clad in shining armor and black leather, they looked impressive. All four were tall and solidly built, like most Sorvinkians, but the knight riding in front was particularly imposing. He was a good head taller than everyone else. Telling the other knights to stay behind, he brought his horse a short distance from mine and stared at me through the slits in his gilded helm. He had vibrant blue eyes, I noted. "In the name of the King, relinquish your weapon," he boomed, his deep voice amplified by his helm. I stared at the imperial crest embossed on his armor, divided in three sections it depicted a rose beside a black eagle over a bear. Then I looked at the soldiers. They wore the blue uniform of the Sorvinkian army, and they too carried the imperial banner. I was confused.

"In the name of which king?"

"King Eric the Fair. Ruler of Sorvinka."

"I don't believe you. King Erik would never allow my men to be slaughtered in such a way. This is the action of a vulgar bandit."

"You tell me so," he said while pulling off his helm. Gray-streaked blond hair fell about his shoulders. I looked at the strong line of his square jaw, at his straight nose and his blue eyes. There wasn't a doubt in my mind, this was King Erik. I recognized his rugged looks from paintings I had seen of him. I let out a sigh of relief. "Prince Amir, your arrogance is quite shocking to me," said the king. "Not satisfied to surround my daughter with Farrellians—Sorvinka's most deadly enemies—

and bring them to my doorstep, you have the impudence to call me a vulgar bandit. Kings have been vexed at far less."

I felt my face blanching. "Farrellian enemies? I don't understand."

"Don't you dare blame your actions on ignorance. The fact that Farrell and Sorvinka are at war is well known. News of it had been sent to my sister, Princess Livia, months ago."

"Princess Livia knew of this! But... she..."

The King's eyes narrowed. "Prince Amir, do not try blaming my sister for this either," he hissed through clenched teeth.

I looked at the dead eunuch guards. Princess Livia had handpicked them for their looks, had had special costumes made for them so their nationality would be unmistakable. Princess Livia had gotten her revenge after all, I thought. I could see no way out of this precarious position... except one. I bowed my head. "My most sincere apologies, Your Majesty. The fault is entirely mine."

Apparently appeased by my apologies, the king nodded. He gestured for the knight on his right to approach. The knight moved beside the king while removing his helm. In a clunk of metal hitting metal, the king slapped his gloved hand on the knight's armored shoulder. "This is my nephew, Lars Anderson, Duke of Kasaniov. I'm sure my daughter mentioned him to you."

I bowed my head at Lars. I had certainly heard of him, Eva's cousin—*twice removed*, she always insisted on that detail—and the presumed heir to the throne. Fair of skin and of hair, Lars was a robust young man of my age. His eyes were pale blue, his chin pointy, and he had a slightly upturned nose. Even with the constant grimace of disgust twisting his face, as if something smelly was stuck under that upturned nose of his, he wasn't ugly. For some reason, I had expected him to be. Loud shouts coming from the back of the caravan made me turn. To my utter dismay, I saw that the king's soldiers had invaded the last carriage where our three wounded eunuch guards were resting. When the soldiers began pulling the wounded guards out, I knew that if I didn't intervene they would be killed. As I aimed to go to their aide, Lars drove his warhorse in front of my mare, blocking my path.

"Stay put, young prince," The king warned.

Feeling powerless and outraged, I could only watch as two of our guards perished at the hands of the soldiers. But when I saw Ely being thrown to the ground, I couldn't remain quiet anymore. "Your Majesty," I pleaded, "he is Eva's most loyal guard. He served her well. Please, Your Majesty, this man poses you no threat."

Unmoved by my plea, the king nodded to the soldiers surrounding Ely, and, at once, they pierced the wounded guard's body with their lances. When it was over, and Ely had expelled his last breath, the king turned toward me and said, "Now this man *truly* poses no threat to me."

Biting my tongue, I squeezed my eyes shut. Poor Ely, he didn't deserve this fate. At that instant, my thoughts turned to Milo, who was still inside the carriage with Eva. He too was doomed... then again, maybe not. I turned to the king. "Will you permit me to fetch your daughter?" The king nodded. Within moments, I was off my horse and entering the carriage. I was met by Milo's blade and nearly got my throat slit. "Careful!" I said.

"Oh, my prince, you are safe," he breathed in relief, lowering his blade from my neck.

"Sheath your sword, Milo." I ordered.

"What?" Milo looked at me as if he thought I had lost my mind.

"Amir, explain yourself," Eva said. "Tell me what's happening."

"There is no time." Then turning to Milo, I blurted, "If you want to live, you will do everything I say, starting by sheathing that blade and unloading my luggage. As for you, Eva, your father's awaiting you outside." For a woman encumbered by three layers of petticoats, Eva dashed outside with stunning speed. Milo shot me a sideways look. At that moment I knew he wouldn't obey my orders. As a eunuch guard, Milo's loyalty was to Eva, not to me, and it would remain so until he saw her safely under the king's protection. Before I could stop him he was out behind her. "Oh lord!" I said, and followed in their tracks. Sure enough, once outside I found Milo with his back against the carriage and three lance tips to his neck.

"Father!" Eva exclaimed. "What are these manners?"

"Eva, go inside," the king ordered.

"No! Not until I know what is happening here."

The captain of the soldiers approached Eva and whispered something into her ear. Her face turned as pale as snow, and without the captain's firm grip on her waist, I believe she would have collapsed on the ground. "Bring her inside, quickly," ordered the king.

Suddenly docile, Eva let herself be carried away without protest. Having lost my only ally, I turned to the king. "Majesty, that one is my valet. Please, tell your men to lower their lances. He is harmless. Look at him, he's not Farrellian."

Lars dismounted from his horse, marched straight to Milo and inspected him from head to toe. "I don't know. He looks half-Farrellian to me. That's enough to merit death."

With a hand on the grip of my sword, I stepped forth. Milo turned a gaze toward me, filled with a mixture of fear and determination. "My lord, don't risk yourself for me," he said in his light airy voice.

Lars grimaced at the sound of Milo's voice, then abruptly plunged his hand into Milo's crotch. "Aagh!" he exclaimed, leaping back in disgust. "This one's a gelding."

I looked at the king. His face displayed no emotion, yet I thought I saw a hint of disapproval in his eyes. "I thought eunuchs were made to guard the harem and serve women," the King said.

"No," I quickly rectified. "White eunuchs serve the Sultan… and princes as… as personal valets. None are better."

"And what tasks are these personal valets supposed to perform."

"Hmm... hmm. They attend to one's grooming needs, baths, daily washing. They help one dress."

Lars let out a loud cackling laugh, while the other men present were more discreet and just chuckled behind their hands. The king however remained dead serious. After a brief glance at Milo, he turned his attention to me. "Prince Amir, in Sorvinka, men dress themselves. But as you seem incapable of accomplishing this task by yourself, I will permit you to keep your servant. Because you are a guest in my castle, I am obliged to respect your customs, no matter how strange they may appear to us."

"Your Majesty is too kind," I said, bowing quickly to hide the redness of my cheeks.

"Don't thank me yet, I'm not done. One thing must be clear, Prince Amir. Maybe in Telfar a prince can have his servants fight his battles, but in Sorvinka servants aren't allowed to carry swords. And as long as you'll be a guest in my castle, you will live by my rules."

"Yes, Your Majesty." With obvious pleasure, Lars swiftly disarmed Milo. Then he slammed the sword on his armored knee several times, in an attempt to break it, I presumed. His efforts were useless—the sword was made of Telfarian steal, hence of too good a quality to be broken this way. Frustrated by his failure to destroy Milo's weapon, Lars shoved the sword into the hands of the nearest soldier. The king shook his head, then turned his horse around and headed back toward the castle. Once he reached the gate, he pivoted in his saddle and shouted, "Oh yes, I forgot. Welcome to Sorvinka, Prince Amir."

I looked at Milo, who was rubbing the sore spots on his neck where the lance tips had dug into his flesh. I looked at the corpses surrounding the caravan, then finally at the stern, hostile face of the king. In my opinion, this was the coldest welcome I had ever received in all my life.